Yellow Metal

Simon Sharpe

Copyright © Simon Sharpe, 2015

ISBN: 978-1-326-41564-8

Cover design by Sophia Di Martino

PublishNation, London
www.publishnation.co.uk

For Miyuki,
Tom, Arthur and Sarah

Prologue

Epilogue

Prologue

2

EARLIER

The snow tyres of the customised black Mercedes four-by-four ground through the patina of ice as the vehicle sped along the M32 stretching from Samara in southern Russia towards Uralsk just across the border in Kazakhstan. For the first twenty or thirty miles the road had been lined with stands of birch or pine, capped or coated in snow and frost, but now the road skated in a dead straight line for hundreds of miles with not a contour nor sign of vegetation to disturb the white winding-sheet laid over the landscape. At this time of year, the temperature on the steppes was minus ten even at this cut-glass high point of the day. The solitary vehicle luged on through the crisp and desolate expanse.

After a further forty miles, a lone Chrysler Jeep came into view idling at the roadside. The Mercedes slowed and the driver and his companion craned forwards to see the occupants of the new vehicle. The driver of the Jeep gave a curt nod and set his vehicle in motion, turning off the M32 and onto a line of tyre tracks which broke through the snow at right angles to the main road. The two vehicles scudded along the tracks for several miles until a line of snow-clad fir trees confronted them. The tracks turned to run parallel with the trees until, a mile further on, there was a break in the vegetation. The Jeep led the way through the gap. The occupants of the Mercedes spotted a huge steel-tracked vehicle, like a tank with no turret, concealed among the trees. Moments later its function became apparent: the Samara river, meandering tributary of the distant Volga, lay before them with a military-style extending bridge projecting across its frozen waters. The Jeep and its follower clattered across the steel bridge. Dense forest lay ahead.

Two or three miles into the frosted gloom, the two vehicles came to a small clearing. The clearing itself was deserted, but hidden among the surrounding trees were several more off-road vehicles and a couple of trucks. The forest suddenly seemed to stir and it became apparent there were dozens of heavily armed men in winter camouflage dotted among the trees. From their equipment and

3

comportment, it was quite clear this was no rag-tag bunch of thugs, but a private army of highly trained men, most likely all ex-Spetsnaz or past members of other elite units.

The Jeep came to a halt and the front-seat passenger stepped out. He waved the Mercedes to park under the trees. Having concealed their vehicle, the two men from the Mercedes clambered out and crunched over towards the Jeep. One of the two men carried a laptop zipped into a black leather holder. The Jeep passenger indicated for the men to halt. He carried out a rapid but thorough pat-down search for weapons and inspected the contents of the leather holder before ushering the two men into the back of the Jeep. The Jeep sped off deeper into the forest.

In due course, as the vehicle turned into a much wider clearing, a large wooden country lodge loomed into view. Several vehicles were again concealed under the surrounding trees. A helicopter squatted beneath a winter camouflage net in the centre of the clearing. At the approach of the Jeep, there was again a stirring among the trees which revealed another contingent of heavily armed men exuding an air of menacing competence. The Jeep pulled in under the white canopy of fir trees and the four men disembarked.

The men stamped the snow off their boots as they ascended the front steps of the dacha. Entering the lodge, they were flooded with warmth and the scent of pine – a log fire blazed in a giant stone hearth which dominated the entrance area and central main room. But any sense of welcome was shortlived: the way into the main room was barred by a denuded branch upon which crouched an emerald-eyed lynx – rather magnificent in its brindled winter pelt, but poised in readiness to pounce with bared fang and claw. The two guests skirted this trophy of a past hunting trip and coolly took in their surroundings.

The first of the two visitors, perhaps in his forties, was a little below average height, yet square-shouldered and with a martial stance. His hair was neatly cropped, but he had a gathering shadow about his jaw and possessed eyes like the tundra in winter. He removed his cashmere greatcoat and dropped it on a chair. Beneath the coat, he wore a dapper Savile Row suit. His companion, probably a decade older, was an inch or two taller, but of slighter build. He

4

was flinty featured, wore rimless spectacles and had oiled-back hair. Beneath his leather, fur-trimmed coat, he too wore an expensively cut suit.

Two burly bodyguards advanced upon the guests and conducted another pat-down search, followed by a sweep first with a hand-held metal detector and then with a wand designed to detect anything emitting a radio signal. The laptop was taken from its leather holder, the battery removed and replaced and the machine then powered up and switched off again before being returned to its owner. At this moment, a door on the far side of the room burst open.

"Gentlemen, gentlemen, welcome, welcome, welcome!" boomed forth. The speaker was built along heroic Soviet lines – indeed appeared to be something of a throwback to that bygone era. A brawny stakhanovite, he too was clad in a suit, but one which looked as though it might have been laid down in a naval dockyard, most probably with its present occupant as the chief welder. He had a bristle of grey hair, tiny eyes and an anvil of a chin. He shook the hands of his guests and clasped them in a hug. "Refreshments! Can I offer you refreshments after your journey?" He turned and indicated with a sweep of his arm a pot of coffee set out with little cakes on a low table in the centre of the room and, on a side table, a large silver basin containing a glistening block of ice drilled through to take a couple of bottles of vodka and hollowed out on top to hold a tureen of caviar. Beside the basin, a silver salver held a plate of blinis and bowl of sour cream.

"We have a plane to catch," said the guest with the rimless glasses. "May we proceed straight to business?"

The host seemed briefly taken aback at this dismissal of his hospitality.

The stockier guest eyed his companion coldly. "I will take a coffee," he said to their host, though the smile he offered up with this concession also showed little sign of warmth.

"Coffee, coffee, wonderful, wonderful!" said the blacksmith of a host. He snapped his fingers at one of his retainers. As the coffee was poured, he waved his guests into leather armchairs around the low wooden table. "Since you wish to proceed straight to business, may I first make sure we are perfectly clear the two million dollars you have already paid is a non-returnable access fee and nothing more – it merely buys you the right to sit here and discuss. I trust that was fully understood and does not present a problem?"

"If you have the materials," said the stockier guest, "that does not present a problem."

"I do of course have the materials," said the host. "Is that not after all why you are here?"

"And when can we see them?" asked the narrow-faced man with the oiled-back hair.

The stakhanovite leaned forwards in his chair and held his impatient guest for a few seconds with a frosty look. His guest remained stonily impassive. Suddenly, the host beamed, leant back in his chair and clapped loudly twice. Silence descended upon the room as the seated group waited for a response.

But, seemingly impatient of the silence, the host suddenly again lunged forwards in his seat and fixed an interrogative stare upon his visitors. "Payment will not come through Dubai?"

"Payment will not come through Dubai," affirmed the shadow-jawed visitor.

"Last time, payment was through Dubai and payment did not come at all."

"Payment will not be through Dubai."

"Those who orchestrated that little farce will not be making further payments of any kind," said the host pointedly. He paused. "And not through Qatar or Riyadh, I hope ... nor through Islamabad? I'm assuming we're dealing with ...?"

"The payment will not come through the Middle East; it will come through Moscow or London. Our buyer has connections in London."

"Hm." The host was apparently content with this answer. He nodded in deliberation for a second. "You are ready to transact now?"

"Not yet. We will let you know when."

"And delivery instructions?"

"Those will also come much closer to the time."

A moment later, two men entered through a side door carrying a large steel casket. They placed it on the floor in front of the host, who bent down and snapped open the locks. He lifted the lid and, settling back in his chair, eyed his two guests.

The older, flint-faced man, who was seated closest to the casket, angled forwards to inspect the contents. A tiny spark of surprise flickered across his face. The host gave a little clap and emitted a "Hah!" of delight – clearly he had been anticipating this reaction.

The stockier visitor seemed to pick up on the meaning of this exchange. He turned to his colleague. "Yours?"

The older man raised an eyebrow a millimetre and inclined his head the merest fraction to indicate that it did indeed seem to be so, though he found this hard to believe. He looked at his host. "This should be under lock and key."

"Should be," chortled the host. "But isn't."

The narrow-faced guest indicated his laptop.

"Please," said the host.

The man opened his laptop, located the desired programme and, leaning forwards to take careful note from the contents of the steel casket, entered a lengthy serial number. His expression hardened. "No. I have the latest audit. It is still there. Whatever you have here is not what it purports to be. We cannot deal on this basis."

The host did not seem perturbed. "Which audit are you consulting?"

"The latest one, six months ago."

"A new audit was made three days ago. Please take a look at that."

"You have internet ... wi-fi?" The man cast his eye around the lodge as though he might see the radiowaves.

"We have satellite ..." The host pointed helpfully towards the roof. "... and, yes, wi-fi. The password is lynxlynx – as in the cat ..." He nodded towards the animal guarding the entrance. "... nineteen seventeen – one nine one seven. You can gain access to the audit?"

His guest nodded.

"Our revered authorities' competence in matters of security is sometimes a disgrace." The host beamed in mingled approbation of his guest and self-congratulation.

The head of oiled-back hair bent over the laptop in concentration for some minutes. When the visitor finally looked up, his expression had once again darkened. "The latest audit is also in order."

"But of course it is in order ... however ..." The host gave the wooden table-top a little rap of pleasure with his knuckles and wagged a triumphant finger. "... please check the inventory item by item."

The visitor leant towards the casket and retyped the lengthy serial number. He stared at his screen for several moments. "Hm," he acknowledged.

"And you might like to re-check the audit of six months ago – just in case anyone should go back and compare."

The visitor typed again and inspected the result. This time his expression gave no immediate clue to his thoughts, but he switched off and closed his laptop. He turned to his colleague and gave a wordless nod.

"Splendid, splendid, splendid!" beamed the host. He snapped the casket closed and waved at his staff to remove it. Turning back to his guests, he indicated the ice-encased bottles of vodka. "I cannot tempt you?" It was clear he could not. "Well, then ..." He drew a deep breath of satisfaction. "... it is just a matter of price." He leant back in his chair and gazed at the ceiling for a protracted while, holding his guests in suspense. He finally brought his gaze back down to them. "Two hundred and fifty million dollars."

Neither of the visitors showed a trace of emotion, but stared at their host as though intent on turning him to stone. They matched his suspenseful silence ... they outdid it ... Finally, tundra-eyes spoke.

"Fifty million."

"Oh, come, come ... you surely appreciate what risks we have run in obtaining this?"

"We appreciate the risks. But we know what it is worth."

Anger suddenly flashed across the face of the stakhanovite. He rose from his chair and marched to the front door. Throwing it open, he stabbed a finger towards the clearing as though he were about to cast out his guests. Instead, he fulminated, "This kind of security does not come cheaply. And, by the way, it is for your benefit as much as mine."

"Our negotiation payment covers the cost of the security many times over."

The host slammed the door and came back into the centre of the room. He paced in front of the hearth. He stopped and grimaced. "Two hundred million. That is a huge concession."

Permafrost-in-the-soul directed his hard-as-iron stare at his host for several seconds. "Seventy-five. And that is our limit."

The stakhanovite removed his boiler-plate jacket and threw it over the back of his chair. He strode to the side table and helped himself to a blini, larded it with sour cream and added a huge dollop of caviar. He stuffed it into his mouth. He turned to his guests and waved towards the little buffet. "No?" he invited them, spraying a few sturgeon's eggs onto the floor. It was clear his guests still had no interest in this inducement. The host took one of the bottles of vodka, poured himself a shot, knocked it back and poured himself another. He thrust the bottle back into the ice. He stared at the wall for a second and then advanced back into the centre of the room. He stood for a further moment before knocking back the second shot and then resuming his seat. He nursed his empty glass while seeming to wrestle with his thoughts. Suddenly, he banged the empty glass on the table. His eyes lit up, but his expression was otherwise one of impatience. "One hundred and fifty and then will you join me?"

"Seventy-five is our limit," came the cool reply.

"One hundred and fifty is mine."

Without a word, the two guests rose, retrieved and put on their coats and walked towards the front door. The host stared after them in angry astonishment. Seeing the discomfiture of their boss yet not knowing quite what to do, the stakhanovite's band of men bristled in readiness like the crouching lynx but like the cat remained rooted to the spot. However, the young bodyguard closest to the front door, finding himself in the path of the abruptly departing visitors, in panicky confusion drew his Makarov pistol and pointed it at the stockier guest. At this, the other henchmen also made for their weapons. But the host urgently held up splayed hands to arrest this unwanted development. The young bodyguard, however, did not seem to see this, but was rather transfixed by the glacial stare of the visitor at whom he continued to point his gun. The visitor turned and

9

looked with disdain at his host before turning back to the bodyguard. The young man now glanced across at his boss ... in this instant, the stocky visitor executed a movement so swift, deft and contemptuous that no one else in the room could immediately take in what had happened: he disarmed the bodyguard with a barely perceptible flick of the wrists, briefly pointed the gun at the young man as though he might shoot him, but instead quietly placed the weapon on a side table. He turned back to the host.

"We did not pay two million dollars to come here and be threatened. I trust you will teach this oaf some good manners."

Brushing the young man aside, the visitor and his colleague stepped out into the cold. The two men walked silently across the clearing to where the Jeep was concealed beneath the trees. The soldiers, wraith-like among the trees a moment before, suddenly became palpable and stood in watchful guard before the two men.

The visitors were kept waiting in the freezing air for several minutes before the driver of the Jeep and his companion came out to them. Without exchanging a word, the four of them climbed into the Jeep. The vehicle backed into the clearing and then sped off along the forest track. As they entered the smaller clearing, a satellite phone at the front of the car suddenly carilloned. The front-seat passenger picked it up and listened for a second before passing it back to shadow-jaw.

"Yes?"

"One hundred million. I do not believe you will pay less for a nuclear weapon."

I   Hedgie and Oligarch

ONE

"Gilded, but damned," rasped the police inspector. "Why do they do it? Every advantage in life and they kill themselves with drugs." Inspector Hunt was a grizzled bear of a man – in former years a Metropolitan Police rugby team prop forward, but now baggy and jowly with middle age and booze. He turned to the pallid young forensics officer. "You're done?" The officer nodded. Hunt replaced the white bathrobe over the naked body of the young woman.

They were in the Mayfair flat of Charles Draper, one of the City's top hedge fund managers. The apartment – remodelled by an architect, interior designed, laden with modern art and equipped with every electronic device – was the epitome of fashionable taste where expense was no object. A marbled and mirrored hall led into the large open plan living area. Here the walls were hung with silvery slub silk and adorned with Damien Hirst sketches for his shark in formaldehyde and his pickled sheep. A Marc Quinn frozen blood head meditated in a temperature-controlled glass tank on a black marble pedestal. Set into an opposite wall were a large plasma television and metre-high speakers. The polished parquet floor was inlaid with huge roundels of different woods – cross-sections carved from the felled methuselahs of ancient forests. The flat was as glintingly clean as an operating theatre and the placement of every item was as neat and precise as a binary code. Hunt and the two forensics officers stood among the cream leather couches and armchairs of the sitting area. The girl lay at their feet tidily aligned beneath her white robe in the middle of a large oriental silk rug.

At the far end of the living area, Charles Draper himself sat at the glass-topped dining table and stared blankly at the view of Green Park. A young policewoman sat opposite him, tight-lipped. The mid-morning traffic could be heard rumbling below. Even seated, Charles towered over the policewoman. Broad-shouldered and with a massive head, he had a swept-back mop of brown hair and refined and handsome features, though these were now pulled into a bleak expression of grief. He wore a crisp white shirt and a pair of bespoke denim jeans.

The front door of the flat was open and footsteps could be heard ascending the stairs. There was a thump and a muffled "Bugger!" A couple of moments later a fresh-faced young man of about thirty appeared at the threshold. He wore a suit, but had the look of an untidy schoolboy and was dabbing a bleeding lip. He ducked beneath the police tape stretched at an angle across the doorway. Hunt advanced towards him.

"Slipped on the damned stairs and bit my bloody lip," said the young man.

"I'm sorry, sir, this flat is off-limits just at the moment. Can I help with anything?" Hunt's arms were outstretched as though to scoop the intruder back outside.

The young man produced an ID from an inner pocket.

"Ah," grunted the inspector and then with a note of surprise and lowering his voice to a gravelly rumble, "MI5? I took this as just a case of a drugs overdose – albeit with slight peculiarities. Is there some security angle involved?"

"It's simply that she's the daughter of a cabinet minister. Can't imagine there are wider implications, but anyway I've been sent along. Actually, I think my boss just wanted to get me out of the way for the morning." The young man was still dabbing his lip. "Has anyone got a tissue or anything? Bloody thing won't stop."

Charles Draper turned and rose from the dining table, revealing his full height of six foot six. He disappeared into a bedroom and returned with a box of tissues, which he placed on a glass side table next to the visitor.

"Thank you," said the young man.

"Mr Draper ..." Hunt consulted the young man's ID once again. "This is Mr Lemon."

"Tim Lemon, Security Service assigned to the minister." Tim Lemon reached forward a hand in greeting.

Charles Draper lifted a hand which might have belonged to some outsized stone monument. Tim braced for a bone-crusher of a handshake, but met only the briefest clasp from the huge span.

Charles responded to Tim's words of greeting with a sombre nod of the head and then returned to the dining table.

"Inspector Hunt, by the way." The inspector removed a latex glove and offered his own large and shaggy paw.

Tim shook the inspector's hand and retrieved his ID with a "Thank you". He stepped past the inspector into the living area. Looking down at the young woman, he turned back to Hunt. "Well, Inspector, please could you give me a rundown."

"What we have so far, Mr Lemon, is Lucy Trenchard, daughter of the Home Secretary and girlfriend of Charles Draper here …" He nodded in Charles's direction. "… lying dead apparently from a drugs overdose. It seems Mr Draper made a brief trip to Monaco yesterday and returned on a flight from Nice early this morning. He came directly back to the flat, arriving here at around eight thirty a.m. Upon entering the flat, he found Miss Trenchard lying on the living room floor, as you see, with evidence to suggest she had shot herself up with what we take to be heroin."

Tim noticed drug paraphernalia on a glass coffee table – plastic sachet still with traces of something inside it, metal spoon, disposable lighter …

"Mr Draper called an ambulance," continued Hunt, "tried to give Miss Trenchard mouth-to-mouth, but – as the ambulance boys noted – she had clearly already been dead for a little while by the time they arrived. We were summoned."

"You said there were peculiarities." Tim lowered his voice. "Are you saying Mr Draper took his time to call an ambulance?"

Hunt led the young man into a study where they were out of earshot of Charles Draper. The study was equipped with multiple computer screens, though these were all switched off for the moment. The walls were hung with the Chapman Brothers' grotesquely comic mutilations of Goya etchings.

"No, I'm not saying Mr Draper took his time. If you want my snap judgement, I'd say he's not implicated in any way and is genuinely shocked by what's happened. Furthermore, we had a pathologist here a short while ago and he estimated time of death as the early hours – probably around two a.m. That puts Draper comfortably in the clear – we've checked his flight details and have confirmed he was indeed on the plane from Nice this morning. No, I think what we have here is just another case – another *tragic* case – of a privileged young person throwing her life away. I remember a similar case when I was a teenager – Tory cabinet minister's daughter OD-ed at a party in Oxford. But the peculiarity is this – and it rather contradicts my central assumption ..." Hunt drew a step closer to Tim. Tim could smell coffee and cigarettes on Hunt's breath. "... according to Draper, neither he nor she ever touched drugs. She didn't smoke, hardly drank and would never touch anything else. Of course, we'll do an autopsy – and we'll run a blood test to check him out as well – but he says this came completely out of the blue. It's true, in this business, one often finds people lead secret lives which even their close families know nothing about, but I get the impression Draper really believes what he's saying. One develops a nose for these things."

"May I take a quick look at her and speak to him?"

"If you must."

Hunt led Tim back to the body. The police inspector lifted the white bathrobe and stood back.

"Beautiful girl. *Was* a beautiful girl." Hunt shook his head. "Terrible, terrible waste."

She was indeed a very beautiful young woman. Lying on the silk rug, she looked strangely composed and serene and unblemished – apart from a tiny puncture wound on her left forearm. Her body lay quite straight; her blond hair fell to her shoulders; her right arm rested gently on her midriff, while her left fell to the side. Tim saw that a syringe had rolled a few feet from her left hand.

"She looks oddly peaceful, doesn't she?" commented Tim. "This is probably nothing, but she must have injected herself with her right hand, yet the syringe seems to have rolled away from her left."

Hunt shrugged. "She could easily have changed position or passed the syringe from one hand to the other."

"Hm. Thank you." Tim indicated that he had seen enough. He went over to Charles Draper. "Mr Draper, I really am most awfully sorry. The inspector has explained to me what happened here."

Draper nodded, but said nothing.

16

"Forgive my pressing the point," continued Tim, "but I understand Miss Trenchard usually kept well clear of drugs?"

Draper drew in a deep breath and exhaled a long and tremulous sigh. He stood and went to the window. "I just can't understand it." His voice was a forceful baritone, though now breaking with emotion. "Lucy was as good and pure and clean as they come. She never touched drugs. Never. I thought I knew her and I thought we were happy together. Whether she meant to do this awful thing or whether it was a horrible accident, either way, I just can't understand it. From what dark place this came, I just can't, can't imagine." Charles's gaze was suddenly drawn to the street below, where two further police cars and a black Jaguar had pulled up. He gulped another deep breath and began to shake a little as he put his hand to his mouth. "Oh God, I think it's Henry and Juliet."

"The minister?" asked Tim.

Charles nodded.

A moment later, the voice of a woman could be heard on the stairs distraughtly and endlessly repeating to herself, "Oh no, oh no, oh no ..." When Juliet Trenchard entered and saw her daughter, she emitted a wail which pierced everyone in the room. The forensics officers, who were just bagging the evidence, stood back from the body. Hunt, however, stepped between Lucy and her parents.

"Mrs Trenchard," said Hunt, and then to the minister, "sir ... I do apologise, but we must preserve the integrity of the evidence."

Juliet Trenchard gave Hunt a look of incredulity.

"Officer," said Henry Trenchard, "this is not just some piece of evidence, this is our daughter."

The minister's wife barged past Hunt and, falling on her knees, took her lifeless child in her arms and continued to wail. Hunt raised his hands in token protest, but ceded to the force of Juliet Trenchard's emotion and the superior rank of the minister. Henry Trenchard, himself in tears, knelt by his wife. He put one arm around his wife and began to smooth his daughter's brow, whispering, "Oh Lucy, oh Lucy." Charles closed his eyes in an expression of grief-stricken pain while, witnessing the parents' distress, Tim, even Hunt himself, and the rest of the police team found themselves struggling to maintain their professional distance and detachment.

17

As Juliet Trenchard's wailing gave way to sobs, the minister looked towards Charles with an expression of anger. "Charles, in the name of Christ, can you explain what happened here."

Charles opened his mouth, but just shook his head.

Hunt stepped forward. "Sir, we are all truly and deeply sorry for what has happened. I can't be definitive at this stage, sir, but Mr Draper has explained that he flew into London this morning, found Miss Trenchard in this condition and promptly called an ambulance. Although it's a terrible shock, sir, it seems for reasons unknown Miss Trenchard in the middle of the night took an overdose of what appears to be heroin."

"That's just ridiculous, officer. It makes absolutely no sense at all. Lucy was not remotely, remotely that kind of girl. I absolutely can't accept that and you'd damn well better keep looking until you come up with a much better explanation than that."

TWO

Unlike the gleaming steel and glass Security Service offices of much television and film lore, the interior of the MI5 building was in fact more like a drab 1970s hospital, with snot green walls and, in place of mopped floors, heavily stained carpet tiles – many of the stains contributed by Tim. However, the technology at least was closer to its fictional representation.

Tim sat at his desk clicking through his emails amidst an untidy clutter of documents, pens minus their tops, a three-quarters eaten cheese and pickle sandwich, yellow post-it notes, knocked-over and thankfully empty paper coffee cup, swimming goggles with a snapped strap poorly held together with staples, the stapler, right at the back an unopened but completely crushed packet of biscuits, business cards ... Tim was expecting the police report on Lucy Trenchard. He was not in the best mood. Lucy Trenchard's death was of course a terrible tragedy for her family and no doubt for Charles Draper too, but it was surely an isolated incident and not in any way a matter of national security. It annoyed Tim that just because he was called Lemon and had a habit of bumping into things, his section chief, Gordon Walker, tended to treat him as incompetent and assign him less important tasks. Such as this one. Tim had not encountered this attitude since his first years at school, when his lack of physical coordination had for a while been misconstrued as deliberate troublemaking. Tim did not think he had given Gordon, nor indeed anyone else in the Security Service, reason to doubt his effectiveness. He had entered the Service eight years earlier with a perfectly respectable degree in History from the University of Exeter and had always been a hardworking and reliable member of the team. Looking back, he might not have played a leading role, but he had been instrumental in foiling at least one jihadist plot; he had helped trap a scientific research assistant who was attempting to sell to the Chinese confidential laboratory data on the newly developed wonder material graphene; he had played a slightly larger role in helping to close down the British links in an international arms cartel which had sought to broker the sale of chemical weapons technology to various Middle Eastern and African governments ... He had never put a foot seriously wrong in terms of his work, even if he had two left feet when negotiating a projecting chair leg or stray waste paper basket. At worst, he could occasionally be a little impetuous. Yet Tim felt his career had been held back during the couple of years since Gordon had taken over as section head. Somehow Tim needed to demonstrate to Gordon that clumsiness did not equate to slow-wittedness. But Lucy Trenchard surely did not provide the means to do this.

The rest of Gordon's team, meanwhile, were engaged in the crucial work of identifying the members and in particular the head of a string of Islamist terrorist cells dotted around the country. Leading this project was Tim's peer, Helen Stride. She sat to his right at a desk which, in sharp contrast to his own, had not an item upon it apart from her mobile phone and a rather impressive bottle of premium *daiginjo* sake containing a snow-shake of *kinpaku* gold flakes. The bottle had been presented to Helen by an inebriated Japanese businessman as an awkward peace-offering after a misguided attempt to pick her up at the bar of a Japanese restaurant. Efficient, intensely focused on the job, ambitious, rarely giving much of herself away, Helen was encased in a formal grey pinstripe suit and austere white blouse – though Tim could not resist the observation that this businesslike attire did not wholly disguise the curves of her figure. Her face – shaped rather like the softly described outline of a heraldic shield, Tim thought – had an angular beauty enhanced by large and strikingly green eyes. She affected a tough-as-nails attitude and would frequently announce, particularly after a drink or two, that she was ready to kill someone 'if I have to' or 'if the occasion demands'. Tim was quite sure Gordon had a severe weakness in the trousers for Helen – which Helen's combination of personal reserve and professional hustling somehow seemed not to discourage. But then perhaps all the men in the office had an eye for Helen. Tim himself included, though he didn't especially warm to Helen as a person. Tim generally lacked confidence when dealing with women – both inside and outside the office – and Helen's terse professionalism did nothing to help him overcome this awkwardness.

On Tim's left, partly hidden by a neat little barricade of files, sat Trevor Wilde. He was a couple of years older than Tim and Helen and had transferred from MI6 a year earlier. He had been kidnapped in Lebanon and held in a windowless room somewhere in Gaza for two years. He insisted he was over his ordeal, but could be rather morose and taciturn – though he was also wont to display signs of a dry sense of humour. His preference for dark suits with black or brown shirts added to his saturnine aura. With a narrow, rather vulpine face, he possessed an odd tendency to curl his upper lip and bare his front teeth whenever he had just cracked a joke. He also had a habit of slipping quietly from the office for a few hours, sometimes returning with a vital piece of information, sometimes with a *macchiato* from the nearby Caffè Nero. Tim found him rather creepy, but felt sorry for him after what he had been through.

The police report arrived in Tim's inbox. He opened the report and hit 'print'. He stood to collect the report from the printer.

"Tuck your shirt in, Lemon."

That was another of Helen's affectations – she called everyone in the office by his or her surname. Except for Gordon, to whom Helen showed the appropriate respect – though not, Tim would have had to concede, unthinking deference.

Tim stood at the printer beside the desk of Margaret Harcourt. Actually, Helen also called Margaret by her first name, but then Margaret was half a generation older and had a much greater depth of experience. A little taller than average, Maggie was maternal of feature and becoming a little matronly of build – though you could still readily imagine she remained captain of the ladies' tennis team at her local club. If she had not taken a twelve year sabbatical to raise a family, Maggie would certainly have been at least section chief and probably in the much higher echelons of the Service. She had a very sharp mind, but was quietly unassuming and friendly to everyone. She was also unflappable. She had recently been on late evening duty when a careless junior minister had realised he had allowed a press photographer a glimpse of a briefing document which contained details of an impending police raid on a terrorist cell in Bradford.

21

Within the hour, Maggie had coordinated a lightning early hours raid which had caught all the suspects asleep in their beds before the morning papers had hit their doormats or they had switched on their televisions or computers. Gordon had stepped forward to collect the accolades, but everyone in the unit knew it was Maggie who had salvaged the situation. Tim glanced at Maggie's desk and noticed that, unusually for her, she had left The Times crossword untouched.

"Not able to do the crossword this morning, Maggie?"

"No, I've done it," she said, not taking her eyes off the report she was typing on her computer screen. "Just the train was rather crowded – I had to stand the whole way."

"But it's blank."

Maggie handed Tim the newspaper and a pen. While still working at her report and not taking her eyes off the computer screen, she reeled off in quick succession the answers to all the clues. "Serendipity. Blacksmith. Cicero. Isotope. Phantom limb. Saxi-frage…" Tim had to scribble to keep pace.

"Very impressive," he said, returning the completed crossword and pen to Maggie. She acknowledged the compliment with a tilt of the head and a little smile.

The police report was ready. Tim gave the pages a shuffle to square them off and returned to his desk. It did not take many minutes of reading to realise that the report largely confirmed what had been said or surmised on the morning of Lucy's death. The autopsy revealed that, while her system was flooded with a massive overdose of heroin, her liver was not that of a habitual drug user or heavy drinker, nor were her lungs those of a smoker. Toxicological analysis of hair samples similarly yielded no evidence of past drug use. The pathologist confirmed that Lucy appeared to have led a very healthy life prior to the overdose. Police interviews with a number of her friends similarly amounted to a chorus of disbelief: every friend echoed the view that Lucy never went anywhere near drugs and that she was a well-balanced and happy young woman whom one could not imagine taking an overdose – or any dose – of heroin, whether accidentally or deliberately. Charles Draper had also willingly submitted to a blood test and medical examination which confirmed that there was no evidence of his being a drug user and certainly no sign he had taken anything in the hours or days immediately preceding Lucy's death. The police conclusion was that the tragedy was the result of a young woman's private experiment which had gone disastrously wrong.

There was one outstanding item in the report. The heroin itself had been tested: its composition was much as other street heroin commonly available in London, except that it contained microscopic traces of brewer's yeast. The police did not recognise this signature and wondered if the heroin had come from an unusual source. Lucy had been a frequent traveller – in fact, had been to New York and Paris in the month before her death – so the police had sent the results to the FBI and DEA in the US and to the French police and Interpol. The FBI and DEA had already replied that the traces of brewer's yeast were as unfamiliar to them as to the British police. Responses from the French police and Interpol were still pending.

Tim could see little point in his pursuing the matter any further. He picked up the report and went over to Gordon Walker's office. He put his head round the door.

"Gordon, have you got a mo for this Lucy Trenchard thing?"

"Two seconds. Just got to send off some instructions to Tabi." With his scarlet braces and paunch, Gordon firmly believed the security of the United Kingdom – and perhaps of western democracy as a whole – rested on his shoulders. The truth was he relied upon Margaret for sound advice and upon all the team for hard work. Tabi Shah, to whom he was sending a memo, was the team's IT wizard, who also happened to speak a handful of the languages of the Indian subcontinent plus Persian and Arabic.

"So, Timbo," said Gordon, "what do we have?"

Tim handed the police report to Gordon. "Not a great deal. The police think it was a one-off tragic experiment by a girl who never usually touched the stuff. There's a scrap of a clue about the provenance of the drug – it contained microscopic impurities which the police haven't seen before. That's about it. I have to say I can't see any implications for the minister or for state security. I think we can leave the police to tie off the one loose end and I can get back to helping the rest of the team."

"Tim, do you possess an ironing board and an iron?" Gordon was staring at Tim's shirt. "I mean, it's not the highest priority, but your shirt looks not so much as though you slept in it, but rather as though you slept with it scrunched in a ball beneath you." Gordon shook his head. "And, no, sorry, we've got to do a bit more digging on Lucy Trenchard. The minister is demanding different answers from the ones he's being given … and so too is the PM. As I'm sure you know, Trenchard is a close political ally of the PM and I also discovered this morning that Lucy was the PM's goddaughter. I dare say you're right that this is primarily a police matter and, as you quite correctly suggest, we are servants of the state and not gumshoes hired to act on the minister's private behalf; however, the Director General has insisted that we give this our close attention and Trenchard himself has called me personally to ask that we indulge him in this tragic matter and lend every possible assistance – and I'm afraid that means you. How about this Draper character? Anything on him?"

"He seems clean. The innocent and unlucky boyfriend."

"Well, give it some more thought. See if you can come up with something. At the very least, we need to show willing." Gordon turned his attention back to his computer, indicating that the conversation was over and Tim was dismissed. "Oh, and could you ask Margaret to pop into my office when she has a second."

Tim returned disconsolately to his desk, on the way letting Maggie know that Gordon wanted a word.

Helen leaned across to Tim. "Are you done with that report? Can you help us piece together who's who among these fanatics?"

"Sorry," replied Tim. "Gordon's getting pressure from on high to find answers to Lucy Trenchard's death – where there clearly are none, I might add."

"Gordon should spend less time worrying about the powers that be and more time worrying about terrorism. After all, he's the one who's always puffing out his chest and talking about defence of the realm. He should understand better than anyone what we're up against in terms of limited resources at our disposal versus the virtually unlimited task we have to perform. I mean, look, where do we stand so far? … Several thousand individuals somewhere on our radar screen, a hard core of two or three hundred under more intensive surveillance and now, thanks to

24

our efforts to date, of these, twenty ..." Helen leant forward and looked at her screen. "... twenty-seven under round-the-clock watch. And all of that generating hundreds of thousands of pages and thousands and thousands of hours of internet traffic, emails, phone calls and, in the top priority cases, bugged conversations and photographs or video logs of their meetings – all of which we have to read, listen to, look at, watch, sometimes get translated and then read the transcript ... Even if Shah's software helps with the sifting process and even if we can delegate some of the monitoring to others ..." Helen waved an arm in the direction of the surrounding desks, where additional staff sat hunched over their screens, some with earphones clamped in place, all in varying postures of intense concentration. "... the core responsibility lies with us. We need to be on top of *everything*. We're the ones who have to interpret, prioritise, determine what action to take ..."

"Yeah, well, you're preaching to the converted, but I'm afraid I'm stuck with Lucy Trenchard for the moment." Tim let loose a plosive sigh of frustration. "I'm heading out for a coffee and a breath of fresh air."

Margaret, meanwhile, knocked on Gordon's open door.

"Gordon?"

"Margaret, come in." Gordon narrowed his eyes as though casting his mind back. "Maggie, am I right in thinking that you used to work with Martin Chilvers – who's now with MI6 in Moscow?"

"Ages ago, yes ... for a couple of years, in fact."

"Sensible chap?"

"Yes, absolutely. Why – is something amiss?"

"Not really clear, but he keeps sending me breathless messages that a key contact of his in the Russian government has requested an urgent meeting on a matter of great importance to British domestic security. Seems Chilvers hasn't yet managed to arrange this meeting and his contact is now travelling for a day or two."

"No, Martin's a very level-headed chap. I think you should take him seriously."

"Hm. Okay, thank you. Guess we'll just have to sit tight and see what he comes up with when his friend returns."

THREE

Tim stood, coffee in hand, leaning on a wall by the riverbank and watching the Thames drift by. He put aside his frustration and pondered again the scene of Lucy's demise. He had found something about it disconcerting – beyond poor Lucy's death, of course – but he could not put his finger on what. He turned to head back to the office. On the street, he passed a modern furniture shop and glanced in the window at the neat display. He stopped. Somehow the display chimed with the distant thought he was struggling to grasp. And now he realised what was troubling him: Draper's flat had seemed too impossibly composed – as though made ready for a photo-shoot for a glossy magazine. Quite undisturbed by tragedy. And Draper himself, seemingly distressed yet somehow quite unruffled in his crisply laundered shirt ... wasn't his immaculate turnout a bit incongruous with his girlfriend lying dead on the floor? But perhaps it was simply that Tim lived in an untidy little flat and wore rumpled clothes and couldn't imagine the life of a wealthy man whose wardrobe was full of pristine shirts. He felt he still hadn't quite put his finger on it. He paced back and forth for a few minutes before returning to the office.

At his desk, he picked up the report. There were several photographs of Lucy which had printed poorly. He went back to the file on his computer to take a proper look at the photographs. He clicked open the first: Lucy lay neatly positioned on the oriental silk rug, seemingly peaceful as a saint and strangely decorous as a mannequin. And now it struck Tim clearly: the problem was Lucy. She too looked quite unnaturally composed. And the drug paraphernalia neatly placed on the coffee table and the syringe on the floor ... it was almost artful. Shouldn't a drug overdose be ugly and messy? The tableau he saw was somehow of a piece with the tasteful lines of the flat's interior design. He sat back in his chair. But what did that amount to? Perhaps he should at least find out a bit more about Draper.

Google and various press searches revealed multiple references to Draper and to Wave Capital Management, his London-based hedge fund. He had set up the fund in the late 1990s and had prospered. He was reckoned to be worth a billion, perhaps even a billion and a half. Resident of Monaco, but homes everywhere. Prior to the financial crisis, he had received considerable publicity as one of the activist investors who would take a stake in an underperforming company and then press vociferously for corporate change. During the course of the crisis, there had been numerous articles identifying Wave Capital as one of the few hedge funds which had profited handsomely from global distress by consistently and massively shorting bank stocks – which, Tim discovered, meant Draper had sold bank stocks which he had borrowed but didn't actually own and had then bought back the same stocks after their share prices had collapsed, thereby 'covering his short', in the jargon of the business, and reaping huge profits. Draper was clearly an extremely skilled and successful investor. But none of this seemed to be taking Tim anywhere. He resolved to go and have another chat with Draper. He didn't really know about what, but perhaps he would get some further measure of the man.

Nick Braithwaite, at twenty-five the youngest member of the team, had meanwhile wandered over to Tim and Helen. He struck a pose. "What do you think, Helen?"

"What, the hair?" she asked.

Nick's blond mane stood in a vertical shock.

"No, the suit." He strutted back and forth, buttoning and unbuttoning the jacket, adjusting the sleeves and striking fresh poses.

"What is it, Armani?"

"Armani! Pur-lease! No, it's Gieves and Hawkes."

Nick was rather the opposite of Tim. He had once flirted with the idea of becoming a male model and now seemed convinced that the prerequisites for a successful secret agent included an account in Savile Row and a weekly visit to a celebrity hair teaser who might sculpt his coiffure into ever more novel convolutions.

"Well, it's very nice, Braithwaite, but do you think you could concentrate on the job in hand," said Helen drily.

"Yeah, actually, that's why I came over. Tabi's locked in to some very useful chatter. Take a look at what he's sending you." Nick indicated Helen's computer.

Helen clicked open a window on her screen and scrutinised its contents for a few moments before turning back to Nick. "How are you getting on with south London?"

"To be honest, I'm finding it quite difficult to distinguish between would-be jihadists who mean what they say and might pose a real threat ... between them and common-or-garden loudmouths who are just trying to big themselves up in the eyes of their mates."

"Yes, well, making those sorts of judgements is precisely the job we have to do. If you're not sure, come and discuss. If in doubt, we treat them as suspects. I'll buy you a large beer if you can figure out exactly what's going on in south London before I do."

"Actually, I've also been a bit distracted because Gordon asked me to do some research into this ecological protest group whose website keeps causing red lights to flash in Cheltenham."

"Gordon's not tying *you* up with minor stuff as well, is he? He should pass anything like that on to another team – or even leave it to the police. I'm convinced we have an active jihadist cell in the Lambeth area – you need to be wholly focused on that." Helen stood. "I'll go and have a word with Gordon – we can't be wasting time on these sideshows."

Tim had been following this conversation. Several months earlier, Gordon had packed Tim off to observe the police handling of a mass demonstration by anti-capitalist agitators on the occasion of the last G8 summit in London. Tim wondered now whether Nick's group might have been one of those involved in the protest. Not that Tim would be in any position to help Nick with his research. At the time, Gordon had not asked Tim to work on identifying any of the agitators, nor to pursue any kind of further investigation – it had rather been another case of Gordon sidelining Tim for the day.

Tim turned back to his current low priority and unwanted task. He picked up the phone to call Draper's office.

FOUR

Tim was in the St James's office of Wave Capital. He had just sunk into the deep leather armchair in the reception when the receptionist – tall, slim, tanned, fine-featured and expensively coutured – indicated that Draper was coming. A glass side panel in a wooden door darkened and Draper emerged.

"Mr Lemon." He proffered his hand. "Come through."

Tim was struck again by Charles Draper's immense size. Charles led Tim through a small trading room which contained about a dozen desks, each piled with screens and manned by casually dressed young men and women who scanned their computers or spoke on the phone. Charles's office was about the size of the trading floor and contained a very large desk, again piled with screens, a conference table and chairs and a leather sofa and armchairs arranged around a coffee table. The styling of the office was as immaculate as the hedge fund manager's flat. Charles wore another crisp shirt, though today it was powder blue, and neatly pressed beige chinos. He gestured Tim to the couch.

"Coffee, tea, water?"

"Coffee would be great."

"Regular, cappuccino, latte ...? I recommend the cappuccino."

"Cappuccino sounds good."

Charles buzzed the receptionist and asked for two cappuccinos.

"I'm sorry to bother you again," began Tim.

"If there's anything I can do to shed light on Lucy's death, I'm more than happy to help."

A young trader knocked on Charles's door.

"Yup?"

"Gold's back below fourteen hundred."

"Hoover it up," said Charles.

"The whole position?"

"If you can buy below fourteen, then the whole position."

The receptionist entered with two cappuccinos and placed them on the coffee table.

"Thank you, Claudia."

Resting on the froth of each cappuccino, in place of the usual sprinkle of chocolate, was a slender dark chocolate coin with a wash of gold highlighting the embossed relief. Tim noticed that his coin was a pound, while Charles's was a dollar.

"That rather puts other cappuccinos in their place," remarked Tim. He picked up his chocolate coin to pop it into his mouth. The melting chocolate slipped from his fingers and plopped on his shirt front. "Oh, bugger."

Charles leaned forward. "Let me ask Claudia to bring you a wet cloth."

"No, honestly, don't worry." Tim popped the chocolate in his mouth and gave his shirt a wipe with the little napkin which had come folded under the coffee cup. He merely succeeded in turning the neat chocolate ring into a smear. "Never mind, that'll do." He looked up at Charles. "Well, to business …"

"Fire away."

"I'm sorry to repeat questions and I'm not sure what progress we can make, but Henry Trenchard is demanding satisfaction of some kind."

"I can imagine. Poor Juliet. I'm sure she's still completely distraught."

"Please rack your brains again and think if you have any tiny clue as to where, when, from whom Lucy might have obtained the heroin."

"If I'd had even the tiniest suspicion of what was going on, I would have intervened at the outset. I have simply no idea where or how Lucy could have got the awful stuff."

"Hm. And can you describe again exactly how you found Lucy and what you did?"

"I'd had business in Monaco the previous day, flew into London first thing, came straight home to the flat … of course, as soon as I stepped in I saw that Lucy was lying there on the living room floor. I didn't know whether she was just unconscious or … well, I couldn't believe she was dead. I called an ambulance. I've never done first aid, but I tried the mouth-to-mouth thing and the pumping the chest – of course to no avail."

30

"The bathrobe?"

"Yes, when she didn't revive and with the ambulance coming, I draped that over her. Partly out of modesty, I suppose, and also I think I had some notion of keeping her warm."

Tim knitted his brows. This was just repetition and not leading anywhere. He changed tack. "Tell me about Wave Capital Management."

"What would you like to know? How well do you know the hedge fund business?"

"I know little more than I read in the papers."

Charles rose, took a pamphlet from a side table and handed it to Tim.

"This is us. I'm the senior partner. Others ..." He nodded towards the trading floor. "... are also partners. We trade everything – equities, bonds, commodities, futures, options, other derivatives, listed, unlisted. We invest in private equity. We invest globally, twenty-four hours a day. We have multiple strategies: long/short equity funds, event driven, quant ... The hedge fund industry is self-regulated and has greater freedom than others to invest however it wants. Though, of course, after the financial crisis there's blame flying and a huge debate raging about how to rein in the industry."

"Do you have any particular areas of focus or specialisation?"

"We go wherever we think we can make a profit."

"Did I gather you've been one of the few to negotiate the financial crisis rather successfully?"

"I was very bearish early on and stuck with it."

"'Bearish' meaning you expected prices to fall?"

"Yes, exactly. Sorry – we in the financial markets always talk about bulls on the upside and bears on the downside."

"And your view now?"

"Still bearish."

"Hm." This wasn't leading anywhere either. Tim held up the pamphlet. "May I keep this?"

"Of course."

"Well, thank you and sorry to have interrupted your day."

"Not at all. Let's hope we can draw a line under this horrible business as soon as possible – Lucy's death, I mean."

31

"Indeed. Good luck with your gold buying. Should I be buying?"

"If you're as pessimistic as I am on the global economy, yes, you certainly should."

"Aren't we past the worst? Haven't markets already turned?"

"Hah!" exclaimed Charles. "There's plenty more to come out of the woodwork."

FIVE

Once more at his desk, Tim logged back on to his computer. As his screens popped up, he flicked through Charles's pamphlet. It painted the same picture as Charles himself had done, but in greater detail. The pamphlet also mentioned the firm's role as an activist investor. It mentioned a strong presence in the East European markets and especially in the Russian … it seemed there were areas of focus, even if Charles had made light of this.

Among Tim's emails was a follow-up from the police. Interpol had identified the heroin as possibly originating with the Moscow mafia, who were known to use an old brewery on the outskirts of the city as a processing and distribution centre. Not one of the usual sources of heroin for the streets of London, but barely worthy of note and surely another dead end. Unless …

"Lemon, we need your help." Helen interrupted his thoughts. "You've got bird shit on your shirt, by the way."

"It's chocolate."

"Whatever. Shah's unleashed a stream of data. We need all hands to the pump to analyse what's going on."

Two minutes earlier Tim would have leaped at the invitation to get involved with the serious business, but now he wondered if he had found a connection – even if a tenuous one – between Charles and …

"Lemon, pull your finger out. I'm sending you a feed."

"But, Helen, you know what Gordon said to me."

"Forget Gordon. I need your help."

It was several hours before the team had worked through all the data, fitted one or two more pieces of the Islamist jigsaw into place and set aside much that was deemed inconsequential. They did not have the impression that terrorist action was imminent and had done as much as they could for the day. Helen with her sharp suit and sharper tongue had gone home, as had Margaret, Tabi and Nick. Trevor, who was almost always the last to leave, was still tapping at his keyboard. Gordon had retreated to his side office.

Tim ran a search for Wave Capital Management plus Russia. He came up with a couple of Financial Times articles, one referring to Wave as an early and committed investor in the Russian market and a second mentioning Wave's investment in companies controlled by the oligarch Alexei Andropov. Wave appeared to have investments in a bank and a mining company run by Andropov and a notably large holding in Andropov's Taiga Oil. Tim printed off these articles and put them together with the police report and the pamphlet he had received from Charles. With these in hand, he went and knocked on Gordon's door.

Gordon looked up from his desk. "Terror or Lucy Trenchard?"

"Lucy."

"Something to report, I hope?"

"Well ..." Tim hesitated. "I have the merest suggestion of a link."

"Go on."

"Interpol reckons that Lucy's heroin might have originated with the Russian mafia, which is a bit unusual here in London."

"Comes from everywhere nowadays."

"It also turns out Draper is quite a significant investor in the Russian market – particularly in companies run by Alexei Andropov."

"And ...?"

"Well, that's it."

"Andropov's practically a British citizen these days. He's just about the cleanest of the oligarchs. Are you suggesting he supplied the heroin?"

"At this stage, I'm not suggesting anything." Tim hesitated again. "I don't suppose this is enough to justify tapping Draper's phone and trying to get a look inside his computer?"

"Absolutely not." Gordon drew himself up in his chair. "But let's do it anyway. I've got the Director General breathing down my neck and I've had the minister's office calling me all day – and even the PM's office has called to ask for an update. I can understand poor old Trenchard's agitation, but even the DG and the PM seem to think getting to the bottom of the poor girl's death is more important than fighting terror. I'll take care of all the tiresome Regulation of Investigatory Powers paperwork. As soon as that's all signed off, go ahead and set things up. Install a tap on Draper's phones and talk to Tabi first thing tomorrow about getting into Draper's computer. Let me know whether Tabi can do it remotely or whether he needs to gain access to Draper's office to insert a program manually."

"If we need direct access, Draper's office might be difficult. He mentioned that they trade twenty-four hours a day – there's a risk someone could be in the office at pretty much any hour. I'd rather suggest his flat. When I was there, I saw that he has what looks like an outpost of his office set up in his study. If we can hook into his network from his flat, we can probably gain access to everything anyway. And if he's involved in anything other than investment, he's more likely to do it from home."

"Fine. Sounds sensible. And, actually, if memory serves, there's a major hedge fund charity bash the evening after next. See if Draper's on the attendance list. If he is, you know you've got a clear window when he'll be out of his flat."

Tim nodded and turned to leave.

"Oh, and, Tim ..."

Tim turned back.

"You've got bird shit on your shirt."

Tim turned away again. He raised his eyes in exasperation. Thanks, Gordon, he said silently to himself.

"Just trying to be helpful."

SIX

Next morning, Tabi confirmed that manual insertion of a program was preferable since this would allow him to clone Draper's entire network onto Tim's computer, whereas remote access would merely allow Tim to read Draper's emails and to trawl around inside the network in the hope that he might fortuitously light upon something of interest. Tim ascertained that Draper was indeed due to attend the charity dinner. The visit to Draper's flat was accordingly set for the following evening. But Tim thought it would first be prudent to do another recce of the flat. He was also impatient to know how frequently Draper met his Russian contacts and when he had last seen them. He needed an excuse to see Draper at his flat that day.

Tim ran a search on Andropov: multi-billionaire with business interests right across the Russian economy, service in the Russian army under the old communist regime, slightly murky period immediately post glasnost from which he had emerged as one of the band of oligarchs who had successfully gained control of swathes of the liberalised Russian economy. In recent years, he had steadily increased his commercial and property holdings in the UK, France, Switzerland and the US. Various references suggested the financial crisis had exacted quite a significant toll on his diverse holdings. He had recently divorced his wife, who now had possession of their house in Belgravia. The oligarch, meanwhile, was undertaking massive refurbishment of a huge mansion overlooking Regent's Park – though he seemed to be temporarily homeless in London while this work was going on. He also owned a fleet of private yachts, including the world's largest. Photographs of Andropov suggested a businesslike figure of middle years who nevertheless remained in athletic trim. His expression was invariably enigmatic, as though his thoughts were elsewhere – preoccupied with weightier matters than those immediately before him.

While Andropov presented himself as a clean-as-a-whistle westernised businessman, his behind-the-scenes right-hand man and general fixer was known to be Mikhail Vasiliev, an ex-KGB and

FSB agent whose name tended to come up whenever and wherever dirty work was afoot – his name had been mentioned in connection with both the Litvinenko polonium poisoning in London and the assassination of the crusading journalist Anna Politkovskaya. A small handful of photographs revealed Vasiliev to be shorter and stockier than Andropov, with a jaw permanently darkened by five o'clock shadow and with a stare of such icy intensity it might despatch to the gulag forever anyone unlucky enough to catch his eye.

Tim sat back and chewed his pen top. He could surely construct an excuse to pay Draper another visit. He picked up the phone.

"Good morning. Wave Capital." It was the voice of Miss Cappuccino.

"Oh, hello. Please could I speak to Charles Draper."

"Who may I say is calling?"

"It's Tim Lemon. You probably remember I came by yesterday."

"Just a moment, sir."

A moment's silence followed.

"Charles Draper speaking."

"Charles, hello. It's Tim Lemon here."

"Tim. How can I help?"

"Well, I'm sorry to pester you again, but I wonder if I could see you for another very brief chat?"

"I'm not sure what I can add, but yes of course."

"Actually, this is not about Lucy – it's a rather different and confidential matter where you might be able to help us."

"May I ask what?"

"I'd rather speak to you in person and it might be better if we meet at your flat rather than in your office."

"Sounds mysterious."

"No, not really, but I'd rather the conversation was kept private."

"Well, all right."

"Will you be at home this evening?"

"From seven or so."

"If I come over at seven thirty, would that work?"

"I'll see you then."

37

SEVEN

As Tim ascended the stairs to Draper's flat, he wondered whether he was being an imbecile: the conversation he was about to have would alert Draper to the fact that the Security Service was aware of and interested in his Russian connection. In the remote eventuality that Draper's Russian contacts did have some bearing on Lucy's death and especially if Draper himself were implicated in some way, it would put Draper on his guard. But then Tim's questions were not going to be about Lucy, nor about the heroin. He hoped his line of questioning would seem sufficiently innocuous and off-the-point not to arouse undue suspicion.

Draper greeted Tim at the door. Tim removed his light coat.

"Let me hang that for you."

Charles put the coat in a cupboard adjacent to the front door. Tim noted the keypad of the flat's alarm system just inside the cupboard.

"Can I offer you anything?"

"No, honestly, this will be very quick."

They sat in the living room. Tim felt slightly uncomfortable with his feet resting on the spot where the body of Lucy Trenchard had lain.

"Sorry to be conspiratorial over the phone. I just wondered if you might be in a position to help us with one thing. I saw from your pamphlet that you invest in Russia and I gather you're quite a significant investor in companies controlled by Alexei Andropov?"

"Indeed. Has Andropov been up to something?"

"No, no, not at all. Andropov's very much above board. At the same time, even these days there's a fair amount of undercover argy-bargy between us and the Russians. We like to try and keep on top of things – or one step ahead, if we can. It's actually as much to protect prominent Russian businessmen as anything else, particularly after the polonium affair. Andropov and his entourage have been slightly more difficult to look after since he moved out of his house in Belgravia. I was just wondering, do you see him or his associates very frequently?"

"A few times a year."

"And have you seen him recently?"

"Last time was a few months ago in Moscow."

"And the last time in London?"

"Some months before that."

"Do you happen to know if he has a favourite hotel here?"

"I really have no idea. I last saw him at the Alanborough."

"There's really nothing at the moment, but if we have concerns on Andropov's behalf and if there's a possibility you might be able to help us, would you mind if I got in touch with you?"

Charles gave a guffaw and rose from his armchair. "Goodness me! Enlisted in undercover work by MI5!"

"Well, no, it wouldn't be undercover work. I'd probably just ask if you happen to have any clue concerning his schedule on a particular day, for example."

"But he's over here the whole time and I only see him occasionally."

"Sure. But you never know …"

Charles shook his head in continued disbelief. "Well, fine. I can't imagine I'm going to be any help, but yes …"

"That's it, really," said Tim, rising from the sofa.

"No more on Lucy?"

"It continues to look like an altogether out-of-character private experiment which went tragically wrong."

"It's just so hard to believe …"

Charles handed Tim his coat. They shook hands.

"Andropov," said Tim, turning back at the door. "Do you know how he's fared in the financial crisis?"

"Like a number of the Russian oligarchs, he's taken a bit of a hit – but then a fair proportion of the world's business titans have taken a hit. However, Andropov's interests are well spread across the economy. I'm sure he's weathering the storm."

Once outside in the street, Tim asked himself again if he had done the sensible thing. Even if the heroin and Draper's Russian business contacts were in some way connected – which still seemed very unlikely – Tim had surely given Draper no particular cause for wariness. Tim headed for Green Park tube station. He couldn't help feeling he was clutching at straws and almost certainly wasting his time. But a thought suddenly occurred to him … He spun on his heel and set off along Piccadilly in the direction of Knightsbridge and the Alanborough.

EIGHT

As he strode along Piccadilly, Tim rang the office. Trevor answered the phone.

"Trev, could you help me with a couple of things. Could you see if we know Alexei Andropov's current movements – try the Alanborough as a starting point – and please could you send a headshot of Charles Draper to my mobile.

"You're on to something?"

"I doubt it, but no stone unturned and all that …"

"Okay. Call you back shortly."

As Tim reached Hyde Park Corner, Draper's photograph came through to his mobile and Trevor called back.

"Alanborough is right. Seems to be Andropov's home from home in London these days. He seems to have a floor to himself on a semi-permanent basis. You got the shot of Draper?"

"Yup, perfect, thanks."

At the entrance to the Alanborough, the burly, uniformed door-man sized up Tim's untidy appearance and delivered a stern look.

"Can I help you, sir?"

"I'd like to see your duty manager."

"Is he expecting you?"

This was tiresome. Tim did not want to show his ID and risk setting below-stairs tongues wagging.

"It's a private matter."

The doorman gave Tim a look which made clear he doubted his word and ushered Tim towards the reception desk.

"May I speak to the manager, please."

The manager glided over. "Sir?"

Tim discreetly showed his ID. "Do you have a private office where we could speak?"

"Of course, sir. Anushka, will you mind the desk."

They entered the manager's office.

"How may I help?"

"A couple of questions about one of your guests and in particular a visitor he may have had. Alexei Andropov – am I right in thinking he is a guest here?"

"We are lucky enough to have Mr Andropov here, yes sir."

"May I ask how often you see him here?"

"He has kept a floor of the hotel for the past nine months. I believe he finds it convenient to use us as his base in London."

"And is he usually here himself?"

"He spends several days a month in London."

"Is he here at the moment?"

"He has been with us for most of the past week."

"How about Mikhail Vasiliev, does he also stay here?"

"One of the rooms is sometimes used by Mr Vasiliev."

"Is he here now?"

"He was here a couple of days ago, but I believe he has now returned to Moscow." The manager inclined his head a fraction and gestured with his palm towards Tim. "I'm sorry, it was Mr …?"

"Lemon. Tim Lemon."

"Mr Lemon, may I ask, are our guests in some kind of … difficulty?"

"No, not at all. Actually, I rather wanted to ask you, has this man visited Mr Andropov recently?" Tim held up his mobile displaying the photo of Charles Draper.

"I can't say I recognise him, Mr Lemon."

"If I mention that he's extremely tall, does that help?"

The manager inspected the photograph again. "Ah, yes. I believe he has been to see Mr Andropov on a number of occasions."

"Recently?"

"I myself have not seen him since a month or so ago – but I'm only the night manager. He may of course have been here during the day."

"Do you think any of your staff would be able to say whether he's been here in the last week or two?"

The manager considered for a second. "I believe they usually meet in Mr Andropov's suite. The best person to ask would be the butler on Mr Andropov's floor."

"Could I speak to him now?"

The manager phoned to ask for the butler to be sent down. A few minutes later, there was a knock at the office door.

"Sean, come in." The manager closed the door behind the butler.

The butler was a curious figure: probably in his mid forties, he was not much more than five foot tall and was almost spherical. Though wholly unmilitary in physical appearance, he snapped to attention in front of the manager's desk. "Yessir," he said.

The manager leant across to Tim. He indicated Tim's mobile phone. "May I?" He showed the photograph of Draper to the butler. "Sean, do you recognise this man?"

The butler stepped forward to take a look. "Yessir." He stepped back.

"Has he visited Mr Andropov in recent days?" asked the manager.

The butler looked doubtfully at Tim.

The manager understood. "It's all right, Sean. You can speak freely."

"Guest confidentiality, sir ..."

"Yes, it's all right."

"Yessir. Yes, this gentleman has visited Mr Andropov, sir."

"Recently?" asked Tim.

"Yesterday, sir."

"Yesterday!"

"Yessir." The butler stepped forward. "They took tea, sir. Earl Grey. Mr Andropov always likes Earl Grey in the afternoon, sir." The butler stepped back.

"And this was just yesterday?" Tim asked again.

"Indeed, sir." The butler stepped forward. "Third time this week to my knowledge, sir." The butler stepped back again.

"Is this man always such a regular visitor to Mr Andropov, then?" pursued Tim.

"Certainly has been recently, sir."

"Thank you," said Tim, indicating with a gesture that his questions were done.

The manager dismissed the butler, who snapped to attention again, executed an about-face and marched out.

So, thought Tim, as he descended the steps in front of the hotel, Draper did appear to have something to hide. And not only was he a liar, he was also a much cooler customer than Tim had given him credit for: he had told his barefaced lie without missing a beat or batting an eyelid. But where did this lead? Back to Lucy or somewhere different altogether?

NINE

The following evening, Tim and Tabi waited in a car parked around the corner from Draper's flat, while Nick patrolled the street watching for Draper's departure. Phone taps had already been installed on Draper's home and office lines; the task was now to gain direct access to Draper's computer network. At six thirty, Draper exited from his building's underground car park in his yellow Lamborghini. The distinctive growl rising to a whine of the engine could be heard even in the midst of the early evening traffic. Nick watched as Draper disappeared along Piccadilly and then called through to Tim and Tabi that the coast was clear. The three of them gathered on the pavement.

Tabi, whose silver-flecked goshawk plumage and black jeans with leather jacket effortlessly achieved the cool which Nick strove so hard to attain, stared at Nick. It was not Nick's navy blazer and pale pink shirt, which looked perfectly respectable, but rather what appeared to be a large wedge of yellow cheese or possibly a triangle of multi-layered pastry apparently whizzing from his head.

"You know, you give new meaning to undercover," observed Tabi.

"Right," said Tim. "If Draper lasts the distance at the dinner, we should have five or six hours."

"More than enough," said Tabi.

"But, Nick, keep your eyes skinned just in case he reappears early."

Tabi dealt with the lock on the front door of Draper's building and he and Tim slipped inside. They padded swiftly up the stairs to Draper's door. Tabi chose the appropriate tools to pick the lock – a tiny lever like a miniature crank handle, which he inserted first, and then a wire similar to the wiggly end of a hairpin, which he jiggled inside the lock.

"I'm hopeless with those things," whispered Tim as he watched Tabi.

Nick's voice suddenly came over Tim and Tabi's earpieces. "Guys, quick, get the hell out of there! He's turned back. Shit! He's found a parking space on the street. You haven't got time to get out of the building. Hide yourselves somehow."

"Fuck," said Tabi. He looked around – there was no way out other than the stairs and no place of concealment on the stairs or landings. "We'll have to go into Draper's flat and hide there."

"Don't be daft. The flat's big, but not *that* big and we've no idea how long he'll be in there. And either we set the alarm off or we disable it and he gets suspicious."

"How about the flat opposite?" Tabi nodded at the door across the landing.

"What, break in?"

"Do we have any other option?"

"Someone may be in there …" Tim crept across the landing and put his ear to the door. He gave a gentle knock on the door and listened again. "I think we may be okay."

Tabi got to work on the lock.

Nick hissed into their earpieces, "He'll be at the building front door in ten seconds."

Tabi began to fumble.

"Shit, Tabi, you're worse than me."

"Five seconds," hissed Nick, "three, two …"

The flat door opened just as the front door to the building could be heard opening down below. Tabi and Tim glided soundlessly in. But now they heard the quiet beep which indicated the alarm had been triggered and would go off in seconds if they did not disable it. They both flashed torches around the room.

"Where's the damned keypad?" breathed Tabi.

"The layout's completely different from Draper's flat."

"I need to put the light on."

"Don't put the bloody light on – Draper might see it and he might know his neighbours aren't in at the moment."

They swept the room again with their flashlights.

"There," said Tim, indicating a control panel.

Tabi quickly connected a handheld computer which rapidly found the code and disabled the alarm. They could hear Draper arriving at

46

the top of the stairs. Tim looked through a spyhole in the flat door. He motioned to Tabi to keep still and silent – Draper was standing with an ear cocked in the direction of his neighbour's flat. Draper advanced across the landing, then paused and listened again. The flat doorbell suddenly shattered the silence, causing Tim and Tabi to jump out of their skins. Hearts pounding, they kept still. Through the spyhole, Tim could see Draper give a puzzled look, but then return to his own front door. He disappeared into his flat.

"Phew!" Tim leaned back against the wall. He accidentally jogged a side table. In the darkness, a piece of pottery could be heard beginning to wobble. Tabi flashed his torch and, leaping over, caught the pottery.

"Jesus, Tim."

They swept the flat with their torches again. It was packed with huge stone heads, carved stone reliefs and other artefacts which appeared to have come from the Middle East of ancient times.

"Bloody hell," said Tabi. "Looks like we're in the Mesopotamian room of the British Museum. Or, in fact, this looks like the stuff which was looted from the National Museum in Baghdad."

"If it is, that investigation will have to wait for another day."

"Anyway, just don't bloody touch anything, Tim."

"Guys, what the hell's going on?" It was Nick.

"We're in the flat opposite Draper's," explained Tim. "Now you need to keep your eyes open for someone who looks like a collector of ancient Middle Eastern artefacts."

Tim went back to the spyhole in the front door. They waited one minute, two, three, five …

"Sod this," said Tabi. "You don't think he's given up on the charity dinner? You could scarcely blame him … I mean, with his girlfriend dead less than a week. He can hardly be in a party mood."

"Be patient."

"Well, how long are we going to wait?"

"As long as it takes."

In fact, it was another five minutes before Draper re-emerged from his flat and then left the building. Moments later, the growl of his Lamborghini could be heard in the street. Nick called up to say that Draper really did seem to have gone this time. Tabi reset the alarm on the Mesopotamian flat.

Once inside Draper's flat, Tabi had no trouble disabling the alarm from the keypad in the coat cupboard. Tim led the way to the study.

"Draw the curtains," whispered Tabi.

Tim did so. Tabi angled a desk light over Draper's computer and switched the lamp on. He sat at the desk and powered up the hard drive and the several screens. He next plugged a laptop of his own into Draper's computer. As the screens lit up, Draper's master screen displayed a photograph of a gleaming motor yacht. The subsidiary screens all displayed the Wave Capital Management logo.

"Nice boat," remarked Tim.

"All right for some ..."

"How long's this going to take?"

"Depends. If it's just the usual password protection, it shouldn't take long. If he's got something more sophisticated built in, don't know ... it depends."

Tim paced back and forth.

"Could you stop pacing."

"Sorry."

"And please don't touch anything."

"I've got the message."

Tim went and sat in the living room. The room was dark apart from the street light thrown up from Piccadilly below. Tim stared blankly at the shadowy artworks. The bodiless blood head levitated macabrely in the gloom. Tim could just discern that the figure's frozen lids were sealed closed, as though the head – held in fragile limbo, not alive, undead – had witnessed Lucy's unsought release and could no longer bear to gaze upon the scene. Tim gave a little shudder and tried to look for other distraction in the room. He noticed what appeared to be a couple of invitation cards propped on the mantelpiece above the long, low marble fireplace, which had been restyled along spare contemporary lines with an elongated sliver of hearth. Tim rose and crossed the room to inspect the cards. Shielding his flashlight to cast only a narrow beam, he examined the first. The card bore the image of a work by Sarah Lucas comprising distended female limbs created from stuffed tights and entangled with or emanating from a wooden chair. Printed alongside the image was an invitation from an art gallery in Hoxton to a private preview of new works by British artists. Tim turned his beam on the second card. More ornate, with gilt edging and embossed lettering, this was an invitation from the partners of Petrovka Invest to a performance of Tchaikovsky's *The Sleeping Beauty* by the Bolshoi ballet in Moscow. Tim grimaced – had Draper not seen the distasteful irony of displaying such a card just a few feet from the spot where his own beauty had lain in an ill-fated sleep from which there was no fairytale return? Tim looked again at the card. It listed the names of the several partners of Petrovka Invest. Petrovka Invest – didn't that ring a bell? Hadn't the name appeared somewhere in Tim's earlier internet searches? He returned and sat on the couch. He couldn't remember in what context he might have seen the name. He took out his phone and googled 'Petrovka Invest'. A couple of references came up in Russian and one in English. The latter appeared on an obscure financial website and merely stated that Petrovka Invest was a Russian investment firm with a focus on the natural resources sector. This did not jog Tim's memory. He would have to run a more thorough search when he was back in the office. He sat for a further protracted while, vaguely mesmerised by the pulse of traffic in the street below, and then returned to Tabi.

"How are you getting on?" he asked.

"Got into the Wave network with no trouble. We can see all his business stuff. But there are also private files and a private email account which are heavily protected. However ..." Tabi worked feverishly for another couple of minutes. "We're in." He continued typing rapidly. "Damn – I'm in the files, but it's all encrypted."

"Can you break that?"

"Yes, but it may take a bit of time."

Tim glanced at his watch. "With luck, we should have at least another couple of hours."

"Doesn't matter. I've inserted a program which will allow me to continue working on this remotely from our office. And, in fact, if Draper starts using these files and the email, it should be relatively easy to follow what he's doing. All the Wave Capital stuff as well I can feed through to your desk at work. We don't need to be sitting here."

"Are we done then?"

"Just need a few minutes to check it's all working properly, cover my tracks and tidy up."

Tabi finished up and extinguished the desk light. Tim re-opened the curtains. They reset the alarm and slipped out onto the landing.

"Nick?" Tim whispered into his microphone. "We're done. Heading out."

"Immaculate timing," said Nick. "Unless I'm mistaken that's Draper's Lamborghini just turning into Piccadilly now. I'll tell you when he's in the garage and you can come out."

Tim and Tabi crossed the landing and took a few steps down the stairs. Tim suddenly stopped.

"Hold on," he said, raising a hand. He paused in thought for a second. "I need to go back in there."

"What the …" said Tabi. "Why?"

"You don't have long," warned Nick. "It is Draper."

"I just need to check something on an invitation on the mantelpiece."

"Jesus Christ," said Tabi. "How long have you been sitting there when you could have been checking some bloody invitation? You've practically had time to reply and attend the event."

"Yeah, sorry. I did check, but I just thought of something. Nick, you have to delay Draper for sixty seconds."

"Bloody hell, you guys …"

There was a moment's pause and then Tim and Tabi heard a screeching of brakes – loudly through their earpieces and more distantly outside. They looked at each other in shock for a moment, but then heard Nick's voice through their earpieces …

"Whoah! Sorry mate, really sorry!"

"You idiot! I could have killed you!" It was Draper's voice.

"Yeah, really sorry, honestly mate." Nick for some reason had adopted an Australian accent.

Tabi was standing transfixed.

"Tabi, quick – the damned door," hissed Tim.

Tabi hastily reopened the door to the flat and disabled the alarm. Tim sped into the living room. He shone his torch on the invitation from the Russian firm: the first-named partner was Yevgeny Berezin – *this* was the name which Tim had seen before, not Petrovka Invest. There had been some brief mention of Berezin in connection with Andropov's Taiga Oil. Tim took out his mobile phone and snapped a picture of the invitation before scuttling back to the front door. Tabi reset the alarm.

Meanwhile, Nick continued his Antipodean ramble. "Sorry, had a few tinnies and got a bit lost – wasn't looking where I was going … You couldn't tell me the way to Earls Court, could you, mate?"

Tim and Tabi ran down the stairs and waited just inside the front door of the building.

"Okay, Nick," whispered Tim. "We're at the front door. You can let him go."

A moment later, Nick indicated the coast was clear. Tim and Tabi walked briskly along the side street on the opposite side of the building from the garage entrance and doubled back to their own parked car. Nick appeared a few seconds later.

"Jesus, you guys, you sure like cutting things fine. Nearly got myself run over for you there. Might be one thing to go *at* the wheel of a Lamborghini, but not *under* the wheel …"

"Well, anyway – we're all here and the job's done, thank God," observed Tim.

"Tim, what was that invitation business all about?" asked Tabi.

"I realised there was a name which rang a bell."

"And?" pressed Tabi.

"I don't know – I'm going to have to do some checking."

Tim beeped the lock on their car.

"And, Nick," continued Tabi, "what the duck-billed platypus was with the Australian accent?"

"Dunno, cobber – just came to me."

TEN

Tabi had cleared some space in the midst of the clutter on Tim's desk and was already playing the computer like a Steinway when Tim arrived at the office the following morning.

"Morning, Tim. Draper's business stuff is all up-and-running. You can see everything that Wave Capital is up to."

Tabi showed Tim how to navigate through Draper's various files and information feeds.

"I'll leave you to it. Happy data mining. Meanwhile, I'll see if I can get into the encrypted stuff. Though I should just warn you I've also got a ton of things to do for Gordon and Helen – I might not get round to this till a bit later. Anyway, I'll let you know as soon as I make any progress."

"Great. Thanks, Tabi."

Tabi had set up the computer surveillance program so that Tim could explore Draper's saved files and his email archive and at the same time could monitor whatever Draper was working on at that particular moment.

Helen leaned over and looked at Draper's motor yacht screen saver. "Your man's entry in the mine's-bigger-than-yours contest?"

"Guess so."

"I have to admit I might accept an invitation. Though ..." Helen straightened in her chair. "... I should also say again I think this department ought to be spending all its time and effort on counter-terrorism, not on billionaire yacht owners with dead girlfriends, however tragic the circumstances."

Seventy-two hours earlier, Tim would have been of the same mind as Helen, but now he was becoming intrigued. He settled down to work. Not surprisingly, the vast majority of Draper's files, correspondence and current activity related to Wave's investment interests. Corporate reports, brokers' research and recommendations, trading profit and loss accounts, options strategies – the latter a mass of Greek letters which meant absolutely nothing to Tim ... Draper also had a busy travel schedule, for both business and pleasure, and a full social calendar, again apparently a mix of business and pleasure. As Tim carefully picked his way through file after file and page after page, various threads began to emerge.

Firstly, Draper's correspondence with Andropov and his senior associates was extensive. After the correspondence with Andropov himself, the most frequent was with the finance director of Taiga Oil, Vladimir Popov. Andropov clearly regarded Draper not simply as a key investor, but also as an important ally in his control of Taiga. Furthermore, while it was nowhere explicitly stated, Tim began to get the impression that the global financial and economic crisis had put Andropov in some financial difficulty: he seemed to be looking to Draper for additional financial support. Mention of Taiga Oil meanwhile also prompted Tim to run a separate internet search for Yevgeny Berezin. Tim found the article he had seen before – indeed this was the only reference to Berezin in English which he could find. The piece fleetingly mentioned Berezin as a close ally of the Kremlin and as the third largest shareholder in Taiga after Andropov and Wave Capital. The article seemed to imply that Berezin's relationship with Andropov was ambivalent. Tim returned to his examination of the correspondence between Draper and Andropov and went carefully through the recent exchange of emails again. There seemed to be lacunae in the correspondence – there were references to emails which were not in the archive. Tim wandered over to Tabi.

"Tabi, can I borrow you for a sec?"

"Sure."

Back at his desk, Tim showed Tabi the references to emails which were clearly no longer on file. "Are you able to dig up deleted stuff?"

"I should be able to get into his back-up server, which ought to show whatever was in the files originally. Let's try a couple of the dates referred to in these emails."

It took Tabi a few minutes to access the back-up files. He placed them alongside Draper's current email archive: the missing emails which Tim was looking for did not appear to be in the back-up either.

"Mystery," said Tabi. "We may be stuck on this one."

As Tim continued digging, the second point he noticed was that Draper seemed to be buying very heavily into gold. His purchase a couple of days earlier when Tim had been in his office was by no means an isolated instance. He seemed to have started buying in earnest three or four months earlier and was steadily amassing a huge position. There was an early reference to this in his correspondence with Andropov, but then he was silent on the subject. Tim had the impression that Wave's bullion holdings were becoming out of proportion to the size of the firm and its other investments. Margaret had the best financial brain on the team – Tim walked over to her desk to seek her advice.

"Maggie, please could you help me with this? If I've understood things correctly, Wave has about eight or nine billion quid under management, yet somehow contrives to hold slightly more than that in gold ... and that's before you even consider its other investments..."

"It's called leverage, Tim. It's a big part of what the financial crisis has been all about. Prior to the crisis, everyone was borrowing very cheaply on a huge scale and thereby massively leveraging their investments – or their assets in the case of the banks."

"So Draper can use Wave's own capital *plus* borrowed money to make investments which are bigger than Wave itself?"

"Exactly. Then if things go well, they make a large profit on the overall investment, pay back the borrowings and earn an even greater return on their own capital. For example, if they invest a billion of their own capital plus, say, a further billion of borrowed money – i.e. two billion in total – and if their overall investment rises by fifty percent to three billion, they can then cash in, pay back the borrowed billion plus the cost of borrowing – let's say one hundred million – leaving them with a profit of nine hundred million – in other words, a return on their own capital of ninety percent rather than just fifty percent."

"And presumably the reverse is true – if things go badly wrong, they can be wiped out?"

"Precisely. Hence the financial crisis."

"Hm. But, as you say, the massive leveraging of investments was *before* the crisis, wasn't it? Draper's been building this position just recently. I thought nobody was lending money to hedge funds or anyone else at the moment?"

"You're right. But he must be borrowing from somewhere. Might be worth trying to track down where."

"The other thing is this gold position is now his biggest investment by far. His next biggest seems to be his holding in Andropov's Taiga Oil, which is equivalent to about two billion pounds. Isn't he taking a huge risk staking so much on one investment? I mean, he did tell me he was still very pessimistic about the world's markets and, if he's right, I guess that should mean the gold price will rise. But what if he's wrong? Isn't he courting disaster?"

"Potentially so. But bear in mind his other investments are probably a hedge against the gold position. I mean, if the world's financial markets rally, his other investments will go up, just as his gold investment will go down. Even so, he does seem to be making a very hefty bet. If it becomes too out-of-kilter, I would think it starts to become a wild gamble and possibly a breach of his fiduciary duty to his investors."

Tim stood for a moment frowning in thought. "More basic question and probably a very dumb one. What actually is the point of investing in gold? I mean, it doesn't have any yield and you can't do much with it apart from make jewellery."

"You're absolutely right. Investment in gold is pure superstition. As you suggest, it has a magpie attraction for us ..." Margaret held up her hand to display her wedding ring. "... but otherwise it has few practical applications. Intrinsically it has limited value and yet all of us, from humble brides-to-be to governors of central banks, worship it. If one day we all woke up, cast aside superstition and came to our rational senses, these lumps of shiny metal would be virtually worthless."

"Lemon, phone ..." called Helen.

"Thanks, Maggie, that's all really helpful." Tim returned to his desk and picked up his phone. "Tim Lemon."

"Mr Lemon, good morning. It's Alfred Blair, the night manager at the Alanborough whom you met the evening before last. I hope you don't mind my calling."

"No, of course not. Good morning to you. Is there some new development?"

"Actually, it's Sean O'Hanlon, the butler whom you also met. He'd like to see you."

"Did he say what about?"

"He wouldn't tell me, which is a little strange. He is a slightly odd chap, but I must say he seems unusually agitated."

"Well, I'd be happy to see him. Should I come over to the hotel this morning?"

"Well, no, that's another thing. He wants to meet you outside. He asks if you could meet him at six p.m. in Green Park. I'm sorry to put you to this trouble and I've really no idea what he wants to tell you, but would that be all right?"

"Yes, of course. Did he say where in Green Park?"

"Yes, he suggested the Canada Memorial at the south eastern corner of the park."

"I'll certainly be there."

"Thank you. Please do let me know if I can be of any further help."

Curious, thought Tim. Was the plot thickening or had he sparked paranoia or some conspiracy fantasy in the odd little man? Tim returned to Draper's files.

The third salient item which Tim couldn't help but notice was perhaps just a distraction: Draper's magnificent motor yacht was a relatively recent purchase and there was a great volume of correspondence between him and the boat builders concerning the exact specifications for the craft. Tim succumbed to the temptation to dwell upon the many photographs of luxurious interiors and sleek outer lines. Draper had essentially commissioned a private seven star hotel offering every conceivable watersport and capable of travelling one thousand five hundred nautical miles at a top speed of twenty-four knots.

Helen noticed what Tim was up to. "Lemon, seriously, there is no way you or I will ever set foot on a boat like that. Don't you think you should be getting on with some work rather than drooling over it?"

Tabi was now standing behind them. "She is a beauty, though." He returned to the matter at hand. "Tim, I'm in. Very tough encryption, mind you. I don't know who Draper had to set that up for

56

him, but it's more like what you'd expect from us or the CIA or the FSB or the Israelis or someone like that – not what you'd expect from a private individual or small company. Anyway, may I …?"

Tabi sat at Tim's desk. He added a couple of icons to Tim's screen linking him to Draper's encrypted file and email account.

"Here's the latest email," said Tabi. "Actually, from Andropov. Looks like they're planning some kind of party on an island somewhere."

The email message was displayed on Tim's screen: 'Let's pop the cork on La Isla Bonita mid-June. Will deliver champagne Cassis 1st June.'

"'Champagne Cassis' … does he mean *kir royal*? That's champagne with cassis, isn't it?" asked Tim.

"And now he's discussing cocktails …" sighed Helen, affecting a tone of weary resignation.

"I wonder if he's delivering Russian champagne," continued Tim, ignoring Helen.

Trevor now added his contribution. "Doubt it. Sickly sweet stuff, Russian champagne. Can't imagine they'd want that. I'm quite sure Andropov has a cellarful of the best French stuff to lay on."

"Where's La Isla Bonita?" asked Tabi.

"Spanish probably," replied Helen, finally relenting and allowing herself to be drawn into the debate. "The Blessed Isle? No … perhaps The Beautiful Island? The Bonny Isle? Maybe in the Balearics?"

"Hang on a sec," said Tim. He took over from Tabi at the screen and went back to Draper's unencrypted correspondence with his boat builder. After glancing through a few emails, Tim found what he was looking for. "Thought so." He enlarged to full screen one of a series of photographs of the boat and pointed to the calligraphy on the stern: La Isla Bonita. "It's not actually an island, it's the name of Draper's boat."

"Boys and girls, are we working or are we dreaming of what we can't afford?" It was Gordon.

The huddle around Tim's desk broke up. Tabi, however, resumed his position at Tim's computer.

"One more thing to show you," said Tabi. He reopened the encrypted files. "I haven't been through everything, but I think you'll find the missing emails are all here. Looks like the correspondence went underground, so to speak."

"Thanks, Tabi, you're a star."

"If it would be helpful, once you've got your head around these two characters, give me a list of key names, words, phrases – Draper, Andropov, Wave Capital Management, whatever Andropov's companies are called, the name you found on the invitation if that's relevant, that sort of thing – 'hedge fund' is too broad, but anything clearly and specifically relating to them – then I can write you a program which will monitor our network in case a reference to them pops up somewhere. A hit anywhere on our radar and you'll get an alert in your email."

"You're a magician."

"I'm bloody good, aren't I?"

"And modest with it …"

Tim returned to his task. The encrypted file and correspondence shed further light on the urgency of Andropov's financial problems. It seemed he was in danger of losing control of Taiga Oil and was heavily dependent on Draper's support. Andropov held just over fifty percent of the company, Draper twenty-three percent. Berezin controlled twenty-one percent and was clearly seen as a threat by Andropov. Taiga, meanwhile, appeared to have borrowed heavily over a number of years and to have mistimed its investment in new oil and gas production. The company now needed to raise fresh equity capital from its shareholders in order to pay down some of its debts. Andropov's finances across his whole empire were severely stretched and he was having to make difficult choices as to where he directed his resources. His preference was not to invest more of his funds into Taiga's capital raising. However, this would mean his share of the company would drop below fifty percent. Provided Draper remained firmly in Andropov's camp, this would not be a problem since their combined holding would still be large enough for Andropov to retain effective control. But if Draper were to offer his stake to Berezin, for example, then Andropov would become extremely vulnerable since Berezin would subsequently control almost as much of the company as Andropov himself. As far as Tim could see, Draper did not appear to be in active discussion with Berezin; however, delving further back into Draper's unencrypted emails, Tim unearthed a brief exchange between Draper and Berezin dating from several months earlier and relating to a meeting in Moscow which the two of them had held at that time. The subject of the meeting was not disclosed, but it was surely not difficult to imagine the likely topic. As Tim reverted to the encrypted files, it also became clear that one of the reasons why Andropov's finances were so stretched was because he too was devoting a significant portion of his funds to investing heavily in gold. In addition, it seemed the bank controlled by Andropov, Ruza Bank, though experiencing some credit crisis related problems and bad debt writedowns of its own, was nevertheless funding the gold purchases of both Andropov and Draper. Finally, the encrypted correspondence included a couple of references to 'part two of the gold investment plan' or simply 'gold phase two'; however, there was no indication at all what phase two might entail.

By now it was approaching five p.m. and Tim realised he needed to set off for Green Park. He quickly put together and emailed to Tabi an initial list of key names for Tabi to write into his monitoring program: Draper, Andropov, Wave Capital Management, Taiga Oil, Ruza Bank, Siberian Minerals Corporation, Popov, Berezin, Vasiliev, Lucy Trenchard, Alanborough Hotel, La Isla Bonita (was that worth including?) ... He could add others later if appropriate. As he was readying to leave, Gordon approached.

"Anything useful, Tim, or just photos of superyachts?"

"Well, it seems Draper is a very cool liar. He told me he saw Andropov a few times a year and had last seen him in Moscow some months ago. It transpires that, in fact, over the past week they've been meeting at the Alanborough pretty much on a daily basis. And their email correspondence shows they're working absolutely hand-in-glove. I can't say they're doing anything illegal, but they're clearly thick as thieves."

"And prefer that we don't know about it. Hm, perhaps I should have a word with our friend Draper."

"I have another possible lead – though it might just be a red herring. The butler who works on Andropov's floor at the Alanborough has asked to see me. I'm actually on my way to meet him now."

"Good." Gordon looked thoughtful. "I must confess this little investigation is proving more interesting than I expected. Let me know in the morning what the butler saw."

As Gordon turned back to his office, Maggie caught his eye.

"Anything new from Martin Chilvers and his contact in Moscow?"

"Apparently, they're due to meet the day after tomorrow. I'm hoping all will be revealed then."

ELEVEN

Tim emerged from Green Park tube thirty minutes later and crunched down the gravelly path towards the Canada Memorial. As he approached the huge split wedge of red granite decorated with bronze maple leaves, he could see that O'Hanlon had not yet appeared. Tim glanced at his watch – he was ten minutes early. He slowed his pace. A young couple – he with bouffant afro, she with punky crop dyed pink and peroxide – walked by hand-in-hand. A circle of teenage girls sat on the grass and talked animatedly. A trio among them – their school uniforms subverted by means of shortened skirt hems, neckties knotted fat and pulled loose with a couple of blouse buttons undone and socks pushed down about their ankles – burst into a rendition of the chorus from Rihanna's *Umbrella*, echoing '-ella, -ella …' An old gentleman waited by a stand of trees as his equally ancient cocker spaniel sniffed at the bole of an oak.

Ten minutes passed. Fifteen. Still no sign of O'Hanlon. Tim began to pace back and forth, but then thought he might draw attention to himself. He went and sat on the grass. He noticed he had trodden in dog shit and rose again to find a stick to clean his shoe. At six thirty he called the Alanborough.

"Mr Blair? It's Tim Lemon. I'm at the rendezvous point – actually, I've been here since ten to six – and there's no sign of Mr O'Hanlon. Might he have been delayed at the hotel?"

"No, I'm pretty sure … let me put you on hold for a second." After a brief pause, the manager returned to the line. "No, I've just checked and, as I thought, Mr O'Hanlon left the hotel at five thirty. It's only five or at most ten minutes' walk to where you are, so he should have been with you ages ago."

"Do you know if he was heading somewhere else first?"

"I've no idea, but he's an absolute stickler for punctuality and punctilious to a fault – makes him a very good butler. I'm quite sure he would have been on time unless something unexpected and outside his control intervened."

"You don't think he might have simply changed his mind – thought better of it?"

"No, as I say, I'm sure he would have let us know if there was a change of plan. Very peculiar. Well, I am sorry. I hope we haven't wasted too much of your evening."

"No, that's fine."

"I'll speak to Mr O'Hanlon in the morning and find out what's going on."

TWELVE

Tim was woken next morning by his mobile. He stared at the phone for a second as he struggled to return to consciousness. The 020-7 number displayed on the screen looked familiar.

"Morning. Tim Lemon."

"Mr Lemon, good morning. My apologies if I woke you."

"No, that's okay." Tim looked at his watch. Just after six a.m.

"It's Alfred Blair …"

"Sorry?"

"… from the Alanborough. I'm sorry, I have woken you, haven't I?"

Tim was now wide awake. Moreover, he detected a note of panic in the hotel manager's voice. "No, please, carry on."

"Well, I'm not one hundred percent sure and it's really quite shocking, but I took a call from the police just a few minutes ago and I think they've found Mr O'Hanlon." The previously cool and collected hotel manager was talking very fast – almost to the point of gabbling. "They've found … well, it's just too terrible … but they've found a body floating in the Thames at Canary Wharf. The police couldn't yet confirm the man's identity, but they called me because he's wearing an Alanborough tunic and from the description … well, I think it has to be poor Sean. I just can't imagine …"

"Did the police say where in Canary Wharf and do you know if they're still there?"

"Oh, I'm not sure. I think they said Limehouse Reach – Westferry Road … does that sound right? And, yes, I suppose they must still be there – when I spoke to them, they hadn't even pulled him out of the water. I think he was snagged under a pier and they said divers were just lifting him out."

THIRTEEN

As Tim approached the roundabout at the top of Westferry Road, he immediately saw the line of police cars. A police tent had been erected on the pier to shield the body from curious eyes. Tim drew up next to a police Range Rover. What must have been the diving team was loading dry suits into the back of the car. As Tim stepped out, one of the police divers approached.

"I'm sorry, sir, this area is closed to the public at the ..."

Tim flashed his ID.

The diver gave a surprised look. "You'd probably best speak to Inspector Hunt – standing by the tent."

Tim saw the ursine figure of Inspector Hunt hunched in a one-man scrum-down over a cigarette. He strode over and bade the inspector good morning.

"Mr Lemon! Don't tell me this poor chap was also related to a cabinet minister?"

"No. Just a rather bizarre coincidence." Tim wondered to himself whether it was indeed a coincidence. "Sean O'Hanlon?"

"We believe so. His wife is on her way to identify him – lives nearby apparently. But do I take it you know him?"

"Met him once."

"Please ..." Hunt ushered Tim into the tent.

"Yes, that's him. Poor sod." Tim crouched over the body. Although O'Hanlon had presumably been in the Thames for some hours, there was a faint whiff of alcohol. "Drink?"

"Yes, we noticed that. Can you shed any light on this?"

"I really haven't a clue. He was a butler at the Alanborough – as I think you've gathered. He asked to see me last night – didn't say why. Never showed up. I guess we have the reason."

As they stepped out of the tent, a police officer approached escorting a middle-aged woman. Like O'Hanlon, she was small and rotund. She looked pale and a little terrified and held a handkerchief to her mouth.

"Mrs O'Hanlon?" asked Hunt, doing his best to soften his habitual growl.

She nodded.

"We're most awfully sorry. This must be terrible for you. Please..." Hunt held the tent open for her to enter.

Mrs O'Hanlon stood in silent shock for a moment. Her lower lip trembled and tears began to well from her eyes. "Oh, dear." She spoke with a soft Irish accent. "What happened? Tell me what happened."

"I wish we could say, Mrs O'Hanlon," responded Hunt. "I'm afraid all we really know is that he was spotted trapped under this pier first thing this morning." Hunt allowed Mrs O'Hanlon a moment of silent grief before asking, almost apologetically, "Did he like a drink by any chance?"

"Oh, no. Well, not these ten years – hasn't touched it in all that time. Absolutely teetotal. Are you saying he might have been drunk?"

"Well, we're not sure, but there is a bit of an odour of alcohol."

Mrs O'Hanlon leaned a little towards her husband's body, as though attempting to sniff the alcohol from a distance. "No," she said firmly, "that's impossible."

FOURTEEN

"... and, don't tell me," said Gordon, "the police have identified the alcohol as vodka and the brand as Stolichnaya." He seemed rather pleased with his grim witticism. "A girl who never touches drugs dies of an overdose and a teetotaller of many years' standing suddenly knocks back a skinful and falls in the Thames. Your friend Mr Draper and his friend Mr Andropov are proving unlucky people to know."

Tim sat in Gordon's side office. He had briefed Gordon on the events of the early morning. Gordon paced back and forth drumming his fingers on his paunch.

"Let's haul the bugger in, shake him up a bit – Draper, I mean. Not Andropov, of course – don't want to trigger a major diplomatic row. I shouldn't think Draper will tell us anything interesting while he's here, but we have the inside track on his correspondence with Andropov – might be interesting to see what we stir up."

"You never know," added Tim. "He let drop about the Alanborough ..."

"Any further such helpful hints will be a bonus. You and Nick go and pick him up at his office now."

"Not Nick – Nick, er, bumped into Draper when we planted the spy program in his computer. Nick had to delay Draper for a few minutes while Tabi and I made our escape."

"With Trevor, then."

"Should we put Draper in a conference room?"

"Certainly not. Bung him in an interrogation room and make sure he's left there by himself for a good hour or so before we go and have a chat with him."

FIFTEEN

The Wave Capital receptionist, who as before was Chanel-ed to the nines, put down the phone. She sculpted a smile of polite demur.

"Mr Draper apologises, but he can't see you just at this moment. He'll be engaged with visiting clients for another half hour or so. He asks if you wouldn't mind waiting – or of course you could make an appointment for later on, if that would be more convenient for you."

"That's okay, we'll wait, thank you," said Tim.

"Of course. Please do take a seat. May I offer you tea or coffee in the meantime?"

"I'm fine, thank you. But, Trev, I recommend the cappuccino."

"Well, I'll take the recommendation, if that's all right?"

"Certainly."

The cappuccino duly arrived with a gold embossed chocolate euro resting on the froth.

After twenty-five minutes Draper emerged with his two clients – both Middle Eastern in appearance, one older, portly and with a halting gait, the other in his thirties. Tim and Trevor rose from their seats. Draper mouthed 'with you in a second' towards Tim and Trevor as he ushered his departing visitors out to the lifts. He returned a few moments later.

"Gentlemen. My apologies for keeping you waiting."

"No, we should apologise for barging in without an appointment," said Tim. "My colleague, Trevor Wilde."

The three shook hands.

"Please ..." Draper held open the door to the trading room and then led the way across the trading floor and into his office. Noting that MI5 had come in force on this occasion, he closed the door to his office behind him. "New developments?"

"Actually, with further apologies, we need your assistance for a few hours and would like you to return with us to headquarters," explained Tim.

Draper's features betrayed a moment of puzzlement, but glancing out at his colleagues on the trading floor he chose not to press for an immediate explanation. "Hm. The timing's not ideal. I have a rather full diary this morning. Could we make it end of the afternoon?"

"It's not really something that can wait, I'm afraid."

Draper showed a flicker of impatience, but clearly recognised that he was not being offered much of a choice.

SIXTEEN

Once back at MI5, Tim escorted Draper to a windowless basement room furnished only with a bare table and two simple chairs.

"Sorry – hospitality not really up to Wave Capital standards. Have a seat and we'll be back with you shortly." Tim left.

An hour later, Tim returned with Gordon.

Draper rose from his chair and proffered a hand to Gordon. "Charles Draper. Pleased to meet you."

Gordon ignored Draper, but began to pace back and forth across the cell. Draper resumed his seat.

Gordon suddenly turned and advanced on Draper. He leaned across the table, resting on curled fists in a gorilla-like hunch. Inches from Draper's face, he quietly snarled, "Mr Draper, you may think, as a very rich man, you are somewhat above the law and not required to tell the truth to Her Majesty's servants, but I DO NOT LIKE IT…" Gordon suddenly bellowed and slammed his open palms down on the table, "… when my operatives are lied to."

Draper barely flinched.

"You informed Mr Lemon here," resumed Gordon, "that you last saw Alexei Andropov in Moscow some months ago. The Alanborough tells us that over the past week – and on countless other occasions – you have practically been sleeping together."

"Am I under arrest?" responded Draper coolly.

"No, Mr Draper, you are not under arrest. We asked for your help and you immediately – immediately! – fed us complete lies." Gordon continued to speak through clenched teeth. "We thought you might perhaps like to explain yourself."

"My business affairs and particularly those of Mr Andropov are a private matter …"

"Mr Draper, let me remind you that a dead girl was found in your flat a week ago. You may be unaware, but this morning Mr Andropov's butler from the Alanborough was fished out of the Thames."

At this revelation, Draper looked genuinely surprised.

69

"The dead bodies seem to be accumulating around you and Mr Andropov," continued Gordon. "You are not under suspicion, but I think in your own interests and in those of your business partner, you might choose to be a little more helpful."

Draper paused for a few moments. "All right, I confess. I see Alexei very frequently. I am a significant investor in his companies and we discuss his business on a regular basis. But the reason for my lying to you is very simple and there's no hugger-mugger or conspiracy involved – or certainly not on my part. As I'm sure you know, the Russian oligarchs are all absolutely paranoid about their security and everything else. For them, a trip to the corner shop to buy bread and milk is a secret mission. If Andropov got the faintest whiff that I was talking to MI5 about his movements, how do you think that would affect our business relationship? Of course I didn't want to seem uncooperative and secretive with you, so I agreed to Mr Lemon's request. But the truth is, you place me in a potentially very awkward position."

Tim now stepped forward. "Don't you think it might have been better to explain this at the outset?"

"In retrospect, perhaps. But surely my position is not so difficult to understand?"

"Could you explain to us exactly what is happening between you and Andropov?" continued Tim.

Draper furrowed his brow as though it pained him to divulge the details. "I invest in three of Andropov's companies: Taiga Oil, Ruza Bank and Siberian Minerals Corporation. Taiga is by far the most important – I hold twenty-three percent of the company. The long and the short of it is, Andropov is terrified he's going to lose control of Taiga and he's absolutely dependent on my support. It's true I've been approached by one of Andropov's competitors in particular who would like me to sell my stake to him ..."

Berezin, thought Tim.

" ... but I think Andropov is the best business manager among his peers. I could book a very decent short term gain if I sold out now, but I think Andropov offers the best investment potential for the long term. And, to be honest, I also see myself as something of a business ally for him."

"Where is Andropov now?" intervened Gordon.

"He returned to Moscow two days ago."

"How about Mikhail Vasiliev? Do you know where he is?"

"He was here in London until a few days ago. I guess he returned to Moscow with Alexei, but I don't actually know."

"When are you next due to meet Andropov?"

"We have nothing arranged, but I expect when he's next in London ... I guess in a week or two."

"Do you deal pretty much exclusively with Andropov himself," asked Tim, "or do you also see other members of his management team?"

"I'm due to meet Popov, the CFO of Taiga Oil, for lunch tomorrow. I see him quite regularly – and very occasionally Malkovich, the titular chief executive, though it's entirely Andropov who calls the shots as major shareholder and chairman."

"How about the butler at the Alanborough – small, round chap – do you have any clue whether Andropov had any dealings with him beyond ordering afternoon tea and getting his shoes polished?"

"I've no idea, but I very much doubt it."

"Could the butler have been present when sensitive matters were being discussed?"

"Again, I doubt it – and, I'm sure, like any good butler, he would have been the soul of discretion."

Draper was released with a further, but slightly milder, rebuke from Gordon. Tim and Gordon returned to the latter's office.

"He's quite wrong about the oligarchs' paranoia," offered Gordon.

Tim looked puzzled.

"Well," continued Gordon, "with the lifestyle of a Russian billionaire, I'd say the grandeur was entirely real and not remotely delusional and, similarly, when you're surrounded by people who'd be pleased to serve your head on a platter with your eyeballs glowing in the dark, it's not so much a persecution complex as a cold, hard assessment of reality. However, that's a bit of an aside ..." Gordon pursed his lips and stared into the distance for a moment. "Do you think Andropov's putting the screws on Draper? Do you think Lucy

Trenchard could have been a message to Draper that he should support Andropov or very unpleasant things would start to happen?"

"I hadn't considered that."

"Bit of lateral thinking required ..."

"Draper did seem genuinely upset on the morning of Lucy's death. Though he's pulled himself together remarkably since then." Tim pondered. "I think Draper's first and foremost a money man. Maybe this is unduly harsh, but my impression is he puts his business interests way before any personal ties."

"So where does that leave us?"

"Still pretty much at square one. There's no firm evidence that Lucy was murdered. I've absolutely no idea what O'Hanlon wanted to tell me and, even if he was murdered, I'd be surprised if there were any evidence linking his death to Andropov. Draper's doing nothing illegal in investing in Andropov's companies. There's no law against the two of them meeting. Draper's gold investments are disproportionately large, but that's his lookout ..."

"Continue monitoring his calls and correspondence in case this morning's little discussion provokes anything. Find out where he's having lunch with Popov and make sure we listen to their conversation. See what the police have to say about O'Hanlon. Keep an open mind about the possibility that Draper's being threatened. Keep me posted if there's anything of particular interest; otherwise, let's reconvene in a couple of days. If there are fresh leads to follow, we'll continue. If not, I'll tell the DG and the minister we've done all we can."

SEVENTEEN

Tim returned to his desk and opened up Draper's calendar. His lunch with Popov, the CFO of Taiga Oil, was booked at one p.m. at a Japanese restaurant in St James's, just a few minutes from Draper's office. Tim considered for a moment how best to eavesdrop on the lunchtime conversation. He picked up his phone and called the restaurant.

"Good morning. I'm calling from Mr Draper's office to confirm his lunch at one p.m. tomorrow."

A Japanese girl answered in delicate tones. "Yes, sir. I have booking. Two people. Mr Draper is very welcome."

"Do you have a private room?"

"Is already booked, sir."

"Oh good. Thank you."

"You're welcome."

A private room made life easier. Tim would stop by later and plant a bug in the room. Meanwhile, Tim noticed that Draper had logged back on to his computer and had opened his private email account. He watched as Draper typed a message to Andropov: 'Authorities on alert after finding second body and now aware of our close business ties. Have been asked some tiresome questions, but authorities seem to be grasping at straws – and, of course, have absolutely no idea about gold/champagne. Let's review situation when you return.' Almost immediately a reply came back from Andropov: 'What questions?' Draper typed again: 'Mostly concerning our business relationship. I simply told them the truth – ie that I invest heavily in your companies, especially Taiga Oil, and that I strongly support your continuing control of Taiga.' 'That's it?' 'Pretty much. No cause for alarm.' 'We'll discuss when I'm back in London next week.'

Tim frowned. Was this tantamount to an admission of guilt on Draper's part? Not really, not quite. Was Gordon right to suspect that Draper was being threatened? Andropov's blunt questions and his closing remark had an ominous ring to them. And what about the

73

reference to 'gold/champagne'? Were they planning to corner the gold market? Was that even possible? Had O'Hanlon got wind of this and was that what he had wanted to tell Tim? And was the champagne simply to celebrate their anticipated success on board Draper's yacht? That certainly wasn't how it came across in Draper's message. Increasingly, it seemed that 'champagne' might not be champagne at all, but rather a codeword for something else.

Helen was observing Tim as he sat hunched in concentration.

"Your meeting shaken something out of the trees?" she asked.

"Maybe," replied Tim. "Still not really clear."

"You seem to have half persuaded Gordon that something's going on."

"Yuh – though he's just given me forty-eight hours to come up with more evidence or we drop the case."

"Good. We're closing in on the Islamist hotspots. It would help if you were back on the team."

"Sure," said Tim rather abstractedly. "Sorry, just need a word with Maggie ..."

Tim rose and walked over to Margaret's desk.

"Tim?"

"Somewhat similar line of questioning to last time. Do you have any idea, would it be possible to corner the gold market?"

"I doubt it and, anyway, I'm sure it would be illegal. You're talking about Draper?"

"Yes."

"You mentioned he had about ten billion in gold, yes?"

"Yup. And, I'm guessing, but let's say Andropov has the same."

"I think the gold market isn't huge, but I would guess it should easily accommodate their volumes. If memory serves, over the past decade European central banks have collectively sold several tens of billions of dollars' worth. A couple of tens of billions sounds like a lot, but I can't imagine it would be anywhere near enough to corner the market. My wild guess is twenty billion would be equivalent to, I don't know, a few days' trading on the London market." Margaret ran a quick internet search. "Here we go. Last month daily volumes cleared by the London Bullion Market Association were around twenty-five billion dollars. Ah, but there's also an FT article

74

suggesting the actual volumes traded are significantly higher." Margaret turned back to Tim. "Anyway, the point is, even taking the LBMA figure, twenty billion is less than a single day's volume. Mind you, it also says here annual global production is only about one hundred billion dollars' worth at the current price. I suppose if the whole of Draper and Andropov's holdings were bought or sold in one go, it would temporarily destabilise the market. But if that were the deliberate intention, I'm sure it would qualify as market manipulation and, again, would be illegal."

"On the money, as ever. Thank you, Maggie."

Tim did not feel he was any closer to understanding Draper's gold scheme. On the face of it, the plan seemed exactly as Draper had described it and nothing more – in other words, an extremely bearish view on world financial markets translated into a bullish view on the gold price.

EIGHTEEN

Tim glanced up and down St James's just in case Draper happened to be out and about in the area. The coast was clear. Tim entered the Japanese restaurant.

"Sorry, sir. We closed now."

"That's okay. I'd just like to ask a quick question. Does the restaurant offer any private rooms for lunch or dinner?"

"Yes, sir. We have one."

Tim was equipped to bug a number of rooms, but a single private room again made his job more straightforward.

"How many people can the room take?"

"Eight people."

"Would it be possible to have a quick look?"

"We closed now, sir."

"Yes, but it would only take two seconds."

The Japanese girl looked around hesitantly. "Okay, if very quick."

"Sure, thank you, that's very kind."

The girl escorted Tim up a flight of stairs and through the main restaurant. Tim meanwhile secreted in his hand one of the miniature transmitters which Tabi had provided. The girl drew back paper *shoji* screens to reveal a private room with a floor of *tatami* mats and a low central table with a deep footwell beneath.

"May I?" said Tim, lifting a foot to step onto the *tatami*.

"Ah!" cried the girl. "Please no shoes on *tatami* mat!"

"Oh, sorry," said Tim. He removed his shoes and entered the room. He sat at the low table, slipping his feet into the well. He looked around as though gauging the suitability of the room for a prospective booking. With his back to the girl, he removed a protective film from the underside of the transmitter to expose an adhesive strip. He fumbled. Shit – he accidentally dropped the transmitter into the footwell. He grimaced and gave an intake of breath as though experiencing cramp in his leg. He bent down as though to massage the cramp.

76

"You okay, sir?" asked the girl.

"Yes, fine."

Where had the fiddly thing gone? Tim hoped it hadn't glued itself to the floor. As he furtively groped around near his feet, the transmitter adhered to his fingertip. Thank God. He attached it firmly to the underside of the table. As he withdrew his legs from beneath the table, he made a little performance of finding it awkward.

"Sometimes westerner find it difficult to sit on floor," observed the girl. "Long legs," she added helpfully.

Tim thanked the girl and said he would call if he wished to make a booking.

NINETEEN

The following morning, Tim received the initial police report on O'Hanlon's death. The autopsy revealed that he had been drinking heavily and had also taken a large number of sleeping pills. However, the cause of death was drowning. Minor bruising on the arms and shoulders suggested the faint possibility of a struggle, but was really very inconclusive. On the strength of the evidence, it appeared most likely that O'Hanlon had either deliberately committed suicide or had taken himself to the brink with alcohol and pills and had then accidentally fallen into the Thames. However, Mrs O'Hanlon continued to insist that her husband would not touch alcohol, never took sleeping pills and had absolutely no reason to take his own life. Inspector Hunt observed wryly in a covering note to Tim that they had heard something similar somewhere before.

During the course of the morning, while observing Draper's activity on his screens, Tim noted that Draper seemed to be stepping up his buying of gold despite the fact that the price had now pushed through his earlier limit of fourteen hundred dollars – in fact, Draper had made two purchases above fourteen hundred and fifty.

Tim then went out and bought himself a rather dry tuna baguette for lunch before settling down to listen to Draper and Popov enjoying two hours of black cod in *miso* paste and a succession of other Japanese delicacies while discussing business. Their discussion did not stray from the subject of Taiga Oil. Popov gave Draper a description of the performance of the company over the latest quarter and then dwelt on the state of the balance sheet and the details of the proposed capital increase. It became clear that Andropov was hoping Draper might use the occasion of the share issue to increase his stake by a percent or two. Draper seemed amenable to this suggestion.

In the late afternoon, an encrypted message from Andropov arrived in Draper's inbox: 'Champagne on order, but not yet on ice. Supplier wants to renegotiate terms. Still aiming for delivery Cassis 1st June.' If this really was champagne, it would have to be a vintage of extraordinary rarity and value; otherwise, as Tim had already started to suspect, the term must surely refer not to champagne at all, but rather to something quite different which was somehow connected to Draper and Andropov's purchases of gold.

Margaret passed by Tim's desk. "Did you notice the gold price has spiked up today?" she asked. "Actually, rather against the recent trend."

"Yup. Draper's buying even more heavily."

Tim wondered whether Margaret's crossword solving ability might unravel the champagne mystery. "Maggie, could you take a look at these three messages and see if you can make any sense of them."

Tim displayed on his screens the three messages referring to champagne:

'Let's pop the cork on La Isla Bonita mid-June. Will deliver champagne Cassis 1st June.'

'Authorities on alert after finding second body and now aware of our close business ties. Have been asked some tiresome questions, but authorities seem to be grasping at straws – and, of course, have absolutely no idea about gold/champagne. Let's review situation when you return.'

'Champagne on order, but not yet on ice. Supplier wants to renegotiate terms. Still aiming for delivery Cassis 1st June.'

"La Isla Bonita is Draper's yacht," explained Tim. "At first, I assumed champagne just meant champagne – or, with cassis, *kir royal*. I thought they were planning some kind of celebration on the boat, but it looks as though it's a codeword for something else."

"Well, I would guess Cassis is Cassis in the south of France – little fishing village and resort at the Marseilles end of the Côte d'Azur."

"Ah." Tim felt slightly foolish for having thought it might refer to the cocktail ingredient.

"I've no idea how important Draper and Andropov's dealings could be in the grand scheme of things, but you might suggest to

Gordon that you take a little trip to the south of France at the end of May/beginning of June to see exactly what's being delivered to the yacht." Margaret thought for a second. "If anything, I'd say that champagne is a codeword for gold itself – it has a certain aptness: similar colour, both prized commodities. It looks as though they're making a delivery of physical gold to the yacht. But I can't imagine why they'd want to do that or what they might plan to do with the gold."

"Team." Gordon strode into the centre of the room. He wore his most serious 'defence of the realm' expression and had even flushed slightly purple with the intensity of the moment. He spoke with urgency. "Everyone, conference room, now. Events have taken an unpleasant turn."

II Sward and Scimitar

TWENTY

Gordon leaned forward with his knuckles on the conference table in silverback pose. "Chilvers," he said in a brief aside to Maggie, before turning his attention to the group as a whole. "An alarming development. MI6 in Moscow has just informed me that a 'friend'..." – Gordon marked inverted commas in the air – "... in the Russian Interior Ministry strongly believes that, through the Russian black market, someone is attempting to acquire material for a nuclear device and – key point – evidence in the hands of the Russian authorities suggests this device is destined for Britain. It seems our friend either knows, or at any rate feels able to tell us, little more than that. Actually, Tim, your friend Vasiliev does get a mention – but then he always gets a mention, so we can probably discount that. Of course, the Russian government has always said officially that all of the former Soviet Union's nuclear material is fully accounted for and securely held, but we know that it isn't. For starters, we – or rather the CIA – has recently intercepted at least two consignments of weapons grade material, one in Kazakhstan, apparently on its way to Iran, and the other on the border of Uzbekistan and Afghanistan, apparently on its way to Pakistan.

"If a nuclear device is destined for these shores, we need to consider who has the means to acquire it, the expertise to use it and the motive to deploy it. If this were a properly constituted nuclear weapon capable of producing a chain reaction and a full-scale nuclear explosion, then the number of candidates who could assemble such a thing and who might be prepared to use it is mercifully tiny. By far the greater likelihood is that we're talking about a dirty bomb – in other words, nuclear materials strapped to a conventional bomb, which would not produce a nuclear explosion, but would spray radioactive materials over a wide area. In either case, I think we can rule out the Russians themselves – I believe they would have nothing to gain by laying waste to a part of London or any other British city. Apart from anything else, half of them now live here and even if the other half would like to see the first half

83

dead, it's simply not their style to consider something like this. On the other hand, I think we have to believe it's entirely plausible that nuclear materials could be obtained on the Russian black market. Moscow is seething with Russian mafiosi, ex-KGB and ex-FSB agents, members of the special forces … any of whom would be willing to sell anything to anybody for the right price. Obviously, we must remain alert to all possibilities, but I think we also have to work with the intelligence we have. It seems to me the jihadist groups we've been monitoring are the most likely threat. We know they have financial backing from the Middle East. A dirty bomb would be within their competence. Even if the domestic cells lack the expertise to assemble such a device, it would be straightforward enough to fly in a specialist for the occasion and then fly him out again before the device was deployed. We know for a fact that these misguided lunatics include many who believe they have just cause to perpetrate a terrorist act of this magnitude."

Nick raised a hand.

Gordon raised his eyebrows. "Nick?"

"Could I throw in another possibility. It's a bit left field and a bit unlikely, but just in case … As you know, Gordon – and, Helen, I briefly mentioned this to you as well, but the rest of you I think may not be aware – I've been following an ecological protest group calling themselves the Sward of Damocles …"

"Sword of Damocles?" asked Tim.

"No, 'sward' – as in 'greensward'."

"SOD for short, then," muttered Trevor, before exhibiting his peculiar curl of the upper lip and exposing his front teeth.

"As far as I can tell from their website and from police records," resumed Nick, "they're mostly the usual hippies, beardies, veggies…"

"Oi! I'm a veggie," exclaimed Tabi in mock protest.

"Okay, strike the veggies."

"Strike the veggies!"

"Gentlemen," interrupted Gordon, "this is not the time for tomfoolery. I know we've had any number of false alarms along these lines; however, firstly, we have no choice but to take every instance seriously and, secondly, this information comes not from a one-off encounter with some disillusioned junior civil servant who hopes to make a quick buck out of British intelligence …" Gordon paused for emphasis. "… this comes from one of MI6's most longstanding and trusted sources at the very heart of the Russian government. We understand this individual has had sight of an intelligence report from the FSB."

The room absorbed this in silence for a second.

"Nick, you were saying …?"

"Yes, sorry," continued Nick. "The members of this group are mostly harmless eco-activists, I think – even if they do advocate protest and even if several of their members have been arrested on a number of occasions; however, I mention them because of two people. They have a website which mostly gathers press articles and scientific papers warning of impending ecological doom, but they also have a blog page which regularly includes contributions from someone calling himself Dionysus …"

"Dionysus or Dionysius?" asked Margaret.

"Oh, perhaps you're right – perhaps it's Dionysius, not Dionysus."

"Dionysus is Bacchus, the god of wine. It was Dionysius of Syracuse who suspended the sword over the head of Damocles to remind him of the precariousness of life and the fragility of good fortune."

"You must be right, Maggie. Dionysius. Anyway, the point is, this chap is given to incendiary rants calling for extreme action to shock the world's governments into taking more urgent action to save the planet. The group as a whole is vociferously anti-nuclear – especially after the Fukushima earthquake and tsunami. However, amongst other comments, this Dionysius has suggested that a nuclear accident here in Britain might serve as a wake-up call to the government concerning the folly of pursuing nuclear power as a key source of energy. I assumed he meant sabotaging a power plant, but perhaps he had an even grander gesture in mind. And then elsewhere, on a completely different subject, he attacks the pharmaceutical industry over animal testing and talks about contaminating animal testing sites to put them, in his words, 'off limits for a generation' – which might also fit with a dirty bomb. All a bit counter-intuitive for

85

an eco-campaigner, I admit, but his comments are really quite wild and inflammatory."

"And you said there was a second person?" prompted Gordon.

"Yes, the second person is effectively the sponsor of the whole group – the Marquess of Bowley. In fact, I believe the core of the group lives at Bowley Hall, his country estate – he owns half of Shropshire. You've probably seen him in the papers since he makes a periodic appearance for shovelling his family's fortune up his nose, down his throat and into his veins. However, despite his attempts to squander his wealth, he's still well up on the Rich List. If this Dionysius were to prevail upon him, I dare say he could afford nuclear materials. As I say, I think it's pretty unlikely, but perhaps it's worth investigating further just to rule it out."

"Do they have any Russian connections?" asked Gordon.

"Well, that was the last point and again it's a bit tenuous, but the marquess studied Russian at Oxford and spent a year in Moscow and Saint Petersburg. He travels to Russia very occasionally and periodically receives Russian visitors."

"All right." Gordon paused in thought for a moment. "Ecological extremists sounds pretty unlikely to me, but let's play it this way. Helen, you remain team captain on the jihadist threat. In a moment, I'd like you to brief us to remind us where we stand in our investigations so far. Nick, I don't want to waste too much time on these ecologists and anyway Helen tells me you're doing crucial work on the suspected south London Islamist cell. I don't think we can spare you to pursue this second line of enquiry. But, Tim, you've been concentrating on Draper, so I imagine you're not fully up to the pace on the jihadists at the moment and you've also done a bit of work for me in the past on this type of protest group. I want you to turn your attention to the ecologists – which means you're going to have to put Draper and Andropov to one side for the moment. Whatever financial shenanigans those two may be up to and even if one or both of them is willing to murder to secure his financial ends, the current threat is on an altogether different scale and has to take precedence. I'd like you to take a trip to Shropshire, see if you can infiltrate the eco group, find out whether they pose a serious threat and in particular establish whether or not they could conceivably be

86

in the market for a dirty bomb. Nick can brief you when we're done here. Helen, over to you. Please bring us up to speed ..."

Gordon, seemingly oblivious to the expression of incredulity on Tim's face and the slightly surprised looks of the rest of the team, sat down, giving the floor to Helen.

Tim seethed. Gordon was piling insult upon injury. If Gordon had told Tim to put Draper and Andropov aside while he joined the others in dealing with the jihadist threat, Tim would have understood. Top priority for the team was the prevention of terrorism. But Tim had first of all been dragged off the jihadist case and reassigned to Lucy Trenchard essentially as a sop to the Home Secretary, albeit in circumstances of personal tragedy for the unfortunate politician. And now that Tim appeared to have unearthed tentative evidence that Draper and Andropov were engaged in some form of clandestine and possibly illicit activity, he was again being torn away and fobbed off with the team's least promising line of investigation. To make matters worse, if he were despatched to the deep countryside, he would probably not have the means to cast even the most occasional eye over Draper and Andropov's communications – and that with the mysterious handover in the south of France only a week away.

"Gordon," began Tim, "Draper and Andropov are planning ..."

"Tim," interrupted Gordon, raising a hand, "we know they may be up to something, but we can't just ignore a potential nuclear threat. Even if we place low odds on the likely involvement of a group of ecologists, we need to rule these people out conclusively. Helen, you have the floor ..."

Helen frowned at Gordon's dismissive treatment of Tim, but chose to continue. "Shah, please can you pull my pc up here?" Helen indicated the series of large screens running along one wall of the conference room.

Tabi reached for a keyboard on the conference table. After a few moments, he was logged into Helen's computer with her master screen displayed on the wall.

"Thanks." Helen took over the keyboard. She called up a map of the UK with several cities highlighted on one screen and a series of eight suspect profiles on the remaining screens. The eight characters were all

87

Middle Eastern or central Asian in appearance; some were bearded, some not; some were in ethnic-looking dress, some in T-shirts, one in a suit; one possessed a wide-eyed and fanatical look, others lowered or stared vacantly, a couple looked quite sane and unassuming.

"We have identified a network of eight cells across the country: two in London, one in High Wycombe – as in the case a few years ago – two in Birmingham, one in Manchester, one again in Bradford and one in Sheffield. We have a potential ninth in Leicester – I'll return to that in a second. We believe each cell consists of between three and five people and we're reasonably confident we've correctly identified the members in each case, bar a very few instances where we're still gathering and checking evidence. Each cell contains at least one member who has visited Pakistan or Afghanistan in the past eighteen months. In a couple of cases, we know they attended terrorist training camps; in other cases, we suspect they did so. We believe these are the key people in each cell – the team leaders. You see their profiles displayed here. We don't believe the eight cells are in direct contact with each other; in fact, we don't believe they know each other's identities. However, they do appear to share a central bulletin board and we believe there is a controlling figure behind these groups, though we don't know whom, nor are we wholly sure where this person is located. This brings me back to Leicester. The shared bulletin board is a blogsite attached to the website belonging to a mosque in Leicester. We've been working under the supposition that the figure controlling these cells must be operating under cover of the mosque; however, we've so far failed to identify any individual who would fit the profile. In fact, our next step is to try to infiltrate the mosque to get an inside view."

"Do any of these characters possess the skills to put together a nuclear device?" asked Trevor.

"A dirty bomb, perhaps. A fully-fledged nuclear weapon, I would say almost certainly not. Their terrorist training will doubtless have included conventional bomb-making, but none of these people has a scientific or engineering background or even the academic qualifications which might suggest they could readily assemble a full-scale nuclear weapon. As Gordon said, I think we should assume we're talking about a dirty bomb ... and the most likely probability is that the nuclear material will be shipped in with someone who knows what to do with it."

"I should perhaps ask you the same question which I asked Nick," said Gordon. "Do we have any reason to think any of these people could conceivably have some contact or channel of communication with Russian interests which could then potentially supply the materials?"

"No, not directly. I think all of these people, even the team leaders, are just pawns in a much bigger game. I assume al-Qaeda or another Middle Eastern based terror group will obtain and deliver the weapon. Unfortunately, until we can identify and monitor the controlling figure here in the UK, we're unlikely to discover who's controlling him."

Gordon stood. "Clearly, the top priority is to find out what's going on at this mosque in Leicester. Tabi, I know we don't often send you out into the field and we need you here, but in addition to the obvious reason, your combination of computer and language skills makes you the ideal person to infiltrate the mosque and to find out who's masterminding the blogsite. We'll set you up with a job as an IT consultant at the local council as cover. There's a heavy Muslim representation on the council, so with luck you should rapidly be able to establish contacts who can introduce you to the mosque. But, Tabi, please just make sure you resist the temptation to show off your computer skills to the full.

"All of you, I hope I don't have to stress again that we need to pursue this with the utmost urgency and dedication. The Cabinet Office Security Committee – COBRA as our friends in the media like to call it – is due to meet at Number 10 later today to review emergency procedures. Needless to say, the police, airport authorities, the Channel tunnel, port authorities, coast guard – everyone is being put on the highest level of alert and told of the need for the keenest vigilance. But the key to success lies with us and the intelligence we can bring to bear. If and when these nuclear materials arrive here, we need to be sure that we're fully prepared, absolutely ready and waiting, so that they drop straight into our hands and not into those of the terrorists."

89

TWENTY-ONE

Returning to his desk, Tim found a post-it note from one of the assistants seated nearby: Charles Draper had called – please could Tim call him back. Perfect, thought Tim – Draper coming to him with something at the very moment he had been told to put Draper to one side. Tim screwed up the post-it note. But he was curious to know why Draper had phoned and decided that anyway he could not simply ignore the call. He glanced around the office – Helen and Trevor were still in the briefing room and no one else sat close enough to overhear him on the phone if he kept his voice down. He dialled and was put through.

"Charles, it's Tim Lemon. You called, I believe."

"Mr Lemon. Thank you for coming back to me."

Tim noted that Draper seemed to have dispensed with friendliness and had reverted to 'Mr Lemon'.

"With apologies," continued Draper, "it's my turn to be a little cloak-and-dagger and to ask if we could possibly have another short private meeting."

"Of course."

But, thought Tim with frustration, it wasn't 'of course': he had to leave for Shropshire early in the morning and during the few hours of the day which remained he had to glean as much as he could from Nick concerning the ecologists. Furthermore, Tim was quietly thinking he should do some briefing of his own so that, despite Gordon's injunction, someone on the team would be up-to-the-minute on Draper and Andropov and could at least keep half an eye on their correspondence. Ideally, this would be Helen – her manner might be irritatingly curt and to-the-point, but Tim knew she wouldn't miss anything and he knew he could trust her judgement if fresh developments arose – however, she had her hands more than full with the Islamic extremists and anyway Tim supposed she would almost certainly agree with Gordon that Draper should be put to one side while the country was apparently under threat of nuclear attack. Tabi would no doubt have obliged, but he would be in Leicester.

Trevor was Tim's best bet. Reflecting for a second, Tim decided he would need a good hour with Trevor to make sure Trevor had the full picture. Yet somehow Tim now also had to squeeze in a meeting with Draper.

"Sorry," resumed Tim, "just thinking when would be possible. I'm afraid it would have to be this evening."

"We could do seven thirty at my place again, if that suits?"

"Yes, that's good. Let's go for that."

"I'll see you in due course, then."

Tim reopened Draper's correspondence, both the encrypted and the unencrypted, in case this should provide some clue as to why Draper wanted to see him. Tim was surprised to see that in the short interval while he had been away from his desk there had been a little flurry of emails. After months of silence, Yevgeny Berezin had renewed contact with Draper and had proposed a meeting in either Moscow or London, whichever Draper would find most convenient. Draper had responded that he would be glad to meet, but would prefer a more discreet location. He had suggested Helsinki in two days' time. A lunch meeting had been swiftly agreed and then arranged in a private room at the Hotel Kämp. Reading through the emails, Tim gave a grunt of disbelief. For all Draper's protestations of loyalty to Andropov, he clearly remained amenable at least to discussion with Berezin. Tim wondered whether this suggested Draper might seriously consider cashing in his profit on Taiga Oil and abandoning Andropov or whether he was simply keeping his options open. Tim also now saw that Draper was hastily organising a late afternoon meeting with a Finnish paper company on the day of his trip – which Tim guessed was to provide an alibi in case Andropov should get wind of Draper's visit to Helsinki. Tim leaned back in his chair and chewed thoughtfully on a pen top. He couldn't imagine any reason why Draper would request a meeting with him to discuss Berezin. Did Draper have something to tell him about 'champagne' and Cassis? Surely not. Lucy Trenchard? That seemed most unlikely too. Meanwhile, the correspondence revealed nothing else, or at least nothing new, which appeared in any way untoward. Tim would have to wait until seven thirty.

Gordon, Maggie, Trevor and Helen emerged from the conference room. The first three entered Gordon's office while Helen returned and sat at her desk.

Tim hesitated. Even to ask Helen would be a waste of time: she would say no. Trevor would be willing. Tim leaned towards Helen's desk. "Helen," he said quietly. "Huge favour – and I totally understand if it's more than you can manage at the moment or if you disagree."

"Let me guess," said Helen, also lowering her voice. "... Draper." She saw Tim's look of surprise. "Lemon, it didn't take a mind reader to know what was going through your head in the meeting just now."

"Well ... you're right. I know Gordon said leave it, but Andropov's big delivery to Draper, whatever it may be, is due in only a few days' time. I really don't think we should be taking our eye off the ball just at the critical moment. So, yes, I realise you're already up to your neck with the jihadists and it's asking a lot, but do you think you could possibly manage an occasional glance at Draper and Andropov's emails while I'm out with the rustics?"

Helen considered for a moment. "Providing you understand it's likely to be two minutes twice a day. Draper will be a very distant second priority."

"Totally understood." Finding himself genuinely pleased at Helen's unexpected acceptance of the task and at her willingness to connive in his little subterfuge, Tim broke into a smile. "That's brilliant. Thank you." Tim glanced over and saw that Nick was at his desk. "Right now I have to run through the Swards with Nick and then ..." Tim leaned in closer and lowered his voice further. "...actually I have a meeting with Draper. His request – no idea why. But will you still be around later this evening so I can show you what you need to follow?"

"I can't see myself escaping before ten or eleven today."

"Well, sorry to add to the burden. But I'll try to keep the guided tour brief. Thanks again."

Tim rose and went over to Nick.

"Nick, can we do these tree-huggers?"

"Yeah, let's."

"How long is this going to take?"

"Hour max – I don't have a vast amount of info. It's basically their website – I can show you the blogs which keep triggering the alerts at GCHQ – then a handful of police reports and some background material which I've trawled up from the internet."

TWENTY-TWO

Tim was impatient to hear what Draper had to say and also keen to return to the office before Helen left for the day. He bounded up the stairs to Draper's flat, almost falling victim to the very step which had ambushed him on his first visit. Draper's door was open in expectation of Tim's arrival. Tim knocked and entered.

"Mr Lemon ..."

'Mr Lemon' again. Perhaps it was to be expected after the less than friendly *tête-à-tête* with Gordon.

"Come in. Apologies again for dragging you over here. Can I offer you a glass of something?"

"No, that's fine, thank you."

"Please ..." Draper ushered Tim to a seat on the couch.

Draper was wearing a casual but expensively tailored camel-coloured jacket. He slipped a hand into the pocket and brought out what looked like a small black cockroach glued to one of his own business cards. He placed it on the coffee table in front of Tim.

"I imagine this looks familiar to you?"

Tim felt the blood in his veins slow to a crawl. Draper fixed Tim with an interrogative stare such that Tim felt as though he himself were an insect pinned to a piece of card. Draper had found Tim's bug and he clearly had a pretty good idea who had planted it.

"Generically, I mean – not this particular one," clarified Draper.

Tim quietly took a breath. So perhaps Draper wasn't pointing a finger at him. Unless Draper was simply toying with him.

"Well? ... No?" persisted Draper.

Tim decided the safest course was to acknowledge what it was, but not whose it was.

"Yes, of course ... it's an electronic bug, a micro transmitter. Did you find it here in the flat?"

"No. You may remember I mentioned to you yesterday at our little interview that I was due to have lunch today with the CFO of Taiga Oil ..." Draper again looked pointedly at Tim.

Shit, perhaps Draper was accusing Tim after all.

"... we met at one of those Japanese restaurants where you sit with your feet in a well beneath the table – bit of a struggle for someone of my size to clamber in and out of his seat. When I rose to leave, I brushed my leg against the underside of the table and this thing glued itself to my trouser leg. It's no longer transmitting, by the way. I had a friendly watchmaker ..." Draper briefly flashed a huge and elaborate gold watch at his wrist as evidence of the watchmaker's, no doubt gushing, friendliness. "... – chap just round the corner in New Bond Street – I had him remove the battery."

Tim was still not quite sure whether he was in the dock and, if he wasn't, what Draper was expecting of him.

"Well, yes, I know what it is," repeated Tim, "... but how can I help you? Are you asking if MI5 can come and sweep your flat and your office for bugs?"

"No, no, that's all been arranged for first thing tomorrow morning."

All been arranged? Tim hadn't seen any evidence of that in his last check on Draper's various communications – which Tim had conducted only moments before he had left the office to come to Draper's flat. Having found the transmitter and perhaps fearing wider snooping, had Draper switched to an email service external to his network or to a different mobile phone number – one which fell outside MI5's surveillance, a number registered in Monaco perhaps?

"No, I was just wondering," continued Draper, "– and I expect the security people tomorrow morning may also have some suggestions – but I was just wondering, can anyone buy these things on the internet for example and, do you have any clue, is this of western manufacture ... or Russian perhaps?"

Tim picked up the business card and inspected the transmitter. "I'm really not an expert on this sort of thing ... but I could take it back to the office and ask our tech guys – I'm sure they would have a pretty accurate idea."

"No – thank you, but I'd like to keep it as evidence for the security company tomorrow. I was just hoping you might recognise the type and might be able to give me an immediate clue as to its likely provenance. I'm assuming it must be one of Andropov's competitors – I can't imagine who else would want to eavesdrop on a conversation between me and the CFO of Taiga."

So was Tim off the hook? Draper's comment sounded genuine. But Tim knew that Draper was a skilled dissembler and that one should not necessarily take what Draper said at face value.

"Sorry I can't be of more instant help," said Tim. "But let me know if you draw a blank with your security people and you'd like our guys to take a look." He rose from the couch.

"That's most kind," said Draper as he escorted Tim to the front door. "I may take you up on that."

TWENTY-THREE

Tim cursed all the way back to the office. Did Draper know damn well who had planted the bug and had he just been goading Tim or had Draper meant what he'd said this time around? And, either way, had the discovery of the transmitter caused Draper to switch to a channel of communication not monitored by MI5? And, dammit, if Draper had called in experts to review his security arrangements, was there a risk they would run tests on Draper's network and find Tabi's spy program?

As Tim re-entered the MI5 building, Nick and Tabi, dressed for a game of squash, were about to leave.

"You've got time for a game of squash?" exclaimed Tim. "Helen's letting you go?"

"We think we've cracked it," replied Nick. "Cell of three people in Stockwell. Helen owes me a beer. I realised one of the characters we thought was peripheral actually ties all the evidence together. Helen's still up there, but she said she's ready to call it a day with the jihadists as well."

"What's up, Tim?" asked Tabi. "You're not exactly looking calm and collected."

"Guys, not a word of this anywhere near Gordon – I've just seen Draper. Unfortunately, he's found our bug – though I'm not really sure whether he knows it's ours – but anyway he's calling in security people to do a sweep. Tabi, if they go a step further and examine Draper's network, is it possible they could find your program?"

"Tim," said Tabi, placing a hand on Tim's shoulder, "relax. No private security company will get even a sniff of what we have running inside Draper's network."

"You're sure?"

"Trust me."

"When are you leaving for Leicester?"

"I'm on the last train tonight."

"I think Draper may also have a different mobile or email account which we're not tracking."

"Hm, that's more of a pain. If I had some time I expect I could trace it, but I'm afraid there's not much I can do before we both head north. Besides, Gordon would be less than delighted if he knew we were spending time on Draper and he's certainly not going to authorise any new surveillance. I share your curiosity about what these characters are up to, but I don't think there's much more we can do in the current circumstances."

Nick tapped his watch. "Need to get to our court."

"Sorry, I'll let you get on with it." Tim looked at Nick, but gave a nod in Tabi's direction. "Jahangir here ever let you win a point?"

"Hey, I took a whole game off him last time. Though he did then obliterate me in the following game."

"Off moment," said Tabi with characteristic cockiness, though he also beamed with genuine pleasure at his colleagues' implied compliments.

Nick was a decent enough all-round sportsman, but he had discovered five minutes into his first ever game with Tabi – and first thrashing at Tabi's hand – that his opponent was an England under nineteen triallist and an Oxford blue.

A couple of minutes later, Tim was back at his desk. Only Helen and Trevor remained in the office.

"Do I gather the drinks are on you? Bumped into Nick and Tabi downstairs," said Tim to Helen as he sat down.

"It was actually a pretty good spot by Braithwaite," confirmed Helen. "Dandyish posing and tonsorial exhibitionism notwithstanding, Braithwaite's turning into a really rather useful member of the team." Helen looked at Tim. "But what's up with you? You're not looking happy."

Tim grimaced in acknowledgement. "We might have a bit of a problem. Draper found our transmitter at the restaurant. I'm really not clear whether he thinks we planted it or whether he suspects someone else. He *said* he assumes it was one of Andropov's competitors, but he also seemed to be dropping hints that he guessed it was us. Which potentially creates two problems: firstly, after the interrogation with Gordon and now with this, Draper's much more likely to be wary at every step and, secondly, he says he's called in security people to sweep his office and flat, yet ..." Tim pointed towards his screen, where his window into Draper's network was displayed. "... I can't see any evidence of his having had that conversation. Draper may have another channel of communication which we can't follow."

"Lemon," said Helen, "I know I said yes, but can I just ask ... if you think we might have lost the thread on Draper and if we don't even really know why we're chasing him anyway, do you honestly think he deserves our time and attention when we're dealing with a nuclear threat?"

Tim felt the wind leave his sails. This was what he had expected Helen to say in the first place. And Helen's doubts were entirely rational. But still Tim felt this was surely not the time to give up on Draper. He regathered his resolve. "Helen, the honest truth is I don't know what Draper and Andropov are up to, but I think the moment of revelation may be just a few days away. If we can still keep tabs on them, I really think we should."

"Well, I've said I'll follow their emails and I will. But if Draper seems to have disappeared down a different fox hole, I'm afraid I simply won't be able to go chasing after him."

"Understood. Fair enough." Tim pondered for a second. "Another thing and one which I have to concede might further muddy the waters ... curious thing – bit of a surprise, actually. Draper's meeting Andropov's arch rival, Yevgeny Berezin, for a clandestine lunch in Helsinki in a couple of days' time."

"You think Draper might be double-crossing Andropov?" said Helen with surprise and now showing greater interest.

"Not sure I'd push it that far, but he's clearly going behind Andropov's back. For the moment, I'd say he's just keeping all parties sweet. Anyway ..." Tim raised his hands and looked at Helen. "Is now a good time – shall I take you through Draper's network and correspondence?"

"Let's get it over and done with. But, Lemon, if in the end it turns out Draper is guilty of nothing more than poor judgement in his investments and his choice of friends, then you owe me a large one."

"Sure."

Trevor had been half paying attention to Tim and Helen's exchange. He leaned back to circumvent his little barricade of files. "You're covering for Tim on Draper?" he said to Helen.

"A quick look now and then. Jihad permitting."

"Let me know if I can help. Needless to say, I'm busy with the jihadists too, but I think we've now got a reasonably clear picture on the High Wycombe and Barnet cells which are top of my list."

"Thanks, Trev," said Tim.

Trevor rose from his desk. "Anyone want a coffee from the machine?"

"No, thanks," said Tim.

"Helen?"

"I'm fine thanks, Wilde."

Trevor headed towards the machine in the corner of the room.

Sensing that Helen was in a slightly more approachable mood than usual, Tim sat back in his chair and took a deep breath. "Helen, I really do appreciate your doing this for me, but … could I just possibly ask one other tiny and completely unrelated thing. Don't you think, after all the years that all of us have been working together, it's about time to let up on this Wilde, Braithwaite, Shah, Lemon business? I mean, of course come the tough cookie when you're dealing with the bad guys, but honestly you don't need to practise on us. To be completely truthful with you, none of us buys the performance. How about some first names?"

"To paraphrase the late Monsieur Mitterand, if you prefer to use first names, then by all means do, Lemon."

TWENTY-FOUR

By mid-morning on his first day at the council office, Tabi – or Imran, as he was to his fellow council workers – was feeling frustrated. In the first place, in his cover as visiting IT consultant, he could see that the council's IT system was outdated, cumbersome and lacking in applications. If he had really been there as a consultant, he would have recommended throwing out the whole system and starting again. As it was, he had to restrain this impulse and content himself with the suggestion that his team download a couple of web-based applications which would at least allow the council to improve the user-friendliness of some parts of the website. The second reason for his frustration was that Sharon, Jeff, Terry and Angela – the team he had been assigned to work with – though an entirely likeable bunch, would not have known a muezzin from muesli and were not getting him any closer to the mosque.

At lunchtime, however, an opportunity presented itself. The IT team took Tabi to the canteen. As he helped himself to a vegetable curry, a tall, angular and – most importantly – Asian-looking colleague joined the queue right behind him.

"Hi," said Tabi.

"Hello," said the colleague without any immediate sign of great interest.

"Imran." Tabi held out his hand.

"Raheem. Raheem Hameed." He shook Tabi's hand. "Imran?"

"Yup, Imran Malik. Just joined today. Actually, I'm on secondment as a consultant, but I might be here for a while."

"Uh-huh. Which department?"

"IT. You?"

"HR."

"You been here long?"

"Yeah, five years."

"That's a fair time. You enjoy it, then?"

"It's a job. It's fine."

101

"I'd better rejoin my team." Tabi nodded towards the table where the others were taking their places. "But nice to meet you. Catch you later."

"Yeah, sure."

In mid afternoon, Tabi excused himself, saying he was just going to pop out for a short while. In fact, he went to the HR department. He asked for Raheem and immediately saw his head projecting above the partition of a cubicle by the window. Tabi wandered over.

"Hi, Raheem."

"Oh, hi, Imran."

"Not disturbing you, am I?"

"No, it's very quiet this afternoon."

"Do you mind if I ask you something?"

"Go right ahead."

"I've no idea whether you're the right person, but I was wondering about the local mosque – I'd quite like to attend."

"Sure, yes, I can help with that. I can introduce you if you like."

"That would be very kind."

"I'm not sure about today, but maybe tomorrow evening?"

"That would be great."

"It's a very nice community. And the imam's quite a charismatic figure."

"Sounds ideal."

"What's your extension?"

"Twenty-one, twenty-one."

"Okay. I'll come over to IT or give you a buzz sometime tomorrow."

Tabi wondered whether 'charismatic figure' was a euphemism for Abu Hamza-style rabble-rouser. Helen had provided a few brief details about the imam – Daoud Ziai, a political refugee from the Taliban – but there was nothing in the short profile to suggest he might be a troublemaker. Tabi hoped his visit to the mosque would unveil the truth.

TWENTY-FIVE

Tim's train pulled into Bowley station. The journey from London had taken some hours – the local connection from Birmingham New Street ran only hourly and stopped at every station on the way. Tim was the sole passenger to leave the train at Bowley and he found the platform deserted. The station office was closed – a lone ticket machine stood dutifully at the entrance to the platform. The road leading away from the station shimmered in the heat of the cloudless May afternoon. Bowley Hall was three or four miles from the station. Tim had earlier debated whether he should take a taxi or should walk – he had wondered how well the ecologists might receive him if he rolled up in a cab. In the event, there was no taxi stand at the station and no sign of anyone whom he might ask for the number of a local firm. A quick internet search on his mobile produced no taxi company nearer than Kidderminster, which was some ten miles distant. He consulted the map on his phone and set off.

The country road wound between high hedges loud with the clamour of birds. A fox emerged from the hedge twenty yards ahead of Tim. The animal took stock of Tim for a second and then nonchalantly continued on its way, trotting along the road for fifty yards or so before diving back into the hedgerow. Tim's T-shirt soon became wet with perspiration and his backpack began to chafe. In due course, the high hedges gave way to a view of scattered farm buildings and then a handful of houses. Tim tramped on past the little collection of dwellings. The road became lined with elms and chestnuts. On one side of the road, behind wooden fencing, a field of spring wheat grew to waist height; on the opposite side, a field of yellow rape fanned across a rising hillside.

As Tim drew closer to Bowley Hall, his pace began to slacken. Though a group of ecologists should not be too difficult to deal with, he could not help but feel a little apprehensive. What if they really were crazy enough to contemplate detonating a nuclear device? Surely they might then also be crazy enough to wreak summary vengeance on a hapless Security Service agent if he were foolish enough to let his guard slip and be discovered? Tim would have to keep up his act every moment he was at Bowley Hall. He slowed to a halt on the grassy verge and stared at the road ahead. He immediately gave a little snort of contempt at his own hesitancy. This was not the right frame of mind with which to approach the assignment. Of course he should exercise due caution, but the priority was to deal with this case as fast as he could and to return swiftly to London in order to work with his team on the jihadists and to be in a position to keep a careful eye on Draper and Andropov. He adjusted his backpack and strode off again towards the marquess's family seat.

It took Tim the best part of an hour to reach the front gates of the Bowley estate. Ten foot high and with the family escutcheon mounted on each side, the gates stood wide open. They gave onto a wide gravelled circle surrounded by two very fine coach houses, each a sweeping two-storey semicircle of weathered red brick, punctuated with a neatly regular pattern of sash windows, and each crowned with a white belvedere. An arch connected the two coach houses on the far side of the gravel circle. Tim took out his phone to report in to the office that he had arrived, but discovered there was no signal. He crossed over the gravel and passed beneath the archway. A broad driveway curved gracefully to the right before disappearing among shrubs and trees. Rolling parkland stretched out ahead. Bowley Hall itself could not even be seen from here.

Jack Cane, Tim breathed silently to himself as he paced along the driveway. Jack, Cane, Jack, Cane, he repeated in time to his step and then, for good measure, Charles, Draper, Charles, Draper.

As Tim rounded a corner, the great house came into view: set in the midst of undulating parkland, it was again made of russet hued brick, but stood a very tall three storeys with double height windows on the lower two floors. The façade was ornamented with brick pillars and an arch over the front entrance, but the architecture was not over-elaborate and possessed an appealing symmetry. Solid, square, imposing, the house was at the same time aesthetically pleasing – a mastiff of a building, yet also a show dog.

A further half mile walk brought Tim to the front door. He rapped on a brass knocker. There was no answer. He tried again. Silence from the house, bird call from the park. He made his way round to the back of the house, where he found an open door leading into a stone-floored utility room and big country kitchen. He knocked on the kitchen door.

"Hello? Anyone at home?"

A gruff reply came from within. "Hello. Just a minute." A man of about sixty with venerable aquiline features and with his greying hair tied back in a ponytail shuffled painfully into the kitchen. "Sorry, was having a nap – and arthritis stops me from leaping to my feet."

"Hi. Sorry to make you get up."

"No, it's better to move about a bit. The others are all on the farm." He inspected Tim. "How can I help?"

"Oh, er, yes. I hope this isn't a daft question, but have I come to the right place for the Sward of Damocles?"

The venerable brow furrowed slightly. "Why do you ask?" "Well, I was working until a couple of weeks ago, got made redundant, thought rather than doing another pen-pushing job I'd try to do something worthwhile. I've followed the Sward of Damocles website from time to time and I see it mentions volunteers are welcome."

The older man sized Tim up for a moment before replying. "Sward of Damocles is us. And you're very welcome to help out. To be honest, we could use extra hands in the fields at the moment – we grow pretty much all our own stuff. And we're down to just six of us at present. When we're gathering forces for a campaign, we sometimes have as many as a hundred people camping here in the park. But at the moment we're only half a dozen. Plus Gerald, of course."

"Gerald?"

"Owns the place. He's probably upstairs somewhere – shouldn't think he's out with the others. Anyway, I'm being remiss. I'm George ..."

Tim was on the point of saying 'Charles', but caught himself just in time. "Jack. Jack Cane. It's great to be here."

Tim held out his hand. As George offered his left hand to shake, Tim saw that George's right was slightly clawed with arthritis.

"Come and put your backpack in the snug and I'll make a cup of tea."

The snug was actually a large sitting room with big old comfortable-looking furniture. Tim propped his backpack against a worn leather couch and returned to the kitchen with George.

"Martha – my partner – should be back soon. I expect she'd be pleased if you could give her a hand preparing supper. The others will probably be another hour or so." George picked up a kettle.

"Can I help with that?" offered Tim.

"Don't worry, I can manage. So tell me, Jack, what were you up to before?"

"Insurance broking."

"Brum?"

"No, no, London."

"Long trek up here."

"Yuh. But I'm sure it will be well worth it."

"You're a big ecological campaigner?"

"I'm ashamed to say I'm a bit of a novice. But, like everyone, I read the papers, I watch the telly ... you can't ignore what's happening. I think we all have a duty to do what we can and governments around the world need to do a bit more than just pay lip service to the problem."

"You probably don't realise how right you are. The latest UN report on climate change suggests that within several decades the Himalayan glaciers may have largely melted. They're known as the Water Towers of Asia. They supply forty percent of the world's population with fresh water ... via the Ganges, Yangtze, Yellow River, Mekon and the other great rivers of Asia. And a major environmental study conducted by Columbia University concludes that within forty years seven hundred million people will be displaced for reasons of climate change. Forty years – that's certainly within your lifetime and perhaps within mine. Global crisis is right on our doorstep."

At this moment, Martha walked in. Around fifty, buxom, wearing a billowy dress and wooden sandals, dark haired but for a couple of streaks of grey and dark eyed, she held a bunch of carrots in one hand and a clutch of onions in the other. Though a few lines creased her face, she retained a warm and natural comeliness.

"Hello?" she said. "A visitor?"

106

"Jack," explained George.

Martha put down her vegetables and offered Tim a grubby hand. "Martha. Nice to meet you."

"Very pleased to meet you too."

"Jack's come to help out for a little while. Leaving mammon behind to help us with the issues that really matter."

"Has George already been boring you with his statistics?"

"On the contrary. That's the reason I'm here."

In due course, the rest of the troupe appeared: two brothers in their twenties, John and Mark, the former tall and broad, the latter not quite so tall and somewhat barrel-chested, both seemingly laid back and good-natured; Sandy, also in her twenties, apple-cheeked, pretty and arriving with her arm through John's; finally, Derek, in his thirties, short, wiry and stern-faced.

After their labours in the fields, the three young men and Sandy went off to shower and change. Tim helped Martha in the kitchen while George pottered about.

"That is one Bugs Bunny of a carrot," said Tim as he held up a giant specimen.

Martha took the vegetable from Tim with an indulgent smile. "Fresh from the field," she said as she washed and scraped the carrot before chopping it into a casserole.

Once the casserole was simmering, Martha left Tim in charge of the cooking while she too washed and changed. The big kitchen began to fill with the savoury wafts of stewing chicken, vegetables and herbs and the yeasty comfort of home-made bread warming in the oven.

"You know," said George as Tim stirred the casserole, "I've just been reading today that North Sea cod spawning stock has fallen from two hundred and thirteen thousand tonnes in 1966 to half that in 1986 to less than thirty thousand tonnes today. In a generation, we've rendered the North Sea almost barren. And the Sea of Japan is even worse – it's virtually a marine desert. I could go on and on ... blue and yellow fin tuna will have disappeared from the Pacific in three or four years ..."

The others began to reappear and to help ready the evening meal. When Martha returned, she asked if someone could call Gerald. John

107

duly disappeared and a few moments later the sound of a brass gong reverberated through the house.

As the gathering took their places at table, Gerald appeared. He wore an old and filthy woollen dressing gown – perhaps a relic from boarding school days. The gown hung open with its cord trailing behind. Beneath the gown, he was bare-chested and wore only a tatty and dirty pair of jeans. His hair was unwashed and matted, he was unshaven and his complexion was deeply sallow. His eyes were vacant and his bare feet were black. He looked and smelled like a tramp. Wordlessly, he took his place at table and began to roll a cigarette with trembling hands. He lit up.

"Gerry," said George, "we have a new member. This is Jack."

"Hi. Pleased to meet you," said Tim. He stood and reached his hand across the table.

Gerald slowly half turned his head in Tim's direction. Without looking at Tim, he lifted his chin a millimetre or two in acknowledgement and then resumed his smoking.

Sandy leaned across and took Tim's hand. "I think you've made a good impression," she said in a stage whisper.

Tim smiled politely in response and turned to sit. As he did so, he accidentally knocked over a saltcellar, creating a tiny tumulus of white grains. "Oops, sorry," he said as he righted the little silver pot.

"Better throw a pinch over your shoulder," said George. "Bad luck otherwise."

Martha brought the casserole to the table. "Gerry," she said, "do you mind not smoking while we're eating."

Gerald gave a grunt which might have been a 'yes' or might have been a 'no'. He continued to smoke for a few more moments, then stubbed out his cigarette on the side plate. He took his tobacco pouch and cigarette papers from his dressing gown pocket and, with shaking fingers, rolled another cigarette. He placed the cigarette to one side of his plate, apparently in deference to Martha's request.

During the course of dinner, Tim established that the Sward of Damocles website was run by George. There was no internet connection at the house. Gerald had apparently not paid his landline phone bills for months after some dispute with the phone company and his phone was currently disconnected. And there was no mobile signal on the estate, as Tim had already discovered. Most days George would accordingly drive down to the village, where a little library and the local pub both offered wifi connection. Apparently, George and Martha owned a Prius, which they housed in the stable block. "I would walk if I could," said George. George delivered a further lecture detailing the imminence of ecological catastrophe: "The Arctic ice cap is disintegrating at such a rate that there are five hundred percent more icebergs in the North Atlantic than just five years ago." John, Mark and Sandy listened reverentially. Martha cleared the table, now and then admonishing her partner with a kindly, "George, another subject perhaps?" or "George, dear, Jack has barely been here five minutes …" Gerald resumed his smoking. Derek spat the occasional contribution along the lines, "Governments are all cunts."

After dinner, the group repaired to the snug. A joint was passed around. Tim felt his apprehension return as he awaited his toke: he had only had a few puffs of marijuana at university and he was worried that under the influence his guard might drop and he might give himself away. But he was equally concerned that he would lose the group's trust if he appeared stand-offish and priggish. Sandy, who was sitting on John's lap, drew on the joint and then passed it to Tim. Tim took a drag and felt the room swim. Everyone seemed to be beaming at him indulgently. He beamed back.

After a mellow half hour, Mark asked Tim if he had seen the house. The Swards were occupying what had once been the servants' quarters. Mark took Tim's backpack and showed him to a bedroom on a floor also shared by himself, John and Sandy. He then took Tim back downstairs and showed him the baronial splendour of the main part of the house: a vast marble-floored entrance hall, apparently renowned for its stucco work and the remarkable engineering of its entirely freestanding staircase; the Oak Drawing Room, with its finely carved panelling, and the Inlaid Drawing Room, with its ornate decoration in many different woods, ivory and brass. These state rooms were opened to the public a few times a year. Mark explained that the top floor comprised Gerald's quarters – "But you don't want to go up there," he concluded cryptically.

109

Tim decided to shower before retiring. There was a bathroom just opposite his bedroom. The bath doubled as a shower and had a glass panel to prevent the water from splashing on the floor. Tim undressed and stepped into the tub. As he stood under the flow of hot water, he considered how he might make contact with the office. He thought he would have to hitch a lift with George at some point. With the hot water streaming over him, he wondered too whether Helen had picked up any fresh indications in Draper and Andropov's correspondence. Six days remained until the rendezvous in the south of France. Suddenly, the bathroom door opened and Sandy walked in. She wore a man's check shirt by way of a very short nightdress. Without paying any attention to Tim, she sat on the toilet, peed and, without flushing, rose to leave. Tim stood paralysed in the shower. At the door, Sandy seemed to sense what might be running through Tim's mind. She half turned and said, "Saving water." Then she left without thinking to close the door behind her. She disappeared into what Tim was quite sure was Mark's room.

TWENTY-SIX

Next morning, Tim descended at about six thirty. He was drawn by the smell of baking bread. As he entered the kitchen, Martha was removing a freshly baked loaf from the oven. She placed it on the table on a cooling rack and draped a tea towel over it.

"Morning," she said brightly.

"Morning," said Tim, warmed by Martha's cheerfulness as well as by the smell of the bread.

"Come," said Martha. She took Tim's hand and led him out of the back door. It was another brilliant morning, though still a little chilly at this hour. Martha led Tim along the gravel path which led to the front of the house.

Tim wondered if it was an opportunity to find out a little more about the workings of the Sward. "Is Gerry okay?" he asked.

"No. He's slowly killing himself. George and I have been here for five years. For the first two, we played mother and father, did all we could to help him sort himself out, but there's a powerful force of self-destruction there. Poor chap. He was packed off to boarding school at seven; parents divorced when he was nine, I think; in a horrible twist of fate, both parents and their respective second spouses were then all killed together in a plane crash – a light aircraft, which just to make matters as bad as they possibly could be, his father was piloting. That was sometime in his teens. I don't think he and his sister ever really had love and care during their childhood."

"He has a sister?"

"Yes. Married some rich Argentinian and lives in South America. She's a bit wild as well, by all accounts."

They rounded the corner of the house. The sunlit front lawn lay before them. Tim pulled up short in mild shock. John, Mark and Sandy were standing facing Derek, who was the cause of Tim's surprise. Derek was naked apart from a kind of sumo-style loin cloth. Tim could now see that his earlier impression of wiriness fell some way short of the truth: Derek's torso was like a tightly stacked coil of

111

steel hawser and his arms and legs were like thick steel cables held under extreme tension – all sinew and vein taut to the point of snapping.

"T'ai chi," explained Martha. "Follow if you can, improvise if you can't."

Martha and Tim joined the little group facing Derek. Derek gave a short bow and then began his slow motion martial ballet. The others followed – the two women with a good degree of success, John and Mark with a little less coordination, Tim hopelessly at first but then finding some sort of rhythm. Derek drew his performance to a slow motion conclusion and bowed again. His disciples bowed in response.

"Good way to start the day, don't you think?" said Martha to Tim.

"Makes a nice change from fifty lengths of the pool."

Sandy took Tim by the arm. "He's a karate black belt, you know. Maybe he'll give you a demo some time."

Over breakfast, Tim enquired whether he might thumb a lift with George down to the village. He explained that, before leaving London, he had dropped off a set of keys to his flat with his parents and had promised them he would call sometime to let them know he had safely found the group he had set out to join. George said that would of course be fine. However, John asked if it could possibly wait until the following day – they needed to bring in as much produce as possible today in order to take it to the local market the next day. Tim felt that as a new joiner he had little option but to accede to John's request.

TWENTY-SEVEN

"Hm. I've found the problem." Helen was peering at her screen.

"What?" asked Trevor.

"There's absolutely no mobile coverage of the Bowley estate – which is vast, by the way. I've checked all the mobile grids. I also checked Bowley Hall's phone record – there's been no landline service there for months."

"Bit of a nuisance."

"We'll just have to be patient until Lemon finds a way of getting in touch." Helen nodded towards Trevor's screen. "Nothing new from any of your Islamist cells?"

"All the ones I'm monitoring are ominously quiet at the moment," replied Trevor.

"And presumably we've heard nothing new from Moscow on the rogue nuclear material?"

"Gordon hasn't mentioned anything, so I guess not."

"Anything from GCHQ?"

Trevor shook his head. Straightening in his seat, he glanced around the room. He leaned across Tim's empty desk and lowered his voice. "You're following Draper?"

"I'm glancing at what he's doing every now and then."

"He hasn't gone quiet after finding our transmitter?"

"Not that I can see. All his usual channels of communication seem to be up-and-running as normal."

"And?"

"He's still shipping in the bullion. Otherwise, I can't see much of note. He's actually on his way to Helsinki this morning to meet this Berezin character – but Lemon reckons that's just a sideshow." Helen clicked open the window to Draper's network, stared at it for a moment and then closed it again. "You know, if you want my brutally honest opinion, I think Draper's just become a distraction. He and Andropov may conceivably be running, I don't know, some kind of investment scam and they may even be nasty enough to bump off anyone who gets wind of what they're up to, but I really don't think it's MI5's business to be pursuing them. When Lemon gets back, I think I'm going to suggest he has a word with Gordon and then hands everything over to the police … if, that is, we have anything to hand over to the police. I mean, as far as I can tell, we don't actually have a single thing which would stand up as evidence of wrongdoing."

TWENTY-EIGHT

Tabi sat with Raheem on the bus. He wondered whether he would need to use his Persian in his meeting with the imam – or whether he might be better off concealing his knowledge of the language so that he could eavesdrop with impunity if any illicit matters were discussed in Farsi in his presence. If he needed to use the language and if this prompted questions, he would simply explain that he had studied Persian at the School of Oriental and African Studies in London – which was in fact the truth. He turned to speak to Raheem, but saw that Raheem had his head against the window and seemed to have dozed off. Tabi took out his phone to check his messages, but then thought better of it and put his phone away again. He stared out of the window.

Tabi's degree in Persian and Arabic from SOAS was not his first university qualification. He was blessed with a precocious intelligence – though of a different type to Margaret's, for example. While Margaret possessed a wide-ranging general knowledge and was adept at weighing the pros and cons in determining a course of action, Tabi was rather a narrowly and intensely focused problem-solver. He had gone up to Oxford to study Mathematics and Computer Science when barely seventeen and had graduated with a double first while still shy of his twentieth birthday. A Harkness scholarship had then taken him to MIT in the States, where he had continued his studies in maths and computing with a Master's degree. During Tabi's childhood, his parents, who ran a post office in the East End of London, had assumed he would become a successful doctor or engineer; by the time he was at university, they had moved on to believe he would found the next Google or Facebook – and, indeed, Tabi himself had occasionally boasted to this effect during his years at Oxford. Upon his return from the States, however, Tabi had stunned his parents by quietly announcing that he proposed to join the security services.

Tabi's Damascene conversion had come while at MIT and had been prompted in the first instance by reasons of the heart. Tabi had

115

fallen in love with a second generation American girl, Noor, whose family were of Pakistani origin. Noor's father had come to America as a visiting professor of Political Science at Boston College. He had brought his young family to America; they had stayed and in due course had adopted American citizenship. Noor was a fellow student at MIT and, like Tabi, fiercely intelligent. Her subject was Biological Engineering, but she could have used this to enter virtually any field she chose. Tabi had discovered, through Noor and more widely, that while for the average Brit patriotism was a quietly confident attitude of mind, for many Americans patriotism was a burning emotion. Noor was passionate about her adopted country and, especially as a comparatively recent arrival, had felt a powerful need to demonstrate this. She had decided that she would sign up for a short service commission in the US military before returning in her late twenties to civilian life and a full-time career. Tabi had at first gently mocked Noor's fervour and had chided her for squandering her intellectual talents. But he had found her unshakeably in earnest and this had set him thinking. At the same time, the US security services were actively recruiting graduates in Tabi's field at MIT.

Tabi had hitherto taken his national patrimony for granted, but under Noor's influence he had begun to reflect that his own family's adopted country, though small in size and population, had made a disproportionate contribution to the world over the past half millennium. During that period, two of the five seminal thinkers in the first tier of the scientific pantheon, at least in Tabi's mind, were Englishmen: Newton and Darwin, keeping company with Copernicus, Galileo and Einstein. British inventions had dominated the Industrial Revolution and during the past century Britons had invented or discovered stainless steel, television, the jet engine, antibiotics, carbon fibre, the theoretical model and prototype of the computer, the first electronically programmable computer and the internet, to name just a few. And it was not simply in the sciences. 'Shakespeare bestrides Parnassus', as a girl at Oxford had had tattooed around her ankle. Britain had created the first modern parliamentary democracy. With the benefit of hindsight, one could argue the rights and wrongs of colonialism, but tiny Britain had had the administrative capability, in addition to the military and economic, to run a large part of the world for two hundred years and to dominate for a century – and, just as important, upon the waning of empire, had had the good grace peacefully to relinquish its power. If Tabi thought of his own ancestral homeland, India, from which his parents had come to Britain before his birth … the sole aphorism worth retaining among George W Bush's gaffe-strewn pronouncements was that India was a country of 'a billion people, a million problems, and still a democracy'. It was truly remarkable that a country of India's size and population, with such diversity of language, culture, religion and ethnicity, and with such problems of poverty, inequality, bureaucratic inefficiency and corruption, it was astonishing – and a beacon to the rest of the developing world, surely – that India was a functioning democracy with an independent judiciary and an unfettered press. And these shining virtues were a legacy of British rule. Britain today punched far above its weight not only in scientific innovation, but in finance, popular music, fashion… As if all that were not already enough, a significant proportion of the world's favourite sports had originated in Britain – among them football, rugby, cricket, golf, tennis and, Tabi's own sport, squash. And perhaps more important than any of this, why did so many flee from the world's repressive regimes to this crowded island? The clichés were true: Britain offered one of the most tolerant, law-abiding, fair and good-humoured societies on earth. Wasn't that worth defending against the forces of medievalism and the violent and disruptive use of the tools of the twenty-first century?

Somewhere in his heart Tabi still carried a flame for Noor, though they had parted midway through his time in the States. The torch of patriotism lit by her, meanwhile, he had brought back to England. Upon his return, he had applied to join the security services. With his computing and already apparent linguistic skills, he was an ideal candidate. Tabi's aptitude for language had been clear from infancy. His family spoke Hindi and Gujarati in addition to English and some of his uncles, aunts and cousins, with whom he played often as a child, spoke Bengali. From the earliest age, he had displayed a ready grasp of all three Indian languages, in addition to his principal native tongue, English. While at MIT, to impress Noor, he had started to teach himself Urdu, which was the ancestral tongue of her family,

117

and then, when he had discovered that the security services would sponsor the study of foreign languages, he had applied for the course at SOAS. At SOAS, it had at first been the Iranian dialect of Persian which he had studied, but during his year abroad he had been seconded as an interpreter to the British forces in Afghanistan and, by the end of his tour, his fluency in the coarser, more guttural Afghan dialect had overtaken his proficiency in the more musical Iranian.

Equipped with his impressive panoply of academic qualifications, Tabi had first been dispatched to GCHQ for a year. After this, he had been sent to Stockholm for six months to work with a Swedish company in the development of software which could trawl the internet in hundreds of languages with a capability not only to identify obvious trigger words, but also to infer from context what subject was under discussion and even to gauge whether emotions were running high: it could lay bare a plot even when this was wrapped in circumlocution or dressed up as something quite different and could sound the alert when blood was up and violence potentially imminent. And, yes, never slow off the mark, by the end of his six months in Stockholm, Tabi could chat up a girl in Swedish. Already a globe-trotting veteran at the age of twenty-seven, he had then returned, this time not to GCHQ, but to Gordon's team. That had been eighteen months earlier.

Raheem stirred and stretched. He turned to Tabi. "Sorry. Forty winks." He glanced out of the window. "Next stop."

TWENTY-NINE

Tabi and Raheem alighted from the bus and walked the last hundred yards to the mosque. The mosque was not purpose-built, but occupied a former primary school. As they entered, Raheem showed Tabi that the assembly hall had become the prayer room. It was carpeted, but otherwise bare of furniture or ornamentation.

"The imam will be expecting you, so best to go in and see him first."

Raheem gently knocked at an office door.

"Come in."

Raheem gestured to Tabi to enter, while he himself quietly and respectfully withdrew.

Tabi entered to find a plainly furnished office. The imam sat in a rather threadbare armchair in front of a coffee table. His trimmed grey beard gave the impression he was at least sixty years of age, though a large and completely opaque pair of dark glasses made it slightly difficult to tell. He wore a soft white cap on his greying head and a simple blue smock over loose trousers. A pot of tea and two cups sat waiting on the table.

"Forgive me if I do not rise," said the imam in perfect and barely accented English. "My legs are not too good." He motioned Tabi to the sofa beside him. "It's Imran, yes?"

"Yes," replied Tabi.

"Well, Imran, please help yourself to tea and please be so kind as to pour a cup for me too."

Tabi obliged.

"I understand," continued the imam, "that you have just arrived from London and would like to join our community and worship here?"

"Exactly."

"Well, you are of course most welcome. Where did you worship in London?"

"To be honest," said Tabi, "I've been very lax and didn't really attend anywhere. But I thought I should make a new start."

119

"Well, that's to be commended. Prayer meetings are held here at the appropriate hours every day – you are welcome to join whenever you wish. We also have a number of community activities if you wish to join those. You might look at our notice board to see what is on offer."

Tabi did not want to press too hastily, but nor did he wish to delay. He might not have another opportunity to sound out the imam. "Do you mind if I just ask …" he ventured. "I'm not quite sure how to put it, but … where do you stand doctrinally?"

"That's an interesting question for a new joiner. Do you have particular issues in mind?"

"No, sorry, what I really meant … for example, in London the Finsbury mosque has a reputation for being a hotbed of, shall we say, Islamic fervour …"

The imam laughed. "Well, I hope that's not what you're looking for?"

"No, no, on the contrary …"

"That's good to hear. No, we are at the opposite extreme. We are very moderate. I do not wish to shock you, but …" The imam lowered his dark glasses to reveal empty, scarred sockets. He put the glasses back in place. "The Taliban put my eyes out with a hot poker and also broke my legs for speaking against them. I advocated moderation and an enlightened approach."

"That's awful – what the Taliban did," said Tabi, who was genuinely taken aback at what he had seen. "I'm so sorry."

"No, if anything, I was the lucky one in my family. My father, mother, brother, sister, all killed by the Taliban. We were an educated family. My father was an engineer – actually studied at Imperial College here. My mother studied English here. I was a Koranic scholar. Afghanistan has a reputation as a benighted country of goatherds and opium farmers who, if not at war with external parties, will feud among themselves. There is truth in this, but it is by no means the whole truth. I'm sorry, I'm straying from the point …"

"No, I'm very interested to hear."

"Well, my point was I am a strong believer in moderation, education, enlightenment, citizenship, working together … You may be surprised to hear that two of my closest friends are the local vicar

120

and his wife. He often attends our prayer meetings and I often attend his church services. Of course, we have doctrinal differences – to return to your original question – but we both recognise that there is a far greater truth which we both share. Sometimes he brings members of his congregation here and I sometimes take members of the Muslim community to his church. In fact, I think I may even say that those are perhaps the occasions when all feel that God or Allah – call Him what you will – that is when we feel He moves most powerfully among us."

Tabi continued his discussion with the imam for another half hour and, to his surprise, left the interview feeling really quite moved.

Raheem was waiting for Tabi in front of the notice board.

"I see what you mean," said Tabi. "He really is a most impressive man. Thank you for making the introduction."

"No, my pleasure. You mentioned you were also interested in the computer club." Raheem tapped the notice board. "It meets tomorrow evening. I know the guy who runs it – I can introduce you to him too. I'm not much of a computer geek myself, but I know he's supposed to be quite good – he designed and maintains our website."

Once back in his hotel room, Tabi called Helen.

"Helen, hi. Caught you at a good moment?"

"Yeah. Still in the office – with a takeaway. What have you discovered?"

"Well, I'm pretty sure you can rule the imam off your list."

"Your Farsi coming in handy?"

"No need – he speaks perfect English. He's actually a highly educated and hugely impressive man."

"Oh no, they're not turning you, are they, Shah?"

"It'd take a bit more than that to shift an old cynic like me. But seriously … he's a very moderate, eminently reasonable and deeply spiritual man. If all clerics – of all religious persuasions – were like him, the world would be a very much better place."

"Allah be praised. What about the website?"

"Actually, I'm not joking, Helen. He was really quite moving to listen to."

"They have turned you."

Tabi ignored the further jibe. "The website is next on my list. They have a computer club which meets tomorrow. The guy who runs it also runs the website."

THIRTY

Tim's back was aching after a day of unaccustomed manual labour pulling up carrots and onions and cutting cabbages. His clothes stank of the cabbage and onions and of his own sweat – and the sole of his left trainer was cleft into an open flap beneath the toe after a wayward stroke of the cabbage-cutting knife. Tim had also caught the sun. He had gladly accepted first turn in the shower and was standing under the coolly refreshing spray. Gathering vegetables in the fields, he had not garnered a word to suggest nuclear conspiracy among the Swards. As the day had progressed, his mission had seemed increasingly remote. Draper had entered his thoughts from time to time, but the financier too now seemed a world away. Tim adjusted the shower temperature so that it was just warm and began to lather a bar of soap. The bathroom door opened and Sandy entered. She slipped off her clothes, letting them drop to the floor, and – to Tim's complete confusion – joined him in the shower. She took the soap from Tim.

"Let me help," she said.

Though still in a state of mild perturbation, Tim found he had an enormous appetite at supper that evening. And Martha's food – freshly gathered, beautifully cooked – was wonderful. Gerald, though still in dressing gown and jeans, was a little more animated this evening and had appeared at the table with a case of Château Lafleur Pomerol dating from 1976. Tim could hardly believe he was drinking such wine. When George reminded the gathering that since 2004 ice shelves the size of Northern Ireland and Rhode Island had broken off Antarctica and melted, Tim found himself compelled to agree that something urgent had to be done. By the time a second joint was passed around the snug after supper, Tim was struggling to remember who he was supposed to be and why he was there. Fortunately, all the others seemed to be in a similarly beatific state.

A little later, lying in his bed deeply relaxed and now and then whistling quietly to himself the refrain from *Norwegian Wood*, Tim wondered whether he had in truth stumbled into an idyll worth living and a cause worth fighting for. Dimly recalling his mission, he thought it was surely the height of absurdity to suppose that these well-meaning people, even if they had the faintest notion of how to obtain a nuclear device, would ever dream of detonating such a thing.

He was just drifting off when his door quietly opened. Martha stood in the doorway in a diaphanous nightie.

"My turn," she said softly.

Tim sat up in astonishment and even slight panic. "Are you … I mean, I'm not sure if this is right."

"Don't worry – George doesn't mind. He's cool with it."

Martha lifted off her nightie and slipped into bed beside Tim. He could still smell the marijuana in her hair.

THIRTY-ONE

With light shafting in around the edges of the curtains, Tim lay by himself in his knotted sheets in waking reverie – excited, confused, guilty, carefree … If Sandy had been uninhibited, Martha had been the full Woodstock. Tim stretched. This was not the life he had led and he had no idea what to make of it. He looked at his watch. Shit! It was past eight! He jumped out of bed, sped across to the bathroom to take a pee and splash his face, hurriedly dressed and, wondering how on earth he would bid good morning to his two seductresses and their various paramours, hastened downstairs. He found Martha alone in the kitchen.

"Morning, sleepy head," smiled Martha.

"Christ, I'm sorry. Are the others all working already?"

"Relax, relax … John, Mark and Sandy have taken the produce to market. George isn't going into the village for another hour or two yet. There's no rush today."

Martha made breakfast for Tim and sat drinking tea with him. No mention was made of the night before. Tim gradually calmed down and, under Martha's benign influence, even began to feel their relationship had grown warmer and closer. When Tim had finished, Martha took him outside. She led him up a path to the top of a hillock. A lone wooden bench sat on the crest.

"Look," she said. "The Malvern Hills and over there the Clee Hills and there, in the far distance, that's the Black Mountains and Brecon National Park." The morning sun softened the parkland, the surrounding trees and fields, the distant hills. "Isn't it achingly beautiful? Isn't it such an English beauty?" She stood in contemplation for several seconds. "I bet you all over the world people could take you to places in their own countries which have their own quite distinctive and yet similarly heart-stopping beauty. And yet we're putting a blight upon it. Our children, certainly our children's children, won't see this. Every statesman needs to come here – or to his own equivalent beauty spot – and needs to be made to understand that unless he returns to his desk and makes this his first priority – not from tomorrow, but from the very hour he returns to his brief – he needs to understand that his children's and grandchildren's lives are at stake and if he doesn't act with life and death urgency, this will be gone. Gone forever. Thousands of species have already perished, thousands more are on the brink. And, finally, us among them. Across the planet, whole eco-systems hang by a thread. That's what we mean by the Sward of Damocles. The name is not tongue-in-cheek. It's this."

They sat down in silence on the wooden bench. After perhaps twenty minutes, Martha took Tim's hand and led him back towards the house through an ornamental part of the garden. Rounding a hedge, they came upon a lily pond. Tim stopped in surprise. A stone dolphin spewed water into the pond: sitting at the base of the fountain, in the lotus position, again naked but for his loin cloth, with the torrent of water pounding on his head, was Derek. Martha merely smiled and led Tim onwards back to the house.

Within moments of Tim and Martha returning to the house, Derek appeared at the kitchen door. He was still dripping wet, but was wiping himself down with his shirt.

"Jack, come, I'll show you," he said.

Derek marched towards the stables. Tim followed. Finding a pile of bricks, Derek set down two in parallel four or five inches apart and then lay across these a stack of half a dozen others. A few yards further on he built two parallel stacks of several bricks about a foot or so apart. He found two short planks of wood and rested one of these across the two parallel stacks. He stood Tim a few yards beyond the bricks.

"Brace yourself like this," said Derek, standing with one foot forward, one back and with his arms outstretched as though he were pushing an immovable object.

Derek placed the second plank in Tim's outstretched hands and then retreated to a position a couple of yards back from the first little edifice of bricks. He gave Tim a short bow and then began to tense his body. He seemed to turn into a knotted bundle of writhing serpents and a look of frenzy came into his eye. He suddenly took two fierce strides forward and with a 'hyah!' brought his elbow crashing onto the first stack of bricks, which instantly cracked and

126

slumped beneath his blow. With a further two strides and another cry, he splintered the first plank with the blade of his hand. He held his pose for a second, shaking as though possessed with a barely containable strength and energy and with his mouth in rictus and his eyes wide and white. Then he ran two steps and with a whirling leap smashed his bare foot into the plank held by Tim. The plank sundered as a jarring shock slammed along Tim's arms and tore at his shoulder joints. Derek stepped back and gave Tim another little bow.

"That's what I think of cunting politicians," he hissed. "We should teach the cunting fucks a lesson."

Jesus Christ, thought Tim, if meditation is supposed to create inner peace, it doesn't seem to have worked for him.

Derek cracked his knuckles. "I have connections, you know. Powerful people who can show the cunts."

THIRTY-TWO

After Derek's slightly terrifying exhibition, Tim was relieved to be joining George in the car for the trip to the village – though he also felt a touch of apprehension in case George showed any signs of resentment over Martha's nocturnal visit to Tim's bedroom. George brought the Prius round from the stable. As Tim was climbing in, he saw a large BMW with blacked out windows approach along the drive.

"Who's this?" asked Tim.

"Gerry's grocery delivery."

"Groceries?"

George merely nodded towards the BMW as it came to a halt in front of the house. A swarthy and stocky man in a loose white shirt, tight leather trousers and a festoon of bling jewellery emerged from the car. He held a large McDonald's takeaway bag in his hand. He rapped on the front door. After a further couple of raps, Gerald appeared in his dressing gown and jeans. He handed over what appeared to be a wad of notes and took the paper bag. The man returned to the BMW and drove off at speed down the driveway.

"I see," said Tim.

"We can't stop him," said George. "We have tried."

George and Tim set off as the BMW disappeared from view around the bend in the driveway. Settling into conversation, Tim was relieved to find that George was as equable and affable as ever.

"I do feel guilty driving," said George, "but even ecologists have to make some concessions to modern life. You know, we human beings create twenty-seven gigatonnes of carbon dioxide per annum. The average American produces twenty-two tonnes, the average European eleven and the average African four. I actually think ordinary people understand what's going on and would welcome bold action by politicians – but the politicians are all too cowardly, too beholden to different interest groups, too preoccupied with day-to-day matters to see the big picture and take decisive action. For example, why don't they just ban all private vehicles with an engine size of more than, say, one point six litres? I really think a government that did that would be massively popular. Sorry, am I boring you?"

"No, not at all. Your knowledge on the subject is incredible."

They were silent for a few moments.

Tim resumed. "Is it just you that does the website?"

"Mostly. But the others do contribute."

"I noticed at least one of your bloggers regularly calls for quite radical action."

"Really?"

"Yuh. Dionysius, I think he called himself."

"Oh, right. No prizes for guessing who that is."

"Who?"

"Think of the obvious person."

"It's not you?"

"Certainly not! God forbid. No ... Derek, of course."

"Oh, I see."

"I don't agree with what he says, but I don't see it as my place to censor him – or anyone else. To be honest, I think he has serious personal issues unrelated to the fate of the planet. Gerry likes him for some reason."

"Has he been with you long?"

"Several months."

"Where did he come from? I mean, how did he come to join up with you guys?"

"Just appeared one day – rather like you a couple of days ago. I don't know a huge amount about him. He keeps to himself quite a bit and not all of what he says makes sense. As I said, I think he's a somewhat troubled individual."

"Derek ... what's his surname?"

"Barnes. At least, that's what he says. But who knows. We don't pry. We work on a principle of live and let live. I mean, you might not be Jack Cane, for all I know."

Tim gave a little laugh, which came across as forced. He glanced at George. George did not seem to have noticed.

"And Gerry ... does he just fund everything?"

129

"We make a bit of money on the farm produce – but then the farm is Gerry's as well. Actually, all of this surrounding area is owned by him and farmed professionally. We just have a few fields near the house. But, basically, yes, Gerry is our banker."

"What, just hands you a blank cheque when you need it?"

"As a matter of fact, that's exactly what he does. I'd actually prefer it if he took a closer interest and saw exactly where his money was going."

"He seems to manage his grocery bills."

George grunted in assent. "Come to think of it, perhaps I should have mentioned ... there is a phone at the house. Gerry has a satellite phone which he uses to call in supplies. But it's almost always lost. We have a panic every now and then when Gerry needs to place an order and he can't find the phone. His flat on the top floor is a complete mess."

"Who looks after his affairs?"

"Oh, he has private bankers, accountants, fund managers, farm managers ... I just hope they're not all taking advantage of him."

"Didn't I read in the papers that Gerry's a Russian scholar or something like that?"

"'Scholar' may be going a bit far these days, but, yes, he reads Russian. Had a couple of Russians staying at the house for a few days a month or two ago."

"Business contacts?"

"No, no – one was a sculptor and the other ... actually, I wasn't quite clear about the other, but as far as I could gather he was some kind of journalist. Rather taciturn and disconcerting fellow." George turned to Tim. "Lot of questions from you this morning!"

"Yeah, sorry. It's just you seem to have such an idyllic existence here – I can hardly believe it's true."

"We are lucky – but we try to use our good fortune to achieve serious ends."

They arrived in Bowley village. George planned to spend an hour at the library. Tim could make his phone call – he could see that his phone now had a signal again. They would meet up at the pub in an hour's time. George dropped Tim in the centre of the village and continued on the short distance to the library. Tim walked over to a little cobbled square with an old iron water pump at its centre. There were a couple of benches, but the spot was deserted. He called the office.

"Tim!" It was Trevor who answered. "We've been getting worried about you."

"Yeah, I'm afraid there's no mobile signal and the house phone has been cut off."

"So we gathered. Is everything okay?"

"I think these guys are pretty much all in the clear. They seem genuinely and peacefully devoted to ecological issues. Did you know, for example, that the Himalayan glaciers are melting away and that they supply forty percent of the world's population with fresh water?"

"I can't say I did."

Helen was now also listening in to Tim's call. She rolled her eyes at Trevor.

"Are *you* okay?" asked Trevor.

"I'm fine. Having an unexpectedly good time, actually. Breathtakingly beautiful scenery. Fantastic home grown food. And the women … Jesus! Yesterday one of them … how shall I put it politely? … administered oral relief in the shower and … well, I'm not even going to tell you what another one did to me later on. And his lordship – who, by the way, is completely stoned out of his brain the entire time and could barely run a bath, never mind a terrorist plot – his lordship produced this 1970-something *grand cru* claret. I'm afraid I've also had to puff a couple of joints to keep up appearances."

"Jesus H Christ," Helen interrupted. "We send Shah to infiltrate a mosque and he turns into a proselytising religious fanatic; we send Lemon to infiltrate a bunch of eco-maniacs and he turns into a dope-smoking, free-love eco-groupie!"

"Morning, Gordon," said Tim, affecting a tone of weariness.

"Lemon, it's not 'Morning, Gordon'." Helen mimicked Tim's tone of voice. "We're in the middle of a goddamn national emergency. Honestly, I can scarcely believe this is you I'm talking to, but if you're at some hippie holiday camp blowing your mind and

131

shagging your nuts off, then get the next bloody train back here and help the rest of us."

"Yeah, yeah, fair enough, keep your shirt on ... Being serious, I'm pretty sure most of the group here is completely above board. The marquess himself, as I said, is just totally out of it. However, there is one guy who seems a bit of a psycho and who told me this morning that he has powerful connections. I think he's nothing more than a fantasist, but I'd like to press him a bit further just to be sure. If that leads nowhere, I'll play the sick relative card and leave tomorrow."

"What's this guy's name?" asked Helen.

But George had drawn up in the Prius and Tim had lowered his phone and did not hear the question.

"Sorry, Jack," called George from the car window. "Library's closed."

"Got to go," said Tim into his phone. "Lots of love to you and Dad. I'll call you again tomorrow." He cut his phone and went over to the car.

"Seems the librarian's off sick," explained George. "And the pub doesn't open for another hour. I guess we'd better just head back. I hope you've managed to make your phone call at least?" He noticed Tim's expression. "Is everything okay?"

"Not great, actually. Apparently, my dad's in hospital. My mum says he's fine, but it's a bit of a worry."

"Do you need to head home?"

"Well, I think Dad's okay, but if you wouldn't mind, please could we come to the village at the same sort of time tomorrow – so I can call again."

"Yes, of course. I'd be coming here anyway."

Climbing back into the car, Tim realised with annoyance that he had missed an opportunity to ask Helen if she'd seen anything new from Draper and Andropov.

THIRTY-THREE

Nick had overheard Trevor and Helen talking to Tim. He strolled over to their desks.

"Tim okay?" he asked, while picking up Helen's bottle of sake, turning it on its head and then righting it so that a snowfall of reflecting gold flakes fluttered down through the clear liquor.

"Sounds like your first guess may have been right," said Trevor.

"My first guess?"

"Dionysus rather than Dionysius – Tim seems to have pitched up in the middle of some Bacchanalian orgy."

"Damn!" said Nick. "And by rights that should have been my assignment!"

Maggie had also come over to hear the news from Tim. "So long as it doesn't turn into the Euripidean version where the frenzied Bacchantes first rip cattle apart and then fall upon the young man who's come to spy on them and tear him to pieces as well."

"From what Tim is saying," observed Trevor, "squeezed Lemon, yes, but sliced Lemon … it didn't sound like it." He bared his front teeth in a wolfish grin.

THIRTY-FOUR

Tim lunched with George and Martha, who were particularly solicitous of his well-being. After helping Martha with one or two chores, Tim then took himself off for a ramble – ostensibly to explore the estate, but in fact in search of Derek, who had wandered off during the course of the morning, as was seemingly his wont. Tim followed a path which ran alongside a fence at the edge of the fields. On Tim's left, neat furrows of potatoes gave way to a field of barley; to his right, woodland crowded up to the path in a tumble of beeches and oaks, ferns, brambles and fallen branches covered in lichen. As Tim walked along, it occurred to him that he should have given Derek's name – or his alias, if that was what it was – and his description to Helen and Trevor, so that they could try to unearth any information about him. Tim glanced at his phone – as usual there was no signal. The path became increasingly overgrown. Tim came to a stile. He could continue on the same path or could clamber over the stile and follow a track between the field of barley and an adjacent field of wheat. He leaned on the fence. A light breeze swished through the crops and lifted up to Tim a dusty odour redolent of old barns and high summer. The fields fell away towards pasture grazed by a flock of sheep and, beyond this, a line of trees which marked the course of a stream. A mile or more distant, a church spire and the roofs of a few houses nestled among the trees. The scene was bathed in sunlight and caressed by the occasional shadow of a cloud.

While Tim stood gazing over the fields, a figure appeared in the sheep pasture. Tim saw straightaway that it was Derek. He was again dressed only in his loin cloth. As he advanced into the field, the sheep trotted out of his way with the occasional bleat. Derek took up position in the centre of the field and stood motionless. The sheep became accustomed to his presence and milled about closer to him. One sheep cropped at the grass a yard or two in front of Derek. Suddenly, Derek unleashed an explosive movement, taking a stride forwards and then bringing the blade of his hand crashing onto the

134

head of the sheep. The poor animal slumped onto its knees and then collapsed as the other sheep ran bleating to a corner of the field.

"Jesus fucking Christ," whispered Tim to himself as he instinctively recoiled and ducked behind the fence. Tim held his breath as he peered back over the fence. He saw Derek bow towards the sheep and then return across the pasture in the direction from which he had come. Tim could not tell whether the sheep was stunned or dead, but it lay absolutely still. The rest of the flock huddled, still bleating, in a far corner of the meadow.

"Sodding hell," exhaled Tim as he hastened back along the pathway, shaken at what he had seen. Whether or not Derek was a potential nuclear bomber, he was clearly a psychopath. Tim decided he had to find Gerry's satellite phone and call the office. They should identify who Derek was and send someone to arrest him for his probable killing of the sheep.

But when Tim arrived back at the house, he found John, Mark and Sandy had just returned from market: they immediately enlisted his help in unloading the empty crates from the back of their van and then in stacking them in an outhouse. When this was done, Martha asked for Tim's help in the kitchen. The afternoon passed without Tim finding an opportunity to slip upstairs in search of Gerry's phone.

THIRTY-FIVE

Tabi and Raheem left the office at five and hopped on the bus. In his pocket, Tabi concealed a USB carrying a program similar to the one he had installed in Charles Draper's network.

"The computer club starts at six," said Raheem, "but best to get there beforehand and then I can introduce you to Shahid before he gets distracted by the other club members. He's always there early."

The club room was a former classroom. One wall was lined with cubicles, each of which was equipped with a desktop computer. There were four or five rows of old school desks and on several of these laptops sat waiting. The teacher's desk was equipped with its own desktop with a pair of screens. Behind the desk sat Shahid.

"Hi Shahid," said Raheem as he and Tabi entered.

"Raheem, hi." Shahid rose from behind the desk. He was about the same height as Tabi, but three or four times the volume. He wore a loose Hawaiian shirt.

"This is Imran," said Raheem. "He's another geek, so he'll probably give you a run for your money."

"Surely not possible," beamed Shahid. "How do you do, Imran."

"How do you do," said Tabi as they shook hands.

"I'll leave you two to compare notes. Catch you a bit later," said Raheem.

Shahid began to demonstrate to Tabi the website which he had set up and to explain what the computer club had to offer. Tabi, as ever, was keen to get to the point of his visit.

"I couldn't help noticing that the tone of some of the stuff on your blogsite is a bit different from the rest of the website," observed Tabi. "Looks like you have a few fundamentalists in your midst?"

"Oh, that's not us," said Shahid. "I don't know who those idiots are, but it's no one from here. I've told the imam I can shut them out if he wants, but his view is that everyone should be free to express his own opinion and fools should be allowed to condemn themselves out of their own mouths."

"Most commendable."

"I'd be a bit less tolerant myself. We sometimes get quite inflammatory comments. But the imam's words fall like a balm upon the community."

"Very poetically put."

"Actually, I'm quoting the imam." Shahid clicked open a page on the website. "Here we are: 'Let us not poison with angry words the well whose waters we share with our brother citizens; rather let our words fall as a balm upon troubled communities'."

"He is an inspirational man, isn't he."

"He truly is. Whereas some of the bloggers ..."

Shahid clicked open the blogsite and scrolled through a couple of messages. As he did so, a fresh contribution popped onto the site. Tabi froze. At the same moment, his phone began to vibrate in his jacket pocket. Tabi stared at the screen.

"Someone calling?" Shahid nodded in the direction of Tabi's vibrating pocket.

"Email," said Tabi. "Nothing urgent, I'm sure. I'll check in a mo." It was of the utmost urgency, Tabi knew.

Tabi's attention was held by the short message newly displayed on the blogsite: 'Allah calls upon his firstborn to stand ready'. During his time at GCHQ, Tabi had run an exhaustive back-search of Islamist internet chat prior to the 7/7 bombings in London. He had found just such a message, again containing the unusual reference to 'firstborn', and had concluded that this had been an advance signal to the bombers to prepare themselves. A couple of days after the first message, on the sixth of July, a second had followed from the same source to the effect that Allah was ready to receive his firstborn. On the seventh, the bombers had struck. Tabi was in no doubt that his phone was vibrating because his own internet monitoring program was sending him an alert concerning the very message which had just flashed up on the mosque's blogsite. Tabi needed to get on the phone to Helen and team as fast as possible to let them know that the terrorist wheels were seemingly already in motion and it was likely the security services had only a day or two to thwart the intended attack. If he could insert his program into the website, it would become a great deal easier to track where this new message was coming from and whether any other messages appeared to be a coded

137

response. This might then provide clues as to who was involved and what was planned.

Fortunately, Shahid came to Tabi's aid. "Would you like a drink? Coke, Fanta ...?"

"Coke would be great." Tabi took out his wallet and rummaged for suitable coins.

"Oh, don't worry about that," said Shahid.

"Do you mind if I just look at the website while you're getting the Coke?"

"Be my guest."

Shahid headed off to the drinks machine, which Tabi had seen was only about thirty yards down the corridor. Even with Shahid's all-the-time-in-the-world rolling gait, Tabi had at best a minute or so to upload his program. He inserted his USB, clicked open his program and hit 'enter'. "Come on, come on," he said under his breath. Suddenly, Raheem appeared in the doorway of the classroom.

"Hi. Shahid abandoned you?"

"Oh, hi, Raheem. No, he's just getting us a drink."

Raheem advanced into the room. Shit, thought Tabi. He glanced down: only forty-five percent uploaded.

"Er, Raheem, you couldn't do me a tiny favour, could you?"

"Sure."

"Please could you tell Shahid I prefer Diet Coke if the machine has it. I forgot to tell him. If he's already bought ordinary, that's fine."

"Yeah, no problem."

Raheem disappeared in Shahid's direction.

Sixty percent, seventy percent. Tabi went to the classroom door and peeked down the corridor. Shahid and Raheem were chatting at the drinks machine. Tabi went back to the computer. Eighty-five percent, ninety, ninety-five. It was done. He removed his USB. But now he had to restart the computer. He hit restart just as Shahid and Raheem reappeared at the door. Tabi still did not want Shahid to come over and see that he was running a restart. He quickly rounded the desk and intercepted the two with their drinks half way into the room.

"Diet Coke," said Shahid. "Raheem was just in time."

Tabi needed to stall the pair for a further few moments.

"Thanks, Shahid." Tabi popped open the can. "Cheers!" He took a sip. "So, Raheem, you're not one of Shahid's disciples in the computer club?"

Shahid laughed good-naturedly at the implied compliment.

"Oh, I do come along," said Raheem, "but I'm sure I'm a rather slow student."

"On the contrary," smiled Shahid.

"And, Shahid, where did you learn your computer skills?"

"Oh, school, college, taught myself ... You?"

"Yeah, same."

Tabi had surely held them back for a sufficient time with this banter. He allowed Shahid to resume his place behind the teacher's desk.

"Strange," said Shahid. "Website's gone."

"Oh, sorry," said Tabi, "did I accidentally close it?"

"There," said Shahid. "Back up again."

"Guys," said Tabi, "I hate to be rude, but actually I have to scoot off. Just got a message from head office." Tabi waved his mobile as evidence. "Turns out that email was urgent after all, Shahid – some stuff I need to attend to right away. You've both been really great. I'll catch you later on."

Tabi left the two looking a little surprised. He hurried down the corridor as fast as he could without breaking into an unseemly run. As he passed the drinks machine, he dropped his half drunk Coke into a bin. Once out on the street, he broke into a run. He rounded a corner into a quiet side street and took out his phone.

"Helen?"

"Shah ..."

"Helen, listen. In fact, put me on speaker. Tell everyone to stop what they're doing."

Tabi could hear Helen telling the others to pay attention.

"Okay, you're on speaker."

Tabi spoke with urgency. "Hi everyone. The good news is the Leicester mosque is in the clear – they're nothing to do with it – just their blogsite is being used by others as a message board. I've uploaded a program so that as soon as I'm back at my desk, I can

139

monitor everything and with a bit of luck can trace where the messages are coming from. The bad news is I've just this minute seen on their blogsite a message which is nearly identical to one shortly before the 7/7 bombing. You should all have the blogsite on your systems already or just go to the mosque website and look at the blog page. Something to the effect that Allah is calling his firstborn to make ready. If it follows the same pattern as 7/7, this is the pre-signal. The actual signal to attack will follow in a day or two and will take the form of Allah calling his firstborn to him. If I'm right, in the worst case, we have less than thirty-six hours to neutralise this. Even in the best case, we only have two or three days. My advice is we should launch raids on every known cell late tomorrow or pre-dawn the following morning. I don't think we can afford to hang around." Tabi could hear someone in the background asking a question. "What's that?"

Helen spoke: "We were wondering if you have any clue whether this is the nuclear attack?"

"Helen, this is one cryptic line on a blogsite. I have no more idea than you what sort of attack it will be. Anyway, I'm heading back to London now. See you all in a few hours. Helen, small favour ..." Tabi could hear Helen switching back to the handset.

"Yup," she answered.

"I guess before tomorrow we ought to send a message to the council apologising and saying I've been reassigned – please could you arrange that? Right now I need to call a cab, grab my stuff and head straight to the station."

"Sure."

"And maybe could also you get a personal message to Raheem Hameed?"

"Who?"

"Raheem Hameed – the guy who introduced me to the mosque. Something along the lines of 'Apologies for disappearing – I have been reassigned by my company. Very many thanks for all your kindness and help. Best wishes to all at the mosque. *Salaam alaikum.* Imran'. Imran – that's me."

"I know your cover, Shah."

"Something like that. Did you get it all?"

140

"I did. But, Shah, you're going soft – you should just cut contact with these guys."

"Okay. Never mind, perhaps you're right. I'll call again or email when I'm on the train."

THIRTY-SIX

Only when the others were readying themselves for supper did Tim finally have an opportunity to slip into the main part of the house. He bounded quietly up the magnificently engineered staircase, which took him as far as the first floor. At the end of the first floor landing, he found a more modest staircase leading up to Gerald's quarters. Well before he reached the open door at the top of this second flight of stairs, he was struck by the fetid smell emanating from within the flat – a combination of smoke from cigarettes and joints, unwashed clothes, body odour, bad breath, unflushed lavatories, rotting food and an unidentifiable cheesy sickliness, all trapped in unventilated rooms. Trying not to breathe too deeply, Tim knocked on the open door.

"Gerry?"

There was no sound. Tim crept into the flat. He passed an open bedroom door – yellowing sheets were roiled on the bed and dirty clothes were strewn all over the stained carpet despite the fact that Gerry only ever seemed to wear his dressing gown and jeans. A plate of uneaten and mouldy food also sat on the floor with a half drunk cup of coffee balanced at an angle in the middle of the food. Tim noticed several pills of different types scattered under a bedside table, itself piled with a jumble of filthy plates, cups, a wine bottle, a rock music magazine, a rolled but unsmoked cigarette, CDs, more pills ... The next door along was just ajar, but the stench from within caused Tim to gag and immediately revealed that this was a bathroom with a lavatory of Augean filthiness. Tim came to the living room. Gerald was slumped face down on a couch. The room was an even more chaotic jumble of clothes, CDs, books, food plates, wine bottles – empty and half drunk, standing and fallen – brandy and vodka bottles, DVDs, rock music and other magazines, ancient trainers, unopened mail ... Tim stared at the scene: his own flat in London might suffer visitations from the imp of untidiness, but the marquess had seemingly renounced his quarters to the fallen archangel of misrule. That morning's McDonald's bag sat on a huge and no less disorderly oak coffee table, upon which was arrayed a witch's pharmacopia of powders, pills and desiccated leaves plus another bottle of the same *grand cru* claret. Rather incongruously, two fine bronze lions, each about a foot in length, faced each other in lordly pose in the midst of the debris. On the floor close to Gerald lay a syringe and rubber tourniquet and, for good measure, a crack pipe with its contents spilled onto the Wilton carpet.

"Gerry?"

No response. Tim approached the prostrate figure.

"Gerry, are you okay?"

Gerald gave a tiny snort or snore and shifted a little. He was clearly far from sentience, but apparently not in much worse condition than usual. Tim surveyed the shambles. The satellite phone could be anywhere in the flat. He began to root through the jumble of belongings, but found no sign of the phone. He opened the top of a walnut writing bureau: it appeared to contain nothing but a slew of unopened mail. Tim prodded at the cascade of envelopes just in case the phone was concealed among or beneath them. One of the larger envelopes caught Tim's eye: to his surprise, he saw that it bore the logo of Wave Capital Management. Like all the envelopes this one remained sealed, but judging from its bulkiness it contained some kind of printed publication. Digging further down into the pile and finding a second envelope identical to the first but dated exactly six months earlier, Tim guessed that these were most likely Wave Capital's semi-annual reports. And, it struck Tim, this very probably meant that the marquess was an investor in Draper's fund. Tim's immediate thought was that this was a remarkable coincidence, but then he reflected that it was surely not really surprising at all that one of the country's richest men should invest at least a small portion of his fortune in one of the country's most successful hedge funds. And looking again at the untidy stack of mail and in particular at the envelopes which bore some kind of identification, Tim saw that there were several communications from a private bank and from at least one other investment fund. The management of Gerald's wealth was clearly entrusted to a range of financial institutions and not only to Wave Capital.

Tim closed the top of the writing bureau and pulled open the first two drawers: one contained assorted stationery items, the other a single yellowing newspaper. Tim removed the newspaper. Dating from February 1990, the paper devoted half the front page to the death of Gerald's parents. There was a photograph of the wreckage of a small plane in a field and a formally posed family portrait of Gerald's parents with himself and his sister as infants. The lower two drawers of the bureau contained a miscellany of old documents. Among them, Tim found a tied bundle of Gerald's termly school reports from Eton. From the topmost one, he noted that Gerry's date of birth was listed as 24th December 1974 – poor sod, thought Tim, bet he only ever got one lot of presents. Tim also wondered to whom these school reports would have been addressed after February 1990. He was tempted to dip into them, but realised he needed to hurry in his search for the phone. He returned the reports to the drawer. A large manila envelope lay beside the reports. He peeked inside the envelope – it contained letters and a folded page from the Financial Times. Time was passing. He replaced the envelope beside the school reports and closed the drawer. He stopped. Had he just seen...? He reopened the drawer, took out the manila envelope and, opening the top of the bureau and securing the writing table in position, shook the contents of the envelope onto the opened panel.

The design of the logo was quite different from the current one and so had not been instantly recognisable, but the letters were again from Wave Capital. Or, rather, this time from Draper himself – and, in fact, one of the letters, with no corporate logo and bearing a private address in West Hampstead, was handwritten. All of the letters dated from 1998 and 1999. Tim unfolded the page from the Financial Times. This too was dated March 1999. Tim briefly scanned the headlines on both sides of the page, but could not immediately see what among the economic and political commentary could have been of interest to the marquess. He returned to the handwritten letter. Draper was writing to 'Dear Gerry' to explain that he proposed to launch his own hedge fund and to ask if his 'old school chum' – they must have been at Eton together ... well, okay, now Tim had to admit that this was something of a coincidence – to ask if Gerald would consider becoming a founding investor in the new fund. From subsequent letters, it was clear that the marquess had indeed become not simply a founding investor but, at that very first stage, the cornerstone of the fund: he had contributed fifty million pounds of the seventy million with which Draper had launched Wave Capital. Tim again picked up the page from the FT and studied it more closely. On the reverse side of the page in the bottom right hand corner, he spotted a tiny news item:

'**Sacked financier launches own fund**. Charles Draper, dismissed six months ago by Hephaestus Investment Management, has announced that he is to launch his own hedge fund, Wave Capital Management, having successfully raised £70m from investors. This signals a remarkable comeback for Draper, who left Hephaestus under a cloud after 'reckless and unauthorised trades'. At the time, some commentators considered that Draper was lucky to escape prosecution and a possible ban from working in the City.'

Tim let out a silent whistle of astonishment. Nothing in Tim's earlier research had suggested that, at the outset of his career, Draper had narrowly escaped an exit from the City in disgrace. Draper's subsequent success had seemingly swept away all memory of his earlier transgression. Tim wondered if this gave new point to Maggie's observation that if Draper's investment in gold became too disproportionately large in relation to his other holdings, it could become wildly risky and constitute a breach of Draper's duty to his investors. It seemed Draper had form in this respect – even if he had held the tendency to recklessness in check during the decade and more when he had so successfully built up his fund. Perhaps that success had gone to his head and he had now reverted to type.

Tim's curiosity was piqued. He was tempted to open the latest Wave Capital report, which he had tucked back among the heap of letters. He had seen a silver letter opener in the stationery drawer – if he could slice the envelope cleanly, it was unlikely Gerald would ever notice that in the midst of his unread correspondence this one item had been opened. Tim retrieved the Wave Capital envelope and took the silver paper knife from the drawer. He carefully severed the

145

upper edge of the envelope and removed the contents. Accompanying the printed six monthly report was a standard covering letter; however, at the foot of the letter Draper had penned a couple of lines in his own hand: 'Dear Gerry, I'm convinced that a further catastrophe awaits the global economy and that our bet on the yellow metal will come good. Thank you for your unflinching support. Kind regards, Charles.' Tim glanced towards Gerald – he was certainly unflinching. In fact, Tim was now suddenly concerned again that the marquess seemed utterly motionless and might have stopped breathing. Tim crept towards the couch. There was a loud crunch as Tim accidentally trampled on a plastic CD case. He stood stock still. But Gerry did not seem to be stirring at all. Tim approached the inert form of the marquess and bent closer. Tim could just hear Gerry taking muffled breaths into the fabric of the couch – he seemed all right.

Tim went back to the writing bureau and considered again the couple of handwritten lines from Draper. Draper's message was consistent at least – this was pretty much what he had said to Tim. However, while Tim laid no claim to financial expertise of any sort, he couldn't help but feel that Draper's continuing black pessimism concerning the global economy was starkly at odds with increasing signs of stability and a return to growth. Yes, the financial crisis was not yet wholly resolved, but to expect 'further catastrophe' was surely to take a quite extreme view. And then to bet the ranch on that view …? Tim picked up the fund report and scanned the summary. He was surprised to see that the overall value of Wave Capital's investments had actually fallen over the preceding six months – and precisely because during that period the fund had been continuously accumulating gold while the gold price had been steadily falling. Tim had missed this point when he had been monitoring Draper's network. Tim continued to feel puzzled. He was aware of the investment adage 'buy low, sell high' – if Draper's positive view on the gold price should in due course prove correct, he was doing the right thing in taking advantage of recent price weakness to buy. But if Draper should turn out to be wrong … And, Tim now suddenly thought as he looked again at the Wave Capital covering letter, did the little handwritten note imply that Gerald was somehow involved

146

in Draper's scheming? No, surely not – Gerry hadn't even bothered to open Draper's recent correspondence. And if there were any active discussion between them, via Gerald's satellite phone for example, Tim would surely have seen some evidence of this in Draper's phone records or would have found some reference to the contact in Draper's email correspondence with others. Gerald's investment in Wave Capital Management was coincidence, not collusion. But, debated Tim as he reminded himself of the mission in hand, if Gerald had once provided financial means to the disreputable, might he now be willing to do the same in support of the unconscionable? Tim decided this was also highly unlikely: the step from backing an old school friend with a questionable record – or from providing shelter and support to a group of ecologists – the step from there to sponsoring nuclear terrorism was surely far too great.

A carriage clock – a rather fine antique with a highly ornamented silver and brass face, but which now acted as a bookend on an untidy shelf – suddenly chimed the quarter hour. Gerald showed no signs of reacting, but Tim felt a moment of panic. He had become distracted and the search for the satellite phone was taking far too long. He took out his own mobile phone and hastily snapped photos of the summary in the Wave Capital report, Draper's handwritten couple of lines, the brief news item in the FT, Draper's handwritten letter of 1998 and a subsequent letter under the header of the newly established Wave Capital which confirmed Gerald's investment of fifty million pounds and the successful launch of the fund. Tim then put back in the bureau all the items he had removed and closed the writing table and the various drawers.

As Tim hurriedly picked his way back among the detritus on the floor, his eye was caught again, this time by a couple of sheets of paper protruding from a magazine which had been discarded beneath the oak coffee table. He knelt by the table and reached for the sheets of paper. Gerry shifted on the couch. Tim paused and held his breath. Gerry lifted his head a fraction, grunted and settled back into his stupor. Taking care not to rouse Gerry any further, Tim quietly took the sheets of paper from the magazine and stood to inspect them. Though Tim could not read Russian, he had immediately recognised the script as Cyrillic. One of the sheets carried what looked like a

147

numbered inventory; the second was set out in short paragraphs such that it might have been a list of instructions. Had Tim dismissed Gerald too easily? Was it conceivable that the shadowy Russian journalist who had visited Bowley Hall a month or two earlier was not a journalist at all? Tim looked again at the ravaged figure of the marquess. Nuclear conspiracy was surely too far-fetched. Still, he set the two sheets of paper on the coffee table and, taking out his mobile phone, photographed each of them. He replaced the sheets in the magazine and then quickly surveyed the room again in case he had missed anything else of potential importance. As far as he could tell amidst the disorder, he had not.

Returning along the corridor, Tim pushed open another door. His gorge rose as he was hit by the sickening smell of long soured milk. The room was a small kitchen and the offending carton of milk sat open on the draining board beside a teetering pile of unwashed crockery. Tim noted that the crockery was all fine bone china adorned with the Bowley family crest. There was again no sign of the phone.

Tim tried the next room. To his surprise, it was completely tidy and uncluttered. A mahogany dining table and eight high-backed chairs sat in the middle of the room. Against one wall was a large oak sideboard with carved front panels depicting a hunting scene. Two empty crystal decanters huddled on a large silver salver turned pewter in colour through tarnish. An oil painting of Bowley Hall hung above the sideboard. Tim advanced into the room. And there, lying in the middle of an otherwise bare dining table and inviting use like the shrinking potion in *Alice in Wonderland*, was the satellite phone.

"Bingo," breathed Tim as he seized the phone. It was switched off. He pressed the power button. Nothing. Dead. Tim cursed quietly – now he needed to find a charger. There was clearly none in the dining room. Power sockets, he thought to himself – check if the charger is still plugged into a socket.

An inspection of the wall sockets in the sitting room drew a blank. Gerald meanwhile remained immobile on the couch. Tim glanced in the kitchen and then tried Gerry's bedroom. Here, finally, he found what he was looking for. The charger was plugged into the wall beneath the bedside table. Tim also spotted that among a tumble of books lying on the floor under the bed, there appeared to be several

148

weighty tomes in Russian. Tim took the phone and charger and went along the corridor to the room furthest from the sitting room and from Gerald. It was another bedroom and, like the dining room, relatively tidy – though the bed appeared to have been slept in and there was an empty suitcase on the floor. Tim plugged in the charger and the phone. The phone came to life. 'Enter PIN,' it demanded. Damn. Tim hadn't thought about a PIN code. He tried 0000, 0123 and 1234 – to no avail. He racked his brains for a moment. Birthday? Too easy? He entered 2412. No, that didn't work either. Or 1224? Success! Jesus, this had all taken time. Tim moved to the window. The phone registered a signal.

"Helen?" he whispered.

"Lemon? Where are you?"

"I'm at the house. I discovered that Gerry – the marquess – has a satellite phone. Listen, three things. Firstly, on the nuclear question … I'm in Gerry's private rooms and I've just found a couple of sheets of paper in Russian – one looks like a list and the other could be a set of instructions."

"In Russian? Can you send those straight through to us?"

Tim looked at the phone in his hand. "I'm afraid the satellite phone doesn't have a camera. I've photographed the documents with my own mobile – I'll send them to you as soon as I'm somewhere with a signal. But …" Tim paused. "… let's not get too carried away here. My assessment is still that the marquess isn't remotely capable of orchestrating any sort of nuclear attack. I'm just saying we should check what these documents are in order to be absolutely certain."

"Of course."

"Second thing is a bit of a weird coincidence, but it turns out the marquess is a founding investor in Draper's hedge fund."

"Hm," grunted Helen, apparently taking some interest while also reserving judgement as to whether Tim's discovery was relevant or significant. "So you think he might be tangled up with Draper and Andropov in some way – especially with this Russian connection?"

"No, no, that's not the point. No, I think he's just a passive investor in the fund. The interesting thing is the marquess has an old newspaper cutting about Draper. It transpires that fifteen years ago, before Draper launched his own fund, he was fired by his previous employer and nearly got himself kicked out of the City altogether for, I think it said,

149

'reckless and unauthorised trading'. Draper's not the untarnished golden boy he'd have everyone believe – he has a history of making questionable investments, even if it's buried some way back in the past."

"Well, maybe he's learnt his lesson. And, anyway, how does this help us? I'm afraid we really don't have time to go digging around for Draper's rogue investments from fifteen years ago."

"Yes, I know … but I just thought it threw an interesting sidelight on the case." As he said this, Tim realised his comment sounded lame and he felt slightly foolish for getting excited by his discovery. He sensed, as well, that Helen was feeling under pressure. However, he persisted. "Have you managed to take a look at Draper's network? Does it look as though he's still using all the usual channels after finding the bug and have you seen any sign of anything new on the handover?"

"I've been doing my best to keep an eye on things and, yes, all the usual channels seem to be fully in use. The external call to the security company which you were worrying about must have been a one-off precaution. However, apart from Draper flying to Helsinki and back yesterday, I haven't seen anything new."

"No developments with Berezin?"

"Not that I've seen, though I haven't had time to check Draper's emails since early this morning. What was the third thing you were going to tell me?" Helen was sounding increasingly impatient.

"Yes, sorry, I should have told you when we spoke before … the potentially dangerous lunatic I mentioned … his name is Derek Barnes – or that's what he claims. This afternoon I saw him kill a sheep with his bare hands – with a karate chop. Kind of a ritual killing. He clearly is a psychopath."

"Do you think this guy could somehow be taking advantage of the marquess to obtain nuclear materials?"

"No, no, I really don't think so – I think he's just a violent nutter who should be hauled away in a straightjacket. I honestly think there's no whiff of nuclear conspiracy here. The majority of these guys are just live-off-the-land – or rather live-off-the-lord – eco-campaigners … with a drug-addled patron and with one wacko who's drifted into their midst. My plan is still to leave tomorrow. But to be absolutely on the safe side, please check the Russian documents as soon as I get them to you and please also check out this Derek Barnes. He should probably be arrested for killing the sheep."

"Were there any other witnesses to the killing?"

"No, I don't think so. Just me."

"I don't think we want to put you on the witness stand over a sheep killing – not worth compromising your cover just for that. But give me the guy's details and I'll have him checked out."

"Fair point. Anyway … Derek Barnes. White male, about five foot five or six, slight but muscular – very wiry build, brown hair, karate black belt, also does T'ai chi, detests politicians, arrived here several months ago … that's about all I have."

"Okay, I'll follow up. We'll have the Russian papers translated the minute you send them through. But I really think you should forget about Draper for the moment and I'm afraid this Derek Barnes character is also going to be very low priority. You need to be aware that the jihadist situation has moved to red alert. Shah called in a little while ago – he's identified a signal putting the Islamist cells on standby for action. We believe they're going to strike within the next day or two. I need to focus on that – and unless it turns out the marquess really is shopping for nuclear materials, you need to switch your attention to the Islamic extremists too. We need you back here asap."

"So does that mean we're now pretty convinced it's the jihadists who are about to launch a nuclear attack?"

"We still have no further clue about that. Anyway, call me when you're on the train tomorrow. And, Lemon …"

"Helen …?"

"Don't have too much fun on your last night at the holiday camp – you need to be fully *compos mentis* when you get back here. Really, I mean it …"

"Yeah, yeah, no need to lecture. I'll send you the photos and call you from the train in the morning and then I'll see you later in the day."

Tim replaced the phone and charger in their original positions and hastened back downstairs.

THIRTY-SEVEN

Tim found supper in the final stages of preparation. Mark went to summon Gerald with the gong. Tim assumed that Gerry would not appear and was duly astonished when he came shuffling into the kitchen a few minutes later and took his place at the table – albeit still in a state of semi-stupefaction. It seemed the distant gong had penetrated more deeply into Gerald's subconscious than minor disturbances nearer to hand and had succeeded in hauling him back to consciousness. Gerald rolled a cigarette, but – perhaps remembering Martha's injunction – left it by the side of his plate.

Over supper, Tim explained that he couldn't help worrying about his father and had decided to head back home the following day. But he hoped he would be able to return to Bowley soon. The others were all completely understanding. In the snug afterwards, he declined the habitual joint – and, again, the others all understood that he was not in the mood. However, thought Tim, whilst he was among the Swards and even though he now suspected nothing of an extremist nature, he might as well press Nick's original investigation one step further. He asked how they went about organising their protests and when the next one might be. George explained that the Sward acted as a focal group rallying support for ecological demonstrations and marshalling forces on the day of protest. He regretted, however, that they couldn't always control all the elements who typically participated and events frequently got out of hand. And the police sometimes didn't help – sometimes they seemed more intent on provocation than containment.

"Cunt-fucking pigs," interjected Derek.

George got up and began riffling through a shelf of DVDs next to the television in the corner of the snug. He turned to Tim. "We often film ourselves so we have counter-evidence if the police get too heavy-handed. I have a perfect example here. It was the last G8 summit in London. We were just peacefully standing around when the police suddenly charged into us. Here we are ..." He picked out a disc and put it into the DVD player beneath the television. Unsteady images gradually came into focus on the screen.

Tim suddenly went cold and felt the hairs stand on his forearms. Sweat began to prickle in his armpits. Fuck, this was the very demonstration which Gordon had sent him to observe. What if he appeared on the film? He should prepare his excuses just in case. Thank God he had kept a clear head that evening. Amateurish shots of milling demonstrators alternated with sweeping takes of the lines of police confronting them. Oh, shit, there he was – standing behind the line of policemen. He was wearing a yellow police tabard. Once you had spotted him, he was unmistakeable. At least his position behind the line of police was unobtrusive. He glanced around the room. The others were all mellowed out and not paying too close attention to the recording. Except perhaps Derek, who sat on the edge of his seat and occasionally muttered through gritted teeth, "Gash-wipes" and "Cunts." After a few minutes, the recording moved on to a different street scene. Thank Christ, no one seemed to have noticed Tim.

Everyone began to drift off towards bed. Martha and Sandy in turn squeezed Tim in a sympathetic hug, but then, mindful of his father and respecting his emotions, bade him goodnight. Tim followed the others, though he noticed Derek remained behind in his chair.

THIRTY-EIGHT

Though it was late, the MI5 team were all still at their desks. Two or three half-eaten and now cold pizzas lay discarded on top of a row of filing cabinets. Preparations for simultaneous raids on all the identified Islamist cells were rapidly taking shape. However, there was still absolutely no further clue as to whether, where, how or by whom a nuclear device might be deployed.

An email headed 'Derek Barnes' popped up on Helen's screen. She clicked it open, but in the same moment and before she had looked at the email, Tabi strode in.

"Helen," he called as he entered.

"Shah. Good, we need you to track down that signal."

"I'm on it. I can run it from your desk."

Helen made way for Tabi at her desk.

"I'll put it up on the big screen," said Tabi, indicating a pair of large wall-mounted screens which were showing respectively Sky News and Al Jazeera. "Please could you change the channel on one of them to External 1."

Helen went and picked up a remote control from the top of a cabinet. She changed Sky News to External 1. For the moment the screen was blank.

Tabi looked at Helen's screen. There was an open email: 'Derek Barnes is a paranoid schizophrenic. He was convicted of killing a policeman with a blow to the head in September 2012 and was remanded to Rampton secure psychiatric hospital. However, he escaped custody while in transit and has not been seen since. He is considered highly dangerous. If there is any reason why we should not immed...'

"Shah?" Helen called from in front of the screen.

"Yeah, it's coming." Tabi closed the police email. It was clearly nothing to do with the job in hand. He began typing furiously. After a few moments, a stream of internet protocols began to cascade down Helen's screen. Tabi hooked up the display to the screen on the wall. All eyes in the room turned to the stream of data.

154

"Shah, what's this telling us?"

"Sorry, can you switch the other screen to External 2. I'll put it up in map form."

A map of the world appeared and lines instantly began to zigzag back and forth from one point on the map to another.

Tabi came and stood by Helen. "Bouncing the bloody thing all over the place," he observed.

Abruptly, the cascade of data and the zigzagging on the map stopped. Helen and Tabi studied the final point on the map.

"Gaza," said Tabi.

"Hamas," added Helen.

"Or anyone working under their protection – al-Qaeda conceivably." Nick had joined Helen and Tabi at the screen.

"Shah, can you send this IP address to all of us. Braithwaite, can you send it on to GCHQ and explain to them. Wilde, can you liaise with the CIA and Mossad. Let's see if we can pinpoint this exactly."

"Couldn't we just prevent them from sending out the instruction to attack by blitzing them with spam and crashing the site – like the Russians did to prevent the dissemination of information in Georgia?" suggested Nick.

"That would just tell them we were on to them," replied Tabi. "And, anyway, they'd simply switch to a different address for the next message."

"And it's better that we leave the channel open so that we can monitor their traffic," added Helen.

"True," acknowledged Nick. "Dumb suggestion on my part."

THIRTY-NINE

When Tim descended for breakfast the next morning, he found the others were all in the kitchen. George, Martha, Sandy and Derek sat at the kitchen table. John and Mark stood. There was no food on the table – only a closed laptop computer at Derek's elbow. Everyone was silent. No one returned Tim's "Good morning." Derek cracked his knuckles.

Derek opened the laptop and turned it towards Tim. It flickered into life. Frozen on the screen was the image of Tim behind the line of policemen at the demonstration.

"Is this you?" asked Derek.

Tim did not instantly answer.

"Jack," said Martha, "– if indeed you are Jack ..." She looked at him intently. "If you are a policeman, we understand and respect that you have to do your job, but I must say we feel rather betrayed and feel our hospitality has been abused."

Tim needed to hold his nerve. He lifted his hands, hoping the others did not notice they were trembling very slightly. "I'm not a policeman. It is me and I'm sorry I didn't mention it last night. I just didn't think it was relevant."

"How could it not be fucking relevant?" snarled Derek.

"As I told you, until a couple of weeks ago I was working for an insurance company." There was the faintest quaver in Tim's voice. "We insured one of the buildings that was damaged in the demonstration. The owners called us that morning to tell us they would be lodging a claim. I was sent along to assess the damage in order to make sure any claim was appropriate and was proportional to the damage actually caused by the demonstration. In fact, I also got a bit shoved around by the police, but when I told them what I was doing, they put me in that jacket and told me to keep out of the way."

"You said you worked for an insurance broker, not an insurance company," said George.

"Yes, that's right. But we sold the policy and any claims were processed through us."

"I still don't see why you couldn't have told us this last night," said Mark. "Especially if you got pushed around by the police – that was the whole point of George showing you the recording."

"The fuck's lying," growled Derek. "If there's one thing I hate more than cunting politicians, it's cunt-shiteing policemen."

Derek rose from the table and came striding round to Tim. John and Mark leapt to restrain him just as he unleashed an explosive lunge towards Tim's head.

FORTY

After a few hours of fitful sleep, Helen and team were back at their desks.

"No sign of Gordon yet?" asked Trevor.

"The DG summoned him to the COBRA meeting," explained Helen.

"At Number 10?"

"I think they're in the bunker this time. He's due back any minute." Helen turned to Margaret. "Maggie, what's the status with the police armed response teams?"

"They're all ready and on standby – except Sheffield. Apparently, roadworks all over town are holding up some members of the team."

"They'd better get their act together before we give them the green light. We'd all look like prize idiots if Sheffield were flattened because an elite police squad couldn't get round a hole in the road. Have we got someone with that team yet?"

"Brian Thompson from the regional office is on his way to them."

"ETA?"

"Any minute, I hope."

"Here we are," said Trevor, rising to his feet and allowing a note of excitement to enter his usually Eeyore-ish tones. "The IP address sending out the instructions to the bombers ... the Israelis reckon they know exactly who and where it is. They've already been monitoring these people for months. Not Hamas proper, but a splinter group calling themselves the Righteous Scimitar of Allah – or perhaps it's Allah's Righteous Scimitar, in which case let's not think what the acronym would make these fanatics." Trevor briefly bared his teeth. "They're actually more extreme than Hamas and occasionally at loggerheads with them. But clearly no friends of the Israelis."

"Nice of our friends in Tel Aviv to keep us informed," observed Helen.

"Our friends in Tel Aviv," continued Trevor, "would be more than happy to send a message of their own and reduce the building in question to rubble."

"Sometimes I think the Israelis are the trigger-happy ones," mused Nick.

"However," said Helen, "on this occasion, I think we should gratefully accept their help."

"We should make sure any Israeli attack is timed to coincide exactly with our raids here," cautioned Margaret. "If the Israelis attack prematurely, word could get back to the cells here, which would at the very least put them on the alert and might prompt them to move early or to initiate even more extreme action."

"You're right," acknowledged Helen.

At this moment, Gordon walked in. His face was grimly set in a burden-of-high-office expression. "Morning everyone. Conference room, please."

Within a few moments the team had convened around the conference room table. Gordon stood at the head of the table.

"Following my advice, the PM and COBRA are taking this threat with the utmost seriousness. The Cabinet, the Royal Family, senior civil servants, the Governor of the Bank of England and his deputies – basically all of the A List – will be evacuating from London during the course of the day. Other MPs are being discreetly directed to return to their constituencies, unless located in at risk areas ..."

"Gordon, sorry to interrupt," said Margaret, "but does this mean we have confirmation that the impending attack is nuclear? We've seen no more intelligence on this here."

"Unfortunately, the answer is still that we don't know – we have nothing new. MI6 is trying to get an update from our source in Moscow, but he or she has gone quiet. As you rightly observe, neither we, nor MI6, nor GCHQ and not the CIA either, none of us has picked up any further references to nuclear materials."

"Are we being too alarmist?" asked Nick.

"We have no option but to assume the worst and to work on that basis. Thanks to Tabi's intelligence, we're pretty sure a multiple Islamist attack is imminent. The timing of the nuclear tip-off may

159

just be a coincidence, but we have to work on the assumption that two plus one-and-a-bit makes four."

"What about the general public?" asked Maggie.

"Difficult. Very difficult. No one wants to initiate a mass evacuation unless we're absolutely certain there's a significant and credible threat of major loss of life – otherwise, future would-be terrorists know they only have to say 'boo' and we'll do their work for them by causing major disruption. Having said that, COBRA did debate the contingency plans for a large scale evacuation. But it's not straightforward … apart from the question of the credibility of the nuclear threat and the costs of unwarranted disruption, we fear sounding a general alarm might create panic which would very likely cause problems of its own – perhaps even deaths. And, for example, huge disorderly crowds at railway terminals would present the bombers with prime targets, possibly increasing the number of casualties even for a conventional attack. And, of course, it would immediately alert the bombers to our knowledge of their attack, so they might focus on other targets or keep their powder dry for another day."

"Well, at least we're poised to launch raids on all the Islamist cells," said Helen.

"On the eight cells we've identified, yes," said Gordon, "but what if there are eighteen cells?"

"I take the point about not wanting to set a precedent for bowing to terrorist threats," intervened Maggie, "but if COBRA does decide to take action with respect to the general population, has the committee considered going about things in the opposite way?"

"Meaning?"

"Instead of attempting to evacuate people *from* London, rather make an effort to keep people *out of* London. The resident population of the West End and the City is a tiny fraction of the daytime population. If we engineer overnight a general stoppage of all public transport – or at least all public transport inbound to London – and at the same time issue strong advice that everyone outside London should stay at home, we would at least limit the numbers potentially exposed. The same will be true of the other targeted cities, albeit to a lesser degree. And, with no inbound public transport, any intending

160

bombers who had slipped through our net would quite possibly be stymied, if only temporarily. It would at least buy us more time to pursue any other leads which might emerge from tomorrow's dawn raids. Of course, we'd have to bring transport managers and union leaders into the loop, but in such circumstances I'm sure we could count on their understanding and discretion."

"Hm." Gordon furrowed his brow. "I'm sure such a scenario is among the various contingency plans at COBRA's disposal; however, when I left the committee, the discussion was all about evacuation. We hadn't given thought to preventing people getting into London – and the other cities at risk."

"Shouldn't be a problem bringing the transport system to a grinding halt," mused Trevor, half to himself, "happens all the time."

"The committee is still sitting," resumed Gordon. "As soon as we're done here, I'll call through to make sure the relevant plan is also under consideration in line with your suggestion, Margaret. Meanwhile, Helen, what's the status on the raids?"

"Police teams are on standby – except in Sheffield, but with luck they'll also be in place by the time we've finished this meeting. The current plan is to strike simultaneously at all cells at four-thirty a.m. And one more thing ..." Helen turned to Trevor. "Wilde ..."

"Yes ... Gordon, we've just heard from the Israelis. They're very confident they've identified the source of the instruction to the bombers as a Hamas splinter group calling themselves the Righteous Scimitar of Allah – a new one to us, but apparently familiar to Mossad. Tel Aviv is willing to launch a missile strike. We haven't gone back to them yet – this came in literally as you walked through the door five minutes ago – however, our thought was to request that they go ahead while asking them to make sure they time the hit to coincide exactly with our raids here."

"Good," said Gordon. "Good. COBRA will be pleased to hear of that. If we can take out the ringmaster, perhaps the circus will fold its tent ... if only for the moment."

The team returned to their desks. Gordon ensconced himself in his side office.

With the raids on the Islamist cells all but poised to launch, Helen decided she could spare a brief second for Draper. Over the past

161

twenty-four hours she had barely had time to devote the promised two minutes twice a day to Draper's activities; however, she had rapidly scanned his emails before leaving the office the previous evening. She had seen that, following his trip to Helsinki, Draper had sent a message to Berezin thanking him for their meeting and, as Draper had written, 'for your proposal, which I will continue to bear in mind.' As Tim had suggested, it seemed Draper's discussion with Berezin was an exercise in keeping options open rather than an outright betrayal of Andropov. And, in fact, as Helen now reopened the window to Draper's correspondence, she saw that Draper had just moments earlier received a new message from Andropov via their encrypted email: 'Terms agreed – unchanged. Expect delivery of champagne in next 24 hours. On track for Cassis.' Helen had no more idea than Tim as to what exactly was going on between Draper and Andropov and she retained her scepticism over the need for MI5 involvement; however, she dutifully took note of this latest message. Finding nothing else of particular significance, she closed the window on her screen and returned to finalising the plans for the impending raids on the jihadist suspects.

Some minutes later, Trevor happened to glance up from his computer to see Gordon emerge from his office. Gordon's features were contorted in a harrowed expression. He walked slowly into the middle of the room and leant on a nearby desk.

"Oh, God, no," said Trevor under his breath, "it's happened already."

Helen looked up.

"Oh fuck," she whispered. "Fuck. It's gone off. The bomb's gone off. Which city's been hit? We've missed the bastards completely."

Helen and Trevor rose from their desks.

"Everyone," Gordon began to say. He cleared his throat. "Everyone. Bit of a setback." He suddenly seemed to realise what was running through everyone's mind. He held up a hand as though to arrest the erroneous thought. "No, no, it's not the bomb." He paused. "It's Tim. He's been attacked."

FORTY-ONE

All eyes were on Gordon as he continued.

"It seems one of the eco-group is a violent schizophrenic and convicted murderer who escaped police custody several months ago. Derek Barnes. The police say they sent us a warning about him last night."

Helen's expression suddenly turned to one of horror. "Oh God." She sat and began hastily scrolling through her email. "Is Lemon all right?" she asked in rising dread as she searched for the email she thought she had briefly seen. "The email's here. I didn't read it."

"Tim was set upon by this man," said Gordon. "According to the police, the eco-group suspected Tim was a police mole."

Tabi, who had come over and was now standing near Helen, suddenly paled. "Helen, it's my fault. I saw the message and closed it when I sat down at your desk just after I came in last night."

"Helen, Tabi," said Gordon, "calm down ... fortunately, Tim is not in overly serious condition. He's in hospital with mild concussion. It seems for once his habit of falling over things was his saving. Apparently, this Barnes character is a martial arts expert who killed a policeman with a karate blow. And some local out walking his dog yesterday also reported to the police that he'd seen Barnes kill a sheep. Anyway, this madman went for Tim, but it seems Tim stumbled and cracked his head on a table. The other members of the group overpowered Barnes before any worse damage was done. The ecologists called an ambulance, the ambulance crew called the police. Tim is being kept under observation for a few hours, but all being well he should be on his way back to us before the end of today. I just thought you would all want to know straightaway. I'll let you know if I hear anything new." Gordon looked around the team who, though relieved, all stood rooted to the spot. "Well, duty calls – noses back to the grindstone, please."

"Gordon," said Helen, holding him back as he was about to return to his office. "Can we reach Lemon? Is he able to speak on the

163

phone? I'd ... I'd like to check that he's okay ... and also he has the photographs of the marquess's Russian documents on his mobile."

"Good point. Thank you for being on the ball, Helen. I haven't spoken directly to Tim since the police called, but, yes, see if you can reach him on his mobile."

Helen dialled immediately.

"Lemon? You're all right, you're in one piece?"

"I'm fine, Helen."

"Where are you? Still in hospital?"

"No. Everyone's been making a completely ridiculous fuss – I was only unconscious for about thirty seconds. I've discharged myself and I'm on my way to the railway station."

"Thank God. You gave us all a bit of a scare." Reassured, Helen returned to business. "You haven't sent the photos of the marquess's Russian documents yet?"

"Oh, no, sorry – completely forgot about that."

"You're really okay?"

"Yes, yes ... sending them now. Hold on." Tim was silent for a few seconds. "Okay, on their way. Helen, I have to get to the station. I'll call you later or anyway see you before the end of the day."

Looking up, Helen saw that the rest of the team had been listening to her conversation. "He sounds fine. He's discharged himself and he's already on his way back." Helen straightened in her chair as she saw the email from Tim arrive in her inbox. "Shah, I've got the marquess's Russian documents from Lemon's phone – should I run a translation programme?"

Tabi came over. "Could do – but there are several Russian speakers downstairs who would surely do a much better job."

"I know Victor Blachowski," said Trevor. "I'll give him a call."

A few minutes later, Vic Black, as he generally called himself, appeared on the floor. He was swarthy featured and wore a heavy check shirt, jeans and a dark grey donkey jacket. He looked like an off-duty navvy or merchant seaman. The two pages of Russian text were projected onto the wall screens and all members of Gordon's team, including Gordon himself, gathered round in expectation. Victor stared at the two pages of text.

"Well?" asked Gordon impatiently.

Victor pointed to the first item on the page consisting of short paragraphs. "All hap ..." he barely began.

"All happy families resemble one another, but each unhappy family is unhappy in its own way," leapt in Margaret. "Sorry ... interrupting. And showing off. Tolstoy – the famous opening lines of *Anna Karenina*."

"Quite so," said Victor. He looked at Maggie, gestured towards the text and raised his eyebrows – inviting her to continue the translation.

"No, sorry," she said contritely. "I can't read or speak Russian – I just guessed that was what was coming."

Victor studied the texts again. He indicated the first page. "I think this is all quotations from Tolstoy." He turned to the second. "And this is just a list of books the person who wrote this wants to buy – the first item is an anthology of modern Russian poetry, for example."

Gordon shook his head. "No misquotations, odd transpositions of words ... nothing to suggest a concealed message?"

"Well, I don't know all these quotations off by heart," said Vic, "but it looks very straightforward and correct to me. I think it is what it is."

Gordon scowled. "Complete and utter bloody waste of time. Thank heaven Lemon is all right at least. Victor, thank you. Please do just run a check on those quotations and book titles to be absolutely sure. Otherwise, case closed. Team, back to work please. We might have ruled this one out, but the Islamist threat still demands our full attention."

Nick stepped forward a little sheepishly. "Gordon, sorry, this whole ecologist thing clearly had nothing to do with the nuclear issue. Totally wrong call on my part."

"No, no – no need to chastise yourself. Ignore my intemperate comments. You did the right thing. Much better to investigate and cross off the list than to ignore or overlook and live to regret it."

The team settled back down to work. Gordon returned to his office ... only to reappear at his door ten minutes later with a further announcement.

"Margaret, COBRA is adopting the contingency plan along the lines you suggested. London and other target cities will effectively be cordoned off. A select team at the Home Office under Keith Parker and Section D here will share responsibility for immediate preparations. However, the plan will only be put into effect if and when we confirm that the bombers have received the signal to attack."

Trevor and, over at his desk, Nick suddenly and simultaneously leapt to their feet. They spoke at once. "Gordon, everyone, looks like this is it," from Trevor, while from Nick, "Guys, isn't this the signal?"

All eyes went to the Leicester mosque's blogsite, which every team member had kept open on his or her screen: 'Allah summons his loyal firstborn to his bosom as joyful martyrs for their faith.' It could hardly be clearer.

"Right," said Gordon, his face flushed with the momentousness of the hour. "I'll alert COBRA. Maggie, please speak to Keith Parker at the Home Office and Alan Wright in section D, so that civil preparations can get underway immediately. Trevor, give the Israelis the green light, but make sure they observe the timing." He looked at Helen and again Trevor. "You two are joining police teams on the raids, yes – plus Tim, assuming he's fit and back here in time?"

"And Braithwaite," said Helen. "Lemon's joining Barnet, Wilde's High Wycombe, Braithwaite and I are Stockwell. Our colleagues in the regional offices are taking care of the other cities."

"Tim will be fully briefed and will know what he's doing?" Gordon looked doubtful.

"I'll make sure of it," confirmed Helen.

"And, Maggie, you're coordinating?" Gordon turned back in Margaret's direction.

Maggie, who was already on the phone to Keith Parker, gave a curt nod.

"This is it, then. All of you make sure you keep in mind that if one of the cells does indeed possess a nuclear device and if it's primed and has some kind of manual trigger, then any false step or hesitation on our part could have dire consequences. When we strike, we must do so swiftly and with absolute decisiveness. Good luck everyone."

FORTY-TWO

It was late afternoon and Helen and Nick were in a secure basement room in Brixton police station. They and the police armed response team had just watched a video of the street where the suspects were located. The street comprised a row of terraced houses with tiny front gardens. The three Islamic extremists in this particular cell occupied a ground floor flat in the house at the end of the terrace. A helicopter shot had shown the small and mostly untidy gardens behind the row of houses. An eight foot brick wall separated the garden of the jihadists' house from the adjacent sidestreet. A live video relay of this seemingly innocuous residential street continued to play on a television in the corner of the police briefing room. Photographs of the street and the end-of-terrace house were pinned to the wall alongside mugshots of the suspects. A floor plan of the flat – and, in case of need, of the first floor flat above – were laid out on the table for the police team to commit to memory.

167

FORTY-THREE

Tim, meanwhile, apparently not significantly the worse for his latest contretemps with a piece of furniture, was going through an almost identical briefing procedure in High Barnet police station. There was, however, one important difference: while the Islamist cell again numbered three suspects, this time they were located at two different addresses. The two members of the cell who were living together had very recently rented a semi-detached house in a downmarket residential area. The third member lived in a flat above a newsagent with main access via a narrow front door beside the shop, but also with a fire escape at the back. To complicate matters, the suspect who lived by himself had not been seen for two days and the surveillance team which had been tracking his movements, having earlier said he was in his flat, now conceded that they were not one hundred percent sure whether he was still there. The surveillance team watching the other pair were certain the elusive third member had not joined these other two at their address. The uncertainty of the lone suspect's whereabouts created a far from satisfactory situation – indeed, Gordon had made a furious phone call to the head of the surveillance team who had potentially allowed their quarry to give them the slip – however, there seemed little option but to raid the two addresses as planned and to assume that the third suspect was at one address or the other. Tim would join the raid on the semi-detached house.

Tim felt there was a certain rightness or symmetry in his being here with the police team. While he now had no thought of swapping his role as guardian of national security for one of protector of the public from crime, throughout his early years his firm intention had always been to join the police force. His reasoning, or perhaps more accurately his instinct, had been uncomplicated: his diet of television and films had persuaded him that the cops were generally the good guys – not always perhaps, but generally so – and more often than not they cleared the streets of the bad guys. It was only when Tim had visited his university careers office to ask how he should go about applying to join the police force that a careers officer had mentioned the Security Service as another option and had thereby set Tim on a different path.

As Tim and the senior member of the police team jointly briefed the assembled squad, Tim felt his adrenalin begin to rise. His detour to Shropshire had achieved next to nothing of value to MI5, but perhaps the coming hours would provide him with a better opportunity to demonstrate something of his worth to Gordon.

FORTY-FOUR

Trevor and the High Wycombe team also faced a complication in tackling their suspects – a lesser complication perhaps, but one which required careful handling. The cell was again divided in two: a trio lived in a flat in the centre of Wycombe, while a fourth member lived with his family – his parents, brothers and sisters and grandparents – in a quiet and respectable residential area on the outskirts of the town. The lone member had to be seized with the same speed and decisiveness as all other suspects, but his family – who were almost certainly wholly oblivious to their son's jihadist involvement – needed to be firmly contained during the course of the raid, yet also treated with appropriate care and sensitivity during this action and throughout the ensuing process. In the extreme event that shots were fired, it would of course be essential to ensure that only the suspect was in the line of fire. Though there were three suspects at the central Wycombe address, Trevor assumed responsibility for the more delicate task of the raid on the family house.

FORTY-FIVE

Shortly after four a.m., the three London armed response teams, the two High Wycombe teams and teams in the five other cities across the country rolled quietly into place in unmarked police vans. They took up initial positions in streets adjacent to their targets, but out of the line of view of any suspect who happened to take a wary look up and down his own street.

Four twenty ... four twenty-five ... twenty-eight ...

"All units, standby. Two minutes." Margaret's authoritative voice came over every earpiece.

Four twenty-nine ...

"Wait!" It was Tim. "On the livecam. Someone approaching the suspects' address on a scooter. Could be our missing man."

"All teams, hold!" commanded Margaret. "Barnet Unit 1, can you actually see the suspect? Can you identify?"

"I'm going out to him," said Tim. "Watch on the livecam. If I take him down, launch. Otherwise, let him pass, then we launch."

"All units, standby to launch on my instruction." Margaret hesitated for the briefest moment. "Barnet, I advise against interception – if this is the suspect, he will anyway identify himself by approaching and entering the property."

But Tim had already slipped out of the back of the van and was running along the street. With the blood rushing in his ears, he barely registered what Margaret was saying. He raced to the corner of the road, then on turning into the suspects' street slowed to a brisk walk. Unlike the police team, Tim was in civilian dress. Though he was on the street at an unusually early hour, there was no particular reason why he should arouse suspicion. The man on the scooter was approaching from the opposite direction. He came to a halt ten or fifteen yards short of the suspects' house and stepped off his scooter. He wore a helmet and was looking down – Tim could see nothing of his face. He also wore a bulky jacket – it crossed Tim's mind that if this was a bomber, he might just possibly already be wired with explosive beneath his jacket. Tim drew level with the man.

"Morning," said Tim – almost in a whisper, but in a casual and friendly tone.

The man looked up. Damn. His helmet had a darkened visor and still Tim could see nothing of his face. Tim had a split-second to make up his mind. Pumping with adrenalin, he decided it was no time for scruples. He smashed a punch into the man's throat, sending the man flying onto his back.

"All units, go, go!" Margaret's distant voice came over Tim's earpiece.

The scooter rider, while clutching at his throat, began to scrabble backwards on the ground. He snapped open his visor. "*Police ...*" he gasped only half audibly as he struggled for breath after Tim's blow, but then finding his voice, "POLICE!"

For a confused second, Tim was not quite sure whether the man was sounding the alarm to his confederates or calling to sleeping neighbours for help. But realising he could not afford to hesitate, Tim leapt on the man's chest, pinning down the man's arms with his knees. Tim rammed the boxy muzzle of his Glock 17 handgun into the man's mouth.

"Silence," he hissed.

In the pre-dawn half-light, with much of the man's face still obscured by his helmet and with his eyes wide with fear and his mouth contorted around the barrel of the gun, he could have been almost anyone.

Tim heard the pounding approach of the police officers. He glanced towards the suspects' house. Shit – a face had appeared at a net curtain and instantly vanished. A light went on in the front room and there were sounds of commotion in the house. Members of the armed response team streamed around the house, four of them advancing on the front door with a hand-held battering ram.

At the same moment, an officer joined Tim. The biker's helmet was torn off to reveal that ... yes, it was the elusive third suspect. Tim had been right. He felt a moment of jubilation as a meaty police hand was clamped over the suspect's mouth and one arm yanked behind the man's back. But Tim held up a hand in silent caution. He gingerly opened the suspect's jacket ... thank God, no explosives. The man was handcuffed and hauled to his feet. Only now Tim realised that his knuckles were raw and bleeding and were starting to burn with pain – he had raked the bottom of the helmet when he had punched the man in the throat.

The armed response team's battering ram meanwhile burst the lock on the front door … in the next instant, a blinding yellow flash erupted in the front room of the house, emitting a boom which hit like a thump in the chest. The battering ram team was flung from the front door as shards of glass, splintered window frame and chunks of brick showered into the street followed by a billowing cloud of brick dust. The windows of the adjacent houses and of the houses directly across the street had also shattered and a car alarm launched into witless complaint. Partially deafened and covered in fine debris, but otherwise unhurt, Tim was vaguely aware of Margaret's voice urgently crying out for more police back-up and for ambulances. Lights began to come on along the street; screaming and wailing emanated from some of the houses.

FORTY-SIX

Meanwhile, in Stockwell, on Margaret's instruction, Helen, Nick and team had rushed the terraced house. Helen and two police officers took the sidestreet, while Nick joined the team making the frontal assault. At Helen's insistence, Nick had put on a bulletproof vest. In the sidestreet, one of the policemen gave Helen and the other officer a leg-up onto the top of the wall, from whence they leaped into the small, unkempt and rubbish-strewn back garden. Within moments of Helen and the policeman landing in the garden, one of the suspects, clad only in his underwear, came crashing through a closed window in a shower of glass. He scrabbled in the broken glass and other rubbish to find his footing and then attempted to leap a wooden fence into the neighbouring garden. But Helen and the policeman were already upon him and dragged him to the ground, quickly subduing him. The back door of the house was kicked open by a heavy policeman's boot, the lock splintering through the doorframe. When the policeman saw that Helen and the other officer had the suspect under control, he returned inside.

While Helen and her police colleague had clambered into the garden at the rear of the property, in a simultaneous offensive, the frontal assault team of four police officers, with Nick following closely behind, had burst through the main entrance. They quickly found two of the suspects still asleep in a bedroom and three of the police officers immediately seized the men and hauled them from their beds. The fourth police officer plus Nick, hearing the remaining suspect in the kitchen at the back of the flat, sped along the hallway. But the commotion had by now alerted the suspect: in panic and having no other route of escape, he flung himself through the closed kitchen window. Nick dived into the kitchen after the man, while the police officer raced along the hallway to the back door, which he smashed open with a hefty kick. Seeing that Helen and the officer with her had apprehended the fleeing suspect, the policeman at the rear door turned back into the flat just as a fourth man – a fourth! there should only have been three! – shot from the kitchen. The

174

police officer threw himself upon the man, bringing him crashing to the floor. Leaping instantly to his feet, the policeman took hold of the man by the arms and dragged him, writhing and noisily protesting, down the hall into the front room – where the two suspects from the bedroom already lay face down with wrists bound and under police gunpoint.

"Fucking infidel pig shite," spat the newly apprehended suspect as he twisted in the policeman's grip and glared with insane-eyed hatred at his captors.

Helen was close on the heels of the officer in the hallway and followed him and his unruly prisoner into the front room.

"Four of them?" she exclaimed as she rapidly took stock of the situation.

"Seems so," growled the police officer as he restrained the panting and gurning additional suspect.

"Show me their faces," said Helen, nodding towards the two men on the floor.

The two suspects were rolled over so that Helen could inspect them. At such close quarters, it was belatedly apparent that one of the two on the floor and the fourth suspect, though not identical, were of very similar appearance – almost certainly brothers. From a distance, they could easily have been mistaken for one another. And quite conceivably the timbre of their voices would have sounded similar to the surveillance team listening in. Helen now also noted that on a threadbare sofa were what looked like two lifejackets – but in place of inflated airbags were wired-together packs of explosive.

"Control?" said Helen into her mouthpiece.

"Yes, Stockwell, go ahead."

"We have four – repeat four – suspects, not the expected three. However, all now apprehended. Also we have vests packed with conventional explosive, evidently for use in a suicide attack … but only conventional explosive, nothing more."

"Other units are reporting the same." Margaret chose not to distract Helen with an account of the debacle in Barnet.

As Helen's police colleague who had covered the rear of the property with her escorted the blood-streaked would-be runaway into the front room, Helen suddenly looked around the assembled gathering of armed response officers and their subdued and sullen or, in the case of the fourth suspect, still struggling charges.

"Where's Braithwaite?" she asked.

FORTY-SEVEN

Trevor and Wycombe Unit 2 had decided to adopt a slightly less brutal approach to entry. They had noticed one or two lights were already on upstairs in the house. They rang the doorbell. A tousled, sleepy-looking middle-aged man in pyjamas and dressing gown duly appeared at the front door. The first policeman seized him, clapping a hand over his mouth, while the remaining officers streamed silently into the house. Trevor and one of the policemen sped upstairs to what they believed they had identified as the suspect's bedroom. As they passed a closed door, they heard coming from within the sound of someone shitting profusely and uncontrollably into the toilet. Trevor indicated to the policeman to stay in front of this door. Trevor padded a few doors along the landing. The suspect's bedroom door was ajar and the light was on. Trevor darted his head and handgun around the door. The room was clearly empty. Trevor returned to the policeman and indicated for him to force the bathroom door. The policeman swayed back and then delivered a hefty jolt to the door with his shoulder. The door sprang open to reveal seated on the lavatory a skinny young man with a shadow of bum-fluff on his upper lip. He looked up in wide-eyed terror at the armed men as his bowel erupted again. He was already shaking and now began moaning.

"Let me finish," he pleaded. "Please let me finish."

"Quick," hissed Trevor, not taking his gaze from the terrified youth.

The young man tried to wipe himself clean, but could barely hold or tear the toilet roll, he was shaking so violently, and his efforts were constantly interrupted by renewed attacks of diarrhoea. After perhaps a minute, he seemed to achieve some kind of respite.

"Enough," said Trevor.

The policeman dragged the young man to his feet as the boy tried to pull up his pyjama trousers. The boy turned to the washbasin in an effort to wash his hands, but the policeman hauled him out onto the landing. Trevor and the policeman marched the young man downstairs.

The father was still held by a policeman in the doorway to the sitting room. He struggled free of the hand clamped over his mouth.

"What in heaven's name is going on? What are you doing to my son?"

"We are detaining him under the …"

"My son has done nothing wrong," interrupted the father. "Qasim, you have done nothing, have you? He is unwell – he has been up half the night in the toilet. What are all these … these armed policeman?"

The mother now appeared on the stairs, tying a dressing gown. "What on earth is happening? What is the meaning of this intrusion?"

Qasim was still shaking uncontrollably and, Trevor realised, was now shitting in his pyjamas.

"Oh no," said the mother. "Can't you see the poor boy is sick?"

The father suddenly turned a sterner gaze on his son. "Qasim, you have done nothing wrong, have you?"

The boy began to wail. "I'm sorry, Dad. I'm sorry."

"What have you done?" His father was now beginning to look aghast.

"I'm sorry," sobbed the boy.

Trevor suddenly wondered whether he could take small advantage of the situation. He turned to the father. "Ask your son who he is working with."

The father stared at Trevor and then at his son. "Who are you working with?" he asked his son in growing horror.

"Three men in Wycombe. You don't know them."

"Ask him their names and where they are."

The father asked. Qasim gave the names of the three men in High Wycombe and their address.

Trevor had the confirmation he was looking for. He turned to the father again. "And who is all of that group working for?"

The father nodded at his son to answer the question.

"I don't know," said the young man forlornly. "We just followed instructions. Some website gave us instructions."

178

"To do what?" whispered the father.

Qasim hung his head.

Trevor saw that the grandparents and three younger children were now standing at the head of the stairs looking down.

"To do what, Qasim?" repeated the father with anger in his voice.

"We were going to let off bombs in London," whispered the boy barely audibly.

The mother, who had been standing transfixed at the foot of the stairs, suddenly seemed to be gasping for air. She reached for a hall chair and slumped in the seat. The grandmother hurried down the stairs to help her daughter or daughter-in-law, while the grandfather ushered the other children back to their bedrooms. Trevor told the policeman at the front door to summon the ambulance team which had been standing by at a short distance. However, before the paramedics appeared, the mother was already back on her feet.

"Let me at least clean him up," she said.

FORTY-EIGHT

Gun in hand, Helen darted back along the hallway to the kitchen. A quick glance was sufficient to confirm that the room was empty. But one wall had been partially opened up to create an archway into an adjoining dining area. As Helen advanced into the kitchen, she saw a pair of Church's welted brogues projecting from behind the archway. In rising horror, Helen stepped into the dining area. Nick sat slumped against the wall. What looked like a bread knife had been plunged deeply into his neck at an angle and just above the collar of the bulletproof vest. The vest, Nick's clothes, the wall, the floor, all were covered in blood. Nick was motionless and staring vacantly. Bubbles of blood popped at his lips.

"Braithwaite ... Nick," gasped Helen. Kneeling beside him, she grabbed his wrist ... could she still ... surely ... surely she could still feel the faintest pulse. "Braithwaite, stay with me," she commanded, stilling her own dread. Then, craning back through the archway and forgetting the microphone at her throat, she yelled with the full force of her lungs, "AMBULANCE! OFFICER DOWN! CALL A FUCKING AMBULANCE!"

Ambulances had been on standby just around the corner from the outset and it was no more than seconds before paramedics came rushing through the flat. Helen stood back, biting her lip, as the paramedics knelt beside Nick. One took Nick's wrist, searching for a pulse, then put a finger to his neck. The paramedic looked around at the quantity of spilled blood. He drew a deep breath, turned to Helen and slowly shook his head. At Nick's mouth, the tiny carmine sacs, last desperate pellicle-wrapped ransom of the mortal flesh, repositories of final whispered adieus, had ceased to pop.

FORTY-NINE

Gordon stood at Margaret's desk. The morning's first shafts of sunlight hit the office windows. The immediate jihadist threat, at least as far as MI5 was able to identify it, had been successfully quashed; however, neither Gordon nor Margaret could find reason to celebrate.

Gordon summarised in a sombre tone of voice. "The team has suffered one shocking loss." He succumbed to a moment of silent reflection before continuing. "Miraculously, no fatalities in Barnet apart from the two jihadists – though we do have four police officers in hospital with injuries of varying severity … fortunately none life-threatening. I shall speak to Tim as soon as he gets in. Otherwise, all suspects in custody. Conventional explosives found. Attacks clearly planned for today in London – by all three cells in the area. Both cells in Birmingham also primed to go. Two other cells, in Sheffield and Bradford, with conventional bomb-making equipment, but this apparently not intended for use today. Final cell, in Manchester, seemingly not equipped and unprepared for action." Gordon considered for a moment. "The question is, are we confident enough to recommend to COBRA that the transport stoppage should be called off?"

Margaret paused before responding. "Two outstanding consider-ations. Firstly, have we accounted for all potential bombers? Yes, we've got all those on our hit list for today, but that leaves hundreds of other potentially active militants – some whom we know about, some whom we suspect, doubtless some who remain unknown to us … are we totally confident that we've hit every active cell? Surely, the prudent answer is 'no'. Secondly, as you point out, our raids have uncovered an alarming number of cells poised or equipped to carry out conventional suicide or car bomb attacks, but there's no sign at all of nuclear materials or nuclear intentions. Do we simply rule out the nuclear threat as a red herring – or at least as a quite separate issue? Again, surely the prudent answer is that we have to assume the worst. Precautions are in place: let's recommend to COBRA that we keep them there for today."

181

FIFTY

As soon as Helen returned to MI5, she asked Gordon if she could speak to him in his office.

"Gordon, I feel awful about Braithwaite. His death is completely my responsibility. Deploying him on the raid was wholly my decision – but he clearly wasn't ready for field work of such danger."

"Helen, stop, stop ..." chided Gordon gently. "Nick's death is awful, but it is absolutely not your responsibility. It is sadly a feature of the job we do that very occasionally we suffer a tragic loss such as this. Nick had undergone all the necessary training – it was entirely appropriate that he should participate in the raid."

"But ..."

"No, no, Helen – your sentiments are admirable, but misplaced. We are fighting a war and it's in the nature of war that there are casualties. Unless a commander is negligent or reckless, he cannot be held to account – should not hold himself to account – for individual casualties. You were not negligent or reckless – on the contrary, this and all the raids were meticulously planned by you and all were carried out to the letter ... with one exception perhaps. If I had to blame anyone, it would be the surveillance team who failed to spot that there were four suspects in the house, not three – though I understand in slight mitigation that two of the suspects looked practically identical. But, anyway, I don't think this is the moment for recriminations. No doubt there will be a careful review of what happened, but it is perfectly clear that no part of the responsibility for Nick's death rests with you." Gordon realised he had unintentionally become a little hectoring in tone. He softened his voice. "If you need to take time out, I would completely understand ..."

"No, there's certainly no need for that," said Helen. "Nor would I dream of leaving my desk with the nuclear threat still hanging over us."

"Good. Then let's have no more talk of you being in any way accountable for this tragedy." Gordon exhaled a short breath. "Tim on the other hand ... could you send him in, please."

182

Tim felt like the proverbial schoolboy summoned before the headmaster as he entered Gordon's office a few moments later. Gordon was standing at the window with his back to Tim. Gordon turned. His expression was one of incredulity and exasperation as much as anger.

"Tim, I suppose you deserve a modicum of credit for spotting the scooter driver, but what in God's name possessed you to go charging out there? All you had to do was wait for a few seconds to see whether or not the biker went up to the house – as Margaret was telling you, by the way – and then the armed response team could have done its job."

Tim was not sure what to say. He had thought he was doing the right thing.

"Well?" persisted Gordon.

"I'm sorry … I just thought it would be easier to grab the scooter driver in the street and then deal with the other two in the house. I didn't think he'd have any opportunity to raise the alarm."

"Tim, we have strict protocols for these operations – which you and everyone else had rehearsed. Yes, the biker's sudden appearance necessitated a few moments' stay of execution, but there was no call for you to go dashing out there by yourself, thereby launching the raid at half-cock and putting your own life and those of your colleagues at risk." Gordon stared grimly at Tim. "I realise this was a misjudgement made in the heat of the moment, but I am debating whether some form of official reprimand is called for. At the very least, I hope it's clear to you that you have not covered yourself in glory." Gordon nodded towards the door. "For the moment, back to work. I shall be briefing the whole team shortly."

Tim trudged unhappily back to his desk – cursing himself, cursing Gordon, angry with the world, but also feeling deeply relieved that none of his police colleagues had lost life or limb. Whereas Nick … the thought of Nick's death instantly swept other emotions aside. Tim looked around at his colleagues. A heavy silence hung over the whole team. Tim noticed that Helen was looking especially stern and saw that, as he approached, she quickly brushed a tear from the corner of her eye. She turned to him as he sat down.

"Bollocking?" she asked, not unkindly.

183

Tim grimaced by way of confirmation.

"Lemon, I can't say I might not have done the same in that situation."

Tim knew that Helen would not have done the same – she was decisive, he was rash, that was the difference. But he was grateful for her moral support. A little surprised to receive it as well. He felt marginally better.

"Thanks," he said.

Unable to find any fresh enthusiasm for the fight against jihadist terror, Tim clicked into Draper's network instead. Helen had already pointed out to Tim Draper's non-committal note of thanks to Berezin and also the one recent update from Andropov in the encrypted email. As Tim now looked, Draper and one of his trading team were exchanging emails about an options strategy in technical language quite alien to Tim. The discussion clearly had no relevance to Tim's investigation, but its impenetrability increased his feeling of impotence and frustration. Making something of Draper and Andropov was his best chance of redeeming himself.

Gordon appeared. "Team, could we gather in the conference room."

Tim was about to close his window to Draper's network when he saw a new message arrive in Draper's encrypted email. It was a further update from Andropov: 'Champagne received in past hour. Cassis as planned.' Tim closed the message and followed the rest of the team into the conference room.

FIFTY-ONE

Gordon stood at the head of the table. He spoke in sober tones.

"We've all been knocked back this morning by what happened to Nick – it's truly a shock for all of us. I know it takes time to come to terms with the loss of such a close colleague. Nick was a bright and lively young man and a good friend to all of us. However, there will be a time to mourn Nick properly. For the moment, we must press on with our job. Otherwise, hundreds or perhaps even thousands or tens of thousands of people among the general public could soon find themselves experiencing the same emotions which we now feel for Nick. We can't let that happen. Let's turn our respect for Nick into continuing professionalism and dedication in protecting all the law-abiding people of this country."

Gordon surveyed the team, who sat with heads bowed in solemn reflection.

"I think," he continued, "that we can allow ourselves at least a small measure of congratulation for having correctly identified a number of jihadist cells and for having successfully apprehended all the relevant suspects – apart, of course, from the two who blew themselves up. But we should consider that this may not be the conclusion of the matter. The morning is not yet over, let alone the day, and grave dangers may remain. Tomorrow may be incubating new threats of its own. It's true we believe we've neutralised all of the front-rank extremists and our initial interrogations this morning have tended to confirm what we suspected rather than open up entirely new avenues of enquiry. In addition, I understand, Trevor, that the Israelis have confirmed that they've wiped out the target in Gaza?"

Trevor nodded.

"And, Tabi," continued Gordon, "I believe you said the relevant internet address now seems to be unresponsive?"

"I've tried bouncing signals off the IP address all morning. Of course, it could just be switched off or disconnected, but given continuous activity in the past, my hunch is it's dead."

185

"So," resumed Gordon, "with the streets of London as quiet as first thing on a Sunday morning, there's a great temptation to relax. But we must not. Vigilance remains of paramount importance and our intelligence remains the key to anticipating and dealing with any remaining threat. It is entirely possible that there are terrorists out there who have successfully evaded our attention. And, most important of all, if there is indeed a nuclear elephant sitting somewhere in the room, we have so far failed ..." Gordon was interrupted by the buzzing vibration of his mobile, which he had placed on the conference table in front of him. He snatched up the phone. "Yes?" He furrowed his brow. "That's it?" He gave a grunt of acknowledgement and clicked off his phone. He pursed his lips. "Well, the pile of elephant dung just got a little higher and steamier. Our contact in Moscow has passed a message to MI6 that the nuclear transaction is rumoured to have taken place somewhere within Russian borders during the last hour or so."

"It seems to me," said Margaret, "that the jihadist threat which we've been addressing this morning and the putative nuclear threat are playing out according to quite different and entirely independent timetables. We may be dealing with two wholly unrelated things."

Tabi was staring fixedly at his mobile. He turned to Tim. "Tim, pick up the alert on your phone."

Tim took his mobile from his pocket and opened the relevant email. His expression froze. The hairs on his bare forearms stood like porcupine quills.

"Enlighten me," said Gordon, turning first to Tabi and then to Tim, with a look of slight irritation.

"I wrote a program for Tim," explained Tabi. "We identified twenty or so key words relating to Draper and Andropov. The program monitors all traffic on all the security services' servers – ours here, MI6, GCHQ – and then sends us an alert if any of the key words crops up."

"Tabi," huffed Gordon, "that's very enterprising of you, but if you're setting up a program to trawl the entire security services' network, do you think you could possibly let me know in advance?"

"Oh, sorry, Gordon. Yes, of course. I thought this one was innocuous enough ..."

186

"Well, is it innocuous?"

Tabi held up his phone. "The program has just sent an alert – looks like the message originated with the National Security Agency in the US, was passed to Langley, then to Cheltenham. Tim ..."

"It seems a Cayman Islands account which the CIA is monitoring has just this morning received a payment of one hundred million dollars ..."

"Go on ..." urged Gordon impatiently.

"... from Ruza Bank – Andropov's bank." Tim stood. "Could I just go and double-check something on my computer?"

"I can get it for you here," volunteered Tabi. He pulled the console on the conference table towards him and in moments had called up Tim's screens on the large wall display. "Let me guess," he said, "... Draper and Andropov's encrypted correspondence?"

"Exactly," confirmed Tim. "The most recent message."

'Champagne received in past hour. Cassis as planned.' The message appeared on the wall display.

"I am clearly a step behind here." Gordon looked at Tim with annoyance.

"We thought 'champagne' was a codeword for something – possibly gold bullion, which Draper and Andropov have been buying in massive quantities. The two of them have a rendezvous in Cassis in the south of France on the first of June, when the 'champagne' will be delivered to Draper's yacht. Oh, and then an earlier message told us that they planned to 'pop the cork' on Draper's boat a couple of weeks later. Now, this morning, we have three pieces of intelligence indicating, firstly, that Andropov has taken delivery of whatever this 'champagne' may be, secondly, that his bank has just made a payment of one hundred million dollars to a suspicious Cayman Islands account and, meanwhile, thirdly, according to our mole in Moscow, that a transaction in nuclear materials has just taken place somewhere within Russian borders."

Gordon – and indeed the rest of the team – looked dumbfounded. "Are you suggesting ...?"

"It does seem highly improbable," admitted Tim.

"But it makes no sense," interjected Helen. "Why on earth would Draper – or Andropov for that matter – why on earth would they want to

187

set off a nuclear device, presumably here in London? They both live here, their livelihoods are here, Andropov's children are here ..."

"Draper's actually a resident of Monaco," said Tim. "And he has houses all over the place. He could live on his boat if he wanted to. Same with Andropov – houses everywhere, even bigger boats ... not to mention private jets – he could whisk his family off anywhere at the drop of a hat. And Draper has offices elsewhere and anyway all he needs to get on with his business is a laptop and a mobile phone. Andropov's businesses are based in Russia ..." Tim held up his hand. "And another little thing ..." He began to click through the photographs on his mobile phone. "... when I was at Bowley Hall, I found out the marquess and Draper went to school together and the marquess is an investor in Draper's fund. I discovered a brief handwritten message from Draper. Here we are ..." Tim enlarged the relevant section of the photograph on his phone. "I read it as Draper saying he expected 'further catastrophe' to hit the global economy, but what he actually wrote was he expects '*a* further catastrophe' – maybe he couldn't resist a boastful hint to an old school friend."

"But Draper and Andropov's businesses depend on the financial markets," insisted Helen. "If London were hit with a nuclear bomb, the markets would go into a tailspin."

"But not gold," intervened Margaret.

"Exactly," exclaimed Tim. He pointed to the photograph on his mobile phone. "That's precisely what Draper says. Here, I quote: 'I'm convinced that a further catastrophe awaits the global economy and that our bet on the yellow metal will come good.'"

"The gold price would probably rocket," resumed Margaret. "The scenario seems quite unthinkable, but it would explain why the two of them have been buying as much gold as they can afford despite increasing signs of stability and recovery in the global economy. Their gold investments could make them tens of billions of dollars – and meanwhile the markets would be littered with distressed assets available at giveaway prices. Gordon, I think you should immediately despatch Tim to Cassis to observe the clandestine handover. And if we're right about the delivery, we should then have the navy ready to intercept the cargo once it's heading our way."

188

"Quite so," spluttered Gordon, still looking somewhat nonplussed. "Good grief!"

"If this is all correct," continued Margaret calmly, "this could actually be a positive turn of events: we know who, we know where, we know when; for what it's worth, we can even guess why. To intercept a yacht on the open sea should be a great deal easier and entail much less risk than carrying out speculative raids in the middle of the city …"

Gordon stood with his mouth open. The team could almost hear the painstaking ratchet of his mental Enigma machine as he caught up with events. He shook his head. "Tim, you've done a satisfactory job with Draper so far, but I really think, Helen, you should now take over on this one. I'd like you to assume responsibility for Draper and Andropov and to head down to the south of France."

Tim could not believe what he was hearing. Indeed, the whole team stared at Gordon. After a couple of moments of silence, Helen gave voice to their common thought.

"Gordon, I'm very happy to work on Draper and Andropov, but surely this is Tim's case – shouldn't he continue to take the lead?"

Gordon, still looking off balance after Tim's revelation, pulled a face. He hesitated. "The two of you come to my office. We'll continue the discussion there."

As the team filed out, Margaret held Gordon back.

"Gordon, I agree Tim should have handled Barnet differently and of course the decision is yours, but don't you think Tim has done extraordinarily well in bringing us this far with Draper and Andropov – from a starting point of absolutely nothing? It's a crushing put down if you give the case to Helen now."

"Yes, Tim has done a reasonable job with Draper – all right, he's done *well* with Draper – but Helen is a thoroughgoing professional. If we're dealing with a nuclear threat, I'd feel much more confident with matters in her hands. I mean, look at the way Tim went hoofing out to intercept that scooter driver …"

"I agree Tim can be a bit headstrong, but he's doggedly determined and without his efforts we'd be totally in the dark over Draper and Andropov."

Gordon gave a non-committal harrumph. "Anyway, I'll speak to them both."

189

III   La Isla Bonita, part 1

FIFTY-TWO

The Hôtel du Port, situated on the Quai des Baux just across from the waterfront, lived up to its name, but barely to its two stars. The centuries old harbour of Cassis was surrounded by a tightly packed arc of ancient, narrow, three and four-storey buildings, each one different from the next, most painted in varying shades of peach and apricot, all capped with terracotta tiled roofs. Narrow streets, some cobbled, disappeared among and behind the huddled buildings. The Hôtel du Port was one of these edifices, four storeys high, a dusty umber in colour, wide enough only for two small guest rooms at the front of the building and one at the back on each floor.

Tim, in a lingering fury with Gordon for doubting his ability to follow through successfully with Draper and Andropov, had secured a top floor room which met the essential requirement that it overlooked the harbour and the Mediterranean beyond. The room was otherwise very basic in its amenities: bed, table and chair, small television on a stand, narrow wardrobe, washbasin in the room, tiny adjoining room into which were squeezed a shower and toilet and which smelled faintly of drains. Tim had quickly discovered that there was no broadband connection: he had plugged his laptop into the phone socket, but had found the internet to be excruciatingly slow and intermittent. His mobile phone was proving similarly recalcitrant when he attempted to use it to log on to the internet. He had sent a brief message to London requesting delivery of a broadband mobile dongle registered to one of the French networks in the hope that this would solve the problem; however, at this early hour of the morning he had not yet received it.

Tim had flown into Marseilles late the previous evening – the evening of the thirtieth of May. After the morning conference in London and the follow-up conversation in Gordon's office, when Gordon had finally conceded that Tim should retain the lead on Draper and Andropov, Tim had returned to his flat, hastily packed a bag and headed straight to Gatwick. An MI5 quartermaster – a grey-suited and grumpy civil servant – had met him at the airport and had handed him high-powered binoculars which offered both conventional optics and thermal imaging, a monocular which allowed night vision and a digital camera with high-powered lens. Tim's flight had subsequently been delayed and he had not reached Cassis until shortly before midnight. He had slept for a few hours and risen at dawn.

First light revealed to him the harbour and the small multitude of its inhabitants: opening the shutters to his window, he saw that the little port had netted a teeming shoal of sailing boats and motor yachts. He scoured the bobbing ranks of motor cruisers. The one he sought was not among them. He lifted his gaze further afield, taking in far off to his left the white limestone cliffs plunging dramatically into the sea, the open expanse of ocean and then, closer to hand, the harbour wall and arc of houses disappearing off to his right. His eyes returned to the tranquil azure of the Mediterranean. Some distance out to sea, aloof, a grander yacht than any in the harbour lay at anchor. Tim took his binoculars and adjusted the focus: sleekly powerful as a killer whale, with upper decks sparkling white and lower glistening black, like an orca basking on its back, the vessel glinted on the water. As the boat swung on its anchor, Tim trained his binoculars on the stern: the motor yacht's dark purpose was belied by the innocent charm of its name ... La Isla Bonita.

Tim took a series of photographs of the yacht and then attempted to relay them to London. The inadequate phone line failed him again. Taking up the binoculars, he spent fifteen minutes observing the yacht. There was no sign of activity. The delivery of 'champagne', if running to schedule, was at least twenty-four hours away. Still, Tim did not wish to leave his post for a minute in case he missed something. He decided to call down for breakfast.

A sheet of card on the table boasted of twenty-four hour room service, though this seemed to consist of only three options:

- ❖ *Petit déjeuner (pain, patisseries, confiture, café)*
- ❖ *Salade Niçoise*
- ❖ *Steak aux frites*

194

Tim summoned his best schoolboy French. *"Est-ce que je peux commander un petit déjeuner, s'il vous plaît?"*

"Oui, monsieur, bien sûr," came the response with a Marseilles twang on the *'bieng'*.

"Et avec du thé, s'il vous plaît. Du thé au lait."

There was the briefest hesitation. *"Oui, monsieur."*

Tim looked out of his window. The restaurants and cafés circling the harbour were beginning to come to life. Just below him and one building to his right, a waiter was setting out tables on the pavement. He spread out red tablecloths and clamped them in place before disappearing inside and then returning to plant a menu in the centre of each table. People began to emerge from the sidestreets and one or two came ashore from the boats in the harbour.

There was a knock on Tim's door.

"Bonjour, monsieur. Vous avez bien dormi?" *'Bieng'* again.

The proprietor of the hotel, receptionist, provider of room service and very probably chef as well was a middle-aged man, shortish, nut-brown, with a bristly salt-and-pepper crew cut which came to a sharp 'V' on his forehead and with an upper lip adorned by a rather extravagant and luxuriously curly moustache. He contrived at once to be thin-faced and stringy of limb while also sporting a slightly protruding pot belly. He wore dark blue trousers and a check shirt. He set down the breakfast tray on Tim's table.

"Voilà, monsieur."

Tim noticed that the man also brought with him a faint miasma of French cigarettes and body odour beneath an overlay of aftershave or perfume of some kind – sandalwood, perhaps. The effect was not too excessive or overpowering, but Tim nevertheless felt it constituted a minor olfactory invasion of the confined space of his room. And now Tim realised that another odour was also faintly troubling him. He looked at the breakfast tray.

"Ah ... j'ai dit du thé, monsieur, pas du café ..."

The man stared at the coffee with an air of haughty bewilderment. He proceeded to insist, with shrugs and gesticulations, that Tim had surely ordered *café au lait*, that now that it was prepared and brought up to Tim's room wasn't *café au lait* anyway perfectly acceptable and, finally, that he could not understand what Tim was struggling to say to him. Tim relented.

La France un, l'Angleterre zéro, mused Tim to himself as the proprietor turned to leave.

The hotelkeeper paused at the door. *"Vous avez de la blanchisserie ou du repassage à faire?"*

Tim was blank for a second, but then realised that the man was referring to the untidy mound of clothes on Tim's bed. The clothes were in fact all clean, though Tim had to concede that to the unaccustomed eye this might not be apparent. At the same time, thought Tim, what in buggery was the world's obsession with ironing? He was hard pressed to think of a bigger waste of time and energy. *"Non, merci. Pas pour l'instant."*

"Si vous voulez la faire, il y a un sac dans le tiroir." The man nodded towards the drawer in the little table. He turned and took his leave.

When Tim had eaten, he settled himself in the chair at his window and periodically lifted his binoculars to see if there was any sign of life on La Isla Bonita. For the moment, there was none. Tim's mind began to wander. His ill temper over Gordon's slight subsided a little and his thoughts turned instead to poor Nick. The rapid unfolding of events over the past twenty-four hours had allowed little time for reflection on Nick's death. Sitting here by himself, Tim felt Nick's death was quite unreal. He pictured Nick in his navy blazer, Tabi teasing him about his hairstyle. Tim drew a slow breath and then expelled it in a short, sharp sigh. He thought about Helen and her shedding of a secret tear for Nick. He wondered whether Helen was not quite the kick-arse tough cookie she affected to be. Tim flexed his right hand and looked at his raw knuckles where he had struck the motorcycle helmet of the jihadist biker: perhaps, thought Tim, conversely to Helen, he possessed greater reserves of physical courage than he would have previously supposed.

FIFTY-THREE

"*Citron*, morning. Any signs of the pirates of Piccadilly?"

"Morning, Trevor. The boat is certainly here, but no sign of life on board just yet. Any new developments at the London end?"

"You've missed a bit of excitement here this morning." Trevor did not sound particularly excited. "The press has mostly been pretty favourable – we thought we might get some flak for bringing half the country to a standstill, but on the whole everyone seems to agree we did the right thing. And then the PM was here a few minutes ago – said a few thoughtful words about Nick before delivering the nation's thanks for our hard work and sacrifice in ensuring public safety. Gordon looked suitably chastened over Nick, but when the PM spoke about the country's debt of gratitude to us for preventing multiple atrocities, Gordon's chest swelled to the point I really thought the buttons on his shirt were about to start pinging around the room."

"I hope Helen was given due credit – she organised everything. And you, Tabi, Maggie, all of us – we all played our part."

"Gordon was magnanimous to all ... while leaving the PM in no doubt that it was he, Gordon, who had masterminded the whole proceedings."

"Typical. Anyway, is herself about?"

"Two seconds ..." Trevor waved his phone in Helen's direction. "Helen ... *Monsieur le Citron* – seems *un peu pressé*." His delivery was deadpan, but his upper lip adopted its characteristic curl as he looked to Helen for a reaction. "*Citron pr* ..."

"Yes, yes, *très drôle*," rejoined Helen as she picked up the phone. "Lemon, morning. Any sign of things happening?"

"Well, I just explained to Trevor that La Isla Bonita is indeed sitting resplendent in the bay, but with no sign of activity on board at the moment. I'll send you some pics when the dongle shows up – assuming that works. Any idea when it's likely to appear?"

"Not for a while yet, I think. Our usual man in Marseilles, Eric Carter, is back here on home leave at the moment. He suggested asking an associate, Geoffroy de Beauregard … Comte Geoffroy, I think he is, actually. Anyway, *Monsieur le Comte* has said, yes, he'll see to it as soon as possible."

"Which probably means if he gets hold of a dongle this morning, he'll pause briefly for a four-hour lunch, stop off on the way to shag his mistress and get to me by late afternoon. I'd go and buy one myself, but I haven't got a clue about signing a French mobile contract and, anyway, now I'm here in my eyrie, I don't want to take my eye off the boat."

"Let's hope de Beauregard doesn't live up to your expectations. But, anyway, the key is for you to have the thing before tomorrow, so that we can analyse your photos of the handover of the contraband. Where exactly is the boat?"

"It's not actually in the harbour – it's moored, I'd say, a mile or so out to sea … perhaps a bit less."

"Part of a flotilla or just sitting by itself?"

"Very much sitting by itself."

"Okay, good, presumably that gives you a clear view and it should help us locate it and lock on to it with a satellite – then we can track it later if things really do start to happen."

"I'll keep you posted as soon as I see anything of significance."

"Yup." Helen was silent for a second.

Sensing her change of mood, Tim adopted a softer tone. "How are you, Helen – I mean after Nick?"

"I think it's still sinking in. There's still a bit of an atmosphere of shock and unreality here."

"Yuh, that's exactly how I feel."

"Well, let's not dwell on it," said Helen more briskly. "Give us another bell as soon as you have anything to report."

FIFTY-FOUR

Though it was not yet the tourist season, by nine-thirty the waterfront was becoming animated with shoppers, people attending to their boats, workmen and sightseers. One or two young mothers with pre-school children were heading towards the town's beach, the near end of which Tim could just see from his window. Shortly after nine-thirty, Tim caught sight of movement on La Isla Bonita. He raised his binoculars. After several minutes of observation, he concluded that there were two crew members on board. Both wore the same livery of navy blue shorts and white polo shirts. Though it was a little difficult to gain a precise impression at this distance, both looked stocky and both were fair-haired, one appeared to be about forty and the other perhaps ten years younger. They seemed to be toing and froing fairly busily, but Tim could not see what they were doing. At moments when they came on deck and were more clearly in view, Tim took a series of photographs. He wondered whether the two men were simply innocent crew members – hired ship's hands not knowingly involved in whatever Draper was up to. Tim supposed it was a long shot that his colleagues in London would be able to identify them. By midday, the two crew members had again disappeared inside the boat. Tim thought he once or twice caught sight of their silhouettes through the windows of the bridge of the yacht.

Meanwhile, enticing smells of cooking were beginning to drift up from the restaurants around the harbour – grilled fish and grilled steak, perhaps with a little accent of *herbes provençales*. *Bouillabaisse* – hadn't Tim read somewhere that this fish soup was the local speciality? Tim suddenly started to feel exceptionally hungry. He wondered if he dared abandon his post for an hour. The restaurants were there on his doorstep and if he picked the right table, he would probably still have a view of La Isla Bonita.

As he was gazing down at the restaurants, a reflected flash of sunlight from the direction of the motor yacht caught his attention: there were signs of activity at the rear of the boat. Taking up his binoculars, Tim could see that the tailgate of the yacht had opened, allowing the two crew members to lower a small motor launch into the water. The two men stepped aboard the launch and, as the tailgate levered closed behind them, cast off from the yacht. The launch turned towards the harbour and then spurted forwards. The trip to the harbour took the speeding launch only a couple of minutes. As it entered the harbour, it disappeared from view among the larger boats. Damn. Tim had completely lost sight of it. He scanned the harbour, alternately with and without binoculars. Would it be better to go down into the street to see if he could locate the two men and determine their purpose in coming ashore? Just then he caught sight of them walking along the harbour front. They were coming in his direction. He snapped several photographs – much clearer ones than those taken when the men had been out on the boat. The crewmen's purpose very soon became apparent: they settled at an outdoor table at the restaurant just next to Tim's hotel. A red awning obscured many of the restaurant tables from Tim's view, but the two men chose one which he could see clearly. Lunch menus appeared, quickly followed by a bottle of red wine, a bottle of mineral water and a basket of bread. Was this a perfect opportunity for Tim to take a table adjacent to them and eat a decent lunch while also listening to their conversation? He resolved to do so, but strained for a moment to listen from his window. The crewmen were ordering in French, but their accents were clearly not French – rather had a glottal quality. The two men completed their order and resumed conversation between themselves. Curses, muttered Tim … the language certainly wasn't English and to his ear, from the few words he could catch, it sounded like Russian. Tim could no more speak Russian than read it. He would gain nothing from sitting beside the men – well, apart from a good lunch. But they would see him. That didn't matter in the least at the moment – they would have no idea who he was – but if, for example, he needed to follow them at some stage, it was better that he meanwhile preserve his anonymity.

Tim resigned himself to the hotel's twenty-four hour room service. *Steak aux frites* was fine – it was probably what he would have ordered anyway. He picked up the phone.

"Un steak aux frites, s'il vous plaît, monsieur."

"Ah, désolé, monsieur. Le steak aux frites, ça, c'est pour le soir. Le déjeuner, c'est la salade Niçoise. D'ailleurs, c'est très bonne." Bugger. *La France deux, l'Angleterre zéro.* He would have to make do with the salad. *"Eh bien, la salade Niçoise. Avec du pain, s'il vous plaît."*

"Volontiers, monsieur."

Would he get the bread, Tim wondered, or had that been too much to ask? He looked out of the window at the two crew members. He trained his binoculars on their table. Dammit, one of the men was having a *salade Niçoise* as an *hors d'oeuvre*! And the other had a whole trolley of different types of *pâté* parked in front of him and was apparently free to take as much as he wanted! After several minutes, Tim's salad arrived – with bread. At least that was something. He sat at the table and pulled the tray towards him. The *salade Niçoise* and the bread did actually taste very good. But having polished off his frugal meal in a couple of minutes, he still felt hungry. He went back to the window. Oh, this was cruel! The crew member who had had the *salade Niçoise* was now tucking into what was surely a *steak au poivre* with a mountain of *frites*! And the one who had gorged on *pâté* was now ladling onto his plate the contents of a steaming cauldron of what could only be *bouillabaisse*! Tim could taste the bloody, slightly metallic tang of the steak, heightened by the palate-provoking peppercorns; the aroma of steaming fish stock lifted up to him – what might it be? – sea bass, bream, langoustines, clams, fresh *provençal* vegetables and herbs …

Tim started to feel slightly depressed and his anger rekindled. Where, by the way, was bloody de Beauregard? No doubt, Tim had been right and *Monsieur le Comte de la Merde* de Beauregard was off somewhere burying his face in a five-hour banquet eaten off the naked body of his sun-tanned and Pyrenean-breasted mistress. Tim looked disconsolately into the street – as though de Beauregard might suddenly appear with the dongle and a present of chocolate éclairs. De Beauregard did not appear. And Able Seaman *Niçoise-and-steak au poivre* was now tucking into what Tim guessed was a *tarte aux abricots* with *crème Chantilly*, while Able Seaman *pâté-and-poisson* was obviously so stuffed he could eat no more and was content with a double espresso. Tim photographed the dessert trolley which was alongside the table.

The two men in due course ordered a *liqueur* and seemed in no hurry to leave the restaurant. Tim closed his windows and retreated into the room. He called the office.

"Hi there, Lemon. I was about to call you."

"Hi, Helen."

"What's up? You don't sound too cheerful?"

"I'm feeling hungry and pissed off."

"Why? Get some food."

"I've had some food. But everyone in Cassis seems to be stuffing their faces with a gourmet lunch, while I'm stuck with a crappy room service menu which offers only two options and you can't choose the one you want. And, meanwhile, *Monsieur le Con* de Beauregard hasn't shown up with the patiss ... I mean, the dongle."

"Lemon ..." Helen sounded exasperated. "Honestly, I can't believe you guys. Firstly you join a bunch of swampies and turn into a let-it-all-hang-out hippie, then Tabi infiltrates a mosque and comes home with a prayer mat and a compass pointing to Mecca and now you spend less than a day in France and already you've turned into a gastronome whose sole preoccupation is food. You're not there for the cuisine, Lemon, you're there because, utterly improbable as it might seem, your friend Draper may just be on the point of taking delivery of a nuclear bomb which he plans to sail up the Thames."

"Yeah, well, thanks for the lecture, Helen. You said you were about to call?"

"Yes, partly to see if you had anything new to tell us and partly because, one, we have a satellite lock on Draper's boat; two, we have an SBS team with fast assault craft on standby in Gibraltar and we also have a frigate with a chopper and second SBS team on its way from Plymouth."

"Is there no frigate in Gib?" interrupted Tim.

"I'm afraid Her Majesty's fleet now includes only thirteen frigates worldwide, with none currently in port in Gibraltar and with the nearest one – in Malta – out of action because of engine repairs. Plymouth was the closest available warship. Then, third reason for my calling you, de Beauregard has just contacted us to say he'll be with you sometime this evening, but he couldn't say exactly when."

"Surprise, surprise."

"Apart from the wretched food – or lack of – is anything happening at your end?"

"Just one development. La Isla Bonita has a crew of two. They're actually here in town at the moment – in fact, they've just polished off a sumptuous feast at a restaurant about thirty feet directly below my garret." Tim heard Helen theatrically draw breath. He could visualise her shaking her head with impatience, though she was managing to restrain the urge to repeat herself. "Anyway, when I have the blessed dongle, I'll send photos so you can check whether these two mean anything to us. From the scraps of conversation I've been able to hear, I think they might be Russian."

"I thought you couldn't speak Russian?"

"I can't. Which is obviously a drawback. They're both well-built, fair-haired ... one's about forty, one maybe thirty-ish. They spent the morning pottering about on the boat and then came into town for lunch." Tim peered through the closed window. "Shit, they're on the move. I'll call you again a bit later."

The two men walked fifty yards along the harbour front and then turned up a sidestreet. Tim grabbed his room key and shot from his room. He summoned the iron cage which served as a lift. The lift rattled slowly up to him and then, with Tim on board, it rattled slowly back down to the ground floor. It would have been quicker to run down the stairs. Tim sped out onto the street. As he circumvented the outdoor tables of the adjacent restaurant, he cracked his knee on the dessert trolley, which still projected onto the pavement. He swore and directed an *"Excusez-moi"* in the general direction of the nearest waiter. Great way not to draw attention to yourself, he thought. He tested his knee with a couple of limping steps before resuming the chase at a swift walking pace. He turned into the cobbled sidestreet which he thought the men had taken. No sign of them among the few people wandering up and down the road. Had it been the next street? He walked as fast as he could. No sign of them there either. And this was surely too far. It had been the first turning. He sped back and walked up the cobbled street. Side alleys wound off in different directions. A *camionnette* emerged from a courtyard with a hoot at Tim, forcing him back against the wall. He came to a Casino supermarket. He didn't suppose they would be in there. Unless perhaps they needed provisions for several days' voyage ... He entered the supermarket. Crates of ripe peaches and a display of local cheeses set off Tim's taste buds again. A woman in an apron offered him a small sample of cheese. He took it. He shouldn't have done. It tasted too good.

"Ça, c'est du chèvre, monsieur," explained the woman. *"C'est bon, n'est-ce pas?"*

"Oui, très bon," nodded Tim.

He went from aisle to aisle. He backtracked. He almost collided with a trolley. *"Excusez-moi,"* he said without thought. Then abruptly came up short. Oh, Christ, it was them – their trolley he had almost walked into. Luckily, the men paid no attention to Tim – they ignored his apology and carried on with their shopping. Tim had glanced at the men just long enough to notice that the older one had some strange deformity of the left eye socket.

So Tim's guess had been correct. This afternoon at any rate the men were shopping for groceries, not for nuclear weapons. Tim grabbed a bag of *petits pains*, one of the goat's cheeses he had tried, a couple of peaches and a bottle of Badoit. His hands were full. He paid at the checkout and headed back to his watchtower.

Ensconced once more in his seat at the window, he waited and watched the street. Sure enough, after about twenty minutes, the two crew members emerged from the sidestreet laden with carrier bags. They walked along the harbour front, descended to a wooden jetty and disappeared from view. A few minutes later, Tim saw the little motor launch nose out from among the larger boats in the harbour and head out towards La Isla Bonita. The launch docked with the motor yacht and the men unloaded their supplies. Tim continued his observation for several minutes. It seemed reasonably clear that no further developments were to be expected for the moment.

Tim helped himself to two of the bread rolls he had bought, a hunk of the cheese and one of the peaches. He suddenly felt obscurely triumphant and childishly happy.

204

FIFTY-FIVE

"This is absolutely not what we tossing need," muttered Tabi to himself. He carried a sheaf of printouts and was heading towards Gordon and Helen, who were in conference at the latter's desk. "Gordon, Helen, not good news. We're suddenly picking up a cascade of messages similar to the one that signalled to yesterday's bombers that they should prepare for action. The sources all seem different and the messages are hitting websites and blogsites all over the place. If we take this at face value, it suggests a whole wave of new attacks are on the point of being launched ..."

Gordon took the printouts from Tabi, glanced through them and passed them to Helen. Trevor and Maggie also came over and looked through the messages.

"We could haul in every single suspect we know of," suggested Helen.

Gordon grimaced. "With yesterday's lot, we had a fair idea of what they were up to and the evidence uncovered has vindicated our actions. But after that front-line group, even if we take just the next tier of, what, two, maybe three hundred Islamists whom we already have under close observation ... sure, they've attended hard-core meetings, they've been heard to make inflammatory remarks, one or two have done time for petty theft, pushing drugs, possessing weapons and, yes, a number of them have visited relatives or maybe it's 'visited relatives'" – Gordon described inverted commas in the air – "in Pakistan or elsewhere, but we don't actually have any concrete evidence that they're plotting anything. We could haul them all in and maybe we'd strike lucky somewhere, but we could also make grand fools of ourselves."

Maggie entered the conversation. "More than that, Muslim hackles are already up in some quarters because of yesterday's arrests – obviously with no justification at all given what the raids have exposed – but if we then carry out a huge sweep, detaining hundreds of more or less innocent Muslims, we risk a real backlash."

"Exactly my point," said Gordon, though actually it hadn't been, not exactly.

"But we can't just ignore this," said Helen, waving the sheaf of printouts.

"No, I wouldn't suggest we ignore it," said Maggie. "I know it's not ideal, but I think we just have to intensify surveillance on every higher priority suspect and also keep an extremely close watch on the remaining few thousand Islamists whom we already have under some lesser degree of observation ... but not actually arrest anyone unless they give us clear reason to believe that they're about to take action of some kind."

"Exactly," said Gordon again.

"But our resources are stretched to the limit," said Trevor. "We don't have the manpower to tail every suspect, listen in to every phone call, read every email ..."

"Well, the technology can help with the latter two," said Tabi.

"Of course, but someone still has to review everything the software throws up as potentially suspicious," rebutted Trevor.

"We can enlist the help of the police again," pointed out Helen. "That puts much greater manpower at our disposal."

"Yes, but the whole plan would be far from fail-safe," continued Trevor.

Tabi indicated the printouts. "We should also take account of the possibility that these guys might deliberately be sending us on a wild goose chase. They may have realised that we're on to their messaging system, so now they're flooding the internet with bogus signals in order to send us scurrying around pointlessly – and then perhaps making us ignore a genuine signal next time around."

"By the way, with messages coming from all over the place, does that mean it might not be these Righteous Scimitar people, but some quite different and probably larger group?" asked Helen.

"They could be part of a larger group operating from multiple bases or it could be multiple groups acting in concert," offered Maggie. "The Israelis were pretty clear Righteous Scimitar was not Hamas proper, but a splinter group acting under Hamas's protection. We may be dealing with something of a hydra."

"Yuh, but again not necessarily," said Tabi. "These messages could all be originating from a single source who's successfully hacked into hundreds or thousands of computers and is using them as a relay so that he can spam the hell out of us with anonymity."

Gordon held up his hands. "This isn't helping. We're wasting precious time. Maggie is right. We need to stick to all known suspects like flypaper – but obviously without advertising that we're doing so. Maggie, Helen, Trevor, divide up the list of suspects and liaise with the relevant police forces to make sure everyone is under close surveillance. If you encounter any problems, let me know and I'll get the DG or, if necessary, the Home Secretary to speak to chief constables. Tabi, obviously you take charge of the electronic monitoring. Keep me updated on progress. I'll alert the DG and he or I will inform the PM and COBRA."

As Helen turned back to her desk, her phone rang.

"Hi again, Helen."

"Lemon, I don't really have time. We've got a bit of another crisis. We're being flooded with jihadist signals. Unless you have anything urgent?"

"Not really …"

"Okay. Talk to you later, then."

FIFTY-SIX

Tim was again feeling disgruntled. Partly because of the brush-off from Helen and partly because he was getting bored. The remainder of the afternoon had passed uneventfully. Nothing of interest was happening on the boat. Tim had paced around his small room. He had switched on the television, but there was no satellite, only French terrestrial channels, all of which seemed to offer nothing but excruciatingly verbose and dull debates which Tim could not begin to follow. A couple of books lay discarded on the shelf below the television. He had given them a brief glance: the first was soiled and dog-eared and, judging from the crude illustration on its cover, seemed to be a cowboy adventure; the second, a slim volume with spine unbroken, bore the cryptic title *Quelque part quelque chose est* and was apparently a philosophical treatise by one Rémy Desplanches. *Monsieur le philosophe* vaunted himself in a photograph on the back of the book: with his flowing locks, suntan and white blouson shirt open to the navel, he seemed a creature more of base desire than of lofty abstraction. Only the French, Tim had thought, as he had tossed the books back onto the shelf. Later in the afternoon, he had chanced another five minute stroll along the harbour front, but had realised that, firstly, nowhere offered him the clear view of La Isla Bonita which he enjoyed from his room and, secondly, he would be extremely conspicuous if he stood in the street for any length of time with a pair of binoculars trained on the yacht. Of necessity, he had returned to his room. As dusk approached, he noted that deck lights came on aboard the motor yacht. Tantalising odours from the street below began to tease his appetite once again. At least he could order steak this time. He did so. *"Tout de suite, monsieur."* Might he also order a green salad? *"Bien sûr, monsieur. Vous buvez un verre de quelque chose?"* Tim resisted the temptation. He wanted to remain fully alert. *"Non, merci."*

Thirty minutes passed and there was no sign of Tim's food. He rang down again. *"Monsieur? J'ai commandé un steak il y a à peu près trente minutes ..."*

"Oui, monsieur. Ça arrive. Vous étiez un tout petit peu trop tôt pour le dîner, mais nous serons là en quelques minutes."

Another thirty minutes passed before *La Moustache* appeared with Tim's steak. A lettuce leaf wilting beneath the steak appeared to be doing duty as green salad – though there were also a few *haricots verts* and a couple of slices of carrot. It would do. Tim could not be bothered to complain again. Meanwhile, the hotelier eyed Tim's bread and cheese with a look of disdain – as though these were illicit items smuggled in and displayed as a deliberate reproach to his hospitality. He left.

Tim ate his steak, followed by more of the bread and cheese and the remaining peach. He kept an eye on La Isla Bonita. In the gathering twilight, cabin lights had come on. Tim caught glimpses of the crewmen passing back and forth inside the yacht. Shortly before ten, the lights inside the upper decks were extinguished, leaving still burning only the external deck lights and lights in a couple of forward cabins. Tim exchanged his binoculars for the monocular with night vision and scanned the decks for several minutes. No sign of activity – the crew had surely headed to their bunks. Tim thought he should do the same – tomorrow was the big day. But looking down at the street, Tim saw that, though custom was thinning, the restaurant below was not yet closed. He was tempted by that dessert trolley. He scanned the yacht for another couple of minutes, then went down to the restaurant.

"Est-ce que je peux prendre un dessert?"

The waiter, who wore a black apron with a picture of jagged white cliffs encircling an inlet, consulted his watch. *"Nous sommes sur le point de fermer, monsieur."*

"Mais je voudrais seulement un dessert ..."

The dessert trolley was beside the waiter. He relented. *"Qu'est-ce que vous voulez?"*

The apricot tart still looked good. *"La tarte aux abricots, s'il vous plaît ... avec de la crème – crème Chantilly, s'il vous plaît."*

The waiter indicated a table to Tim, took a plate from the bottom of the trolley and served Tim with his dessert.

"Vous prenez un verre de quelque chose, monsieur?"

"Un thé au lait, s'il vous plaît."

209

As Tim sat eating his apricot tart and drinking his tea, he again felt a quite disproportionate wave of satisfaction and beamed fatuously. He watched as a gaggle of teenage boys and girls passed in front of the restaurant, the boys strutting and joshing each other, the girls gossiping and flicking back their hair to impress the boys. An elderly couple slowly made their way towards the harbour. A tall and aristocratic-looking gentleman in blue blazer strode by ... Tim sipped his tea. He wondered at what time tomorrow the delivery to La Isla Bonita would take place. He should be up at first light just in case it was due to happen in the early hours. He paid for his dessert, leaving a generous tip, and returned to the hotel.

"Monsieur!" The hotelkeeper hailed Tim from within his little *conciergerie* behind the reception desk. *"Il y a un petit paquet pour vous, monsieur."* The man picked up the package from behind the reception desk, but instead of handing it straight to Tim, went to the front door of the hotel. *"Le monsieur était là il n'y a que trois minutes."* The hotelier looked up and down the street. *"Non, il a disparu."* He returned to the desk and handed the package to Tim. *"Voilà, monsieur. Bonne nuit."*

The dongle! Tim had almost given up on Geoffroy de Beauregard. He opened the package as the iron cage rattled up to his floor. Damn ... that must have been de Beauregard passing in front of the restaurant – the tall gentleman with the blazer. Never mind – the dongle itself was the essential. As soon as Tim was in his room, he powered up his laptop and plugged in the mobile USB. He had to run through several steps to register the device. It would have been easier if de Beauregard had been there to help him with the French instructions, but after twenty minutes Tim was up and running. He inserted the memory card from his camera into the computer and despatched his photographs to London with a brief covering message.

Feeling he had at least accomplished something, Tim readied himself for bed. He left his shutters wide open and set the alarm on his mobile for four a.m.

210

FIFTY-SEVEN

Nervous apprehension concerning the day ahead had kept Tim tossing and turning and had prompted him to rise occasionally to check the yacht. He had finally succumbed to sleep sometime after two a.m. The beeping of his alarm now wrenched him from deep slumber. There was light in the room, but the sun had not yet risen. Tim hauled himself out of bed and went straight to the unshuttered window. In the half-light of pre-dawn, La Isla Bonita bobbed on a placid sea. The deck lights were still on, but the cabin windows were all dark and there was no suggestion of activity. Tim sat at the seat in the window for twenty minutes watching the silent boat before deciding to shave and take a shower.

Four forty-five a.m. ... no doubt still far too early to summon the twenty-four hour room service. Tim stood at the window. The harbour too was silent apart from the ticking of a loose lanyard against a mast and the gentle slap of the sea against the hulls of the tethered boats. Tim sat down at the little table and powered up his laptop. He logged on to his office email, though his mobile already showed him that there was as yet no response to his photographs. Along with the rest of the team, Tim had been copied in on the flurry of emails concerning the apparent jihadist messages. He wondered how Helen and the others were dealing with this new and potentially redoubled threat. As far as he could see, surveillance of numerous suspects had been intensified, but so far no more dramatic action had been taken.

At six, Tim rang downstairs, but there was no answer. At seven, his bedside phone trilled.

"*Vous avez appelé, monsieur?*"

Tim ordered breakfast. He didn't bother to ask for tea. A short while later, the tray appeared. In contrast to the previous day's air of haughty disdain, the hotelier's manner this morning was one of twinkly-eyed complicity. Tim wondered what this might herald. He was pleasantly surprised.

"*Du thé, monsieur. Lipton. Avec du lait. Bon appétit.*"

Tim took his breakfast sitting at the window. La Isla Bonita slumbered still. At eight fifteen, his mobile rang.

"Morning, Lemon."

"Morning, Helen."

"May I first just ask the import of the dessert trolley?"

"The what of the what?"

"The dessert trolley – you sent us a photo of a dessert trolley."

"Did I? Oh, sorry – I should've deleted that one. Yeah, sorry, that was when I was feeling a bit hungry and pissed off ..."

"Are you okay?"

"Yeah, yeah, I'm fine."

"Any news on the boat?"

"No. So far this morning all is quiet at sea."

"Well, your photos have produced one interesting result. The older of the two crew members is one Ivan Markov, ex GRU – Russian military intelligence, in other words – and a known associate of Andropov's *eminence grise*, Mikhail Vasiliev. Not too difficult to recognise because a bullet took a chunk of bone out of his left eye socket and sliced the top off his left ear. The other guy we can't identify. But it looks as though Draper's boat is crewed by two of Andropov's henchmen."

"*Nom de Dieu.*"

"*Nom de Dieu* indeed. I have to admit your theory suddenly starts to look a degree more credible."

The two of them were silent for a few moments as they pondered this revelation.

"How about the jihadists?" asked Tim. "What's going on there?"

"Yeah, sorry if I was a bit abrupt with you yesterday."

An apology from Helen ... and for being abrupt! Tim was very surprised.

Helen continued. "We've had a torrent of signals on the internet apparently alerting suicide bombers left, right and centre to ready themselves for action. But we're coming to the conclusion it's probably all a bluff. They've overplayed their hand – so many signals it's become a bit ridiculous and beyond credibility. However, we're continuing to take it seriously, just in case. Basically, we and the police are closely shadowing every single known suspect."

"Well, good luck with that."

"Yuh, you too. Talk to you again in a bit."

Another hour passed before Tim caught sight of one of the crew appearing on the deck of the motor yacht. He and the other crew member in due course continued about their business on the boat as they had done the previous day – they gave no indication that today was to be any different. However, as lunchtime approached, there was no sign of the little launch and no sign that the men might once again come ashore to eat. Tim called Helen.

"Still all quiet, but it looks as though they're not coming ashore for lunch today – so perhaps they're standing by for delivery."

"We're watching Draper's encrypted email for you. He and Andropov have exchanged messages about Taiga Oil, but not about anything else – so no further clues there."

"Guess I'll just have to sit and wait and see what transpires."

"If you're stuck there, why don't you ring down to that restaurant and see if they can send something up to you?"

"That's a thought – if they're willing and if my French stretches that far."

"I could have a try for you – my French isn't too bad. Or, tell you what, better still, I'll ask Véronique, the girl downstairs who liaises with the DCRI, the French security service. I'll ask her to see if she can exercise her charm on the maître d' on your behalf. What's the name of the restaurant?"

Tim could not remember. He peered out of the window and looked at the red awning. "*Les Calanques.*"

"Spelling?"

Tim spelt it out. "I think I read on the internet it's what they call the rocky inlets along the coast here."

"And what would *monsieur* like to order?"

What had come over Helen? Tim was mildly astonished. "*Pâté* for starters would be good, then *bouillabaisse* would be great and then ..." Tim paused for thought.

"I've got the dessert trolley here," said Helen. "I think I can see profiteroles ..."

"Profiteroles! That would be perfect."

"And then perhaps a *rosé provençal* to wash it all down?"

213

"I'm staying strictly sober."

"I wasn't serious about the wine. But I'll see whether *la charmante* Véronique can rustle up the rest of it for you."

"You're a star, Helen. Thank you." Tim thought his planets must be in some especially propitious alignment today.

"Well, don't thank me yet, Lemon. The restaurant might say no."

The planets moved out of alignment. The restaurant said no. Helen called Tim back after twenty minutes to say that Véronique had tried her best, but the restaurant insisted it was not equipped to deliver food – not even to next door – and, anyway, the hotel itself served food and it would be unthinkably rude to deliver a meal under the nose of the proprietor, who was also a friend.

"Oh, well, thank you for trying. Not to worry – the *salade Niçoise* is okay and I've still got some bread and cheese which I bought. I'm not going to starve."

Tim kept his eye on La Isla Bonita. Two o'clock passed, three o'clock … still nothing of note. One or two other vessels glided in and out of the harbour, but none of them passed anywhere near Draper's yacht. Tim started to worry. Had he mistaken the day? He knew he had not – and, anyway, here was the boat moored just outside Cassis at the appointed moment. Nevertheless, he called Tabi to ask him to double-check Andropov's message. Yes, it said the first of June. Now, a worse thought occurred to Tim: might the delivery have taken place during the brief period in the small hours of the night when Tim had slept? Three a.m. on the first of June was just as much the first of June as midday or three p.m. Shit, he should have gone to bed as soon as the crew members had done so – instead of going downstairs and stuffing his face with that bloody apricot tart – and then he should have risen at midnight. Tim started to feel a little nauseous and began to sweat. But then, he reasoned, if La Isla Bonita had already taken delivery, wouldn't it have set sail by now? This thought calmed him somewhat. Four o'clock passed … five o'clock approached and the sun was just beginning to dip. Fuck, what if he had missed it …?

FIFTY-EIGHT

In the late afternoon light, Tim saw a large naval vessel appear in the distance to the east. He assumed it was a French destroyer on its way to Marseilles. He looked through his binoculars, but the ship was still too far away to make it out clearly. After observing the ship for ten minutes or so, Tim began to get the impression it was actually heading straight towards Cassis. He continued to train his binoculars upon it. Now Tim began to notice odd things about the warship. It was not battleship grey, as you might expect a battleship to be, but brilliant white. The bridge bristled with radar and communications equipment and there appeared to be a helicopter pad on a foredeck, but there was no sign the vessel was armed. Tim leapt to his feet, knocking over his chair. He could not hold the binoculars steady – his hands were trembling with a mixture of excitement and sudden incipient terror. La Isla Bonita was an impressive yacht, but this new Leviathan spoke of an awesome and, in the wrong hands, potentially terrifying power. Tim's stomach suddenly dropped as the enormity of what might come to pass truly hit him for the first time. He was a simple and rather clumsy human being perched four storeys up in a tiny and quite bare hotel room, yet the fate of the city of London and of the world's financial markets very possibly depended upon him. He tried to steady his breathing. He realised he was completely soaked in sweat. He swapped the binoculars for the camera and took shot after shot of the looming vessel.

The mighty craft seemed to be slowing. If La Isla Bonita was a mile or so out to sea, the huge ship was coming to a halt about a third of the distance again beyond the yacht. Tim trained his binoculars on the ship. An anchor spooled into the sea. As the ship slewed around, for the first time Tim caught sight of the name: Bucephalus. He was sure he was right. He made a fumbling grab for his mobile and nearly sent it spinning out of the window. He called the office.

"Tim?" It was Margaret.

"Maggie … Bucephalus …"

"Alexander's horse."

215

"Sorry?"

"Alexander the Great's horse."

"Oh, yes." Tim paused for a second. "That may already give me my answer. Alexander's proud steed, Alexei's proud vessel … I think Andropov's flagship is also called Bucephalus, isn't it?"

"Andropov's? Yes, I believe you're right. Is there some development?"

"It's here. The rendezvous is really happening."

Maggie went silent for a moment. "Hold on, Tim. I'm putting you on speaker." Tim could hear her calling to the rest of the team. "Gordon, everyone, it's Tim. I'm putting him on speaker. Andropov's megayacht has arrived in Cassis. Tim, go on, we're all listening."

"Hi everyone. Jesus, it's a bloody big boat – pardon my French. I thought it was a naval destroyer." Tim was gabbling.

"Tim," Gordon intervened. "Take a deep breath. Slow down."

"Yuh, sorry. Andropov's flagship – Bucephalus – it's just arrived in Cassis. It's just this minute dropped anchor a little way out to sea – just beyond Draper's yacht."

"Any sign of the exchange taking place?" Gordon again.

"No, no, the ship's literally just arrived this minute." Tim lifted his binoculars. "However, I can see activity on both of the two boats. Hold on, I'm putting my mobile on speaker as well." He put the phone on the table and switched to speaker mode. "Yuh, several people toing and froing on the Bucephalus. And the two crewmen on La Isla Bonita are out on deck watching."

"Take some photos, Tim," said Gordon. "As many of the individuals as you can and then the package when it appears."

"Will do." Tim watched in silence through his binoculars for a second, then picked up his camera and started to shoot.

"Any change, Lemon?"

"No sign of the package yet. Light's beginning to fade a bit for these pictures." Tim took a few more photographs. He lowered the camera. "I've no idea whether this is going to be five minutes or five hours – shall I call you back when it looks as though the exchange is taking place?"

"Tabi, can't we get this on satellite?" asked Gordon.

216

"We're locked onto Draper's boat and I should be able to identify Andropov's beside it, but we've got nothing with high resolution photography overhead at the moment. Tim has the grandstand view."

"Okay, yes, Tim, please call in again when the cargo appears."

"Sure."

"And, Tim, feather in your cap ... but don't miss a thing of what's going on out there."

"Thanks, Gordon. And, don't worry, I won't." Well, grudging praise from Gordon was something at least, thought Tim.

Less than fifteen minutes later, Tim was back on the phone. As before, he put his mobile on speaker mode so that he could continue using the binoculars and camera while talking.

"Hi. Tim again."

"Okay, you're on speaker." This time it was Helen who answered.

"The Bucephalus has just put a launch in the water and it's coming round to a kind of side deck which has opened out from the hull of the ship. Looks like two men in the launch, one on the side deck. Hang on! Here it comes! Two men carrying what looks like a wooden crate – about the size of a large tea chest. Can't see any markings." Tim set the camera to take a continuous sequence of photos and fired off a series of twenty or thirty shots. "Crate's being loaded onto the launch ... Now four men in the launch ... Launch now pushing off and heading towards Draper's yacht. I can see Draper's crewmen on the diving platform at the rear of the yacht – obviously waiting to receive." Tim watched the passage of the launch as it made the short crossing. "Launch closing in ... Okay, the launch has docked with La Isla Bonita. Stern of the boat swinging out of view a bit, but I can see they're unloading the crate ... The four crew from the launch all seem to be coming on board the yacht. Crate being taken into the yacht and all six men going inside." Tim switched the binoculars to thermal imaging. The binoculars registered a faint blurry heat signal from the group of men inside the boat, but gave no clear indication of what was going on. "Can't see much at the moment – they're all inside. Let me send you these pictures, then call you back in a minute."

Tim popped the memory card out of the camera, inserted it into his laptop and relayed the photographs to London. Meanwhile, he kept his eye on La Isla Bonita, but there was no sign of the crew re-emerging. For thirty minutes, Tim held the binoculars or the night scope locked on the boat. When using the binoculars, he alternated between the conventional optical view and the thermal image. He could detect the crew moving about and could see figures apparently descending to a lower level, but for the moment all members of the group remained inside the yacht.

Gordon called, impatient to hear what was happening. Tim reported what little he could see.

"Looking at your pictures," said Gordon, "the crate doesn't give us much clue as to what's inside it, except, as Maggie has just pointed out, it couldn't be gold bullion – if it were gold, two men couldn't lift a crate of that size. On the other hand, unfortunately, it remains perfectly feasible that it could contain a nuclear device."

Shortly after Gordon's call, all six crew members appeared on deck. There was a general exchange of handshakes, back-slapping and embraces. Three of the four men from the Bucephalus clambered back onto their launch, leaving the fourth with the two men from La Isla Bonita. In the dying light, Tim took as many photographs as he could of the man who was remaining behind with the crew of Draper's yacht. As the launch headed back to the Bucephalus, Tim called London and explained what he had seen. At the same time, he relayed through his latest pictures.

"Getting too dark, Tim." Tabi had joined the call. "Can't see much on your photos – I'll have to try and enhance them."

"Sure," said Tim. "Launch now at the Bucephalus … Crew back on board the mother ship and launch being hoisted out of the water."

Within a few minutes, Tim saw the Bucephalus reel in its anchor. With a great churning of the waters at the stern, the mighty vessel heaved about on its axis and steamed off in the direction from which it had come. Tim passed all this on to his colleagues and then, with an apparent lull in the activity, signed off on the call for the moment.

After a further twenty minutes or so, Tim spotted that the three men had emerged and were putting La Isla Bonita's own little launch into the water. Were they bringing the crate ashore? It didn't seem so. The launch set off with the three men on board, but – Tim was pretty certain – not with the crate. The launch disappeared among the

218

boats in the harbour. Tim readied his camera. As he had anticipated, within a couple of minutes the men appeared on the harbour front. The street lights and the light from the restaurants, cafés and shops provided more than adequate illumination for Tim to take several reasonably clear shots of the new member of the crew – perhaps in his fifties, sharp faced, with rimless glasses and slicked-back hair. He saw the three men enter a restaurant – not *Les Calanques* this time, but one further along the street. Tim sent off the photographs with a brief covering message that the men had come ashore, apparently to have dinner.

After his several lengthy phone calls, the battery on Tim's mobile was very low. He plugged the phone into the wall socket to recharge and went back to the window. A middle-aged couple were inspecting the menu of the restaurant which the three crewmen had just entered. A few doors along, the teenage girls whom Tim had seen the evening before emerged from a boutique, pointed excitedly to something in the window and bustled back inside. Tim turned his gaze from the street and again looked out beyond the lights and shadows of the quietly swaying boats in the harbour to the twilit ocean. La Isla Bonita, deck lights twinkling, rocked gently on the inky sea. A thought suddenly leapt into Tim's mind. He pushed it away as faintly preposterous. But surely it wasn't so preposterous: a great opportunity had unexpectedly presented itself. If the crew were having dinner, Tim had at the very least an hour and probably two to swim out to the boat and inspect the crate.

FIFTY-NINE

Tim's head spun for a moment. He tried to keep calm and to think clearly. He should ring London to let them know he was considering swimming out to Draper's yacht and to get clearance from Gordon. He didn't want another dressing down. But there was no way Gordon would sanction such a spur-of-the-moment solo foray. He wouldn't trust Tim to carry out the venture without blundering; he would say the plan was half-baked, Tim was ill-prepared and the escapade was altogether far too risky; he would cite the pile of paperwork needed for proper authorisation ... On the other hand, if Tim told no one, what was the downside? If he came back empty-handed, he wouldn't breathe a word and no one would be any the wiser. But if he found unequivocal proof that the crate contained nuclear materials ... well, sure, he might still get a rap on the knuckles for acting without London's prior clearance, but he would have pretty much single-handedly stitched together all the evidence Gordon would need to order with complete confidence the immediate seizure of the boat and its crew, its owner and his partner in crime. Gordon would be forced to acknowledge that Tim, having been handed nothing more than an unpromising case of a drug overdose, had brought to light a nuclear conspiracy and had successfully pursued the case to a definitive conclusion. Tim was resolved. However, he had to concede that one of Gordon's putative objections was well-founded: his lack of preparedness. Unlike the secret agents of fiction, Tim had no scuba gear, no underwater jet propulsion ... in fact, it had not occurred to Tim that he might need to take a swim and he did not even have swimming trunks. No matter, his underpants would have to do. He reckoned he could swim out to the boat in at most half an hour or so, which should leave plenty of time to find and inspect the crate.

Tim's heart began to thump with rising exhilaration. He craned out of his window and looked off to his left. As far as he could see, the town's beach was pretty much in darkness and seemed deserted. With luck, from the beach he could slip into the water unnoticed. He would need his phone – to photograph the evidence and possibly to call into the office from the boat so that he could immediately describe what he had found ... assuming of course that he could get a signal out in the bay. But how could he prevent the phone from getting wet? He didn't have a suitable waterproof bag. He looked around the little room ... the proprietor had mentioned a laundry bag. Tim opened the drawer in the table. He was in luck – the laundry bag was plastic. He noticed that it had vent holes in the bottom, so he tied the bottom in a tight knot. He disconnected and checked his phone: two bars of charge. If he switched the phone off now, it should allow a brief call from the boat and a photo or two. He held the power button down – the screen faded. He dropped the phone into the laundry bag and tied the top of the bag in another tight knot. He swapped the yellow polo shirt he was wearing for a black T-shirt. The jeans he had on were already his darkest trousers. Slipping his bare feet into a pair of black flip-flops, he grabbed his room key and left the room.

SIXTY

Tabi stared at the photo identification report and exhaled. He forwarded the report to the rest of the team and went over to Gordon and Helen. The three of them were the last ones remaining in the office at this hour of the evening. Tabi leaned across Helen's desk and clicked open the message he had just sent.

"Take a look," he said.

Helen and Gordon stared at the report.

Helen looked up at Gordon. "Doesn't leave much room for doubt, does it? Must say I'm beginning to feel a bit bad for having generally given Lemon such short shrift over Draper."

"I have to acknowledge we've come a long way from Lucy Trenchard," said Gordon. "I know this man by repute."

The report confirmed the identity of the crew member who had joined La Isla Bonita from the Bucephalus. Konstantin Suskin was a former military engineer and munitions specialist, whose expertise extended to nuclear weaponry. He had garnered an unpleasant reputation early in his career during the Soviet occupation of Afghanistan, when he was rumoured to have used Afghan prisoners to test the effectiveness of experimental munitions. He had later graduated to the Soviet nuclear programme, where he was engaged in the design and construction of nuclear weaponry. He was thought to have been involved in Soviet efforts to develop a nuclear 'suitcase bomb' – one small enough for a single individual to deliver to its target. Over the past decade, he had apparently disappeared from the military scene; however, he had quite frequently been spotted placing hefty bets in the casinos of Monte Carlo, which suggested he was somehow earning a more than sufficient living.

"I think we can take it that he's not in Cassis to challenge the crew of Draper's yacht to a hand of *chemin de fer*," observed Gordon drily, as he studied the detail of the report.

"Do you think we should just notify the French security services and send in the French police to seize the boat and the crew?" asked Helen.

"I've been thinking about that," replied Gordon. "I have several reservations. Firstly, we're now pretty sure we know what's going on, but we don't yet have one hundred percent confirmation of what's in that crate and where it's going. I realise the possibility looks increasingly remote, but if the crate contains something innocuous, then we end up looking like right Charlies in the eyes of the French – which I don't wish to happen. Secondly, if we allow Andropov and Draper to play out their hand just a little further – in other words, if we catch La Isla Bonita sailing into British waters with a nuclear bomb on board – then we have pretty much incontrovertible proof of their intentions. Obviously, the mere possession of a nuclear weapon is already an offence, but at the moment we can't actually prove what they intend to do with it. Thirdly, the French rarely say 'Yes, Gordon, we'll do as you ask' – there's nearly always some kind of philosophical debate to complicate matters. Fourthly, the French government may get it into its head that this is a moment to exercise diplomacy with Russia rather than to demand action. I'm hoping that somewhere along the line we can snare Andropov and his cronies as well as Draper – though I think we'll need some luck to carry that one off. We'll probably need Andropov to be in London at the very moment we seize the boat, so that we can bring him in at the same time. If he's safely in Russia, I would guess the chances of extraditing him are nil – as usual. But the overall point here is, if the French become involved, I think the political ramifications become a great deal more complex. Fifthly ... am I on to my fifth point? ... losing track slightly ... anyway, yes, fifthly, we're keeping a close watch on the boat and we expect it to sail straight into our arms. Finally – and this is really a matter of selfish pride and I should probably set this reason aside – ..." Gordon's chest swelled even as he made this disclaimer. "... my feeling is, we've uncovered this plot, we've handled the matter from first to last and we should be in a position to bring the affair to a successful conclusion. We don't need the French to step in at the last moment and claim it as a victory for France."

Gordon stood and went over to a large screen on the wall. The screen displayed a map of Europe, extending from the coast of North Africa in the south to the Arctic in the north and from the Urals in the east to the Atlantic Ocean in the west. A winking red dot just to the south-east of Marseilles indicated the satellite lock on Draper's boat. The SBS team in Gibraltar was marked with a green light and a second green dot rounding the Breton peninsula indicated the frigate on its way to the northern waters of the Bay of Biscay. Gordon turned to Tabi.

"And there's a sub just out in the Atlantic also awaiting our call, yes?"

"Should be, yes."

"Make sure that's a definite yes and get it on the map as well. It should be possible for us to intercept La Isla Bonita in the open ocean well before it enters the Channel." Gordon indicated the general area where the Atlantic met the Bay of Biscay. "Or, in the absolute worst event, to send the bloody thing to the ocean depths."

"Should we be readying other naval vessels and the coast guard, just in case?" asked Helen.

"Well, let's hope the yacht is under our control long before that becomes necessary. And, anyway, for the moment La Isla Bonita is several days' sailing away from Britain." Gordon turned towards his side office. "Helen, give Tim a call and let him know who we're dealing with. I'll go and update the DG, the PM and COBRA."

"Will do, Gordon."

Helen dialled Tim's mobile, but to her slight surprise went straight through to his voicemail. She tried the number of the hotel, but there was no answer. She tried Tim's mobile again, and again went straight through to his voicemail. Upon her second attempt to reach the hotel, the phone was answered.

"Oui, Hôtel du Port. Bonsoir."

"Bonsoir, monsieur. Je voudrais parler avec Monsieur Lemon, s'il vous plaît."

"Un instant, madame."

Helen was connected with the phone in Tim's room. It rang several times before the proprietor came back on the line.

"Je crois qu'il n'est pas là, madame. Je suppose qu'il est sorti. Enfin, c'est l'heure du dîner ..."

"Oui. Alors, merci, monsieur."

"Je vous en prie, madame."

The hotelier's guess that Tim had gone in search of food was most probably correct – particularly in view of Tim's recent gastronomic fantasies. Still, Helen found it odd that Tim had not let his team know he was going out – and especially odd that he seemed to have turned his phone off. Could he be following the crew of La Isla Bonita somewhere? But Tim's last message had said the crew were heading to a restaurant – surely they would only just have started their dinner? Perhaps Tim had followed them into the restaurant and was keeping watch on them while eating at a nearby table? Even if that were the case and Tim did not want to draw attention to himself, he only had to set his phone to silent mode – he did not need to switch it off completely. Helen frowned in consternation.

SIXTY-ONE

Tim had rounded the corner on the Quai Saint-Pierre, the street which skirted the harbour, and had crossed over the Esplanade Charles de Gaulle which bordered the beach. Street lights along the esplanade cast alternating pools of dim light and deeper shadow across the sand and down to the water's edge. Tim descended a short flight of stone steps onto the beach. He startled a young couple embracing in the shadows. The boy and girl stared at Tim for a second; Tim stared back. The couple turned and ascended the stone steps onto the esplanade. Tim saw that the far end of the beach – a couple of hundred yards distant – was in almost complete darkness. He also noted a rocky outcrop where he could hide his clothes. He kicked off his flip-flops, scooped them up and set off along the beach at a jog, while keeping an eye on the esplanade to make sure no one was watching him. A few cars passed by and the occasional pedestrian wandered along, but no one paid any attention to Tim. He looked back and saw that the young couple had disappeared.

Tim stepped in among the rocks and dropped his flip-flops onto the sand. He pulled off his T-shirt and started to unzip his jeans. He suddenly realised his underpants were bright white – he was afraid they might catch the street lights and draw attention to him as he waded into the sea. Should he leave them behind? Even though his whole intention was to be seen by nobody, he somehow felt he would be vulnerable if he abandoned them altogether. What if someone happened upon his clothes and walked off with them? He decided to put the underpants in the plastic bag with his mobile and take them with him. Stripped naked and in a half crouch among the rocks, he glanced about him. He slid his room key into a crevice in the rocks. He bundled his jeans inside his black T-shirt and stuffed them with his flip-flops into a larger but still unobtrusive gap between two boulders. The laundry bag containing his phone and underpants had a drawstring which he tied around his wrist. Before tightening the knot at the top of the bag, he had expelled all of the air, so that he could now just about conceal the bag in his bunched fist. He looked about again, then ran the twenty yards to the water's edge.

He stepped in. Jesus, it was freezing! He hadn't reckoned on the water being so bloody cold. Gingerly, he waded out a little further. He gave a shudder. He was not sure he could make it if the water was this cold. He pressed on. He encountered a warmer current of water. But then as he reached waist depth, the water became freezing again. His scrotum clenched against the cold as he gave another shudder. He looked back at the shore. He decided he would try to swim, but would turn back if the cold was unbearable. He released the laundry bag from his tight grip, so that it floated at his wrist. As he reached forwards into the water, the raw knuckles on his right hand briefly smarted, but the sensation was quickly lost in the cold. He pushed off in a gentle crawl, trying to keep as quiet as possible, but with the laundry bag awkwardly slapping the water at each stroke. Another twenty or thirty yards further out, Tim again encountered a band of warmer water. The action of swimming also seemed to help mitigate the cold.

Tim was a strong swimmer. Any kind of ball sport and he was hopelessly uncoordinated. Middle distance running, he was okay. Swimming, his clumsiness seemed somehow to dissolve away. He had represented his school and university in freestyle and as a member of the relay teams. And the Security Service required their operatives to keep physically fit – not to SAS standards perhaps, but front-line staff were not simply desk-bound pen-pushers or keyboard-bashers.

Tim found a rhythm in his stroke and laboured on for ten minutes, fifteen, twenty … For a while he felt he was keeping the cold at bay, but then he started to feel incredibly hungry. His stomach was suddenly an aching hollow. He realised he hadn't eaten for several hours and he lacked calories to burn. The yacht seemed barely any closer. Only if he looked back to the shore could he see that he had already covered quite a distance. He struggled on … His rhythm slowed as his strength began to fade.

But at last the yacht began to loom. Tim found last reserves of energy and stepped up his rhythm again for the final stretch. This close, the yacht seemed like a house floating at sea. Tim suddenly had an awful thought: would the boat be locked just like a house? Would it be impossible to gain entry? Tim's heart sank a little at the thought as he swam round to the stern. He grasped the diving platform as it rose and fell. As the platform bobbed down, he hauled himself on board and collapsed on the wooden deck. He glanced at his watch: it had taken him thirty-five minutes to get here. It felt like an hour and thirty-five minutes. Cold and exhaustion hit him and he began to shake uncontrollably. But he couldn't afford to rest and the best way to get warm was to dry off and go inside the boat … if he could.

SIXTY-TWO

Tim stood, still trembling violently. There was only the lightest breeze, but it brought his skin out in goose bumps. His teeth chattered. He saw that a short flight of steps led up to the main deck of the yacht. But now it occurred to him that, though he was on a boat, he should probably not leave tell-tale wet footprints everywhere as he walked around. He undid the laundry bag and took out his underpants, then used them as a cloth to wipe himself down. He had to wring out the underpants and repeat the exercise several times before he was reasonably dry. He gave the underpants a final wring and put them on. Cold and damp, they sent another convulsion up his spine.

He ascended the short flight of steps. The first thing he encountered was a neat pile of fresh towels. "Typical," he muttered through still chattering teeth. There were even a couple of discarded towels which he could perfectly well have used without running any risk at all of anyone noticing he had been there. In fact, he was shaking so violently with cold, he cast caution aside and took one of the fresh towels from the pile. He wrapped it around himself. The soft, warm, enveloping material was like a loved one's embrace. He would put the towel back in place before he left.

Now for the door. Tim took the handle, closed his eyes and pushed ... Thank God, the door opened. He stepped into the main living area of Draper's yacht. As he closed the door behind him, his first sensation was one of warmth. Cosseted in the towel and the warm air of the cabin, he felt slightly restored and his trembling began to subside. His stomach still ached with hunger, however. And now he realised there was another problem he had completely overlooked in his impetuous haste to swim out to the boat: the cabins were largely in darkness and, of course, he could not possibly go around switching lights on in case the crew caught sight of this from the shore. The living area he was in was at any rate not quite dark, but rather penumbral – the outside deck lights cast enough of a glow for Tim to distinguish the outlines, light or dark hues and matt or

229

shiny textures of what looked like pale leather sofas and armchairs and glass-topped coffee tables. As he took a step forward, his toes sank into deep carpeting. The entire space seemed to be lined with fine wood panelling, while a huge plasma screen filled one bulkhead. Peering ahead, Tim saw the living area was divided by what appeared to be a carved wooden screen, beyond which stood an elegant glass dining table with seating for a dozen guests. At the far corner of the room, Tim noticed a faint light coming from what he guessed to be the galley.

As Tim's eyes adjusted, he could see that the crate was certainly nowhere in the sitting and dining areas. As he turned to look about, his towel knocked something … Tim held his breath as the barely visible object rattled on the glass top of a side table. He expected a crash, but fortunately none came. He reluctantly decided he should abandon his towel for the moment and dropped it onto the seat of a nearby chair. He would collect it and replace it at the bottom of the pile of towels when he left the boat. He took care to keep the laundry bag containing his phone tightly bunched in his hand. He advanced to the galley. On the counter, there was a well stocked bowl of fruit. Tim decided that a single banana would not be missed from the large bunch which rested on the top. He also noticed a bowl of individually wrapped chocolates and took a couple. Having wolfed down banana and chocolates, he found a rubbish bin and pushed the chocolate wrappers beneath the other waste. He decided the banana skin would be too conspicuous and returned outside to throw it overboard. As he stepped back inside, he felt a new degree of warmth and energy return.

He remembered from the plans of the yacht that the master cabin was on this level at the front of the boat and that guest cabins were on the deck below. The captain's cabin was located on the upper deck behind the bridge and the remaining crew's quarters were accessed via a separate staircase and were tucked beneath the master suite. The crate was surely hidden in one of these several cabins. But Tim needed a torch. He thought about his mobile phone, but decided using it as a torch would kill the battery immediately. A quick look round the galley revealed nothing of use. Tim wondered whether he might find a torch on the bridge. He went back towards the dining

230

area and found the staircase to the upper deck. The interior of the upper deck was in much deeper darkness than the main deck and Tim could not immediately see the door to the bridge. He did his best to visualise the floor plan of the yacht. Feeling his way along and praying he didn't send any unseen object flying, Tim found his way to what he guessed was the right door. He eased it open ... his guess was correct. Furthermore, the yacht's huge bank of instrument panels cast a glow throughout the room. The bridge was an astonishing sight: a temple to marine high technology. Set before the deep leather chairs of the captain and first officer, the bank of illuminated computer screens displayed plans of the ship, gauges measuring all of the ship's functions, radar and sonar, ocean charts ... Tim glanced at the chart currently on display: it showed the eastern Atlantic running from the mouth of the Mediterranean up the coast of Portugal and Spain and then, to the south-west, extending down to the Canary Islands. Doubtless, the crew had been plotting their passage around the Iberian peninsula and on to Britain. Beneath the bank of screens was a series of lockers. The first contained life jackets and flares, the second ship's manuals and charts of the traditional kind, the third an assortment of items including ... a torch.

Shielding the beam with his hand so that light was cast only below window level, Tim quickly inspected the saloon on the upper deck – again, no crate – and then went back down to the main deck. He gave the living area another cursory look now that he had the torch, but his first assessment had been correct. Heading to the forward part of the ship, he pushed open the door to the master bedroom. The room was luxurious almost to the point of caricature – huge bed, leather chairs and leather-topped desk, walnut panelling throughout, massive plasma television and, mounted on the wall above the bed, an etching of a minotaur astride a sleeping woman in a style which looked vaguely familiar to Tim – he peered more closely – a Picasso, no less ... and another above the desk, this time of a naked female toreador tossed on the back of a bull, then displayed on a side table a small bronze statuette of a bull throwing back its horns – bulls were clearly something of a theme in Draper's bedroom – and on another side table exquisite glass ornaments – Lalique? Baccarat? – Tim had no idea. He judiciously gave them a

231

wide berth. Tim thought back to Draper and Andropov's encrypted correspondence: 'Let's pop the cork on La Isla Bonita mid-June.' Did that really mean trigger the bomb on board the boat? Had Draper really spent tens of millions on his motor yacht, lavishing care on its design and stuffing it with treasures, only so that he could vaporise the whole lot shortly after its maiden voyage? It made no sense. Glancing at his watch, Tim realised he could not afford to linger. Clearly, the crate was not here either. He took a quick look inside the ensuite marble floored and wood panelled bathroom with its two person jacuzzi: no, no crate.

Tim ducked out of the master bedroom and took the staircase down to the guest cabins deeper in the bowels of the ship. He inspected the first cabin: not quite as sumptuous as Draper's quarters, but still up to the standard of the very finest hotel room ... but no sign of the crate. Next cabin, the same. So too the third. Fourth and final cabin ... the door was locked. Tim stepped back. Surely, the crate must be here. Where might he find a spare key to the cabin door? On the bridge? He set foot on the stairs, but then froze. The rumble of machinery echoed somewhere inside the boat. Tim held his breath and listened. Was some automatic process underway or, Jesus buggery fuck, was the crew back already? Tim tiptoed up the stairs. He peered round the bulkhead at the top of the stairs and then crept into the living area. He stopped in his tracks. He could hear an outboard motor turning over and the sound of voices. The rumble was the tailgate of the yacht being raised so that the launch could be hauled inside. He was fucked, he was well and truly fucked ... His mind raced. Could he get out onto the deck, creep round to the front of the ship and drop overboard? Even if he wasn't seen, he'd surely be heard hitting the water. It was a ten or fifteen foot drop. He couldn't think of any other option. He crouched and ran to the door through which he had first entered. Still hunched down low, he raised his head a little to check where the crewmen were and to make sure he could make a dash for it without being seen. Oh, shit, shit – one of the crewmen was already coming up the steps to the main deck. Tim had no time to do anything! The crewman stopped and turned back to speak to his colleagues. Tim spun and scuttled as fast he could back to the stairs. He padded downstairs as quickly and quietly as he could. At the foot of the stairs, he stopped and listened again. He heard the door on the main deck open and the crewman calling back to his colleagues. Lights went on in the main living area and sent a sudden wash of brightness down the stairwell to Tim. Tim held his breath and quietly turned the handle to the cabin door nearest to him – the one opposite the locked door. He eased the door open and slipped into the cabin. He stood at the door, keeping it ajar so that he could hear what was happening on the deck above.

A few distant clangs and then a renewed rumble signalled that the launch was stowed and the tailgate was closing again. The voices in the living room above became three. Tim could not understand a word, but the tone was one of jokey banter. Suddenly, the conversation stopped. When it resumed, the tone was staccato, interrogative … Tim suddenly realised that – idiot, idiot, idiot! – he had left the towel on a chair in the living room. The crew were now rapidly moving about the ship, shouting to each other. Tim closed the cabin door. He still had the torch and now flashed it round the room. There was no obvious place to hide: the bed had a solid base; there was a wardrobe which he could probably squeeze into, but he doubted he could keep silent in the awkward, confined and resonating space and anyway the crew might take a look inside to check it was empty … Tim heard footsteps rapidly descending the flight of steps to the guest cabins. He went into the bathroom. He heard the door to the cabin opposite being unlocked … A couple of seconds later, the crewman shouted up to his colleagues – presumably confirming that the crate was there and untouched. But now it seemed the crewman was checking the other cabins. Tim closed the bathroom door. There was a double cupboard beneath the washbasin. Tim opened the cupboard and crammed himself inside the tiny space. The torch and his mobile phone clonked on the floor of the cupboard. He pushed them against the side. He pulled the first cupboard door closed. As he pulled the second towards him, he heard the door to the cabin open and the light go on. He eased the cupboard door towards him, finally using a fingernail … a magnet pulled it the last centimetre and it closed with a click. Tim held his breath. The bathroom door opened and the light went on. Tim could hear the blood beating in his ears. The crewman seemed to stand and listen

233

for hours, though it could not have been more than a second or two. The bathroom light went out, then the light to the cabin; the cabin door was closed.

Tim waited. He didn't dare make a sound. He thought he heard the crewman go back upstairs. Still he waited. He started to feel cramp in his back, his legs, his arms ... He eased the cupboard door open, but could not prevent the click of the magnet. He listened again. He could hear no sound on this deck. He opened the other cupboard door and rolled quietly onto the towelling rug. He lay on the rug listening for a further few seconds. The guest cabins and stairwell remained silent. He stretched out and then stood. He tiptoed to the cabin door and listened once again. The voices of the crew were distant. After several more seconds at the door, Tim eased it open an inch and held his breath. He could hear that the three crewmen were all back on the main deck. The tone of their conversation had settled – with luck, they had convinced themselves that one of them had left the towel on the chair. Tim quietly closed the door.

SIXTY-THREE

Helen sat alone in the office. It was ten p.m. and there was still no new word from Tim. She held her phone against her chin and stared at her unchanging email inbox. Tim's mobile was still not answering; the hotel had still not seen him; he had not sent any message since the email two hours earlier with the photographs of Suskin. Helen told herself her concern was foolish: two hours was not so long and Tim was almost certainly eating dinner in a restaurant where he could keep an eye on the movements of the crew of La Isla Bonita; he had spent much of the early evening on the phone to London and his battery was probably now flat; he hadn't sent an update because for the moment he had nothing new to report.

Helen realised that her concern was partly because she was still thinking about Nick – and also about Tim's close call at the hands of Derek Barnes. In both cases, Helen could not shake off the feeling that some responsibility rested with her. Nick's gruesome death before her very own eyes in particular had affected her deeply. In her eight years in the service, this was the first time a close colleague had been killed. Trevor had suffered two years of captivity in Gaza; a former colleague had been shot in the leg; another former colleague had an unfortunate habit of getting into altercations and, after suffering a broken arm and smashed cheekbone at the hands of a disaffected informer, had been quietly encouraged to leave the Service ... but no one had died. Helen continued to punish herself with thoughts that she should not have committed Nick to the field or at least should have kept him at her side during the raid. And what if Derek Barnes had successfully landed the karate blow aimed at Tim? It was she, Helen, who had missed the police message concerning Barnes ... even though, on reflection, she believed it would have made little difference if she had seen it. Tim had anyway been due to leave the eco-group that morning and had not indicated that he felt himself to be in any personal danger. Even if Helen had read the police message, she would almost certainly have waited until after Tim's departure before sending in officers so that Tim would have been able to make a clean exit without becoming entangled in the police proceedings. Furthermore, it seemed the circumstances of Tim's discovery had been the purest bad luck. And surely Gordon was right about Nick – it was in the nature of the job that officers in the field sometimes faced mortal danger. But somehow Helen's telling herself all of this did little to assuage her feelings of grief and guilt.

Nor was it simply that Helen's thoughts about Nick and about Tim's earlier narrow escape sharpened her concern for Tim now. Over the past few days, she had begun to reassess her whole attitude towards all of her colleagues. Helen's would-be toughness and curtness were not just a silly and affected pose: she truly thought a woman had to be tough and unsentimental to progress in any profession and she considered this to be especially true of the security services. Her attitude came from her mother. Her father had left home when she was three and had gone to live in the States. She had seen him only once every two or three years and felt he was a stranger to her life. She had been brought up by her mother, who had never remarried. Her mother had started her professional life as a lowly legal secretary, but had studied to become a solicitor and was now a senior partner in the law firm for which she had always worked. Helen knew it had taken a great deal of single-minded determination and professionalism for her mother to achieve this position. She felt she owed it to her mother and to herself to be similarly driven and businesslike in the pursuit of her career.

Helen rose and went to a water cooler at the side of the office. She filled a plastic beaker and returned to her desk. A decade or more earlier she had nearly become a travel agent in her home town of Brighton. From the age of sixteen, she had had a Saturday and holiday job working at a travel agency owned by a friend of her mother's. Of her own initiative, Helen had quietly overhauled the agency's filing system; she had discovered that a quite large incentive payment owed to the agency by a major tour operator had never been claimed and had secured the belated payment; after her mother had joined a wine-tasting tour of the Loire, Helen had established links with the wine tour operator and had thereby brought new business to the agency – and all this before her eighteenth birthday and while still at school. She had planned to go directly from school to the University of Sussex to take a degree in Business Studies and French. But at that moment the owner of the travel agency had had the misfortune to discover she was suffering from breast cancer. She had asked Helen if she might consider taking a gap year before university so that Helen could help run the agency while the friend underwent treatment. Helen had agreed. Sadly, her mother's friend had died only a few months later. Helen and her mother had then been a little shocked to find that the departed friend, having no close family of her own, in a newly written will had left the travel agency to Helen and her mother. Helen had briefly considered abandoning her degree to run the agency on a full-time basis, but instead had decided to employ a manager while she pursued her studies, with a view to returning to the business upon graduation. But mid-university two things had happened more or less simultaneously: a larger travel firm, operating across the south of England, had offered to buy out Helen and her mother, and then Helen, tagging along with a couple of university friends, had attended a speech given by Dame Stella Rimington, former head of MI5, on the defence of liberty. Overnight, Helen had reached a decision: she and her mother had sold up – though they still retained a holding in the larger agency and Helen still received regular dividend payments which supplemented her MI5 salary – and, then, upon graduation, Helen had joined the Security Service.

Helen shook her head and looked around the empty office. Where had these nostalgic thoughts suddenly come from? She did not usually indulge herself like this. She realised she had been thinking about Nick, Tim … the rest of her colleagues. Weighing the need to preserve professional detachment against the possibility of closer friendship with the members of her team. After what had happened to Nick and now that she took a step back and thought about it, she realised that her colleagues were the best friends she had. She really liked Tim and Tabi and she had really liked Nick. Trevor was mostly rather dour, but he was not difficult to work with and displayed occasional flashes of wry humour. Gordon was a bit pompous and tended to hog the glory when there was a departmental success – and perhaps he was a bit hard on Tim – but he generally listened to the

237

rest of the team and he certainly treated Helen with professional respect and trust. Maggie was a gem. Why was Helen always so brusque with all of them – and particularly so with the colleagues she liked the best? Why didn't she lighten up a little with these people? Yes, they all went out for drinks occasionally and had lunch or even dinner together from time to time, but she never really let her guard down. Surely, she could remain professional and ambitious, yet allow her defences to drop a little and perhaps give friendship half a chance? And what other intimate friendships did she have? She remained very close to her mother. In her early days with the Service, she had had a fairly serious boyfriend for several months, but he had grown fed up with her irregular hours and sometimes unexplained comings and goings – it hadn't been so much a matter of lack of trust as of inconvenience and the barrier to intimacy. After him, she had managed only a couple of short-lived flings. She saw some of her old school and university friends occasionally, but could not speak freely about her work and felt she had become increasingly distant with them …

Helen pushed aside her brooding thoughts. She looked at her watch: ten twenty. She was achieving nothing by sitting here. She decided to compose a brief message to Tim: 'Tim, mildly concerned…' She saw what she had written. She pulled a face and deleted 'Tim'. She resumed: 'Lemon, mildly concerned at lack of contact. Please confirm all OK and provide update – even if hour is very late.' She sent the message, closed down her computer and left the office.

SIXTY-FOUR

Tim sat on the cabin floor next to the door, which he held open a couple of inches. He was feeling cold and hungry again and now needed to pee as well. The crew were still toing and froing and conversing on the deck above. However, Tim had had time to take stock of his situation and realised he simply had to wait until the crew had all gone to bed. He would then be able to slip off the boat and swim back to shore. It was just unfortunate that the crew did not seem in any hurry to retire for the night.

As Tim continued listening, the conversation on the main deck seemed to break off. He could hear the crew moving to the front of the boat – he guessed they were taking either the forward stairs down to the crew's quarters or else the stairs up to the captain's quarters behind the bridge. Tim eased himself onto his feet. His muscles ached. He opened the cabin door a further six inches and held his breath. There did not seem to be any sound from the main deck. He tiptoed into the stairwell. It occurred to him to give the locked door another try in case the crewman who had checked the guest cabins had left it unlocked – but, again, to no avail. He padded up the flight of steps. Keeping his head at deck level, he peered round the bulkhead at the top of the stairs. Damn! One of the crew – the one who had joined from the Bucephalus – was still in the living room. He was sitting in front of a coffee table studying a laptop computer. Tim pulled back. Just then a mute growl reverberated from the aft of the ship, while a distant clatter emanated from somewhere to the fore. Tim's aching stomach convulsed into a knot. He gave a sudden involuntary shudder. As he listened in horror, the distant clatter came to an end and the growling reverberation found an even pitch. It was difficult to tell from Tim's position in the windowless middle of the ship, but ... oh, fuck ... surely the yacht was in motion. If Tim was going to make a break for it, it had to be now. But there was absolutely no way he could slip past the crew member. And if Tim was going to assault the man, he would first have to cover the several yards from the stairwell to the middle of the living room – which

239

would give the Russian ample time to raise the alarm. Even if Tim successfully overpowered the crewman and made it to the water, once in the water he would be a sitting duck. And if he rushed the man, whatever the outcome, the secrecy of MI5's operation would be blown. The pitching motion of the yacht was now unmistakeable as the boat gathered speed. Tim, clad only in his still slightly clammy underpants and with the laundry bag newly knotted and secured at his wrist in readiness for the anticipated swim, retreated back down the stairs. He quietly re-entered the cabin and stood in the darkness. His life was quite possibly in danger and, even if he managed to escape at some point, his career was surely sunk. He suddenly felt overcome with exhaustion.

SIXTY-FIVE

Helen woke with a start. She had forgotten to set her alarm and had overslept by some minutes. She grabbed her mobile ... no missed calls, no messages from Tim. She called his number and, as before, went straight to voicemail. Genuinely anxious now and angry with herself for having overslept, she hastily showered, dressed and headed in to work.

Helen had made up time and was only moments behind the rest of the team in reaching her desk. She quickly logged on to her screens.

"Anyone heard from Lemon?" she asked the floor in general.

"We assumed you'd spoken to him," said Trevor.

"I've been trying to get hold of him. No one's tried the hotel yet this morning, then?"

"Nope."

Helen dialled the number. *"Bonjour, monsieur. C'est encore la collègue de Monsieur Lemon. Je voudrais parler avec lui, s'il vous plaît."*

"Je crois qu'il n'est pas là depuis hier soir, madame."

"Vous en êtes sûr?"

"Pas cent pourcent, mais ..."

"Eh bien, est-ce que vous pouvez vérifier s'il est dans sa chambre? J'ai un message urgent pour lui."

"C'est à dire ... enfin, il me faudra quelques minutes ..."

Helen could hear that the hotelier was slightly put out by the request to go and make absolutely sure that Tim was not in his room. *"C'est vraiment urgent, monsieur."*

"Ben ... alors, si vous voudriez rappeller en cinq minutes, madame ..."

"Merci, monsieur. Vous êtes très gentil." Helen hoped that would be sufficient to placate him.

"Have you seen the map?" Trevor indicated the wall screen displaying the positions of La Isla Bonita, the Gibraltar team, the frigate and now the submarine as well.

241

"Fuck," said Helen. She could see that La Isla Bonita was no longer on the coast at Cassis, but was a good hundred miles or more out to sea. She waited less than four minutes before calling the hotel again.

"*Non, madame. Evidemment, il n'est pas là.*"

"*Ses affaires sont toujours là?*"

"*Oui, oui, madame, elles sont toutes là ... en peu en désordre peut-être – mais j'ai l'impression qu'il est toujours un peu comme ça. Peut-être qu'il a trouvé une petite amie – une* girlfriend *– quelque part aux alentours, non?*"

"*Alors, merci, monsieur. Désolée de vous avoir dérangé encore une fois.*"

"*De rien, madame. C'est un plaisir ...*"

Shit, thought Helen.

"He's not there?" asked Trevor.

"Him no, all his stuff yes. Hotel proprietor's guess is that he picked up some floozie and spent the night with her – which I have to say, unless Lemon's head has been completely turned by his love-in with the hippies, is about as unlikely a scenario as one could possibly imagine. And meanwhile his mobile's still not responding."

"Plus, the boat has set sail."

Helen went to Gordon's office. "Gordon, problem. We've had no word from Lemon since yesterday evening when he reported the yacht crew coming ashore and then sent us the photos of Suskin. His phone's not responding, even though I've tried to reach him repeatedly, and he doesn't appear to have been in his hotel room since around the time he last contacted us. And, meanwhile, La Isla Bonita has put to sea."

Gordon stood. "I saw the boat was on its way ..." His brow furrowed. "What is the fool up to?"

"I know you're not keen, but don't you think we should alert the French police?"

Gordon read Helen's expression. "Helen, of course the very last thing I want to do is to jeopardise the life of another member of the team, but if we can possibly avoid involving the French authorities..." Gordon studied a corner of his room for a second. "What's the name of Carter's man?"

"De Beauregard?"

"Yes ... who is he exactly? Does he work at the consulate?"

"No, the consulate is basically Carter, who's on holiday, and a secretary, who's manning the desk in his absence. If I've understood things correctly, de Beauregard is ex French military intelligence, now retired from the army; divides his time between Marseilles, where he has a small business, and Cassis, where he has a villa; very Anglophile, trustworthy, close friend of Carter, hankers after the old days and isn't averse to helping out ..."

"Ex French military intelligence ... I'd much rather keep this strictly in-house. However, perhaps we have little choice. See if you can get hold of de Beauregard. Ask him if he can get down there and make some enquiries. Send him pictures of Tim and the three crewmen so that he can ask some questions around Cassis harbour. But don't tell him any more than you have to."

SIXTY-SIX

The evening before, as La Isla Bonita had surged out to sea, Tim had recognised that he had no choice but to alert the office to his predicament. He had realised that he should call immediately, before the boat was too far from shore and the mobile signal lost. It had crossed his mind that the yacht probably offered a wifi link to a satellite connection, but he had assumed that usage would require a password and the facility would therefore be inaccessible to him. Hurriedly untying the plastic laundry bag, he had tipped his phone onto the soft carpet. A trickle of seawater had followed. He had pressed the power button on the phone … to no effect. He had thoroughly dried the phone, removing the battery and drying both that and the battery compartment. He had tried again … with no success. Either the phone had been damaged by the seawater or the battery had lost what little charge it had gained during its brief recharging at the hotel.

A short while later, quietly re-entering the stairwell, Tim had discovered that the lights on the main deck had been extinguished – the remaining crew member had presumably either retired to his quarters or gone up to the bridge to take a shift at the helm. Tim had crept back into his cabin and the bathroom and, with huge relief, had finally dared to take a pee – though sitting on the toilet in order to make as little noise as possible and then not daring to flush. He hoped that he would have an opportunity to flush later or else that this evidence of his presence would not be discovered until it made no difference. He had found a towelling robe in the wardrobe and had gratefully put this on. He had hung his clammy underpants in the shower cubicle to dry.

Conducting a further sweep of his cabin with his torch, he had found the room was equipped with a hotel-style minibar, which contained water, juice, nuts, mini rice crackers and chocolate. But he had also realised that the yacht had the capacity to remain at sea for several days and that these provisions might not be enough. After listening on the stairs for some time, he had sneaked up to the galley and had taken another banana, an apple, a tomato, a bread roll and a brioche, a couple of slices of ham from an already open packet, a couple of Babybel cheeses and a large bottle of mineral water. All of these items were in plentiful supply and he had judged that his little hoard would not be missed. He had used the laundry bag as a carrier bag – and had also thought he could use it later for his rubbish, so that when he left he could leave no trace of his presence in the cabin.

He had briefly debated whether he should also take a weapon in case he needed to defend himself – there was a knife-block containing a neat row of kitchen knives. But if he took one of these, the set would be conspicuously incomplete. And what might he do with it anyway? If the Russians discovered him and resorted to violence, it was most unlikely he could successfully take on all three of them – a knife battle would almost certainly result in his death. And he could hardly creep around in the dead of night slaughtering the crew members, nor even for that matter initiate violence if he was discovered – for a start, he and his team lacked conclusive proof of the crewmen's guilty complicity in Draper and Andropov's scheme and then, even if Tim had been in possession of such proof, it was certainly not his place to despatch summary justice. Dismissal from his job was one thing, imprisonment for murder would be quite another. Besides, it was not the Russians' fault that Tim was trapped on the boat – he had put himself in this position. Concealment and, in the worst event, a plea of foolhardy but innocent curiosity concerning the yacht would serve him better than knife-wielding bravado.

He had retreated unarmed to the guest cabin on the lower deck. By torchlight, he had eaten a frugal meal, which had at least partially restored his strength and his spirits. The boat had been silent apart from the just audible thrum of the engine and the rhythmic slapping of the hull against the sea. Tim could see no reason why the crew should come down to the guest cabins during the night. He had lain on the bed and, succumbing to a vision of himself and Helen holidaying on the yacht with the dessert trolley from *Les Calanques*, he had fallen asleep.

SIXTY-SEVEN

Trevor, phone to his ear, rose from his desk. "He's gone and done a Reggie Perrin," he said half to himself and then, waving his phone and repeating for all to hear, "Lemon's only gone and done a Reggie Perrin."

Gordon turned from his conversation with Maggie. "Trevor, this is hardly the time to speak in riddles."

"They've found Tim's clothes on the beach." Trevor pointed to his phone. "It's Véronique downstairs. The DCRI have just called her to say the French police have Tim's clothes."

Helen stared at Trevor in wide-eyed shock. "Oh, God," she whispered to herself.

"Saints preserve us," muttered Gordon. "What the hell has Lemon gone and done now? And how in God's name did this go straight to the French security service and how on earth do they know that Tim works for MI5?"

Trevor shrugged. "Apparently, they do."

"De Beauregard probably," huffed Gordon. "Trevor, can you ask Véronique to come up here immediately."

Véronique appeared a few minutes later. She was petite, dark haired and dark complexioned. Her exquisite features were defined with a deft touch of make-up. Wearing an extremely elegant dark suit and ivory blouse, she made everyone else in the room somehow look shabby. With a French mother and English father, she was bilingual – or, in fact, trilingual since, for good measure, she also spoke fluent Italian.

"Véronique, thank you for coming up," said Gordon. "Could you please explain what is going on."

"Surely," said Véronique, managing to blend a sweetness of tone with a businesslike manner. "The DCRI called me a few minutes ago. It seems a woman and her young children found Tim's clothes hidden among rocks on Cassis beach. The woman reported this to the police, who then also found Tim's hotel room key somewhere nearby. Of course, once the police had that, they could rapidly

246

identify whose clothes they were. Apparently, the hotel proprietor confirmed that Tim had not been seen since yesterday evening. Somehow the information was passed on to the DCRI, who then called me. They are asking if we know where Tim is and what we would like them to do."

"Damn." Gordon banged a bunched fist onto the desk beside him. "Please tell them ..." He searched for inspiration. "Please tell them that Mr Lemon is carrying out a financial investigation into a British citizen whom we wrongly thought was holidaying in Cassis. Eric Carter ... Trevor, can you get hold of Eric Carter and haul him off his vacation. We need him in Cassis immediately, so that he can take care of this. And tell him to recover all of Tim's stuff – we don't want Tim's laptop falling into the wrong hands."

"It is encrypted," intervened Tabi.

"Tabi, with all due respect for the encryption skills of you or GCHQ or whoever does the security on our kit, if I gave you a foreign agent's encrypted laptop, what would you do with it?"

"I'd decipher the encryption."

"Exactly." Gordon turned back to Véronique. "Sorry, Véronique, where was I ...?"

"Tim is carrying out a financial investigation into a British citizen whom we wrongly supposed was holidaying in Cassis."

"Yes, precisely. We're unsure of exactly where Mr Lemon is at this minute and would be very grateful if the French authorities could let us know if they hear anything new in that respect; however, for the moment, we are not requesting any specific action. In the meantime, Eric Carter, our consul in Marseilles, will be flying back there immediately to lend any appropriate assistance and, if necessary, to collect Mr Lemon's belongings."

"Gordon, that sounds horribly ominous." Helen found her voice was squeezed in her throat.

"Well, this certainly isn't helpful." Gordon turned to Véronique. "Thank you, Véronique. Please pass all of that on to the DCRI and please let me know immediately if there's anything new. Oh, and give my best regards to ... er ...."

"Lebec?"

"Indeed – Lebec."

247

Véronique gave a little nod and left.

As the door closed behind Véronique, Gordon threw out his arms and looked around the room, particularly holding Helen and Margaret in his gaze. "Did I not say so? Is this not the perfect illustration of why I should have sent Helen and not Tim? ... What in the name of Christ can Lemon have been thinking this time?"

Maggie gave a despairing shake of the head. "I hate to say it, but he does seem to be compounding matters."

"And I'd say that's putting it mildly. And where do we think he might be now? Floating somewhere in the Med and posing a hazard to shipping?" Gordon realised he had overstepped the mark. "I just hope the fool is alive and safe."

Margaret frowned in thought for a second. "It seems to me these are the possibilities. We last heard from Tim just as he saw the men coming ashore for dinner. Given the clothes on the beach, I think we have to assume that Tim saw an opportunity to swim out to the boat in order to examine the crate delivered by the Bucephalus. If that's correct, there are several conceivable outcomes. The water is still pretty cold at this time of year: I don't want to entertain such a thought, but it's possible Tim didn't make it to the boat. If he did make it to the boat, the crew may have found him and – though again I truly hope not – may have killed him. Or they may be holding him prisoner on the boat. Our best hope is that Tim is hiding on the boat, but can't communicate with us – either he doesn't have his phone or he can't use it. If Tim has drowned, been killed or is a stowaway – in other words, if he's either dead or relatively safe – then for the moment we should stick to our plans. Only if he's being held captive should we think about accelerating the assault on the yacht and possibly calling in French – or perhaps by now Spanish – assistance."

"Thank you, Margaret, a fair summary," said Gordon a little testily, while also employing a tone and wearing an expression which seemed to suggest that these had been his own exact thoughts and Margaret had merely given voice to them.

"Tim's a very strong swimmer," offered Tabi. "I did one of the physical training courses with him. Shooting, he couldn't hit a barn door and, in fact, he accidentally discharged his weapon into a

248

concrete pillar at one point; on the military assault course, he narrowly escaped breaking his neck when he slipped running across a high beam – somehow he managed to cling on; he tore his clothes and himself to shreds when crawling under barbed wire; but swimming ... swimming, he was really good – best of the lot of us."

"And I haven't taken my eyes off Draper and Andropov's encrypted email," added Helen. "If they're aware of any intrusion, they're managing to keep very quiet about it."

"That's something at least," grunted Gordon. "Let us in that case assume man *on* board, not man overboard. For the moment, we stick to Plan A. Meanwhile, Trevor, get Eric Carter down there prontissimo to rescue Tim's kit." Gordon tried to inject a measure of optimism into his voice, but as he re-entered his side office the team saw him strike the door frame with the side of his fist.

SIXTY-EIGHT

Tim passed a day of tedium and hunger – he resisted the temptation to gorge on his meagre provisions, meting them out carefully. A daily menu of *salade Niçoise* and *steak aux frites* would now have seemed a banquet. He kept everything in the laundry bag, which he stowed in the cupboard under the washbasin so that, if anyone came, all signs of his presence were already concealed. He also worked out a more comfortable position for himself under the washbasin and practised a few dry runs, quickly curling himself into the cramped space and quietly closing the cupboard doors. He was a little worried that the unflushed toilet was starting to smell – as indeed was he. Noxious odours drifting up from the guest cabins might bring the crew just as much as unwonted disturbances. But for the moment, he did not dare to flush, nor to open a window.

Early in the morning, he had briefly seen through his cabin window the far off coast of what he took to be Spain, but that had receded and for the rest of the day his view was one of open water furrowed only by the occasional tanker, container ship or sailing yacht. When night fell and the crew seemed to have settled in their quarters or to be on duty at the helm, Tim again crept up to the main deck. As he glanced into the living area, his curiosity was aroused by a wooden casket somewhat larger than a presentation biscuit box sitting on the glass dining table. He padded over to the table. In the half light, he could see the casket was fashioned from ornate burl wood. He gently lifted the lid, releasing a leathery aroma of tobacco with the sap and sawn-timber perfume of cedar wood. The humidor was packed with Cohiba cigars. Tim quickly and quietly closed the lid, sealing in the aroma – he did not want to leave any additional trace of his nocturnal visit wafting around the deck. He padded back past the stairwell and crept into the galley. Finding a cupboard containing several packets of biscuits, he took the one which looked least appetising in the hope that it would not be somebody's carefully selected favourite and would therefore not be missed. A wine cooling cabinet caught his eye. Though he had no intention of drinking alcohol, he opened the cabinet. There were half a dozen racks of champagne and then half a dozen more of white wine. Tim pulled out a bottle of champagne. He looked at the label. What he saw combined with the chill of the bottle to send a shiver through his arms and down his back. The bottled, a little slick with condensation, slithered in his grip. He cradled the bottle more carefully. He could not read the label, but he could recognise the script: Cyrillic. The champagne was Russian. Was it possible that the tip-off from MI6's contact in Moscow had frothed Tim and his team into a lather of completely misguided speculation ... could it be that the Bucephalus had indeed delivered a crate of champagne to La Isla Bonita and nothing more? Or perhaps champagne and caviar – Tim had seen several tins of caviar in the fridge – but, anyway, provisions for a celebration, not the means to lay waste to London's financial district? The Swards had taken Tim on a largely pointless wander up the garden path; had he now trapped himself on this boat while in pursuit of a still greater fool's errand? His emotions churned in a mixture of hope and relief at the possibility that London might be safe and sudden deepening of his depression at the thought that his ordeal and the whole escapade might be even more of a foolish absurdity than he had already recognised it to be. He replaced the bottle in the rack and checked the other bottles of champagne. There were only a few Russian – the great majority were French: Dom Perignon, Krug, Bollinger, Cristal ... Tim gave the matter further thought: surely to send a yacht the size of a battleship across the Mediterranean to deliver a single crate of champagne and caviar would be ridiculous? But then he thought he remembered reading that Andropov had once had an order of sushi flown by private jet from his favourite Japanese restaurant in London to Kazakhstan, where he was engaged in business. The Bucephalus had anyway probably been parked somewhere just along the Côte d'Azur. Still, there was the coincidence of the hundred million dollar payment to the shady Cayman Islands account ... and how come one cabin was locked on an otherwise unlocked boat? Tim realised that he had to continue working on the assumption that the yacht was carrying a lethal cargo. And, besides, he could hardly go and announce himself to the crew, make his apologies, explain that it had all been a terrible mistake and ask if they could possibly drop him off at the next convenient port.

At this moment, Tim heard a door opening on the upper deck and voices emanating from the direction of the bridge. He froze in alarm. It sounded as though one of the Russians might be heading down towards the main deck ... perhaps on his way to the galley for a drink or a late night snack. There was no place for Tim to hide in here – and the stairwell from the deck above was adjacent to the stairwell leading down to the deck below. Tim seized his packet of biscuits, listened for the briefest second at the galley door and then padded as fast as he could down the stairs to his cabin. With his cabin door ajar, Tim could hear that the crewman had indeed descended to visit the galley. It was four or five minutes before the Russian could be heard returning to the bridge – or perhaps he was now heading to his sleeping quarters. It was some minutes more before Tim felt able to draw a calmer breath and quietly close his cabin door. He hid the packet of biscuits in the cupboard under the washbasin and lay down on the bed.

The night before, exhausted by his swim in the icy sea and by his adrenalin-pumping first hours on the boat, Tim had slept quite soundly. Now that he had recovered from his exertions and with a need to be constantly on the alert, Tim's head lay uneasily on the pillow. At every sound, he rose and crept to the cabin door to listen. It also now occurred to him that he tended to snore – which brought a jolt of retrospective shock as he considered the risk he must have run the night before. He dared not allow himself to fall into another deep sleep.

SIXTY-NINE

The team in London had spent the previous day following the red blip on the map as though it were an indicator on a hospital monitor tracking the vital signs of a close relative on life support. Occasionally, someone would zoom in on the map or zoom out again in a vain attempt to hasten the passage of La Isla Bonita.

The second morning of the yacht's voyage started with the London team in the same state of suspense. However, at around ten a.m., Trevor reported that Andropov had flown into Northolt on a private jet. Gordon and team briefly discussed whether this presented an opportunity to pull in both Andropov and Draper, but realised it was likely word would immediately reach the crew of the yacht, who might then ditch their cargo. The MI5 team needed to wait until the yacht was under the control of the navy and proof was safely in their hands before moving on the two main protagonists. They would have to hope Andropov's visit was more than fleeting. La Isla Bonita was still a couple of days' sailing from Gibraltar and a few days more from the waiting frigate.

Twenty minutes after Andropov's touchdown, an exchange on his and Draper's private email revealed that Andropov was first heading to the Alanborough and would then collect Draper from his office at about one p.m. Trevor immediately set off for the Alanborough with Luke Scott, a newish recruit to the service who had been seconded to Gordon's team that morning. Luke was in his early twenties, red haired, freckled, a little thin – or perhaps just wearing a suit which was a size too large for him. Diffident and polite, he seemed rather in awe of the team and his assignment to work with them.

Trevor and Luke parked fifty yards from the front entrance of the Alanborough. Shortly before noon, a midnight blue Maybach swept up to the hotel. A bodyguard bundled out of the front passenger seat and leapt to open the rear door. Andropov uncoiled himself from the hand-stitched leather depths of the car. He wore a neat grey suit with an open-necked shirt. He was about six foot and lean – lean-faced and lean-bodied. He was in his mid-forties, but his narrow features,

253

hollow-set eyes and skullcap of grey hair made him look a decade older. Yet he walked with an athletic, loping stride and bounded up the steps to the hotel. The burly doorman bowed obsequiously and, with a slightly absurd flourish, ushered Andropov into the hotel.

Trevor and Luke knew Andropov's next destination, so they did not need to wait. Pulling out from the curb, they headed for St James's. A hundred yards from Draper's office, they found a convenient parking space. With fifty minutes to wait, Trevor sent Luke to buy sandwiches.

SEVENTY

At about the same noonday hour, Tim was drawn to the door of his cabin by the sound of an argument on the deck above. He opened the door a few inches and strained to listen. Of course, he could not understand what was being said, but he caught the same phrase repeated a number of times – it sounded like 'long *something*' ... 'long *desha*'? 'Long' sounded English, '*desha*' sounded Russian. It was clearly the focal point of the argument, but Tim had no idea what it might mean. "Long *desha*," shouted one of the Russians again, only to have the phrase thrown back at him in a sneering tone of voice by one of his associates. An uncomfortable thought suddenly crossed Tim's mind. He quietly closed the cabin door and went through to the bathroom. Reaching into the cupboard beneath the washbasin, he withdrew the packet of biscuits which he had stolen from the galley the night before. Emblazoned across the packet was the name of the biscuit: *Langue de Chat*. Tim had eschewed the packets of chocolate biscuits and artisanal oat cookies in favour of this plainest-looking confection in the hope that the theft would pass unnoticed. But it seemed he had unwittingly chosen the very particular selection of one of the crew. At least, thank God, the Russians appeared to be accusing each other of devouring the biscuits, or perhaps forgetting them at the supermarket checkout, rather than jumping to any more dangerous conclusion. Tim returned the biscuits to the cupboard under the washbasin and went back to listen at the cabin door. The argument seemed to have subsided. However, Tim reflected that he had better not make any further nocturnal raids on the galley – or certainly not for the time being. Though he had the biscuits and still a few other provisions, he contemplated the lunchtime hour with gloomy resignation.

SEVENTY-ONE

Meanwhile, in St James's, at one o'clock exactly, the Maybach drew up outside the Wave Capital building. Sixty seconds later, Draper emerged. The chauffeur sprang from the car and held the rear door open. Draper folded his huge frame into the limousine. The chauffeur jumped back in and the car pulled away. Trevor eased into the traffic, keeping some distance from the distinctive Maybach. The blue behemoth turned into Piccadilly and headed west. Taking the underpass at Hyde Park Corner, it entered Knightsbridge, then the Brompton Road. It passed Harrods department store and continued on into the Cromwell Road. For Trevor and Luke, the light traffic created ideal conditions for maintaining a convenient distance from their prey while not drawing attention to themselves. And the limousine itself was so conspicuous it was not difficult to follow. The Maybach continued west onto the M4 motorway, took the M25 to the south and then turned west again onto the M3, all at a stately pace.

Trevor and Luke exchanged little conversation.

"Mr Wilde, do you have any idea where we're going?" asked Luke at one point.

"Not a clue," replied Trevor, and then after a brief pause, "… and 'Trevor' is fine, by the way."

Past Basingstoke, they left the motorway and joined the A303 towards Andover. In due course, Andover too was left behind.

"Quite what an oligarch and a hedge fund manager are doing on Salisbury Plain, I struggle to imagine," volunteered Trevor, but then fell silent again.

After a further ten minutes' drive, Stonehenge's massive lodestructure loomed by the roadside.

"The Canary Wharf of the ancients," observed Trevor. "Or Canary Wharf is the Stonehenge of the moderns – where the Drapers of the world make obeisance to Mammon rather than druids to the sun, obviously."

To Trevor and Luke's astonishment, the Maybach pulled off the main road and came to a halt in the visitors' car park adjacent to the historic site. Trevor and Luke followed and parked some distance away. Trevor was now becoming concerned that the occupants of the limousine, having been tailed all the way from central London and into the Stonehenge car park, would surely at some point notice their shadow. Trevor also feared that if the journey resumed and headed deeper into the West Country, he and Luke would run out of petrol and, forced to stop for a refill, would lose the Maybach.

Draper and Andropov, the broad-shouldered, heavy-headed giant and his lean and loping companion, meanwhile paid a visit to the twenty-first century public toilets, while directing no more than a brief glance towards the prehistoric monument. After a few minutes' stroll around the car park, they returned and stood by the limousine. Trevor noticed that the bodyguard had jogged over to the visitor centre and now hastened back with what looked like tickets to the ancient site; however, the oligarch and his fellow passenger displayed scant interest in making use of them and instead climbed back into the Maybach, which duly set off. Turning back towards London, the limousine retraced its route along the A303 and in due course the M3.

Trevor and Luke had phoned in to the office a number of times to report on the progress of their rather baffling journey. Trevor now called in again and spoke to Tabi.

"Wild goose chase, I think – or Wilde, with an 'e', goose chase, if you'll pardon the pun." Trevor glanced in Luke's direction and briefly displayed his front teeth. "Seems to me that Andropov and Draper have simply been holding a protracted *tête-à-tête* in the securest location they can think of. I wouldn't be surprised if they spotted us at some point and decided to take us for a midsummer jaunt to Stonehenge just to take the piss. Or take *a* piss, which is all they seem to have done there. Anyway, we're going to have to stop for petrol in a minute. We'll try to catch them up, but if they run too far ahead of us, my guess is you'll see them at Draper's place or the Alanborough in about an hour. I assume at that point they will have completed their business for the day."

257

SEVENTY-TWO

Tim had grown accustomed to the constant sensation of hunger: it had faded to an underlying ache. However, in the late afternoon, the wind picked up a little, the sea became choppy and, for the first time, Tim started to feel seasick. The smell from the toilet didn't help. Furthermore, Tim worried that if he were to vomit in the toilet, in addition to the noise he might make, the mephitic vapours from the resulting devil's *bouillabaisse* in the pan might finally invade the main deck. But then Tim realised that the rougher weather was perhaps coming to his aid: the ambient noise about the boat had risen to a point where he might at last risk flushing the toilet. After listening at the cabin door for several minutes, he went into the bathroom, closed the door and flushed. He went back into the cabin and listened again at the door.

For a few moments, Tim thought he had got away with it, but then he heard the members of the crew moving about on the deck above and talking animatedly. An approaching voice indicated one of the crew was advancing upon the stairwell. Tim quietly closed the cabin door and raced into the bathroom. If one of the Russians were to enter the cabin, he would surely detect the lingering malodour even if he picked up no other signs of Tim's presence. Anyway, Tim had no choice but to hide and to pray that the crewman had an insensitive nose. Tim hurriedly folded himself into the cupboard beneath the washbasin and clicked the doors closed just as he heard the cabin door opening. One of the Russians had indeed come to check on the source of the unexpected noise from the lower deck. Tim held his breath as he heard the bathroom door open. In the muffled distance, the drumming of the engine, the percussion of the hull against the waves and the incantation of the wind as it roamed the outer decks continued … but here in the bathroom not a sound escaped the Russian. Tim's insides contracted into an even tighter knot than the one already induced by his being crammed beneath the washbasin. This is it, he thought … the crewman's realised. The towel left on the chair on the first evening, the missing biscuits, now the flushed toilet and the fetid air in the cabin ... the penny had finally dropped. Tim braced himself for the moment when the cupboard doors would be yanked open. What on earth should he say? His mental faculties seized ... But an unexpected odour – something like aromatic wood smoke – reached Tim. Jesus, was there a fire on the boat? Was that the cause of the commotion? Tim heard the crewman turning to leave and in the same instant recognised the smokily fragrant aroma. He barely suppressed a gasp of relief – and was now afraid he had made a noise which must surely have been audible to the crewman. But the Russian could be heard leaving the cabin and closing the cabin door.

Contorted in his hiding place, Tim waited in silence for some minutes – he guessed the Russian would also check the other cabins on the lower deck and Tim did not want to make a sound until he was sure the coast was clear. At last, Tim clicked open the cupboard doors and uncurled onto the towelling bath rug. He sat back against the bulkhead and, shaking his head in disbelief, chuckled silently to himself. Cigar smoke hung in the air. The crewman had entered the cabin no doubt with eyes skinned and ears pricked, but at the same time had himself kippered the very sense which would have served him best. Tim rose from the bathroom floor and went and sat on the bed. The rush of adrenalin and the change in the cabin air seemed to have eased his nausea. That he had successfully maintained his concealment despite an impromptu check from a suspicious crewman lifted his spirit.

A little later, as the setting sun trailed a pennant of chartreuse between the ragged canopy of clouds and the western horizon, Tim noticed that in the far distance under this pale green banner the coast of Spain had once again sailed into view.

SEVENTY-THREE

Tim had been at his window pretty much since first light when he had woken from shallow sleep – the breeze had dropped in the early hours, allowing him at least a brief period of reasonably comfortable rest. Upon rising, he had seen that the boat was now much closer to the coast – perhaps only three or four miles from the shore. A range of low black mountains, carved with ravines, formed a dramatic frieze behind the coastal landscape. The yacht skimmed along, passing a low headland with a lighthouse at its point. Resort villages lined pencil strips of beach; clusters of whitewashed houses receded into the hinterland. Towards mid morning, a larger town came into view. The boat altered course, apparently steering towards this destination. The town appeared affluent: along the seafront, pristine white buildings of several storeys paraded behind an intermittent screen of palm trees; beyond these, glass and steel high-rise buildings towered here and there in testament to wider commercial activity; and, Tim saw, an expansive marina flung a protective arm around a flotilla of yachts.

Tim's heart began to beat faster. If La Isla Bonita were to put in to the marina, he must surely have a chance to escape. With the yacht at berth and the crew occupied, he would surely have an opportunity to leap ashore – or perhaps onto an adjacent boat if that afforded better concealment as he made his escape. He realised he should prepare himself. He had not worn his underpants since hanging them up to dry. He retrieved them from beneath the washbasin where he had secreted them. They were like cardboard, but he slipped them on. He cast off his towelling robe, folded it as neatly as he could and replaced it on a shelf in the wardrobe. It was none too fresh, but this should not be noticed unless someone actually put it on. The laundry bag contained his few items of rubbish: empty plastic mineral water bottles, the apple core and cheese rind, an empty jar which had contained mixed nuts, two chocolate wrappers and an empty rice cracker packet. To this he added the half-eaten packet of *Langue de Chat* biscuits and, from the minibar, a half-drunk bottle of water and

260

a half-consumed jar of honey-roasted cashew nuts. He tied the laundry bag loosely to his wrist. His mobile phone he tucked into his underpants. This way his hands remained free. He smoothed down the bed and went back to the window. His heart sank ... the yacht seemed to be gliding past the marina.

Tim watched anxiously as the yacht sailed on and the more built-up area of the town gave way to still quite densely packed but smaller and more quaintly attractive whitewashed buildings with terracotta roofs. Jumbled layers of whitewashed houses backed up one behind the other on the low hills running parallel with the shore. Now Tim's heart leapt again: another marina, far more impressive than the first, had come into view. Harbouring rank upon rank of superyachts, the marina seemed almost to call to La Isla Bonita. And, indeed, the yacht slowed, the engines churned; the boat slewed around and began to chug slowly into port.

Tim looked around the cabin which had been his involuntary home for the past two and a half days. It had passed muster the evening before and would surely do so again provided no one made too close an inspection. He opened the cabin door a few inches. He could hear the crew busily passing back and forth on the main deck and shouting to each other. He closed the door and went back to the window – he could see that the boat was gently angling its way towards a pier where a refuelling tanker was waiting. The yacht glided to its berth. Tim could hear running footsteps on the deck above and voices calling. He went back to the cabin door and opened it again. The minor commotion above continued for several minutes and then subsided. The yacht fell silent.

Trying to breathe steadily to quell the thumping in his chest, Tim crept to the foot of the stairs and listened. He could hear distant voices on the pier, but the yacht itself was quiet. He padded softly up the stairs and, with his head at deck level, peered around the bulkhead. He could see no one. He strained to listen, but could only hear the blood singing in his ears. With the laundry bag tucked under his arm and keeping low, he edged forwards into the living area. The carved wooden screen dividing the sitting area from the dining section partially obscured his view of the outer deck. Pressed behind the screen, he cautiously peeped around its side. Damn, damn, damn

261

and fuck! The same bastard crew member was sitting at a table on the outer deck and was again playing with his bloody laptop. Tim glanced around, taking in the position of the crewman and the layout of the yacht. There was absolutely no way Tim could escape from the boat without attracting the attention of Andropov's man – in fact, without walking past his nose. As on the very first evening, Tim could rush the crewman, but at the very best this would blow the secrecy of the operation – and do so with the Royal Navy's intervention either imminent, in the case of Gibraltar, or at most only a few days away, if it were left to the frigate. What if the Russians, fearing discovery, immediately put to sea and then ditched the bomb? MI5 would have absolutely nothing of any use to show in evidence against the conspirators. And if the crew took careful note of where they had dumped the cargo, Draper and Andropov might be able to retrieve the bomb in secrecy at a later date – and potentially make use of it at a time when MI5 was wholly unaware of their plans. Tim observed the crew member for a couple of minutes, but realised that the man had no intention of moving – and if he did move, it was very likely he would walk straight into Tim crouched in his hiding place behind the screen. Tim crept back to the stairwell. Concealed behind the bulkhead, he watched and listened for several more minutes. The Russian was clearly going nowhere. His colleagues must be dealing with the refuelling and buying provisions in town while he remained on watch. He had taken up a position where no one could climb onto the boat without passing him. And this meant Tim could not get off the boat either.

Tim retreated dejectedly to his cabin and sat on the bed. He pulled his phone from his underpants and tossed it onto the bed. He picked it up again and idly pressed the power button … the screen came to life! Tim stared at the phone for a moment, not really believing what he was seeing. He struggled to think straight. The phone must have thoroughly dried out after its earlier marination in seawater and had seemingly recovered. The phone indicated it was successfully receiving a signal, but the power indicator showed almost no life in the battery. Tim didn't dare risk a voice call, so he began rapidly typing an email message. He thought about apologising for his ill-conceived actions, but decided to keep to the immediate point.

262

'Trapped on La IB, lower deck, starboard aft guest cabin. Believe crate in opposite cabin (port aft), but door always locked so unable to check. 3 crew – usually on main deck/bridge during day and in crew's quarters/on bridge during night. La IB now refuelling/ reprovisioning on coast of Spain (Marbella??). Escape blocked – unless you can organise immediate distraction of crew? Otherwise, I assume RN assault in due course, as planned. If not, please advise. But please note battery nearly dead.' He paused and then added as an afterthought: 'Surviving on contents of minibar and scraps stolen from galley. Am OK, but will be delighted to see RN.' He hit send. The phone indicated that it was in the process of transmitting the message. The screen suddenly went blank. Fuck. The battery was now well and truly dead. Had the message gone or not?

SEVENTY-FOUR

Helen leaped from her desk with a cry to the team. "Lemon's alive! He's all right, he's bloody well all right! Look at your emails – he's on the boat!"

There was a chorus of excitement around the room. Everyone dived to open Tim's email, there was applause, everyone beamed – even Trevor permitted himself a transfiguring smile, or perhaps it touched Trevor especially, given his own experience of captivity, and Luke too looked delighted, though for the moment he still only half grasped all that was going on.

Helen hastily typed a return message to Tim: 'Fantastic to hear from you. Will revert asap if able to intervene now. Otherwise, RN on track. Good luck and see you soon!'

Gordon emerged from his office. He permitted himself a smile of relief. "Thank God the hothead is alive at least."

"Can we send someone in to get him? ... The Spanish police?" asked Helen.

The floor went quiet. All eyes were on Gordon. Gordon stared at the floor and ran a hand over the dome of his head.

Tabi had zoomed in to close-up on the map. "Tim's almost right. He's actually at Puerto Banus, right next to Marbella ..."

Gordon looked up. He scowled in thought. "We still face the same dilemma ... well, we do have Andropov here under our thumb this time, which is a huge plus. But I'd still rather have the evidence firmly in the hands of the Royal Navy – and, ideally, seize the boat once it's manifestly heading for British waters and its intent is unquestionable. I think we'd still be letting things slip a little from our grasp and going off slightly at half-cock if we weighed in now."

"But couldn't we just get the Spanish police to call the crew ashore to check their papers, so that Tim can escape?" persisted Helen.

"It might work," said Gordon. "However, by the time we go through all the channels, explain just enough, but without giving the whole game away ... the opportunity may have passed. And then we'd be relying on the Spanish police or harbour authorities to strike just the right note with the crew so that no suspicions are aroused; otherwise, the crew might take fright, decide to abort the operation, head out to sea and send the bomb to fifty fathoms for collection at a later date … then we might finish up with nothing." Gordon saw the grim-faced expressions of Helen and the rest of the team. "It's tough, I know. But Tim says he's okay. The SBS team will know precisely where he is on the boat. Depending on circumstances, we might be able to board the yacht as it passes through the Strait of Gibraltar – in which case, rescue is only hours away. Even if we wait on the frigate, the operation is only a few days from conclusion. I think we have to let this play itself out as planned."

SEVENTY-FIVE

La Isla Bonita meanwhile continued with its refuelling. Tim returned to the top of the stairwell and, crouching behind the bulkhead, kept anxious watch for another hour and twenty minutes in the hope that rescue might be at hand. In the end, it was the other two crew members who reappeared. Tim had no choice but to descend once more to his cabin. La Isla Bonita put to sea. Tim was again confined to his hiding place. Feeling rather despondent after the missed opportunity to escape, he remained glued to his porthole. In the late afternoon, he judged from the proximity of the coast, the topography and the greater volume of shipping that the yacht was approaching the Strait of Gibraltar: he hoped that intervention from the Royal Navy was near at hand. The truth was that he was beginning to feel increasingly in need of rescue: his poor diet was starting to give him stomach cramps, his lengthy confinement to the cabin was becoming claustrophobic and his edginess at every sound was fraying his mental resilience. He had donned the bathrobe and now clutched his mobile phone – this was all the preparation he needed for rescue by the SBS. As La Isla Bonita pulled past a container ship, the Rock of Gibraltar loomed into view, thrusting from the coastline.

SEVENTY-SIX

Gordon, Helen, Margaret and Tabi were gathered around the conference room table. One of the large screens on the wall displayed a pitching image with, in the foreground, the stiletto nose of a wave-piercer as it unseamed the ocean and, beyond the prow of the assault craft, in the middle distance, various other vessels – two oil tankers, a container ship, a trawler … and glinting in their midst, La Isla Bonita. The second screen showed a Royal Marines brigadier, wearing the lovat green uniform of the Corps, in the operations room at the headquarters of the Directorate of Special Forces. This officer, Tony Russell, and Gordon were clearly known to each other.

"Tony, could we have your assessment, please," said Gordon.

"Gordon, the wave-piercers can overhaul the yacht in a matter of minutes and we have every confidence that we can rapidly overpower the crew and take control of the vessel. Even if they're armed, we have superior numbers and a certain element of surprise … though we should assume they'll detect our approach once we close in – stealth design does minimise that risk, but their radar might pick us up, we might trigger an alert on their collision warning system or they may simply see us as we draw close – visibility is good as you can see on the screen. Meanwhile, if your man stays in his cabin and keeps out of sight …"

Gordon grimaced.

"… he should be safe. From his message, we know exactly where he's located on the boat. But …" Tony Russell paused for emphasis. "… – and this is a very big 'but' – the one wild card and the one thing we cannot guarantee … if these guys decide to go out with a grand gesture, we can't be sure that we can neutralise the nuclear engineer before he has an opportunity to prime and detonate the device which you inform us may be on board. It's unlikely that he'll have time to do it, but we can't make any promises. Apart from anything else, it depends on the nature of the device and, as I understand it, we have no idea about that?"

"Yes, that's correct," confirmed Gordon.

"Well, as you can see, there is a great deal of shipping in the Strait – not least the two oil tankers which you can see on the screen barely a mile beyond the yacht. And, I don't know whether you caught it as we were coming on air, but a large cruise liner also passed by a few minutes ago. If a nuclear device is detonated, the collateral damage will be significant."

"Do I take that as a recommendation to postpone?" asked Gordon.

"Indeed, Gordon, my strong recommendation would be to leave the assault to the team on the frigate. We can pick the timing and the spot in the ocean so that we avoid all other shipping. Our chances of success will be the same and the risk of collateral damage will be minimised. And, in fact, if there's no other shipping about, the likelihood of the crew detonating the thing will surely be considerably less – as a grand gesture, it would go unseen, and as an act of terror intended to destabilise financial markets, it would be next to pointless."

The conference room suddenly filled with the rushing of wind, smack of the sea and growl of twin eight hundred horse power Seatek engines as the SBS team leader opened his communication channel.

"Sir, we need your decision fairly imminently. The wave-piercers are short-range assault craft rather than long-haul ocean-going vessels – we'll soon be nearing the limit of their operating distance."

Gordon began to drum tensely on the edge of the table, but did not immediately respond.

"Gordon, I think we have to postpone," said Margaret quietly.

Gordon nodded in apparent agreement, but still did not speak for four or five seconds. Then, finally, "Postpone. Please stand down your team. We wait on the frigate."

SEVENTY-SEVEN

Tim scanned the choppy waters at the meeting of Mediterranean and Atlantic. As La Isla Bonita had passed Gibraltar, Tim had thought for a moment that he had caught sight of naval assault craft tailing the yacht in the far distance, but then he had decided they were pleasure boats and anyway he had quickly lost sight of them. Staring from his cabin window and with his expectations still riding high, Tim found himself repeatedly catching his breath in little paroxysms of anticipation. But now the coast was beginning to recede, the congestion of the Strait was easing – the nearest ship Tim could see was at least two or three miles distant – and dusk was starting to fall. Tim clung to the hope that the SBS were waiting for the cover of darkness. But as an hour passed, then two and then three, his hopes dissolved and his spirits sank. He started to feel quite ill. He lay on the bed.

He could not sleep, dare not sleep, but fitful visions came to him. At university he had written a thesis on smuggling in the West Country in the late eighteenth century – a period when the illegal trade in spirits, tea, tobacco and other luxuries was thought to deprive the national exchequer of fifteen to twenty percent of its potential revenue. Draper now merged with Zephaniah Job, smuggler and financier of Polperro in Cornwall. His gleaming motor-powered black and white brigantine was trafficking French brandy, Russian champagne, Cuban cigars, Earl Grey tea, *tartes aux abricots* and nuclear weapons. Tormented by cabin fever and with teeth rattling from scurvy, Tim was a stowaway and was bound to be discovered – in the morning Gordon would surely keel-haul him around the barnacle-encrusted hull of La Isla Bonita. Not even Helen could help him now. Tim woke with a start as he realised he had emitted a loud groan. He lay frozen in terror for a second, then rose and went to the door. He opened the door a fraction and listened – he thought he could not detect any sound issuing from the deck above, but in truth could not tell whether he was listening to silence or to a stress-induced tinnitus of white noise. He quietly closed the door and went and lay on the bed again. Again, the phantoms drew in. Tim was not sure he could maintain his concealment much longer. If his condition worsened, he might have to throw himself upon the mercy of the crew.

SEVENTY-EIGHT

When Gordon entered the office next morning, Helen, Trevor, Margaret and Tabi were gathered around the map, apparently in renewed vigil. But they immediately turned to Gordon.

"Gordon, this makes no sense," said Helen. "The boat should be travelling up the coast of Portugal, but it's gone the other way – turned left after Gibraltar instead of right. It's now off the coast of north-west Africa roughly level with Casablanca. Where the hell's it going?"

Gordon stared at the map wide-eyed. "What the blazes?" He thought for a second. "New York ... are they heading for New York?"

"That doesn't make much sense either," said Margaret. "Tabi, can you zoom out? ... Look, if they were going to New York, it would make much better sense to head west to the Azores, not south-west towards the Canaries. And I'm not sure the yacht has the range to cross the Atlantic from the Canaries to New York."

"Perhaps it could head down to the Cape Verde islands and then across to the Caribbean?" suggested Tabi.

"Perhaps," said Margaret, "but that's still quite a haul across the Atlantic and it's a very roundabout route."

"Maybe they plan to flog the bomb to some African state?" proposed Trevor.

"Jesus, let's hope not." Gordon stared at the map. "Damn and blast – we should have taken them out when we had the chance. What the hell are they up to?" He turned to Tabi. "Is it conceivable the satellite could have mistaken the signal – I mean, jumped to a different boat – for example, in the Strait of Gibraltar where the shipping is congested? Could we be tracking the wrong boat?"

"No, I don't think that's possible," said Tabi. He went to the nearest desk and tapped an instruction into the computer. The ocean tracts on the map displayed on the wall screen suddenly thronged with differently coloured and variously orientated isosceles triangles, each indicating the passage of a vessel at sea. The triangle indicating

La Isla Bonita continued to wink with a red light. "Every vessel of any size has a so-called MMSI – Maritime Mobile Service Identity – a unique signal which it has to transmit whenever at sea so that the maritime agencies and other ships can follow all sea-going traffic." Tabi clicked on the triangle representing La Isla Bonita. A small panel opened on the screen showing a picture of the motor yacht and listing its essential details. "I don't think there can be any mistake." Tabi reverted to the original map which displayed only Draper's yacht and the naval vessels.

"God's hooks." Gordon pursed his lips. "Well, we'd better leave the navy on standby for the moment. Trevor, please get in touch with Brigadier Russell at HQ DSF and explain to him that we're now unclear as to the yacht's destination and intentions. But ask him to keep the frigate on the alert in case we need to despatch it in pursuit of La Isla Bonita or in case the yacht reverts to the anticipated course."

At this point, Luke wandered in, burdened with a small travel bag and a rucksack. "Mr Walker, er, Gordon, someone called Eric Carter just dropped this lot off. Says it's Tim's bags from Cassis."

"Oh, good. At least that's something. Is his laptop there?"

"In the rucksack."

"Thank goodness. Just stuff it all under Tim's desk for the moment."

"I've a suggestion," said Margaret. "This may be a long shot, but, Tabi, why don't you run one of your screens over all of Draper's files to see what references you can find to New York or to any African state?"

"No problem," said Tabi. "I already have such a screen set up – just need to insert New York and the names of African countries. Shouldn't take too long."

Gordon paced back and forth in puce-complexioned bad temper while Tabi ran the screen. It took Tabi thirty minutes to complete the exercise and to print off the hundred or more pages of documents carrying the relevant references. He divided up the little stack of papers and handed sections to each of his colleagues. "New York," he said, handing a wad to Gordon. "More New York, plus bits of Africa." He handed further pages to Margaret and Trevor. "Rest of

Africa for you and me, Helen." He handed Helen half the remaining sheaf.

Everyone bent over the printouts, flicking rapidly through the pages while closely scrutinising the text.

"All travel related," said Margaret.

"Hm ... Canary Islands." Helen looked up at Tabi in slight surprise while indicating one of the sheets.

"Yuh, I put that and all the main islands' names into the screen as well," explained Tabi.

"I see," said Helen.

"Anything?" asked Tabi.

"Not sure." Helen resumed her reading.

"No," said Gordon, discarding his pages. "Nothing here."

"African stuff all seems investment related – apart from a holiday in Mauritius," added Trevor.

"Well ..." Helen looked up again. "... we might have something here. Looks as though Draper bought, I don't know, a villa or anyway property of some kind on La Palma in the Canaries at about the same time that he bought his boat."

"Not the usual place for a billionaire to buy property," said Tabi.

"Maybe he wanted to escape from all the other billionaires," suggested Trevor.

"Well," said Margaret, "even if we no longer understand what's going on, I'd hazard a guess that the next stop for Draper's yacht is La Palma."

Helen was still reading through and now came to the final sheet in her hand. Her eyebrows rose. "I'd say your guess is spot on, Maggie. Draper just booked a private jet to fly him to La Palma tomorrow!"

Gordon stood with his mouth open. He shook his head in bafflement. "When would we expect the boat to reach La Palma?"

Tabi glanced at the map on the wall. "Quick calculation, I'd say sometime around the middle of tomorrow."

Gordon gathered himself up. "Goodness knows what's going on here, but we've let this run long enough. At the very least, we should get Lemon off that boat. Helen, I want you on the first available flight to La Palma. Objective number one, help Tim to escape from the boat. Objective number two, see if you can figure out what on

273

earth Draper's playing at." Gordon pointed to the bags under Tim's desk. "Better take Tim's kit with you. But leave the laptop. Maggie, please see if you can find out what this property on La Palma might be and perhaps tee up the Spanish authorities. Get contact details for the police on La Palma in case we need their help. Trevor, can you stand the navy down one notch, at least for the moment while we try to get to the bottom of this – but tell them to hold the frigate in readiness in case we need to revert to them. Helen, good luck ... and for Christ's sake don't take any unauthorised midnight swims."

IV   La Isla Bonita, part 2

SEVENTY-NINE

Helen walked down towards the waterfront, her sandals clacking on the cobblestones as she passed through the old colonial streets at the heart of Santa Cruz de La Palma. She descended the narrow Calle O'Daly – which the hotel concierge had told her was named after an Irish banana trader – taking in the cool mid morning air in the shade cast by the three and four-storey buildings which stood shoulder to shoulder along the historic street. Almost every building, whether painted white or of natural grey or reddish brown stone, encased its upper windows in balconies of ornate black ironwork or in decorative overhanging wooden loggia. The picture-postcard neatness and tidiness of the perfectly maintained streets suggested civic pride was a virtue highly prized among the Palmeros. As Helen reached the Avenida Marítima, the wider road skirting the waterfront, she noted that more modern buildings began to predominate and the shops, restaurants and bars bore testimony to the contemporary tourist trade rather than to the island's colonial history. She crossed the road to the seafront promenade and leaned against the railings. A narrow arc of black volcanic sand curved towards the harbour wall. The concrete wall projected a hundred yards into the sea and then turned at ninety degrees to run parallel with the coast. The sea itself was placid – barely ruffled by the lightest of zephyrs. Helen tasted the salt in the air and … was it her imagination or was there also a tang of sulphur on the breeze?

Helen had flown out to La Palma via Madrid and had arrived on the island late the previous evening. For reasons of convenience and immediate availability rather than extravagance, Her Majesty's Government had seen fit to accommodate Helen in the best hotel in Santa Cruz – the Hotel de España. The hotel was located just beyond the Plaza de España, the picturesque central square dominated by the classical grey stone portal and whitewashed walls of the Iglesia de El Salvador and bisected by the Calle O'Daly. The hotel itself took its architectural motif from that predominant on the island, with a

277

whitewashed exterior shaded by tall palm trees and with interiors decorated in cool pastels.

Knowing that Draper's yacht was not expected to reach La Palma until later in the day and feeling in need of a few moments' release from the tightening coils of nervous anticipation, Helen had made use of the hotel pool to go for an early swim and then, throwing on a bathrobe, had persuaded herself to take advantage of the extensive breakfast buffet. A short while later, showered, dressed and provided by the hotel with a colourful but not very detailed tourist map and still with plenty of time to reconnoitre, she had ventured out in search of La Isla Bonita's likely landing point.

As Helen now leant against the promenade railings, she struggled to hold in check feelings of excitement mingled with dread at the prospect of the yacht's imminent appearance – God, she prayed Tim was still on board and still safely concealed. She hoped … be confident, Helen, she told herself … she *assumed* the absence of communication after the one short message from Puerto Banus was simply Tim's battery dying as he had warned it might. And, anyway, there would have been no mobile signal once the yacht was too far out from the coast.

She set off along the promenade towards the port. Ascending the steps to the harbour wall, she saw that the near end of the little port comprised a compact yachting marina. A couple of dozen small boats were moored at the wooden jetties – motor launches, sailing yachts and one motor yacht altogether more modest in scale than La Isla Bonita. In fact, it was not clear that the small berths in the marina would be able to accommodate a vessel of the size of La Isla Bonita. However, the outer, much larger part of the harbour, which was clearly commercial rather than recreational in purpose, was of sufficient size to handle container ships and cruise liners – and, indeed, one of the latter now lay quietly berthed alongside the harbour wall. If necessary, La Isla Bonita would have no difficulty finding mooring here. While there were no merchant vessels in evidence at that moment, a few cranes for loading and unloading containers stood in readiness along the quayside and a couple of long, low warehouses lined the wharf.

Helen took out her mobile. "Morning, Shah. I'm at the port in Santa Cruz. I guess this must be where La Isla Bonita is heading. What's the latest on its positioning?"

"Hi, Helen. Let me just zoom in on the map ... yes, I'd say they're still plum on course for Santa Cruz."

"ETA?"

"Not far off now. Should be with you in a couple of hours or so. Within binocular range before lunchtime, certainly."

"And Draper's flight?"

"It's a private jet, so there's no published timetable. However, the La Palma airport authorities tell us it's due soon and they've been instructed to let us know the minute it lands."

"Okay, thanks. Let me know if there's any change in the yacht's bearing or any word on Draper's arrival. Meanwhile, is Maggie there?"

Margaret picked up the phone. "Morning, Helen. Not having much luck in pinning down the location of Draper's holiday home. As you saw, he was dealing with a lawyer in Monaco – whom I have actually managed to speak to this morning, though with only limited result. Not surprisingly, the lawyer was very sticky about client confidentiality. However, I have managed to glean that the transaction was done via another law firm in Madrid, which in turn has an outpost in Santa Cruz de Tenerife. But it seems the branch in Tenerife is basically some semi-retired chap who's rarely in the office. The only potentially useful thing I have is the name of Draper's place – Aprisco de la Cumbre Vieja. Apparently, *aprisco* means sheepfold or something to that effect, though the lawyer referred to 'land and property', and Cumbre Vieja is the name of the mountain ridge which forms the southern half of the island. So ... probably somewhere in the southern part of the island and possibly a converted farmhouse or something like that – unless, of course, it's actually in the middle of town or in some resort development and the name's just an attempt to conjure up a pastoral idyll. One other odd thing, though ... I found a public record of the transaction – which still doesn't tell us where the place is, by the way – however, it indicates a price of only twenty-seven thousand euros, which seems incredibly cheap. But then perhaps La Palma missed out on the

279

Spanish property boom. Anyway, if I can rouse the old man of Tenerife and find out any more, I'll get straight back to you." Maggie changed tack. "And, Helen, while you're there, I'm still trying to puzzle out what on earth Draper and his yacht are doing in La Palma. Obviously, the yacht may be en route somewhere else, which still seems most likely, but it could also be that Draper and Andropov are not intending to use the bomb right now and are planning to warehouse it at Draper's property on the island until a later date. Seems a slightly bizarre choice of location, but maybe that's the beauty of it – no one would dream of looking for a concealed nuclear weapon at a holiday home in the Canaries. Or, I suppose there's still the third faint possibility that we're barking up the wrong tree and Draper just wants to spend time on his yacht in the Canaries and Andropov's supplied some goodies for the voyage … though all the circumstantial evidence – the payment, Suskin, et cetera – all that militates against the idea. I think we still have to take the more sinister interpretation. Sorry, going on a bit … but the point is keep your eyes peeled in case they remove the crate from the yacht."

Helen had hoped that she might track down Draper's holiday property while waiting for the arrival of the yacht; however, a name and only the very broadest indication of location – which might anyway be misleading – were not enough to go on. Her map from the hotel offered little enlightenment: it showed only the towns, larger villages, main roads and principal geographical features of interest to tourists. Even if she had had a detailed address, this map would not have been of much use in helping her to find it. Helen called up a map of the island on her mobile: this provided much better detail, but Helen saw that even here many of the smaller roads were unnamed, particularly outside the towns, and large tracts of the interior were without identified features. She turned back towards the hotel. Passing a tourist shop on the promenade, she went in to ask if they had a map of the island. But they had only the same one which the hotel had provided. Once back at the hotel Helen enquired whether Aprisco de la Cumbre Vieja meant anything to any of the staff. It did not – beyond the fact that Cumbre Vieja was the volcanic ridge which formed the southern spine of the island and which was designated a nature reserve, both of which points Helen had already gathered from Maggie and from the tourist map. Did the hotel by any chance possess a more detailed map, even if generally reserved for its own use rather than for guests? It did not. By now Helen had wasted an hour and was beginning to think she should get back to the harbour with the pair of binoculars from Tim's backpack.

A short while later, Helen was striding towards the port with the binoculars slung over one shoulder ... and with T-shirt and shorts for Tim tucked into her bag – he had after all abandoned his clothes on the beach at Cassis. As she passed through the Calle O'Daly, the yeasty, sugary aroma from a bakery-cum-patisserie brought her up short. She deliberated for a second and then veered into the shop to buy a sandwich and a pastry for Tim. Though a combination of tense anticipation and her recent breakfast left her far from hungry, she bought a sandwich for herself too. She crossed the Avenida Marítima and ascended the steps onto the harbour wall.

Helen checked her mobile for email: still no new word from Tabi on Draper's arrival and none from Maggie on the exact location of the property. And, for the moment, as Helen now looked out to sea, the horizon bore no mark of an approaching motor yacht. Helen started to feel a little sick with apprehension in case the yacht had changed course or – she did not want to think about it – in case anything had happened to Tim. She emailed Tabi to check whether the yacht was on course and whether Draper had landed. 'Yes, should be coming into view,' he replied, 'and no – will call airport if no word soon.'

EIGHTY

Helen scanned the horizon again. The yacht was not coming into view. No distant vessel broke the meniscus at the far lip of the ocean. Helen paced the harbour wall. She stopped. Unless ... Helen clapped the binoculars to her eyes. Yes, surely ... Helen's heart leapt. 'Let that be him,' she said to herself. 'Come on, Lemon, come on.' The speck on the horizon was for a minute or two still too distant to identify, but Helen was surprised at how quickly it hove into full view of the binoculars. White upper deck, black below the main deck, a large and sleek motor yacht ... there could no longer be any doubt. Helen started to shake and found it difficult to hold the image of the yacht in the lens of the binoculars.

Within ten minutes, the yacht was in plain view to the naked eye. It occurred to Helen that if she could see the yacht this clearly, then those on the bridge could surely see her and, as a lone figure on the harbour wall with a pair of binoculars, she must be conspicuous. She descended the steps back to the promenade and walked quickly along the seafront. A hundred yards from the port, she found a row of benches shaded by palm trees and overlooking the ocean. Seated here, she had a clear view of the incoming yacht and would draw no attention to herself.

Helen had assumed the motor yacht would enter the harbour, but as in Cassis it chose to remain aloof and slowed to a gentle drift about half a mile out to sea. Through her binoculars, Helen saw the churning waters at the stern subside. At the bow, the anchor unspooled and hit the surface of the water. As the anchor took, the boat gently slewed around to face the prevailing current. Helen held her breath. For some minutes, the boat rested placidly and there was no sign of activity on board. At last, two figures appeared on deck. They surveyed the scene for a couple of minutes and then returned inside. Helen found her heart was thumping and her hands were shaking again. After several more protracted minutes, all three members of the crew reappeared on deck and this time made their way down to the diving platform at the stern. They raised the tailgate and manoeuvred the yacht's launch out of its housing and into the water. Helen watched intently in case there was any sign of the crate being removed from the yacht. But it seemed the three men were coming ashore without their cargo. The tailgate levered back into place and the launch cast off from the yacht. The launch turned towards the half mile distant harbour entrance and accelerated away from the yacht. Helen would lose sight of the launch as it disappeared behind the harbour wall, so she now needed to return to her earlier vantage point to keep both yacht and launch in view.

While following the progress of the crew, Helen had been continually glancing at the main and upper decks of the yacht and at the foredeck in case a fourth figure should emerge – but there had been no sign of Tim. As Helen hastened back to the harbour wall, she did not take her eyes off the yacht. Ascending the steps and returning to her position on the wall, she could again see the launch carving through the water as it sped to the harbour entrance. Helen's stomach began to churn. The crewmen were all off the boat – why didn't Tim make his escape? It was two full days since Helen and team had heard from Tim. That was a long time to remain secure and undetected in a cabin just yards from his captors. And treading softly – literally doing so – was absolutely Tim's weakest point. 'God, let them not have found him,' thought Helen. 'Let him be alive.'

The launch disappeared from Helen's view for a moment as it rounded the far end of the harbour wall to enter the port. As Helen waited for the launch to reappear, a glint from the yacht pulled her attention back in that direction. She had not been watching at that second, but out of the corner of her eye had she not seen the door on the main deck open and close? There was no sign of anyone on deck. Or was that a head bobbing at the level of the handrail around the deck? A crouching figure appeared at the stern and scampered down the steps to the diving platform. Helen's heart leapt. She found herself biting back tears. 'For heaven's sake, don't cry, you ridiculous woman,' she said to herself, as she wiped her eyes on the sleeve of her cotton dress. And what the hell was Tim carrying? He had a white package under one arm as he slipped into the water. The package could not be heavy and in fact seemed like some kind of flotation device as it bobbed and slapped at Tim's wrist while he swam. Helen glanced back at the launch – it was now chugging through the outer commercial section of the harbour towards the little yachting marina closer to where Helen was standing. She descended a few steps, so that she was not quite so plainly in view of the launch but could still keep watch on its passage while also following Tim's progress. It was clear Tim was heading towards the narrow arc of black volcanic sand which curved between the harbour wall and the promenade.

Tim was still some distance out from the shore as the launch pulled up alongside a wooden jetty in the marina. As the three men disembarked, a port official emerged from one of the low buildings on the quay and approached them. There was a general shaking of hands and presentation of papers. The official gestured amicably for the crewmen to follow him to the port authority building – presumably to stamp passports and complete any paperwork.

With Tim now only a couple of hundred yards from the shore, Helen ran down the steps from the harbour wall onto the arc of sand. She resisted the temptation to call out to Tim and to wave – she did not want to draw attention to the scene. Anyway, Tim had his head down and was concentrating on his stroke. But at about a hundred yards, he stopped for a moment and trod water in order to check where he was heading. Helen raised a tentative hand. She saw Tim stare at her for a second and then plunge back into his stroke with redoubled vigour – despite the strange package still slapping beside his arm. 'Oh, bloody hell,' Helen said to herself as she found herself crying again. She kicked off her sandals and waded ankle deep into the sea. At fifty yards, Tim raised his head again; at thirty, he tested the bottom, but it was still just too deep; at twenty yards, he stumbled to his feet, slapped the water with a whoop of triumph and came wading and high-stepping to Helen.

With five days' beard, looking a little emaciated, wearing a greying and, as soaking wet, slightly obscene pair of underpants and with his laundry sack under his arm, Tim looked like a cross between Robinson Crusoe escaping his shipwreck and a Calvin Klein reject who had been thrown overboard. Helen could not help but offer Tim a hug of overwhelming relief.

284

God, Helen's embrace felt good to Tim. A wave of elation erupted in a laugh as he held her. He was more than a little amazed to find her waiting for him and equally so to be given such a greeting. And, Jesus, it was good to press his toes into the warm sand of *terra firma*.

Tim lifted his head from Helen's shoulder as she released him. He surveyed the immaculately well kept promenade with its line of palm trees and, rising in the distance beyond the town, the volcanic slopes. "Well," he said, "I'd hazard a guess this isn't London, but where the hell are we?"

"Lemon," she said, "you somehow contrive to look even scruffier than usual, you need a shave, your breath smells terrible and I am so, so relieved and happy to see you alive and in one piece." Helen looked about her. "We're in La Palma in the Canaries."

"I thought so," said Tim. "I mean, not necessarily La Palma or even the Canaries, but I thought we were heading more south-west than north-east. What the hell are we doing here?"

"Good question," responded Helen. "And I'm slightly embarrassed to say we still don't really have the answer." She looked at the laundry sack. "What's this?"

"My laundry bag," replied Tim.

"You brought your laundry?" Helen was not entirely serious, but nor was she at all sure what on earth the bag might contain. Tim's clothes, after all, were in her possession.

"My rubbish," explained Tim, "... so I didn't leave any evidence on the boat."

"Ah ..."

Tim untied the drawstring from his wrist and, seeing a rubbish bin at the edge of the little beach, went and lobbed the sack into the bin. He returned to Helen, but stopped short. "Oh, hang on." He went back to the bin and tore open his sack.

For one insane second, Helen thought he might have brought her a souvenir of his voyage, but instead Tim retrieved and held aloft his mobile phone.

"Not sure whether this is going to work and it certainly needs charging," he said.

With Tim safe, Helen now suddenly decided it was high time she took firm control of her emotions and showed some professionalism of her own. "Lemon, here, I have shorts and a T-shirt for you. This may be the Canaries, but semi-transparent budgie-smugglers" – she nodded at Tim's underpants – "are probably not the fashion. Though, sorry, I didn't think to bring you a towel – I assumed the boat would come into port … hadn't occurred to me you might be taking another swim. While you're putting those on, I'll just go and check what the crew of the yacht is up to. I'll be back in two tics. Meanwhile …" Helen took out her own phone and started to dial.

Tim suddenly looked anxious. "You're not calling Gordon, are you? I haven't been fired, have I?"

"Well, I can't tell a lie – Gordon has been less than thrilled at your little escapade. But, no, I am not ringing Gordon and, no, you have not been fired. On the contrary, some of your colleagues have been very worried about you … Maggie, hi. Could you put us on speaker – voice you might all like to hear." She handed the phone to Tim.

"Hi, everyone!" said Tim.

Helen could hear cheering and applause at the other end of the line as she left Tim to speak to the team. She hopped up the first few steps of the harbour wall. The port official was on the quay smoking a cigarette and staring absently at the lapping waters of the marina. The three crewmen had vanished from sight, but their launch was still tethered to the jetty. Clearly, the three men had made their way into the town – or perhaps they were planning to meet Draper when he landed at the airport. Helen descended the steps to the little beach.

"Tabi says Draper's coming here," said Tim, as he returned the phone to Helen.

"Crew's gone into town. Let's head back to the hotel," said Helen. "And, yes, Draper's supposed to be landing about now."

"Tabi said he can't get hold of the guy at the airport who's keeping watch for us. We're not hitting the lunch and siesta hour, are we?"

"Nearly one o'clock," said Helen, looking at her watch. "I've got a sandwich for you, by the way." Helen felt slightly sheepish now as she took out a ham and cheese baguette for Tim.

But Tim looked thrilled and gave a grunt of delight. "You've thought of everything." Tim tore into his baguette and marched along grinning like an idiot. "Draper, then," he chomped. "Have we got no further? Have we seen anything in his emails with Andropov?"

"The only fresh clues we have are that the third crew member you photographed is Konstantin Suskin, a Russian nuclear weapons specialist – which is obviously rather ominous and lends a lot of credibility to our theory – and then Draper owns a property somewhere here on La Palma, but we're not sure exactly what or where. Maggie has a theory that Draper and Andropov may want to conceal the bomb here until they're ready to use it."

"That cabin on the boat is still locked, by the way. I tried the door just before I left."

With his unkempt hair and beard and his damp clothes, Tim drew a few stares as he paraded along the Calle O'Daly … and more still as he sauntered through the hotel lobby. Helen had booked adjacent rooms. She had also asked for second keys to both rooms so that she and Tim each had access to the other's room if need be. She showed Tim into his room and then went to hers to pick up Tim's belongings. When she returned a few minutes later, Tim was in the bathroom and Helen could hear the bath was running. She sat on the edge of the bed.

Both rooms were simply but elegantly appointed, with wooden furniture and with walls painted, in the case of Tim's room, a pale honey colour with white detailing and, in the case of Helen's, a powdery blue with the same white detailing. The beds were an exception to the simplicity of style, having ornate ironwork bedsteads reminiscent of the town's famous balconies.

After several minutes of noisy ablutions, the bathroom fell silent. Helen sat and waited. The bathroom remained silent. Helen rose and knocked quietly on the door.

"Lemon?"

There was no reply. Helen knocked again, this time a touch louder. She called again; again, no reply. She gently opened the door. The bathroom was steamy and filled with the soothing perfume of bath salts. Tim was lying in the bath with a wet towel folded beneath his head as a pillow. He was fast asleep. He had one leg propped on

287

the edge of the bath. Helen saw that the still three-quarters full and unstoppered glass jar of bath salts was held on the rim of the bath at a precarious angle of forty-five degrees by Tim's extended foot. If Tim shifted, the glass jar would fall and shatter on the floor or would tip the other way and spill its remaining contents into the bath. Helen reflected that even asleep in the bath Tim was a danger to inanimate objects. She felt a little guiltily intrusive as she stepped into the bathroom and rescued the glass jar. She glanced at Tim and hesitated, but then gently eased his leg into the warm water so that he didn't move and wake himself with an unexpected splash. Tim barely stirred. Helen found she could not hold back a smile. She retreated to the bedroom, quietly closing the bathroom door behind her. She scribbled a note to say that she was going back to the port to keep an eye open for the return of the crew. She put the note and the pastry from the bakery beside the bed and slipped out of the room.

EIGHTY-ONE

No sooner had Helen stepped into the corridor than her phone rang.

"Helen, it's Tabi. Bloody man at the airport has finally returned our call and apparently Draper landed about an hour ago. He was picked up by three men in a four-by-four of some kind – Mitsubishi Shogun or something like that. Have they reappeared at the harbour?"

"I'm on my way back there now. I'll update you in a few minutes."

Helen hastened back to the harbour, cursing the airport official for his nonchalant attitude and herself for deserting her post – though, in truth, she had not really had much option and had lifted her watch for no more than forty-five minutes or so. As she approached the harbour, she saw in the adjacent car park a Toyota Land Cruiser with a car rental sticker in the window. The car had not been there an hour earlier. Mounting the wall, Helen immediately took in that the launch from La Isla Bonita was no longer moored to the jetty in the marina and, lifting her binoculars, she confirmed that … yes, there it now was, tethered to the stern of the motor yacht. Well, she had missed the opportunity visually to confirm Draper's arrival, but it seemed pretty clear he and the crew were now all on the boat. She called the office to apprise the team before returning to her inconspicuous vantage point among the palm trees on the promenade.

As Helen pursued her vigil, it seemed apparent little was happening on the boat. Occasionally, a figure would appear on deck – and she was pretty sure one of those who briefly stuck his head outside was Draper – but it did not seem as though preparations were underway for a return to shore. Helen realised that she was herself now feeling quite hungry and remembered she had another sandwich in her bag. The afternoon passed slowly and in due course the sun began to descend behind the island at Helen's back. Helen tried to call Tim a couple of times, but his phone was not responding. She should have thought to plug it in before leaving Tim's room. She did not have the hotel number immediately to hand and anyway decided to let Tim rest. So long as he was not still asleep in the bath!

As the light softened towards dusk, Helen's attention was caught by signs of activity on La Isla Bonita. Two of the crewmen descended to the diving platform. Helen held them in her binoculars. But they were not making ready to come ashore – on the contrary, they opened the tailgate of the yacht and winched the boat's launch back into its housing. As the two men returned to the lounge on the main deck, the deck lights came on. Helen kept watch for a further twenty minutes, but it seemed clear Draper and his crew had no plans to return to shore that evening. Helen considered for a moment: if La Isla Bonita were to set sail again, the satellite tracker would pick it up and anyway this seemed unlikely with the Land Cruiser still parked near the quay. But now the thought crossed Helen's mind that it would be sensible to track the Land Cruiser as well. Unfortunately, she had not brought a GPS transmitter to La Palma, but she hoped that Tabi might anyway be able to lock on to the vehicle as he had done with the boat. She dialled his number as she set off towards the harbour car park.

"Hi, Shah. Need your help. If we can, we ought to keep a satellite tracker on Draper's rented Land Cruiser."

"Hi, Helen. Yeah, sure."

"Can you get a visual on the car park beside the marina? I'm heading there now so I can indicate which vehicle. And then will you be able to hold a lock on the Land Cruiser?"

"We have live satellite coverage and … yes, I can see the marina car park. And I guess that's you I can see walking towards it."

Helen waved.

"Yuh, that's you."

There were only a handful of cars in the car park and the Land Cruiser was noticeably the largest. Helen stood beside it and waved again.

"Okay, got it," said Tabi. "So long as we can see the vehicle or consistently pick up a heat signal, we should be able to follow it. Only problem will be if we get heavy cloud cover."

"Well, it's been nothing but sunny and clear since I arrived. But, anyway, you've managed with the boat – can't you do the same with the car?"

"No, we can track the boat's radio signal, but the car's just a lump of metal. If Draper were in the car with his usual phone, we could track that, but I can see his UK-registered mobile is still in London. He must be carrying a different phone and I'm afraid we haven't managed to identify that one yet. Anyway, we'll do our best."

"Understood, thanks. I'm heading back to the hotel now, but Lemon and I will be back at the port before dawn. Give me a bell immediately if you detect any movement in the meantime."

"Sure. Have a good evening, both of you."

EIGHTY-TWO

Back at the hotel, a tentative knock on Tim's door produced only a muffled grunt. Helen opened the door to find Tim lying on the bed in shorts and T-shirt. He had clearly still been asleep, but rose with a start as Helen came in.

"God, what time is it? I crashed out completely."

"Coming up to seven thirty."

"Sorry – I haven't really slept properly for five days."

"No, don't worry. You haven't missed anything. Draper and crew are all on the boat and seem to have hauled up the drawbridge for the night."

"You saw him?"

"To be honest, I'm not a hundred percent sure if it was him, but, yes, it looks as though the crew met him at the airport and now they're all on the boat. I'll check again later, but I think we've done all we can for today. Shall we get some food?"

"I could eat a horse – if horse is on the menu. Hotel restaurant?"

"Well, as I said, I *think* Draper's on the boat, but we should probably keep you out of sight just in case he's wandering around the town. Your cover would be blown – and mine too – if he found us in the hotel bar having a nightcap."

"Hm. Guess you're right. Hope they have a better room service menu here than at the hotel in Cassis."

Fortunately, the hotel had a very comprehensive room service menu.

"I think I might just order everything," said Tim, as he flicked through. "Twice."

Helen looked at the wine menu. "There's a very nice-looking Rioja here – bit outside our usual expenses limit, but I think your safe return deserves a little celebration. Gordon can damn well sign off on it."

"Well, I suppose I have got five days' unused travel allowance…"

Helen phoned room service and placed the order for herself and Tim. In due course, there was a knock at the door. Tim held the door open and offered a helping hand as a gamine young woman in a starched white tunic applied all her weight to manoeuvre a heavily burdened trolley into the room. The young woman laid out the spread and uncorked the wine, before withdrawing with a polite "Enjoy your meal".

Helen poured two glasses of wine and handed one to Tim. She raised her glass. "Well, thank God. Very good to have you safely back with us."

"Thank you," said Tim, clinking Helen's glass. "Very good indeed to be back with you. To put it mildly." Tim surveyed the meal and let out a sigh of appreciation. "Honestly, what an almighty relief. Dry land, a civilised meal in friendly company ..."

"I can imagine. Relief for me too. I haven't been through what you've been through, but I must say I haven't enjoyed these last few days."

"To tell the truth, I was getting really pretty low on that boat. Especially after Gibraltar. I was hoping for an SBS rescue in the Strait – when that didn't happen and then when we seemed to be heading in a completely unexpected direction ..."

"The SBS nearly went in, but there was a ton of shipping and we were worried the crew might detonate the bomb. I actually think Gordon should have sent in the French or Spanish police before it even reached that stage. I did say that to him, but he was determined this should be a British victory and no one else's."

They were silent for a few moments. Helen buttered a piece of bread and glanced at Tim.

"It *was* a daft thing for you to do, though."

"It was bonkers. Never mind getting trapped on the boat – though I must say I didn't expect that to happen ... the sea was freezing, the boat might have been locked, the crate could have been stashed anywhere and anyway it's probably sealed closed ..."

"And the navy was standing by."

They fell silent again as they started on their meal.

"I was just fed up with Gordon never giving me credit," explained Tim as he speared a slice of smoked swordfish. "I thought if I could bring in the final conclusive piece of evidence, then the record would show without any possible quibbling that it was Tim Lemon who had

293

uncovered the conspiracy and had followed through the investigation from start to finish – Gordon would have had no choice but to acknowledge the fact. But I suppose Gordon's now doubly pissed off with me. Are you sure he's not going to kick me out the minute we get back to London?"

"Gordon recognises – as does everyone else, by the way – that this whole case was plucked out of a seemingly clear blue sky by you and he knows full well that without your putting the pieces together and refusing to let go of it, we'd have been completely oblivious to what was going on." Helen looked at Tim. "I do think you should make sure you stick to protocol and refrain from wild adventures for a while, but I honestly don't think there's any likelihood Gordon will let you go." She paused. "If he does, I'm going too."

Tim looked at Helen. "Thank you for saying that."

"I'm not just saying it. I mean it."

For a second Tim thought this was just bold talk, but then it struck him that he was hearing a new note in Helen's voice. He looked down into his glass of red wine, which suddenly seemed a fathom deep. Perhaps it was the sense of release after his incarceration, perhaps it was the first rush of alcohol after his days of fasting, but he felt an unexpected glow. Accidentally setting off an awkward little rattle of cutlery, he lifted his glass to Helen's. "Thank you," he said again.

Helen too sensed that Tim had spoken with genuine feeling. "I…" She stopped.

"What?"

Helen hesitated. "I've suddenly realised who my friends are." But now Helen felt she needed to retrace a step and added a little stiffly. "It's important."

Tim ventured another touch of his glass to Helen's. "Here's to that."

"I spoke to Margaret again while I was watching the boat," said Helen, reverting to business. "She still can't get hold of the lawyer on Tenerife and we still don't know exactly where Draper's property is. If Maggie has no luck in the morning, we should probably see if the local police can help us locate it."

"Agreed. But before that, we need to resume watch on the boat from first light. At least one of us should be there until we see signs of movement. In fact, should one of us be there all night?"

"They've stowed away the launch, so I presume they're not coming ashore before morning. If the yacht itself goes anywhere, Tabi has the tracker running." Helen thought for a second. "We'd better rent a car. If they set off in the Land Cruiser, we should be ready to tail them." She reached for the phone and dialled the concierge. "Good evening. May I ask, are you able to arrange car hire?"

"Good evening, *señora*. Yes, we can do that for you in the morning."

"Could we do it this evening?"

"I'm afraid the car rental office is closed now, but we can call them when they open at nine tomorrow morning."

"I see. In which case, yes, if you could, please. Something like a compact four-wheel drive would be ideal, but whatever they have immediately available is fine."

"I will arrange that for you and confirm in the morning."

"Thank you." Helen replaced the receiver. "Damn, should have thought of that earlier. Car rental office not open till nine tomorrow. Anyway, the concierge will organise it for us."

Tim was still busy spooning second helpings onto his plate, but Helen was done with her food. She drained her wine and rose from the table.

"I'll go and give the boat a quick double-check now. Make absolutely sure Draper and co have retired for the night."

"I'll come with you."

"No, best that you continue to lie low, I think. Just in case."

"Perhaps you're right. Not quite finished here yet, anyway. See you shortly, then."

"Your phone's working now?"

Tim retrieved the phone from the wall socket. "Seems fine."

Helen gathered up the binoculars and the night scope and disappeared into the corridor.

Leaving the hotel and descending the Calle O'Daly, Helen saw that the restaurants on the way down to the port were still lively with

295

custom. But when she reached the harbour itself, she found it deserted and silent. The Land Cruiser was still parked near the quay. La Isla Bonita rolled quietly at anchor and remained in darkness apart from its deck lights. Neither the thermal imager nor the night scope revealed any sign of activity on board the yacht. After watching for a few minutes, Helen returned to the hotel.

Tim had wheeled the supper trolley into the corridor for collection by the staff. Helen knocked on his door and entered. She found him in bed and again fast asleep. He did not stir, nor break the gentle rhythm of his snoring. Helen quietly left and went to her own adjacent room.

Having set the alarm on her phone for five thirty a.m., Helen lay awake in bed. Her mind wove together images of Tim – emerging from the waves, lying exhausted in the bath – with operational planning for the following day. She heard a member of the hotel staff wheel away the supper trolley with a muted clatter. She would need to rise early tomorrow and should sleep now. As her head sank in the pillow, her breathing gradually settled, settled to the same gentle rise and fall as Tim's snoring. She fell asleep.

EIGHTY-THREE

Shocked by the ringing of her alarm, Helen sat straight up in bed. She rose, quickly readied herself and packed her few loose items – clothes, toiletries – into her travel grip. Bag in hand – if La Isla Bonita moved on, she was ready to follow – she went and knocked on Tim's door. Silence. She eased open the door. Tim was splayed on the bed and evidently still in the protean depths of sleep. Helen put down her bag and gave Tim a shake. Tim stirred, rolled onto his back and stretched. He opened an eye.

"Whoah!" Tim propped himself up on his elbows. He saw Helen's bag on the floor. "Did you spend the night here?"

"I certainly did not. Though, Lemon, I am a bit concerned about you – you seem to be in a state of permanent collapse from exhaustion."

"Raring to go," said Tim, as he hauled in a lungful of air, prised his lids open wide and stretched again.

"Well, we need a bit less raring and a bit more going. Time to get up. We have to check the boat."

Tim hastily washed and dressed and he and Helen hurried out of the hotel. As they descended through the sleeping streets to the port, they saw that the horizon was just beginning to lighten, though the sky was otherwise heavily overcast.

"Fuck," exclaimed Helen as they approached the harbour.

"What?"

Helen pointed to the car park beside the quay. "That's where the Land Cruiser was – it's gone."

They bounded up the steps of the harbour wall.

"Shit, shit and fuck … look." Helen indicated the familiar launch, now moored to a jetty in the marina. "We've missed the bastards. They must already be ashore and probably with the crate. I'm such an idiot. You were quite right – we should've kept watch overnight."

"Well, we're both equally to blame – I didn't disagree with you. But, anyway, we couldn't have done anything without the rental car."

297

"Should've organised that earlier as well."

They looked out to the yacht. It bobbed quietly on the current in the pre-dawn twilight. The deck lights had been extinguished and no lights shone within. Helen dialled Tabi's number.

"Shah, morning."

"Morning, Helen."

"Glad you're at your desk. Listen, we've just got back to the harbour. It's barely light yet, but the bloody Land Cruiser's already taken off somewhere. Have you got it on satellite?"

"I'm afraid you have dense cloud cover this morning. I was hoping you were going to tell me the vehicle was still in the car park."

"Unfortunately, not." Helen frowned in thought. "Okay ... Shah, please ask Maggie to let me know if she gets any new word on the location of Draper's property. Otherwise, we'll call you again a bit later."

"No good?" asked Tim.

"Too much cloud." Helen gazed down the deserted promenade and grimaced. "Fuck, now what do we do? We're stuck till the town wakes up."

"There might at least be someone on duty at the police station. We could go and ask if they know this whatever of the whatever ... as you suggested."

"Aprisco de la Cumbre Vieja." Helen nodded in agreement. "Good point ... let's try. I've seen where the police station is."

The police station was in a side street running from the Calle O'Daly. The building exhibited no sign of life, but the entrance was open. As Tim and Helen entered, they looked down a darkened corridor to a counter – illuminated by fluorescent lighting, but at first sight unmanned. However, upon approaching, they discovered a young man in uniform slumped in a chair in contorted slumber. Helen rapped softly on the desk.

"*Buenos días*. Good morning," she said.

The young policeman, still half asleep, screwed up his face and then opened his eyes.

"*Buenos días*," said Helen again.

The policeman consulted his watch and ran a hand through a tousled mane of black hair. He stretched and struggled from his chair.

"Good morning," said Helen for the third time.

The young man came to the counter while continuing a little pantomime of struggling to wakefulness.

"*Buenos días,*" he said finally. "How can I help?"

"We're trying to find an address," explained Helen. "Aprisco de la Cumbre Vieja."

"Cumbre Vieja?" clarified the policeman.

"Aprisco de la Cumbre Vieja," repeated Helen.

"Aprisco?" enquired the policeman.

There was a pad on the counter with a pen standing in a holder. Helen took them and wrote down the name of Draper's property for the policeman. The young man scrutinised Helen's note carefully for a few moments. He looked at his watch again.

"At six twenty-five in the morning?"

"It's rather urgent," explained Tim.

The policeman turned to a row of low cupboards stacked with papers. At one end was a coffee machine. The policeman went to the coffee machine. He removed and discarded the used coffee grounds and replenished the machine with a fresh supply and then disappeared to refill the water tank. As the coffee machine hissed and burbled, the young man studied a large map of the island pinned to the wall while running his hands through his hair in a repeat of his waking toilette. He poured himself a coffee and came back to the counter. He took up the piece of paper bearing the address and considered it at length as he sipped his coffee. Finally, he put it down.

"No idea," he said. Seeing the exasperation on the faces of Tim and Helen, the policeman relented a little. "Cumbre Vieja," he said, walking across to the map, "is all of this area." He waved his hand across the southern half of the island. "But this Aprisco … no idea. Maybe if you come back at nine or nine thirty one of my colleagues will know."

"At nine o'clock?" asked Helen.

"Or nine thirty," repeated the policeman.

299

Tim and Helen went back to the hotel.

"I'm going for a quick swim in the pool," said Helen.

"A swim?"

"Well, we can't do anything else for another couple of hours."

"I've done enough swimming. I'll order breakfast."

Back in Tim's room, Helen took a black one-piece bathing suit from her travel grip and disappeared into the bathroom. She re-emerged a few moments later wearing the costume and pulling a towelling robe around her.

"Yoghurt, fruit, toast and tea for me, please," she said. "I'll be back in twenty minutes or so."

Tim rang down for breakfast. He again ordered a copious amount for himself. He was no longer so ravenously hungry, but after his days of deprivation he could not resist the temptation to take full advantage of the menu.

Only a few minutes had passed when Helen reappeared at the door.

"He's here," she said abruptly, throwing her towelling robe on the bed. "Draper's here."

"He's here at the hotel?"

"He's taking breakfast down by the pool. He didn't see me." Helen was rummaging in her bag as she spoke. She took out a skimpy bikini in blue and white sailor stripes.

"What are you doing?" asked Tim.

"I'm going to see if I can engage him in conversation."

Helen again disappeared into the bathroom. She returned moments later wearing her tiny striped bikini. Tim was quite taken aback. Helen looked magnificent. If her classical namesake had launched a thousand ships, Helen would surely be able to sway the master of a single megayacht. She tossed her black one-piece costume on the bed and wrapped herself in the towelling robe.

"I hope you won't mind..." Tim hesitated. He gave an awkward little laugh. "I mean, I ... I hope you won't mind if I say you look really quite stunning."

"Hah. Let's hope the bikini works on Draper."

"How many swimming costumes have you brought?" There was a note of surprise in Tim's voice.

300

"Just the two."

"I didn't think to bring even one."

"I'll see if I can wheedle out of him where this bloody property is."

"Well, take care. Last girl I saw with Draper and wrapped in a bathrobe was Lucy Trenchard."

"I will. Best you keep out of sight till I get back. Call the office, tell them where we stand."

Helen disappeared. Tim sat down on the bed beside Helen's discarded black swimming costume. He could not shake off the vision of Helen in her bikini. And, just as much as that, she was being so uncharacteristically relaxed in his presence and so considerate towards him. It was a minute or two before he picked up his phone to report to the office on Draper's appearance at the hotel. When breakfast arrived, Tim sat eating in a mixture of confusion and excitement. For the moment, his attention was rather distracted from the mission.

EIGHTY-FOUR

Imposing as an Easter Island statue and animated only by his flicking through news on an iPad, Draper sat by the pool. He wore an ash grey linen blazer with a herringbone stitch, a white linen shirt, pale beige chinos and red deck shoes. A glass of orange juice and a pot of tea sat on the table in front of him. Helen made a point of ignoring him as she collected a towel from the pool attendant and selected a lounger not *too* close to Draper, but close enough for them to strike up a conversation in due course. She shed her towelling robe and paraded past Draper – still pointedly ignoring him … but, ah, she had his attention now – to the end of the pool. She dived in and swam a couple of lengths. Floating to the side, she pulled herself out of the water in front of her lounger – and just a few yards from Draper's now watchful eye. She posed herself on the end of her lounger, arched her spine and tossed back her hair as she towelled it dry.

A waiter approached. Helen recognised him as the same middle-aged man who had served her at breakfast the previous morning.

"Good morning, Miss Stride." He gave a deferential nod. "Would you like something to drink or may I bring you some breakfast?"

"Please," said Helen, making sure that she spoke just loud enough for Draper to hear that she was ordering breakfast. "Please could I have orange juice, plain yoghurt, a plate of fruit, wholemeal toast with honey and English breakfast tea."

"Of course, *señorita*."

At the periphery of her vision, Helen had seen that Draper had been watching her throughout this exchange. Now at last she looked him directly in the eye and turned upon him a smile which artfully blended a suggestion of coy reserve with an inviting radiance – she was a woman of propriety who might succumb to improper advances on a holiday island. Helen could see that she had hit the bullseye. She inclined her head. "Good morning," she said.

"Good morning," acknowledged Draper. He admired Helen for a further brief second. "Would you care to join me?" He gestured at the breakfast things set out on his table.

302

Helen paused for a second as though deliberating. "Well, why not? Thank you, that would be nice."

She stood and wrapped herself loosely in the towelling robe – again putting on a little display of modesty, while in fact leaving her breasts and legs partially exposed to Draper's gaze. She took a seat beside him.

"Charles Draper." He offered her his hand. "Miss Stride – I believe I just heard the waiter say, but …?" He raised his eyebrows in enquiry.

"Helen … Helen Stride. And, sorry, Charles …?"

"Charles Draper."

They shook hands.

"Nice to meet you, Charles."

"The pleasure is all mine."

"You're staying at the hotel?" asked Helen.

"Actually, I have a boat. Just came ashore for a spot of breakfast."

"Not by any chance the beautiful yacht I saw parked outside the harbour yesterday?"

"I guess it must be the very same."

"Goodness. I'm mightily impressed. Stunning boat."

"She is a beauty, isn't she? My pride and joy."

"I'm surprised you could tear yourself away for breakfast."

Draper smirked conceitedly.

"Are you cruising around the islands?" asked Helen.

"Actually, it's just a fleeting visit. The yacht is undergoing sea trials and I'm slightly embarrassed to say I flew over here from London just for one day to see how she was faring."

Helen looked suitably impressed.

"And you?" asked Draper.

"Staying at the hotel … but just for a few days." Helen gestured vaguely in the direction of the Cumbre Vieja. "You know La Palma?"

"First time here."

"Me too."

The waiter reappeared with a large tray bearing Helen's breakfast order and a cooked breakfast which Draper had clearly requested for himself before Helen's arrival.

"So," resumed Helen, "may I ask what you do to own a boat like that?"

"I'm a hedge fund manager."

"Financial hot shot."

"If you like. And you?"

"Actually, I work in a travel agency – hence the bargain break. One of the perks of the job – easy to grab an offer when you see one."

"Indeed," said Draper. "Although ..." He held up his iPad in evidence. "... I guess we can all do that to some extent these days."

EIGHTY-FIVE

More than an hour passed before Helen reappeared at Tim's door.

"Well?" asked Tim the moment Helen stepped into the room.

"Told me nothing we don't know already. Talked about his hedge fund and grilled me on the challenges facing the traditional travel agency business in the internet age … I told him I was a travel agent."

"You managed to bullshit your way through?"

"Well, I was a travel agent once and still own a share in one, so it's kind of home territory."

"You were a travel agent?"

"Have I never told you? Yes, before university and before joining the Service. Anyway, the point is Draper would not be drawn on whether he has some special interest in La Palma. But …" Helen held up a hand. "… all is not lost. He's invited me onto the boat for a glass of champagne. I've said yes. I'll find an excuse to check if that cabin is still locked. Lower deck, port aft, wasn't it?"

Tim nodded.

"His crew will be here at about nine to pick us up and ferry us out to the yacht. I'm due to meet him in the lobby in fifteen minutes."

Helen's hair was wet, but her costume had dried. She brushed out her hair, applied lipstick and threw on a white cotton mini-dress over her bikini.

"Helen, I really hope you're all right doing this. All the evidence suggests Draper's at the very least a cold fish and, if our suspicions are correct, then he's an utterly heartless bastard and would-be mass murderer."

"I'll manage."

"What name are you using?"

"My own. Waiter by the pool recognised me from yesterday morning and addressed me by name. One time we could have done without such good service. Right, I'm off. I'll send you a text the minute we're out of the hotel so that you can go and give the police station another try – in case I get nothing useful out of Draper. And give the concierge a chase on the car in case we need that."

305

EIGHTY-SIX

"Helen." Draper manoeuvred his huge frame out of the recesses of an armchair in the hotel lobby. "My chaps will be here in a second."

As they turned to the hotel entrance, the Land Cruiser drew up outside.

"Indeed, here they are," said Draper.

One of the Russians emerged from the back of the car. Helen saw that it was Suskin. Of average height and build, he had a hatchet face, rimless glasses and oiled-back hair. He carried a laptop under one arm. He pushed through the revolving door of the hotel entrance.

"Konstantin …" said Draper, while also holding out an arm to sweep Helen into the conversation.

Suskin did not reply, but gave Helen an icy look.

"Konstantin, very minor change of plan. May I present Miss Stride. Helen, this is Konstantin, one of my crew. I have invited Helen onto the yacht for a quick glass of champagne."

"Mr Draper, there is no time for this."

"Oh, we can spare a couple of hours. Everything is on schedule, yes?"

"Everything is on schedule."

"Then we have time. I've already put the plane back by a couple of hours." He turned to Helen and explained, "Private jet." He motioned towards the Land Cruiser. "Shall we?"

"I will take coffee at the hotel," said Suskin. From his basilisk glare, he was clearly not at all happy with Draper's impromptu arrangement.

Helen had a text message – 'Leaving' – ready to send to Tim at the touch of a button, but she thought she should now add that Suskin was taking coffee in the hotel. She told Draper that she would just hand in her room key and, while at reception, added a line to her message. She sent the message and rejoined Draper.

The two blond and brutish-looking Russians in the Land Cruiser, the older, who was at the wheel and whom Helen knew to be Ivan Markov, distinguished by fiercely bloodshot eyes, greying stubble and in particular an indentation in the bone of his left eye socket just above the eye and also a missing top to his left ear, and the younger, of Slavic appearance with sharp cheekbones and almond-shaped eyes, eyes which had eerily pale irises and the look of a fish laid out on a marble slab, both of these two reacted with the same stony-faced displeasure as that exhibited by Suskin upon Draper's announcement that they would have a guest on the yacht for an hour or two. Helen's polite greeting was met with granite silence.

EIGHTY-SEVEN

Tim was on the hotel phone to the concierge when Helen's text message came through to his mobile. The concierge confirmed that a rental car for their use would be delivered to the hotel by ten a.m. Tim immediately left his room to return to the police station. On his way out of the hotel, a brief inspection of the common parts revealed that Suskin was on a terrace drinking coffee and, as ever, playing with his laptop.

This time Tim found a number of officers at the police station and one came straight to the counter. However, a brief conference among the officers still did not produce an answer as to the whereabouts of Draper's property. The bulkiest and most senior looking of the policemen leant against the counter.

"I have one suggestion. If you go to the post office and ask for Alfonso. He knows everywhere. The post office is go back into the Calle O'Daly, up the street one hundred metres and into the street on the right."

Tim followed the policeman's directions and quickly located the post office. But when he made enquiries within, an efficient young woman in a crisp white blouse informed him that Alfonso was out delivering mail and would not be back until about eleven. Tim wandered along the Calle O'Daly. He was stymied for the moment. He hoped Helen was all right. Finding himself in front of a bookshop, he went in. Guide books to the Canaries and to La Palma were prominently on display. Tim flipped open several of the books and glanced at the index pages just in case Aprisco de la Cumbre Vieja was some kind of landmark and in case there happened to be a reference to it. There was none. One of the guide books included a map of the island which was rather more detailed than the tourist map which the hotel had given to Helen. Tim bought the book and returned to the hotel and to his room.

Helen's rumpled black one-piece swimming costume still lay on the bed. Tim smoothed the costume so that it roughly took Helen's shape. He sat on the bed beside the costume and opened the guide book. His eyes travelled no further than the opening sentence as the very first words ignited a distant memory and transfixed him in a moment of dreadful epiphany. He felt his insides turn to liquid. "Oh, Jesus." He went back to the contents page and ran a finger down the chapter headings. Sure enough, there it was. He fumbled for his phone. Margaret answered.

"Maggie, it's Tim. I've just bought a guide book to the island." His voice was shaking. "The very first sentence tells you. Here, I'll read it: 'La Palma, also known as La Isla Verde, the Green Island, or La Isla Bonita, the Beautiful Island ...' Maggie, it's not the yacht – well, it is the yacht – but it's also the island. La Isla Bonita is La Palma. I remember seeing ..."

"Holy Mary, Mother of God," breathed Maggie, interrupting Tim. "I know what you're about to tell me. Why didn't I think of this before? This is infinitely, infinitely worse than we thought."

EIGHTY-EIGHT

Draper was showing Helen around the yacht. Upon arrival, he had insisted that the cavilling Russians bring out the two jet skis from the housing beneath the tailgate so that he and Helen could take a spin a little later if the mood seized them. They had then proceeded with a tour of the boat. Draper could not resist boasting about the tens of millions spent on the yacht, its top speed of twenty-four knots and range of one thousand five hundred nautical miles, the months spent with the boat builders discussing the bespoke design, the dozens of craftsmen who had worked on the interior, particularly on the carefully selected wood panelling and fitted furniture, the Italian artist who had created the carved screen in the living area and, yes, those were genuine Picassos in the master bedroom ...

While mindful of her reason for being on the yacht, Helen could not help but be rather agog at its opulence. "This is quite fabulous," she said, deliberately pandering to Draper's ego, but also meaning what she said.

Draper showed her the bridge. Markov sat in the captain's leather chair, coldly eyeing Helen as a komodo dragon might some hapless creature which had trespassed upon its lair. Helen ignored him. She surveyed the impressive array of computer screens set in the midst of wood panelling and leather upholstery – a cross between the bridge of the Starship Enterprise and a gentlemen's club, she reflected. She noticed Markov was making a little show of tapping a message into his mobile. She wasn't sure, but thought he might have just used the phone to snap a picture of her.

"Well," said Draper. "I promised you a glass of champagne. Let us repair to the outer deck."

Draper had not shown Helen the lower deck where the guest cabins were located. They passed the stairwell.

"And down here?" asked Helen.

"The guest cabins," explained Draper.

"Could I see those too?"

"They're not quite as sumptuous as the master suite ..."

"The whole boat is simply unbelievable. I'd love to see ..."

"Well, of course. Why not? Come ..."

Draper ushered Helen down the stairs.

"May I?" asked Helen, taking the door handle of the port aft cabin.

"Please."

Helen turned the handle. The door opened to reveal a guest chamber somewhat smaller than the master suite but almost as splendid, for all Draper's disavowal. But no crate. Helen went through to the bathroom. Pristine – and empty.

"It's like the very finest hotel," said Helen. "Better than. A floating palace."

They went out of the room into the central stairwell.

"And the other cabins?" Helen took another door handle.

"They vary slightly, but they're all pretty much the same. Go ahead." Draper gestured for Helen to enter.

Helen looked into the second guest room. She decided it was clear she was not going to find the crate down here, nor indeed anywhere on the boat – it had been taken ashore, as she had surmised. She was also slightly wary of opening the door to the cabin which Tim had occupied – just in case he had left any tell-tale signs of his presence, laundry sack notwithstanding.

"Wonderful. Your future guests will be hugely spoilt."

"Champagne, then."

They returned to the main deck and visited the galley. The younger Russian was standing scowling in the corner as he scored the peel of an orange with a Sabatier knife so that he could tear off the skin in strips. Draper selected a vintage Krug and asked the Russian to put it into an ice bucket and to bring it out to them with a couple of champagne glasses. Draper then escorted Helen through the living area to the outer deck.

Outside, Draper sat down in one of the stylish dark rattan armchairs plumped with white cushions. He gave a sigh of manifest satisfaction. Helen wandered over to the side rail and pointedly admired the island.

311

"Seems a pity to pay such a brief visit," she said. "Aren't you tempted to stay and cruise around for a while or perhaps spend some time exploring the island?"

"Well," said Draper, "as I explained at breakfast, this voyage isn't really a pleasure cruise. It's rather the first long-haul ocean-going sea trial for the boat. I just popped over to see how it was going. And she's performing beautifully, I'm pleased to say."

"And the island?" asked Helen. "I'd be delighted to go for a hike with you along the volcanic ridge if you could extend your visit a little. The hotel concierge told me it's quite spectacular up there."

"No doubt," said Draper. "And a marvellous suggestion. But I'm sorry to say it will have to wait for another day."

The young Russian emerged with the champagne and plonked it on the table in front of Draper with a minimum of ceremony. Helen noticed there was also a large burl wood cigar box on the table and beside it what looked like a miniature guillotine.

"Thank you, Dmitri," said Draper. He saw that Helen was looking at the guillotine. "My little toy," he explained.

Draper rose from his chair. He took the gilt wrapper and wire cage from the champagne cork, eased the cork with his thumbs and sent it popping from the bottle. He carefully poured two glasses and handed one to Helen. He raised his glass.

"Well, here's to my beautiful and charming guest ... and our all too brief acquaintance."

For a second it flashed across Helen's mind that she did not like the sound of 'all too brief acquaintance.' "Cheers," she said. "Thank you again for the invitation to the yacht." She took a sip before resuming the chase. "I think you told me at breakfast that this was your first visit to the island?" Helen wandered back to the handrail and gazed at the island as though inexorably drawn to its charms.

"Indeed, yes."

"Any special reason for coming to La Palma – I mean, rather than to one of the more popular islands?"

At this moment, Markov appeared and handed Draper a sheet of paper. Draper studied the sheet in silence. He pursed his lips and his expression clouded just perceptibly. Helen wondered whether this was some adverse financial report from Draper's hedge fund team or

312

perhaps an impatient memo from Andropov. Draper turned the sheet of paper over and tucked its corner beneath the cigar box, so that the light sea breeze would not send it fluttering across the deck. He looked at Helen.

"It seems I have a weakness," he said. The warmth seemed to have left his voice.

"Don't we all," offered Helen, hoping a conciliatory word might recover Draper's mood and bring him back to her theme.

Draper stood in thought for a second before reinstalling a chilly smile on his face. "Do you watch much television?"

"Some ... why?"

Draper did not answer, but selected a cigar from the box, rolled it pensively between thumb and index finger, inserted it into the guillotine and triggered the mechanism. With a zip and thunk, the blade severed the tip of the cigar. Draper removed the cigar, took a gold lighter from his pocket and then rotated the cigar between thumb and forefinger as he played the flame about its severed tip. He blew on the tip of the cigar to produce a glow, put the cigar into his mouth and drew upon it three or four times. Puffs of smoke began to uncoil.

Helen was starting to feel uneasy and now noticed that, after a brief whispered exchange in Russian, the two crewmen had taken up position behind her at the head of the two flights of steps leading down to the diving platform and the tethered launch and jet skis. Their positions might have been coincidence, but it was also possible they were blocking her exit.

"My weakness," said Draper, "is for beautiful women: it seems I am far too trusting of them. My Russian colleagues, on the other hand ..." Draper retrieved the sheet of paper from beneath the cigar box and waved it in the air before replacing it on the table and putting the cigar box back on top of it with a slightly menacing clunk. "... my Russian colleagues are altogether more wary. And they have friends in all the wrong places who, for a small emolument, will provide all manner of useful information – no matter that it is generally restricted."

Helen was clinging to the hope that the conversation would suddenly take a sunnier turn, but by now she was beginning to dread

313

the worst. Though the air was warm and the breeze was light, she felt a shiver run through her.

"My first mistake," continued Draper, "was Lucy Trenchard. A terrible waste and a terrible tragedy."

Helen could detect no note of remorse in Draper's voice – rather he sounded grotesquely smug.

"I truly thought Lucy was the one. I started to drop little hints about what I was planning – to test her reaction. She rather held me in awe, you see, and I really thought she would follow me. But instead she recoiled at my suggestions. I realised I had misjudged her. I also realised that, although I had said nothing which would give the game away in advance, nothing which *a priori* was remotely incriminating, when I actually came to execute my scheme, Lucy would immediately realise that I was the perpetrator of the unfolding events. Alas, she had to go. Fortunately, Andropov's man Vasiliev is resourceful in that way." Draper paused. He looked at Helen. "Miss Stride, I can see you are wondering why I am telling you this." Draper tapped the piece of paper beneath the cigar box. "I suppose you are a colleague of that buffoon Lemon and the pompous gorilla with the braces?"

The worst was confirmed. Helen resisted the temptation to tell Draper that it was entirely thanks to 'that buffoon Lemon' that MI5 was onto him and that, moreover, the same buffoon had just spent five days as Draper's uninvited guest on the yacht under the very noses of his henchmen. Helen glanced again at the Russians and now realised that Markov, who had been standing with his hands folded in front of him, was partially concealing a pistol in the palms of his hands.

"Does MI5 specialise in unfortunate names, by the way? Lemon, Misstride ..." continued Draper with a sneer. "And, yes, that is a gun my colleague is holding. I have no idea exactly what you think you are doing here – I can only suppose it is no longer anything to do with Lucy Trenchard – but it is too late in the day for me and my associates to take any chances. I am afraid you will not be leaving this boat. Not alive, at any rate. Today would in any case have ended badly for you, though you would otherwise have been oblivious to the fact." Draper sat at the table with the cigar box. "I might as well

314

afford myself the small pleasure of telling you what is going on." He leaned back in his chair and took several luxuriant puffs at his cigar.

Helen's mind was racing as she struggled to collect her thoughts and consider how she might escape. At the same time, here was the crux of the whole operation: it seemed Draper was about to reveal the full nature of his and Andropov's murderous scheme. She had to hear him out first. But then what? She couldn't summon help – her phone was buried in her bag and this was on the chair next to Draper's. If she leapt overboard, she would be a sitting duck for Markov. Even if she eluded the first bullets, they had the launch and jet skis and could reach her in moments. Could she overpower the two Russians and reach the launch or jet skis herself? And make good her escape before they followed? She doubted it – not unless they let their guard drop for some reason. She would need to choose her moment – and to hope fervently that such a moment came. For now, she gave Draper her attention and tried to conceal that she was trembling.

"I asked you if you watched television," resumed Draper. "You didn't see the programme about La Palma some years ago? On the BBC, no less." He looked at Helen. "Apparently not. Allow me to explain. La Palma is a volcanic island. The entire southern half of the island is divided by a volcanic ridge, which is currently dormant but which experiences minor eruptions from time to time. Most recently in 1949, I believe. The volcanic structure is riven with fissures which contain water. Experts believe that in a major eruption the water would boil and the resulting water pressure would crack the island apart. The entire western flank of the island – half a trillion tons of rock – is liable to collapse into the ocean."

Helen suddenly saw Draper's plot in its entirety. She held the handrail in an effort to steady her shaking, but she could not keep the look of dread from her face.

"Ah," said Draper, "I see I have your rapt attention. Hah – you don't know the half of it yet!"

Helen did know, but she kept this to herself for the moment.

Draper drew on his cigar, but it needed relighting. He took the gold lighter from his pocket and reapplied the flame. The cigar took and Draper exhaled a few leisurely puffs into the breeze.

"Half a trillion tons of rock, Helen, plummeting into the ocean, would unleash a tidal wave which would make Fukushima look like a ripple in the bath. The Fukushima tsunami was about fifteen metres high where it hit the nuclear reactors. I don't know how far it ran inland, but I would guess no more than a mile or two. La Palma would send a mega-tsunami racing across the Atlantic at five hundred miles an hour to the east coast of America. When it hit the US, the wave would be half a mile high – fifty times the height of the wave which hit the Fukushima reactors – and it would continue to run inland with massive destructive force for ten or twenty miles. New York, Boston, Miami, the entire eastern seaboard of the US would be wiped out. Why, I see you are asking yourself ..." Draper waved his cigar at Helen. "... why, if this is the case, don't we all know about La Palma and why isn't the US – and, indeed, all the Caribbean and Central American nations too – why aren't they all taking precautions? The answer is because, following the BBC programme, rival academics came forward and questioned the likelihood of all this. They do not expect these events to happen for another ten thousand years. But here's the beauty of it, we have the means to accelerate geological time – to bring this cataclysm forwards from some remote point in the let's-not-think-about-it future to ..." Draper consulted his watch. "... seven o'clock this evening!"

At this, Helen experienced a sudden involuntary plunge in the pit of her stomach. She was fighting to retain any sort of composure at all.

"You see," continued Draper, beaming the smile of one about to deliver a deliciously forbidden confidence, "we have a bomb. A nuclear device. Right now it is planted a little way below the volcanic ridge and close to what is thought to be the most unstable fault line. I even bought a little plot of land at the ideal spot so that we could set up our device without risk of disturbance. It's primed and ready to pop. My friend Mr Suskin, whom you met briefly at the hotel, is an expert in the design and deployment of nuclear weapons. In fact, in a rather nice little twist, it is even a military device of his own construction which we happen to have laid our hands on." Draper leaned forwards a fraction in his chair. "But why, I am sure you are now asking yourself, why would we do such a despicable thing?"

Helen was not asking herself why. She knew why. She was asking herself how the hell she was going to escape, find the bomb and defuse it or remove it to a safe distance in under nine hours. Otherwise, the world faced its worst disaster in recorded history.

"Gold!" cried Draper. "Pure and simple. Every investor's ultimate safe haven in the event of disaster. Oh, imagine the financial meltdown when the eastern seaboard of the US is wiped out. The gold price will soar, will absolutely skyrocket! My good friend Alexei Andropov and I have been buying up every last scrap of the stuff that we can afford – more than we can afford, to be perfectly honest. In twenty-four, forty-eight, I don't know, seventy-two hours, Andropov and I will be up there with Bill Gates, Warren Buffett and Carlos Slim – except that, by then, those three might be down here among the lesser billionaires if the markets whack their stock ... if the markets are even operating, that is. And here ..." Draper waved his cigar with triumphant emphasis. "... here is the final beauty of the scheme. No one will have a clue what we have done, no one will suspect us for a second. The bomb will trigger a massive volcanic eruption which will obliterate all trace of its cause. What about the radioactivity, you ask? Volcanic eruptions throw up radioactivity! The mushroom cloud? But who will see it and live? The Canaries will be wiped out in the backwash from the collapse of the island. Seismologists? Won't they be able to tell the difference? Oh, come on! 'La Palma has erupted, but we think it was a nuclear bomb' ... give me a break! No one will have a clue. But will people question our massive buying of gold? No, they will not. Just google my name and you'll find a stream of newspaper articles and interviews mentioning how pessimistic I am concerning the global financial markets. Of course I've been buying gold – and why wouldn't't my close business associate Alexei Andropov follow my example? And, oh ..." Draper was positively relishing his tale. "Miss Stride, you are standing right here upon my alibi. Why would I lavish tens of millions of pounds and care and attention down to the last minute detail on this yacht only to blow it up? La Isla Bonita ... you know that's the nickname of La Palma? I named the yacht after the island.

317

The Beautiful Island indeed – the beauty of its destructive power and the untold riches it will bring to me!" Draper was flushed with the jubilation of telling his abominable story, but calmed a little as he reached his peroration. "By the time the bomb goes off, I will be back in London fulfilling an evening engagement and my friends here will have melted into the shadows."

Though Helen was still terrified at what she was hearing, the realisation had gradually come to her that perhaps she did have some cards to play after all. In his hubris, Draper thought he was beyond detection and invulnerable. But clearly he was not. Perhaps Helen could brazen out the situation – launch onto the offensive and just conceivably … perhaps there was just the slimmest chance she could convince Draper that to halt the nuclear countdown and submit himself to justice was his best recourse. Helen took a deep breath and summoned all her steel.

"Draper," she said, "you are deluding yourself in thinking no one will suspect you."

"No one has a clue!" he protested.

"On the contrary. We have been watching La Isla Bonita since it was just outside Cassis. We saw the Bucephalus deliver the nuclear materials to the yacht."

At this, Draper looked slightly taken aback.

"We have photographic evidence of the crate being transferred from one yacht to the other."

Draper recovered some of his composure. "Pah!" He waved an arm dismissively. "I find that hard to believe, but what if you do have photographs? Did you see anything suspicious? No. The Bucephalus was just along the coast, Andropov has kindly furnished me with a crew …" Draper flapped a hand in the direction of the Russians. "Why shouldn't he drop off a few Russian treats for his men? If MI5 really has pictures, it has pictures of a tea chest."

"We know about Suskin."

"*I* told you about Suskin."

"You didn't tell me about his record of torturing prisoners in Afghanistan. And …" Helen turned to Markov. "… you haven't properly introduced me to your bully boy here, but I know he is Ivan Markov and ex GRU."

318

Draper looked a little flustered, but parried again. "So what, so what? Every Russian oligarch is surrounded by people like that. Some of the Russian oligarchs *are* people like that. It doesn't mean a thing."

Helen wondered whether to mention that MI5 had had a man on board the yacht throughout the five day journey from the south of France. If Draper were made aware of this, he would understand that MI5 now had a man on La Palma – was it better to make that clear to him or to keep quiet? Perhaps it was best to let him know that Helen was not alone here, but to conceal that the man in question was Tim – whom Draper would then be able to describe to Suskin.

"One of our operatives was stowed away on board this very yacht throughout the voyage from Cassis."

"Oh, what poppycock!"

"I'm sure if you conduct a close inspection of the starboard aft guest cabin, you'll find some traces of its occupation. And we know too about the hundred million dollar payment made by Ruza Bank on the day that Andropov took delivery of the nuclear materials."

"This is all just meaningless circumstantial trivia. Ruza Bank makes billions of dollars' worth of money transfers every day of the year – you could probably pick any day you like and find one or even many transfers of tens or hundreds of millions of dollars. It means nothing."

It now occurred to Helen that she might be able to sow a little discord among her captors. "Oh, and by the way, Draper," she said in a slightly raised voice, "we also know about your dealing with Yevgeny Berezin … behind Andropov's back."

At this, Draper looked alarmed. He glanced at Markov, who now fixed him with an icy stare. Draper hesitated for a brief second, but then retorted, "You are right that I have met Berezin and it's true that he has several times expressed interest in my stake in Taiga Oil; however …" Draper also raised his voice. "… as Alexei well knows, my allegiance is absolutely and firmly with him – with Alexei – and there is simply no possibility I would sell my stake in Taiga to Berezin. Who, by the way, is a crook of the first order."

The irony of this last comment seemed completely lost on Draper. Markov, meanwhile, did not look wholly convinced; however, his

319

glare seemed to have moderated from glacially accusatory to frostily sceptical.

Helen tried a different tack. "We know about your property here – the Aprisco de la Cumbre Vieja."

Draper was by now starting to look quite angry. Helen tried her last roll of the dice.

"Draper, why do you think I am here? We know exactly what you and Andropov are doing."

"Enough! This is becoming tiresome. I am going to offer you a choice. I confess you caught my eye by the hotel pool – as was no doubt your intention. I had hoped that I and my yacht between us might seduce you, that we might share a glass or two of champagne and then christen the bed in the master suite – give the bed its own little sea trial, if you like. And then I would send you back to the island, happily unaware, to meet your apocalyptic fate along with the rest of the inhabitants. Not a bad way to spend your last day, I would have thought – being fucked by a billionaire on his superyacht? Every woman's fantasy, surely. But clearly it's not going to work out quite as smoothly as that – I can't imagine that you are about to give your free consent to my own little fantasy of screwing you. So I will offer you this choice. Either you indulge me and we spend an hour in the master suite while I take my enjoyment of that delightful body of yours – and I would add that when it comes to fucking, my tastes are straightforward – after which I will persuade these two ..." He nodded towards the Russians. "... to deliver a swift and merciful bullet to the back of the head. Or ..." Draper glared at Helen. "... if you choose not to humour me, I shall hand you over to Markov and Lubashev here, who, I should warn you, are likely to take their pleasure in ways which you or I could hardly imagine, before they feed you to the fish one still quivering piece at a time. Or, if you decide to be really uncooperative, I may even summon Suskin back from the hotel and, as you yourself quite accurately pointed out, by repute he is not a man to whom you would wish to entrust your final hour."

320

EIGHTY-NINE

Tim's phone call to Margaret an hour earlier had galvanised the London team. All had rushed to google 'La Palma tsunami' and had quickly found the transcript of the BBC programme, which confirmed Tim and Margaret's recollection and their worst fears. But the team had also found rebuttals from other academics, who argued that the programme contained factual errors and that if a collapse of the island were possible at all, it was likely to come millennia into the future. Professors at Delft University argued that even if the collapse happened, a mega-tsunami diffused across the vast expanse of the Atlantic Ocean would not be as destructive as the programme claimed. It seemed there were two sides to the discussion.

"Right," puffed Gordon, having directed everyone into the conference room. "Heads together, please. We need to come up with an immediate plan of action. We should get all these learned professors – on all sides of the debate – either into this office or on the end of a conference phone before the end of this morning so that we can determine whether this is just sensationalism or whether the island really is unstable. Trevor and Luke, on that please – as soon as we're done here. How long do we think we have, by the way? What did Andropov's message say?"

"Pop the cork on La Isla Bonita in mid-June," said Tabi.

"Mid-June – that's not helpful – it could mean in weeks or it could mean in days. Where are we now? The seventh. Well, we probably have at least two or three days and, if we're lucky, perhaps a few more. Next item on the agenda?"

"We need to get the Spanish police on board to help Helen and Tim," suggested Trevor. "Presumably, the police will be able to deal with Draper and crew and can help locate the device … or do we need to send in special forces – our own or Spain's?"

"I've already spoken to Madrid," said Maggie. "The Guardia Civil on the islands is the nearest military force and of course has the best familiarity with the terrain. The head of the force on the islands is due to fly across to La Palma from Tenerife this morning to take charge – and he's bringing reinforcements. The local team on La Palma is still unaware of what's going on – no one wanted to cause panic."

"The police on La Palma have no idea where Draper's property is." Tim's voice came over the conference phone. "Someone will be at the post office in an hour or two and he might know. But, yes, please go through the channels to get the police or the Guardia Civil ready to arrest these bastards."

"If there's any risk the nuclear device is already primed in some way, we may need some kind of specialist nuclear bomb disposal unit," said Trevor. "Can we fly in the appropriate people? That's assuming we can find the damned thing, of course."

"Madrid is already assembling a specialist team and expects to have them on La Palma by the end of today or early tomorrow," said Maggie. "Needless to say, I've offered our assistance."

"Is Andropov still in London? Are you able to haul him in?" asked Tim.

"I want the conclusive evidence in our hands before we move on him and create a huge diplomatic ruckus," said Gordon. "But, yes, he's here and we're keeping a close watch on the Alanborough. In addition, I've prevailed upon the Minister for Trade to schedule an appointment with Andropov late this afternoon on some business pretext – with a bit of luck we can get Andropov on friendly turf at the time we want to seize him. Now, what else?"

"Well, all the civil preparations," said Margaret. "Madrid is drawing up plans for evacuation of as many people as possible from the islands. But we need to get straight onto the Americans – and we should warn every other Atlantic-facing nation on the whole American continent ..."

"And every other continent," chipped in Trevor.

"Indeed," said Margaret. "But we should clearly start with the US. I think in the first instance it has to be PM to President for that."

"Christ," said Gordon, holding his head, "on the one hand I hope this whole island story is nonsense and we're chasing a chimera, but on the other we have little choice but to ensure tens of millions of people get evacuated in case it's true."

"Yes, I don't think we can hold back from telling the rest of the world," said Margaret. "With the US and elsewhere having to manage an exodus on that scale, they'll need every hour we can give them."

"Of course," said Gordon. "I wasn't suggesting we should delay. And we may need to take precautions along the south and west coasts of the UK as well."

"And we'll need to do our best to clear the Atlantic of shipping," added Tabi.

"Lord, this is a monumental task." For once, Gordon seemed to be shrinking rather than expanding upon the call of duty.

"Is the DG back from the cyber negotiations in Beijing?" asked Margaret.

"No, unfortunately not," said Gordon. "All flights in and out of Beijing are currently grounded because of sandstorms. The DG has delegated responsibility to me until he gets back." Gordon drew in a breath. "I'll go and talk to the PM right now. He needs to get COBRA back in session and they and the Cabinet need to work out how we're going to handle this with the rest of the world." Gordon leant towards the speakerphone on the conference table. "Tim, needless to say, the minute Helen's back from the boat and as soon as you can collar this chap at the post office, make sure you find out where Draper's hidden the bloody thing."

NINETY

Helen was kneeling on Draper's bed undoing the top buttons of her dress. She had weighed up her situation and had concluded she could not possibly take on all three of her captors at once. Despite Draper's huge size, Helen was less afraid of him than of the two menacing Russians. She had decided her best chance of escape lay in separating Draper from his thugs, dealing with him first and then hoping the other two were preoccupied at the moment she chose to flee the boat. Draper had dismissed the two crewmen at the door to the master suite and had mustered a minimum of civility in ushering Helen into his cabin. He had locked the door behind him and set his jacket on the back of a chair. As they had entered, Helen had noted the bronze statuette of a bull – if she could only bring the heavy sculpture down on Draper's head, that would be the end of it with him. But at this moment Draper was standing between Helen and the statuette. Like her, he was unbuttoning his shirt. He placed it neatly on the chair; his trousers followed, tidily folded over the jacket; lastly his underpants, also neatly folded and placed on top of the shirt. Somewhere at the back of her mind, Helen noted with grim satisfaction that Draper's penis was not built on the same scale as the rest of him, but was actually incongruously small. Helen herself was still only half way down the buttons of her dress as Draper advanced upon her.

Helen dismissed a fleeting thought that she could strike now or she could submit to rape in the hope that, *post coitus*, Draper would be off his guard and an easier target. She was damned if she was going to let Draper steal the slightest moment of pleasure from her. As Draper put a knee onto the bed, Helen gathered every ounce of her strength and unleashed a savage punch at his throat. With Draper's great height, Helen did not connect quite as squarely as she had hoped, but still the impact was enough to send Draper reeling backwards, gasping for breath and with his eyes wide in astonishment. Helen advanced to deliver a second blow, but Draper sent his huge spade of a hand whirling through the air and brought it crashing against the side of Helen's head. Helen was flung across the bed and, as she landed, cracked her head against a bedside table. She was blinded by explosive pain – literally so, for she could see nothing but darkness lit by sparks erupting inside her eyeballs. She felt she was on the verge of blacking out. She was dimly conscious that Draper was dragging her across the bed. She flailed and struggled, but – still blinded and with her head spinning and now with Draper's weight upon her – to no effect. She realised Draper was ripping the remaining buttons of her dress, dragging the dress off her shoulders and now wrenching it from beneath her. Enough vision returned for her to see Draper fling the dress behind him onto the floor. Draper snatched at Helen's bikini top. She saw his great head looming above her and slammed the heel of her palm into his nose. She felt and heard a cracking like the snapping of a chicken's wishbone. Draper snarled with pain and lumbered backwards off the bed. Helen could see blood spilling between his fingers. She vaguely noted that blood was also streaming down her own face from the blow to her head. She was still giddy, but looked about the room. The statuette was out of reach. There was a can of deodorant sitting on a side dresser. Helen lunged and seized it. Draper had had a lighter in his jacket pocket. Helen vaulted over the bed, but her head was still spinning and she came crashing to the floor. As she struggled to her knees and fumbled in the jacket pocket, she felt herself yanked by the back strap of her bikini top onto the bed. Helen spun, flicked open the lighter, ground the flint wheel with her thumb to spark a flame and then pressed the button on the deodorant. A foot-long flame shot from the can. She directed it straight into Draper's face. He roared with pain and staggered backwards, crashing into a full length mirror, which shattered all about him. Helen leapt to grab the bronze bull at last ... but now she heard feet thundering along the corridor towards the master suite. The door handle was tried repeatedly and ferociously while the door was pounded with a fist.

"Draper, what's going on? Draper, are you all right?"

Helen had no time to think. She needed three hands – one for the deodorant, one for the lighter and one to unlock and open the door. She held the deodorant and lighter in her left hand behind her back and reached for the door lock and handle with her right. In one swift move, she unlocked the door and threw it open. The two brutes could not help but stare for a second at Helen in her tiny bikini. Helen reignited her miniature flame-thrower and thrust this into the faces of the men. They reeled back, yelling in pain and clutching at their eyes. Markov raised his pistol and fired a wild shot. It splintered the door jamb beside Helen. She directed her flaming spray at Markov's hand. He howled with pain and dropped the gun. Helen gave the gun a sharp kick, sending it spinning down the corridor and then clattering into the stairwell. She sprayed the blazing deodorant into the faces of the men for all she was worth. The younger Russian unleashed a haymaker in what he thought was Helen's direction, but smashed into the jaw of his own colleague, sending the older man crashing against the bulkhead and then slumping to the floor. Helen tried to spray the young man again, but the deodorant was expended. She flung the can away and assaulted the still blinded younger Russian with a rain of blows, kicks, gouges to throat, eyes, testicles, stomach. Markov was staggering to his feet. The two Russians leaned towards each other. Helen saw her moment. In a single motion, she leapt in the air, grabbed the two Russians by the sides of their heads and with all her might brought their heads cracking together. The two men collapsed on the floor. But now Draper reappeared at his door, pathetically clutching to him Helen's bloodied dress. He bellowed like the Cyclops bested in his lair and, for the moment at least, was just as blind. Helen seized her dress from Draper, sprang over the fallen Russians and ran a few steps along the corridor … but then stopped. The gun was lying in the stairwell on the third step down. She should seize it and finish these three bastards now. She stared at the gun in a moment of paralysis. Draper came blundering in her direction. Helen turned and ran through the living area, across the outer deck – grabbing her bag from the rattan chair as she passed, stuffing her dress into the bag and slinging the bag over her shoulder – and then hurtled down the steps to the diving platform. She unhitched the launch and the jet skis, shoved away the launch, kicked against one of the jet skis and then jumped onto the remaining jet ski. It had a push-button ignition. She fired it up and gunned the throttle. The jet ski bucked, almost

326

throwing Helen into the water, and then went scudding across the ocean. Helen heard yells behind her from the yacht. Pistol shots rang out, but the bullets did not seem to be landing anywhere near her. But now she heard the rattle of an automatic weapon and rounds spat into the sea quite close by. She glanced back at the yacht. Lubashev was holding the submachine-gun, but was shaking his head as though to clear his vision. He raised the weapon and started firing again. Bullets went zipping into the water around Helen's jet ski. She heard one fizz by very close to her head. Suddenly she felt a searing pain like a hornet sting on her thigh. She glanced down, but could see nothing. She banked the jet ski first one way and then the other in a headlong slalom which sent up curtains of spray. As the shoreline approached, the shooting seemed to have stopped. Helen glanced again at her thigh – a red welt three or four inches long had come up and was oozing blood. She couldn't tell whether or not the bullet had entered her leg.

The jet ski careered into the shallows at the arc of black sand and Helen leaped into the water. A startled mother with two small children in tears ran from Helen along the promenade. Helen thought they must have heard and seen the shooting, but then realised that she was standing there clad in her tiny bikini with blood streaming from her head and thigh – the family was probably running from her. She tried to wash away the blood in the sea, but could staunch neither wound. At least it seemed the bullet had only scored the flesh of her thigh and not actually penetrated her leg. She took her blood-stained dress from her bag and threw it on, fastening the few buttons which remained. Fearing that Draper and his men might be in pursuit, she looked back at the yacht. To her surprise, she saw that La Isla Bonita had turned tail, abandoning its launch and the lone jet ski, and was now steaming at full speed away from the island and out to sea. It seemed Draper and his crew were trying to outrun their own mega-tsunami. If Draper's assessment was correct, this was utterly futile.

327

NINETY-ONE

Helen ran across the arc of sand and up the few steps onto the promenade. She sped along the Calle O'Daly, causing passers-by to stop and stare. Reaching the hotel, she plunged through the revolving doors at the entrance and made for the flight of steps up to her first floor room. But then she realised she had handed in her key and Tim might not be in the room. She turned back to the reception desk. She saw that the several guests in the lobby were all standing and gawping at her. She was past caring.

She stood at the reception desk, dishevelled, bruised, bleeding and out of breath. "Key to room 108, please."

The two young women at the desk in their trim dark blue uniforms stared in astonishment.

"Key to 108, please," repeated Helen.

"Shall I call a doctor?" asked one of the receptionists, still looking stunned. "Or the police?"

"Just the room key, please."

The young woman seemed dazed as she retrieved the key and handed it to Helen. Helen grabbed the key and ran. But then stopped and ran back.

"Do you have a first aid kit?" she asked.

The first girl still seemed to be in shock, but the second affirmed that they did and disappeared into an office behind the reception desk. She reappeared with a small green plastic case with a red cross on the side.

"What do you need?" she asked, as she started to unfasten it.

"I'll take it and bring it back. Thank you," said Helen, as she seized the case and dashed for the stairs.

As she ran along the corridor to the refuge of Tim's room, Helen was suddenly overwhelmed with the release of emotions which had been held in check while her adrenalin had been pumping – she experienced a flood of relief that for the moment she was home safe, but at the same time renewed terror at what had happened and at the enormity of what she had been told. She was weeping and shaking uncontrollably as she vainly attempted to fit the door key into the slot. But the door opened for her and there stood Tim.

"Jesus Christ, Helen. What on earth happened? Are you all right?"

Tim scooped Helen into the room. She dropped her bag and the first aid kit onto the floor and fell upon Tim's shoulder, sobbing and struggling to speak.

"The fucking, fucking, *fucking* bastard tried to rape and kill me."

Tim opened his mouth in shock. "I'm going after that piece of shit right now," he growled. "Did he hit you? I can see his handprint on your face. We'll nail these fucking scumbags. Are they still on the boat?"

"Lemon, it's worse …"

"He did worse?"

"No, no, he just slapped me up a bit and I was grazed by a bullet … but I kicked the shit out of the three of them." Helen calmed a little and spoke more evenly. "And now they're on the run on the boat. But, listen, it's the island – La Isla Bonita is the island, La Palma."

"I know."

"You know? How?"

"I bought a guide book. It was in the very first line."

"But you don't know what he's planning to do. It's unspeakable…"

"Yes, I do – we do. I saw this TV programme – Maggie saw it too. He plans to blow up the island and unleash a massive tsunami on the eastern seaboard of the US. I've been on the phone and already all hell's been let loose in London and I should think in every Atlantic-facing nation by now. So he told you?"

"He was intending to kill me. He couldn't help boasting about what he was about to do."

"Did he tell you where the bomb is?"

"It's where we thought – at the Aprisco, which is somewhere near one of the fault lines on the volcanic ridge. But he didn't say exactly where that is."

"Fuck, so we still need Alfonso."

"Who?"

329

"This guy at the post office. He's due back from his mail round shortly and might know where we're talking about."

"We must go then."

"No, first let's get you cleaned up and bandaged and then we can go."

"But, Lemon, we don't have time."

"Yes, we do. First things first."

"No, Lemon, you don't understand … it's today."

"What's today?"

"The bomb is primed to go off at seven this evening."

Tim went completely white. "Holy fuck." He stood dumbstruck for a second. "Holy Christ. Gordon and everyone are assuming we have at least a few days. The Spanish government and the US and other affected countries all think they have time to evacuate."

"We have to get to that bomb and defuse it or get it off the island."

Tim exhaled. "Jesus Christ." He thought for a moment. "Look, Alfonso won't be at the post office just yet. You get cleaned up, I'll speak to London."

Helen stepped into the bathroom. Tim dialled Gordon.

NINETY-TWO

Gordon was stunned into silence for a second and then gave vent to a stream of invective. "We've just heard from Madrid that their specialist nuclear unit won't be on La Palma until tomorrow morning, which of course will be too late – and the Spanish government has barely even begun to draw up evacuation plans for the islands, never mind putting them into effect. And COBRA's just moments ago done a call with its US counterpart – PM, President, Home Secretary and Foreign Secretary, Secretary of State, Homeland, the lot, military top brass … We're going to have to get them all back on the phone right now."

"Gordon, we need to make sure we keep track of the yacht as well," added Tim. "Draper and his crew have fled on the boat. If we can find and disarm the bomb so there's no longer any risk of a tsunami or nuclear fallout, then we should send in the frigate to grab these bastards. But we should also ground Draper's private jet and keep that under police guard just in case he decides to head back and try to escape by that route."

"You're right. I'll get Maggie onto the Spanish police with a request to put a chopper on the yacht's tail and to impound the jet and I'll anyway make sure Tabi keeps the tracker running. As soon as we know it's safe to send in the frigate and the SBS, we'll do so." A softer note entered Gordon's voice. "Look, Tim, is Helen really all right?"

"Bit battered, but, yes, she's all in one piece."

"Thank God for that at least." Gordon reverted to his usual more peremptory tone. "Tim, I know I don't need to repeat myself, but you have to locate that damned bomb. Unless you and Helen can stop it, this is going to be carnage."

"We're on our way. How about Andropov?"

"Sod it, yes. Never mind this afternoon's bogus meeting with the minister – it's time we reeled Andropov in."

NINETY-THREE

Helen emerged from the bathroom with a towel wrapped round her. She dropped her torn and bloodied dress into a waste paper basket sitting beside a chest of drawers. "Lemon, please can you help with the dressings?" She picked up the first aid kit from the floor and sat on the bed. There remained a trickle of blood at her temple, while the wound on her thigh glistened with a translucent ichor still spotted with blood. She looked a little downcast. "Lemon, I couldn't do it…"

"Do what?"

"The gun was right there. I could easily have grabbed it and killed the three of them on the spot. But I couldn't bring myself to do it."

"Helen, you beat the shit out of two Russian thugs and a giant. And maybe the fact that you couldn't finish them off makes you a better human being than they are."

"I suppose so, but it's my job …"

"Come on, you were an absolute fucking heroine." Tim sat beside Helen and dabbed her temple clean. "You might need a couple of stitches here." He did his best to tape the wound closed and applied a large plaster.

With Tim's reassurance, Helen's confidence and her usual businesslike manner returned. "We don't have time for stitches. We have to get going."

Helen held a large wad of dressing against her thigh while Tim taped it down and then wrapped a bandage around it.

"Right, that will do. Thank you," she said.

Helen stuffed a few spare plasters, dressings and bandages into her shoulder bag, took fresh clothes from her travel grip and then stepped into the bathroom to dress. Tim looked at Helen's battered dress hanging from the edge of the waste paper basket. His fury with Draper had barely subsided. Where he had previously been excited at Helen's appearance in her bikini, he now felt only protectiveness towards her. He was pleased that she so evidently felt secure with him.

Helen reappeared and gathered a few more items into her shoulder bag. They left the room.

"Shit, Suskin," said Helen, as she and Tim went downstairs. "We need to get him arrested."

"I think he may have left the hotel. I did a quick scout round when I got back here and he seemed to have gone."

"Let's ask the front desk."

Helen returned the first aid kit and asked the young woman on reception if she had seen a man answering to Suskin's description leave the hotel. The young woman seemed flustered for a moment – as though she had still not worked out the correct response to Helen's earlier blood-covered appearance – but then regained her composure, expressed her relief that Helen now looked a great deal better and directed Helen and Tim to the concierge.

Helen described Suskin to the concierge.

"Ah, yes, the Polish gentleman. Mr Piotr Wasilewski?"

"Yes," said Helen.

"No," said Tim simultaneously.

The concierge looked from Tim to Helen and raised a quizzical eyebrow.

"Yes," said Tim.

The concierge raised both his eyebrows.

"Yes," repeated Tim.

"I booked him on a flight to Madrid a little while ago. Rather short notice, but he was lucky – there were plenty of seats." The concierge tapped at his computer keyboard and eyed the screen. "Iberia flight IB3933. Took off ten minutes ago."

"Thank you," said Tim, while cursing under his breath. "And I believe you have car keys for us?"

Tim and Helen did not immediately need the car – the post office was only a few minutes' walk from the hotel. They hastened across the Calle O'Daly and down the road to the post office.

"Do you think we should get the flight recalled?" asked Tim. "On the one hand, we need to get to the bomb as fast as possible and we can't afford to spend hours getting tangled up with the local police in turning the flight around, plus we can anyway get Suskin arrested on

333

arrival in Madrid, but on the other we might need him to defuse the bomb."

"You're right," said Helen. She dialled London. "Maggie ..."

"Helen! Are you all right?"

"Yes, I'm fine."

"I can't believe what that animal put you through. But you're honestly okay?"

"Yes, honestly. Draper is a bastard beyond imagining – but, really, I'm fine. Maggie, we have to get Suskin. He's just left La Palma on a flight to Madrid. Iberia 3933. He's travelling on a Polish passport under the name Piotr Wasilewski. We need to turn the plane back and get him in custody. We might need him to deactivate the weapon."

"Right, I'll get straight onto it," said Maggie. "And, by the way, the coast guard on La Palma is despatching a helicopter in pursuit of the yacht. They're not equipped to mount an assault, but they can at least make sure we maintain close observation until we have the SBS team in range. And the police are on their way to seize Draper's private jet."

NINETY-FOUR

"Trevor, is that conference call set up?" asked Gordon.

On the large wall screens behind Gordon, Sky News and CNN were carrying first reports that the alert concerning potential seismic activity in the Canaries and the risk of an ensuing tsunami – the official version of events pre-agreed by the British, US and Spanish governments for public broadcast – this alert had now been stepped up to the highest level with a call for immediate evacuation of all potentially affected areas, including the entire eastern seaboard of the US. Helicopter shots of US highways from Florida to Maine showed mounting tailbacks of traffic and there was word of looting in Miami. However, from the Canary Islands themselves the networks seemed to have no live coverage and their reports showed only old file footage of palm trees nodding under a blue sky and aerial shots of the volcanic landscape.

"We can't reach the two professors who proposed the theory," explained Trevor. "Apparently, they're at an earthquake symposium somewhere near Tokyo and as of this minute they're on a side excursion to the summit of Mount Fuji where there's no mobile signal." Seeing that Gordon was building up to a volcanic explosion of his own, Trevor raised a pacifying hand. "However, we do have a colleague of theirs from UCL who did field work with them and who had a hand in the BBC programme. He says he's up to speed on the subject and he's in the top floor conference room now. We've also got someone from Zurich who contributed work on the likely tsunami effect and then, on the opposing side, we have a professor from Madrid University's Department of Seismology and someone from Delft on the tsunami. The call's due to kick off in fifteen minutes."

"All right, good. Tabi, over here, please. Trevor, give Tabi all the participants' details. Tabi, I want you to run the call. I'll be with you up in the conference room in five minutes and I'll formally host it. We'll have both COBRA and the rest of the Cabinet dialling in at this end and a similar representation dialling in from the US. I expect

335

both the PM and the President will be on the call. The Spanish Prime Minister and his Cabinet are currently in emergency session, so won't be participating – but clearly will want to know the outcome as soon as the call is done. Oh and, Tabi, before you head upstairs, what's the latest on Draper's yacht?"

"Still heading out to sea." Tabi gave a nod of acknowledgement towards Maggie. "We have the La Palma coast guard on their tail now as well as the satellite coverage."

"Good. And, Margaret, latest on Draper's jet and on Suskin?"

"Draper's jet is grounded. It's actually not his own plane, nor Andropov's – Draper chartered it for the trip. The pilot is ex-RAF, apparently. He's happy to be at our disposal if the plane's needed for Helen and Tim. Suskin, on the other hand, is not going quite so smoothly: the captain of the flight is saying he's just taken off with a full load of fuel and safety regulations don't permit him to land until he's ditched a significant part of the load. He wants to circle over the ocean dumping fuel."

"Damn. See if you can get an override from someone in Madrid and tell them to persuade the captain to return to La Palma immediately. Where's the head of the Guardia Civil from Tenerife, by the way? We need him on the ground in La Palma."

"He and his men are due there any minute," said Margaret.

"Set up a call with him as soon as he's in situ. Now, Trevor … and Luke …" Gordon waved Luke into the conversation. "… – need you two. It's time we acted on Andropov. I've got sign off from the PM. You two head over to the Alanborough. There are special police units posted at strategic points all round the hotel waiting for the nod from us. Trevor, I'm going to be on the conference call, so I'm delegating to you responsibility for giving the green light. Maybe call in to Maggie first, just to check there's no change, then go in and get him. Right, Tabi, get everyone on line for the call. I'll be up there in two."

NINETY-FIVE

"Alfonso is here," said the young woman at the post office counter in the neatly starched white blouse, "but he's just taking his coffee."

Tim threw up his hands in exasperation. "But we need him urgently."

"He will be with you in a couple of minutes," said the young woman calmly.

Tim paced back and forth. Waving an arm in impatience, he accidentally knocked a revolving display stand laden with leaflets. A handful of the leaflets went flying across the floor. Tim gathered them up and restored the display stand to order. Five minutes passed. Helen spoke to the young woman again. Again, the young woman replied calmly and politely that Alfonso would be with them in a second.

After several minutes more, a tiny and wizened old man in weather-worn dungarees and faded cornflower blue shirt entered through a doorway behind the counter. He looked as though he had been fashioned from the gnarled limbs of an ancient shrub. His spiky grey hair had a disorderly tuftiness which the most artful teenager could not have achieved even with the stiffest of hair gels. His chin and upper lip similarly bristled here and there with random tufts of grizzled beard. He wore a hearing aid and his eyes seemed to be almost closed as though he were squinting against the sun.

"*ALFONSO*," said the young woman loudly, "*AQUÍ ESTÁN LA SEÑORA Y ÉL SEÑOR DE LA POLICÍA BRITÁNICA QUE NECESITAN TU AYUDA*." The young woman turned to Helen. "The Aprisco de la Cumbre Vieja, yes?"

Helen nodded.

"*¿CONOCES EL APRISCO DE LA CUMBRE VIEJA?*"

Alfonso did not react for a moment, but then gave a barely perceptible nod and uttered a barely audible, "*Sí.*" His gaze was directed at the floor and his eyes still seemed to be all but closed.

The young woman turned to Helen and Tim. "He knows where it is." And then turning back to Alfonso, "*¿PUEDES LLEVARLOS AHÍ?*"

"*No hay nada ahí*," mumbled Alfonso.

"He says there is nothing there."

"Nevertheless, we need to go there urgently," said Helen.

The young woman explained to Alfonso at full volume and, after some thought, he gave his barely audible reply.

"He asks if you prefer the shorter route or the longer one," translated the young woman.

Tim and Helen looked at each other as though this might be either a daft question or a trick one.

"The shorter?" said Tim.

"You have a car?" asked the young woman.

"At the hotel," said Helen. "We can be back here in less than five minutes."

The young woman and Alfonso resumed their conversation, respectively bellowed and whispered.

"Alfonso has a moped. He will meet you here in front of the post office in five minutes."

For the first time, Alfonso lifted his gaze in the general direction of Helen and Tim and prised his lids open a millimetre or two, just barely revealing the dark berries of his pupils. Then, without a gesture or further word, he turned and disappeared out of the door through which he had entered.

NINETY-SIX

"Mr President, Prime Minister, ladies and gentlemen." Gordon inflated his chest, but his features were drawn with uncharacteristic anxiety.

The MI5 conference room was large, drab, capable of seating perhaps as many as thirty people around its extended table, but now occupied only by Gordon, Tabi and a gentleman of about forty with a circlet of curly blond hair about his ears and shining pate, round NHS-style spectacles and a tweed jacket with leather elbow patches. The walls were adorned by three large screens which displayed, via video link, respectively a combined meeting of COBRA and the remaining members of the UK Cabinet, the US President and his entourage, and a sharp-suited and neatly barbered professor from the Complutense University of Madrid.

"Firstly, may I present apologies from the Director General. He would of course normally host a call of such importance, but is currently on a delayed flight returning from Beijing – as some of you will no doubt already be aware." Gordon turned towards the bespectacled academic at his side. "Ladies and gentlemen, we are joined here beside me by Assistant Professor Madoc Jenkins of University College London. Professor Jenkins was a member of the team which worked on the original television programme warning about La Palma – you should, by the way, all have a transcript of this programme to hand. On screen, in Madrid, we have Professor Javier Rodriguez of the Complutense University of Madrid's Department of Seismology. Professor Rodriguez takes a much more optimistic view of the potential dangers. On the conference line, we have in Zurich Dr Ernst Pfeiffer of the Swiss Federal Institute of Technology, who contributed work on the tsunami effect, and in Delft Professor Ies Plomp of the Delft University of Technology, who is also a tsunami expert, but again holds a different view to Dr Pfeiffer. Gentlemen, thank you all for joining us at such short notice.

"As a point of housekeeping, I would just mention that Professor Jenkins has signed the Official Secrets Act and our other three speakers have all signed similar undertakings. All are bound not to carry the details of this discussion outside this conference call and all are required to allow the authorities to pursue the course of action which they subsequently see fit without voicing any potential dissent in public – we do not wish the debate to spill into the public arena, thereby engendering confusion and potentially endangering lives. But we may all speak freely during the present discussion.

"Ladies and gentlemen, I do not propose to waste your time with a lengthy recap of the situation. I believe you are all aware that we have very strong evidence that a nuclear device has been strategically positioned on a volcanic fault line on the island of La Palma in the Canaries and we believe it is timed to detonate at seven p.m. today local time, therefore in approximately seven and a half hours from now – for your reference, the Canaries are in the same time zone as the UK. We have operatives on the island at this minute who are trying to locate the device and either disarm it or remove it from the island."

"Any update on that?" barked a slab-jawed, uniformed and much be-ribboned officer seated behind the US President.

"General Bulger, we have identified a local official whom we believe can guide us to the device. As soon as we have located the device, we will make a fresh assessment and update everyone." Gordon paused for a second before resuming.

"Mr President, Prime Minister, the purpose of this debate is to try to establish whether La Palma is in danger of collapse if the device explodes and whether this could unleash a mega-tsunami upon the eastern seaboard of the US and upon other Atlantic-facing states or whether the original theory as expounded in the BBC television programme … whether this employed a certain amount of licence – indulged in a measure of sensationalism – in the interests of creating exciting television."

Professor Jenkins opened his mouth to speak, but Gordon silenced him with a gesture.

"Without wishing to prejudge the debate, I would merely reiterate that Professor Jenkins here and Dr Pfeiffer in Zurich retain the more cataclysmic view. Professors Rodriguez and Plomp are of the view that La Palma does not pose such a threat. I will ask each side to summarise its position and will then throw the discussion open."

NINETY-SEVEN

Blithely ignorant of the gravity of his mission, the local official upon whom such hopes rested had shown no sign of acknowledging Tim and Helen's arrival when they had pulled up in front of the post office in their rented yellow SEAT Altea, but without a nod or a gesture and with his eyes still all but sealed in a squint had puttered off on his moped. Tim and Helen had followed.

The moped seemed to have a top speed of little more than twenty-five miles per hour and Alfonso's route took Tim and Helen along the LP1 main road which ran a mile inland from the coast while circumnavigating the entire southern half of the island. From Santa Cruz de la Palma on the eastern side of the island, the road ran south through the impeccably neat and tidy villages of San Pedro and El Pueblo, the latter with its houses painted in tasteful green and pink pastels like presentation packs of expensive soaps and toiletries. Between the villages, the landscape of La Isla Bonita was one of rugged but verdant slopes falling steeply from the volcanic ridge high above the main road to the west and running on down to the Atlantic Ocean a mile beyond the road to the east. But Tim and Helen were in no mood to enjoy the picturesque scenery as they increasingly chafed at their dawdling progress. The vegetation covering the coarse lava slopes became more sparse as the little procession crawled to the southern end of the island. Passing through the village of Los Canarios at the southern point of the slopes of the Cumbre Vieja, the road swung north, now taking Tim and Helen along the western flank of the island. They passed through another village. The volcanic scarp seemed steeper on this side of the island and was covered with low scrub dotted with pine trees. In due course, beyond the village of El Charco, the pine forest on the mountain slope grew more dense. Finally, after what had seemed like an interminable length of time and had indeed been well over an hour, Alfonso turned off the main road and onto a dirt track which climbed sharply uphill through the forest towards the peak of the Cumbre Vieja.

NINETY-EIGHT

"Mr President, Prime Minister, ladies and gentlemen, distinguished colleagues," Assistant Professor Jenkins had begun in a Welsh sing-song, "when the aforementioned television programme was made a decade ago, we had little thought that we would be confronted by such terrifying circumstances in our own lifetimes. However, I feel it is my bounden duty to make absolutely clear that contrary to earlier insinuation ..." Jenkins looked at Gordon. "... this programme was not a work of sensationalist entertainment, but the product of serious scientific fieldwork and modelling in a laboratory."

"Professor Jenkins, please could we just have the facts as you see them." It was the Prime Minister who had spoken.

Assistant Professor Jenkins stared at the Prime Minister on the video link as though he were a troublemaking schoolboy who had asked an impertinent question. "The facts as I see them, Prime Minister, are as follows. A particularly large earthquake may lift the seabed by, let us say, up to about ten metres, causing water displacement and a tsunami of comparable height. A landslide, on the other hand, causing millions and even billions of tons of rock to plunge into the ocean from a height, can provoke a mega-tsunami theoretically of any size."

"That is correct, by the way," came a voice over the conference phone.

"Thank you, Dr Pfeiffer. In the case of La Palma, we estimate five hundred thousand million – half a trillion – tons of rock could plunge into the ocean. Secondly ..."

"Really, I feel I must interrupt already," intervened Professor Rodriguez. "There is simply no scientific evidence for this."

"Professor Rodriguez, please." Gordon held up his hands as though to arrest the flow of Professor Rodriguez's speech. "You will have your say in a moment."

Rodriguez grimaced and shook his head in annoyance, but kept silent.

"Secondly," resumed Professor Jenkins, "La Palma comprises two volcanoes: one to the north, which is extinct, and one to the south – Cumbre Vieja – which is active, though currently quiescent. Cumbre Vieja is actually a volcanic ridge with vents running for twenty kilometres. Thirdly and perhaps surprisingly – and this is a key point – the volcano is full of water. Vertical layers of impermeable lava alternate with permeable layers of loose rock which are filled with water. In a volcanic eruption, the water would boil creating huge pressure and the water would also act as a lubricant between the solid layers of rock potentially allowing a vast section of the island to slide into the sea with devastating consequences."

"Again, that is correct," came Dr Pfeiffer's voice.

"No, gentlemen, that is not correct." Professor Rodriguez could keep his peace no longer. "The water galleries you mention are in the extinct volcano in the north. There is no evidence of these galleries in the Cumbre Vieja. Two road tunnels have been built through the Cumbre Vieja and these produced no evidence of these vertical formations filled with water. Furthermore ..."

"Professor Rodriguez ..." said Gordon.

"No, let me finish. I can't listen to this nonsense. In the television programme, you cited as evidence that an eruption in 1949 caused a four metre slippage in the western flank of the volcano – but this would have put the coastal towns and villages on the western side of the island under the sea. They are not under the sea. And how is it none of the thirty thousand inhabitants in this part of the island noticed this huge movement of the land? It is simply preposterous – there is no evidence for what you say."

At this point, Margaret hurried into the conference room and slipped Gordon a note. Gordon turned visibly purple and stuffed the note into his pocket.

"The so-called mega-tsunami as well," continued Professor Rodriguez, "... your evidence of a similarly destructive wave was taken from the confined circumstances of a bay in Alaska. Even if there were a huge landslide in the Canaries, its effects would be dissipated across the vast breadth of the Atlantic Ocean."

343

"Now here I feel I must join the debate in support of this view," contributed Dr Plomp of Delft. "Our modelling shows …"

"But," interrupted Dr Pfeiffer, his voice rising, "even if the effect of the collapse is mitigated by the expanse of the ocean, a wall of water half a kilometre high at its inception and crossing the ocean at hundreds of kilometres an hour is still going to reach the US with massive destructive force."

"There will be no such collapse," said Rodriguez angrily. "I repeat there is no evidence for this."

"Gentlemen, we are missing …" said Gordon.

"May I just add …" intoned Professor Jenkins.

"Gentlemen, please." This time it was the President with a call to order. "Mr Walker, you were about to say something."

"Yes, thank you, Mr President. Gentlemen – and Professor Rodriguez in particular – I think we are losing sight of what is possibly the single most important fact. We are not discussing whether and how nature will take its course. We are debating what we think will happen if a nuclear weapon is detonated on the volcano. Professor Rodriguez, in the event of a nuclear explosion, potentially of several kilotons, what would you anticipate to be the effect on the geological stability of the island?"

Professor Rodriguez was silent.

"Professor Rodriguez?" The prompt came from the President.

Rodriguez remained silent for a further few seconds before replying. "No one has modelled such a thing. It is impossible to say. I am not an expert on nuclear weapons."

"If the northern volcano has these water galleries, could a nuclear explosion – and likely ensuing eruption, at least in the south – could this cause the collapse not just of the south-western flank of the island, but of La Palma in its entirety?"

The question had come from the Prime Minister. It was met by silence.

"Professor?"

NINETY-NINE

The dirt track had narrowed to a point where the SEAT could no longer proceed. Alfonso puttered onwards without a backward look, his moped skidding now and then on a gravelly patch or bouncing on a protruding tree root. Tim and Helen had no choice but to abandon the car and to follow on foot. They caught up with Alfonso after about half a mile. He had come to a halt at the edge of a ravine which brought the path to an end and which extended out of sight to right and left. The ravine was steep-sided, though not precipitous, and was thirty or forty feet deep and perhaps fifty or sixty yards wide. It was strewn with rockfalls and overgrown with vegetation. Beyond the ravine, the forest quickly petered out. Past the trees, Tim and Helen could see a black scree-covered slope and then a greener expanse which might have served as poor pastureland. Beyond this, the forest resumed.

Alfonso, still astride his moped, turned to Tim and Helen, opened his eyes a millimetre, turned back towards the ravine and lifted his chin in the general direction of the black slope and the field beyond.

"*Allá*," he said.

Tim and Helen followed Alfonso's line of sight, but could see nothing of any significance – no point of reference, no landmark, no dwelling. With a theatrical shrug, upturned palms, puzzled expression and shaking of the head, Tim indicated to Alfonso that they could see nothing.

"We can't see anything," he said, for good measure, though he supposed Alfonso could neither hear him clearly, nor understand his English.

Alfonso pointed towards the far side of the field where the forest resumed. Tim and Helen narrowed their gaze.

"There!" cried Helen, pointing in the same direction as Alfonso. "Lemon, can you see that old hut beside the trees?"

There was indeed a semi-derelict old stone animal shelter or shepherd's hut nestling at the edge of the trees. The roof timbers of the ancient refuge seemed to have largely collapsed.

"That must be it," said Tim.

Helen looked down at the ravine. "Do you think this is the unstable fault line Draper talked about?"

"I guess it could be … but, shit, we need to get round to that hut somehow. Time's running short." Tim looked at his watch. "Just under six hours. Damn it, we should have asked Alfonso to take us the long way round – that must have been the way to get a vehicle over there. Draper's crew must have taken that route. Alfonso …"

But Alfonso had already turned his moped around and was now seventy yards away puttering off along the track back through the forest.

"ALFONSO!" yelled Tim. "*ALFONSO!*" he bellowed, running a few steps in Alfonso's direction.

Alfonso's moped bounced over a tree root and disappeared from sight as the path wound among the trees.

"Oh, fuck," said Tim, as he kicked a loose stone.

Helen inspected the ravine. "Look, Lemon, let's not panic. The ravine's not impassable. We can climb down over there where it's not so steep and then up those rocks on the other side. Meanwhile, we can ask London to send the local police up here with another chopper if they have one or, failing that, with a four-wheel drive taking the other route. I know we don't exactly have time to waste, but Alfonso will be back at the post office in an hour or so and can give the police the proper directions. If the police know where they're going, it shouldn't take them much more than half an hour even if they're coming by road."

Tim was holding up his mobile phone. "Oh, great – no bloody signal here," he said.

"I've brought two satellite phones." Helen patted her bag. "Might struggle under the trees here, but should be fine once we're over the other side in the clearing."

Tim and Helen began to scrabble down the side of the ravine – clambering down the rockface with the help of dangling roots, slipping, sliding, hopscotching from rock to rock.

346

ONE HUNDRED

Maggie was staring at the news screens on the wall. It was estimated that twenty to thirty million people were attempting to move inland in the eastern US alone. Further uncounted millions were similarly in flight across the Caribbean and in the vulnerable states of Central and South America. The news reports on the evacuation showed desperate families in gridlocked traffic on the highways, while a few city centres had witnessed scenes of anarchy and violence. Aerial shots painted the Caribbean as one vast flotilla of boats, large and small, fleeing to the mainland. There were reports that a ferry-boat from the Bahamas – designed to carry three hundred and fifty passengers, but with an estimated six or seven hundred on board – had capsized and sunk just outside Nassau harbour, with most of those on board still unaccounted for and many feared dead. Observing a hundred and fifty mile tailback on Interstate 78 running from Manhattan through New Jersey, Maggie reflected that the history of the US was one of migration from east to west and that US culture, folklore, literature, movies, the highbrow and the low, heroic, tragic or comic, from the wagon trains of the pioneers to Steinbeck's Okies, Bonnie and Clyde, Kerouac's Sal and Dean, *Easy Rider*, Huck Finn in a fluvial variant, and countless others, right down to the likes of the whimsical *Little Miss Sunshine* or the archly violent *True Romance*, were steeped in the lore of the road. Meanwhile, the eastern US and the nations of the Caribbean had suffered at least their share of appalling natural disasters – in recent years, hurricanes Katrina and Sandy had wrought havoc and taken many lives. But the US and its neighbours had never witnessed, nor even imagined, anything like this.

An outer door banged open. Gordon stormed into the office.

"How in Christ's name …?" Gordon looked around at the mostly empty desks of his mostly absent team. "Where's Trevor now? Someone get him on the phone this instant."

Maggie came forward. "Gordon, it's not Trevor's fault."

347

"Well, whose fault is it? How can we have fifty police officers around the Alanborough and still Andropov gives us the slip? In that ruddy great tank of a car, I suppose?"

"He wasn't at the Alanborough and he didn't leave in the Maybach," explained Maggie. "We found out he arrived at Northolt in a black cab. We managed to locate the cab driver. Andropov was picked up at Claridges – it seems he was staying there."

Gordon stood puce-faced and with his mouth open. "How in hell did we miss that?"

"Unfortunately, we took it for granted he was staying at the same place as always."

"And when did this happen? Where is he now?"

"I'm afraid he had his own private jet waiting at Northolt and he took off hours ago."

"And we missed that too? Jesus Christ … How long has he been in the air? Is he over friendly territory and could we try to force him down?"

"I think he'll be in Russian airspace by now."

"Damnation." Gordon thumped the nearest desk with his fist. "Andropov back in Russia, Draper at large on the high seas … What about Suskin? Have we at least got him back on La Palma and under arrest?"

"Unfortunately, that hasn't gone exactly according to plan either. The Spanish actually got their Minister of Transport to speak to the pilot and the minister explained the truth of the situation. I'm afraid the pilot, instead of turning back to La Palma, did the very opposite. He was absolutely adamant that it was his duty to get his passengers out of the danger zone and safely to Madrid."

Gordon rolled his eyes and looked heavenwards.

"Suskin will be arrested on arrival in Madrid," continued Maggie, "but we're going to have to deal with the bomb ourselves."

"Do we know where Helen and Tim are now?"

"They called in a couple of minutes ago. They're within sight of the shepherd's hut which they think must be where the bomb is, but they're having to cover the last part of the terrain on foot. They expect to be there shortly and will call us as soon as they reach the hut. I've asked the Spanish police to send a helicopter up to them, but unfortunately it seems the only one stationed on La Palma is the one now in pursuit of Draper's yacht. The police are trying to summon another helicopter from one of the other islands. According to Helen and Tim, there's also an alternative road route which they suppose must allow vehicle access – I've asked the Spanish police immediately to send a team up to them by that route as well. And, by the way, Brigadier Hernández from Tenerife is now on La Palma, so he's taking charge of the force on the ground."

"What time are we now?" Gordon glanced at a clock on the wall. "Just over five hours to go. When the call comes in from Helen and Tim, tell me immediately." Gordon turned to his office.

"Gordon." Maggie held him back. "What about the conference call – how was that? What was the conclusion?"

"Fractious and inconclusive, but it seemed very clear we have no option but to assume the worst."

ONE HUNDRED AND ONE

Helen and Tim looked up and down the mountain slope. They were confronted by a two hundred yard wide field of black volcanic cinders, which were razor sharp and, in the midday sun, burning hot. The field of jagged scree extended out of sight both upwards towards the summit of the volcanic ridge and downwards to a point where the slope dipped out of view.

"Better watch our footing on this," observed Helen.

Treading warily and with the occasional unsteady slide, they slowly made progress across the loose basalt rubble. In the baking heat of the black cinder field, they began to pour with sweat. Helen's bandage came loose and started to trail behind her. She rewound it about her thigh and tucked it into itself … but it soon worked its way loose again. She pulled it off and stuffed it into an outer pocket of her bag. The dressing at least was just about holding for the moment, though the tape was starting to curl back at the edges. Tim waited and watched.

"I can help you redo it," he offered.

"Thanks, but let's get to the hut first."

As they trudged on over the unstable terrain, it came to Helen that in a profound sense she trusted Tim – trusted him perhaps more than she trusted herself. Helen did not think of herself as a particularly straightforward person, but with Tim you knew where you were. Yes, he could knock things flying and, yes, he was prone to rushes of blood to the head … but he said what he meant and he had no hidden agenda beyond getting on with his job and getting on with his colleagues. It had taken Helen eight years to realise and some days to acknowledge to herself, but the truth was she felt comfortable with Tim in a way she barely felt even when keeping her own company. She skirted a larger rock, following a step or two behind Tim. Suddenly, Tim lost his footing and, barely keeping upright, started to slide down the slope on the loose crust of barnacle-sharp cinders. Helen sprang forwards and grabbed Tim's arm. They continued to slide for two or three yards in an ungainly *pas de deux*. But with

Helen's knees braced and her weight squarely on her feet, she brought them to a halt.

"Thanks," said Tim. "Nearly came a cropper."

"Bend your knees," said Helen. "Like skiing."

"Helen, can you see me on skis?"

"All right, like standing on a bus, then."

"Standing on a bus I can manage."

In due course, they at last reached the end of the cinder field and stepped onto the scrubby pasture with its dry tufts of grass. They both stood for a second and stared across the field at the Aprisco de la Cumbre Vieja. The grey stone walls of the sheepfold's crude shelter were largely intact, though one end had tumbled down, bringing with it most of the roof timbers. A line of old fence posts, weathered, bare and leaning at odd angles, ran between the hut and the forest.

Tim looked at Helen and glanced down. "Leg okay?"

Helen nodded. They set off at a jog across the rough pasture, occasionally skipping to avoid loose rocks and stones and, two-thirds of the way across, picking their way through a line of fallen fence posts still held together with a tangle of wire, which must have marked the boundary of the old sheep pen. As they approached the hut, they saw a portable solar panel resting on the ground outside the doorway with an electrical lead snaking into the shadows within. Helen and Tim entered the dilapidated dwelling and took in what they saw.

Tim exhaled at length. "Somehow I was still hoping we'd all been caught up in some hallucinatory fiction," he said.

At the far end of the hut, in the shadow of what remained of the roof, a smooth steel canister, the shape of an elongated rugby ball but two or three times the size, rested on a metal trestle. The wooden tea chest lay discarded to one side. As Tim and Helen stepped into the hut and as their eyes adjusted from the brilliant light outside to the alternating light and shadow within the hut, they saw that a laptop computer lay on the ground at the foot of the trestle. It was connected by a lead to an aperture at the end of the steel cylinder. The cable from the solar panel ran across the earthen floor and was also plugged into the computer. Though the laptop was closed, a winking light indicated that it was running. Tim and Helen inspected the steel canister more closely. It had a single seam two-thirds of the way along, but this had been welded closed. There was no other point of access to the canister apart from the USB port to which the laptop was connected.

"Now what do we do?" asked Tim.

Helen stepped back from beneath the vestiges of the roof and dialled London on the satellite phone. "Maggie? Hi, it's Helen. We're here. It's here. It's real. It's a little scary. I think we need Shah probably. But best get everyone on the call. I'm putting us on speaker at this end." Helen described what they could see. "Shah, do you think we can open up the laptop or might that be rigged to set the thing off?"

"I don't know, Helen. Have you got a lead which can connect the phone to the laptop?"

"I have. I've got a second phone as well."

Tim was silently impressed at Helen's forethought and organisation. In fact, he quietly acknowledged to himself that she was almost always exceptionally efficient. As Helen's contemporary, he had sometimes resented the fact that Gordon more often than not appointed Helen as team captain – he had dismissed this as Gordon secretly lusting after Helen's until now tightly buttoned-away physical charms – but on reflection Helen was unfailingly deserving of Gordon's professional confidence.

"About to connect the phone to the laptop," said Helen.

"Hold off a second," said Tabi. "Look guys, even plugging in the phone could have consequences – I really don't know."

"What else can we do?" asked Tim. "Could we just disconnect the computer? Wouldn't that stop the countdown?"

"I don't know," said Tabi. "It might stop it; it might equally trigger the bloody thing."

"Could we just leave the set up as it is, but remove the whole lot and dump it in the ocean?" asked Helen.

"Again, that might be fine," replied Tabi, "but if a trembler or an atmospheric pressure gauge has been fitted then it certainly wouldn't be fine. If I could look at the programme which the laptop is running, I'd have a better idea."

"We have no choice but to do something – we can't just hang around and let the device go off," said Maggie. "Which approach do you think is the lowest risk?"

Tabi thought for a second. "I doubt plugging in the phone would trigger it. Let's try that."

Helen readied the phone.

"About to plug it in," she said.

Helen and Tim looked at each other. Helen shook her head. "Don't say a word," she breathed, so quietly that only Tim could hear. Instead, Tim proffered a hand. They shook. They held their breath. Helen gently inserted the lead into the laptop. She waited a couple of heartbeats.

"It's plugged in. We're still here."

There were audible sighs of relief at the other end.

"Okay," said Tabi. "Dial up www dot Battle of Trafalgar – all one word – dot org on the satellite phone."

Helen did as instructed. After about twenty seconds, Tabi spoke again.

"Okay, got you. Now you just need to give me a bit of time."

"As I know we are all acutely aware, we don't have all day," said Gordon. "Four hours and twenty-two minutes to be exact."

"Looks like the encryption is essentially the same as Draper's, which should make life a bit easier," said Tabi.

Silence fell over the participants at both ends of the call as Tabi could be heard furiously tapping at his keyboard.

"I'm in there."

Silence again – again apart from the frenzy of Tabi's fingers at the keyboard.

"Good thing you didn't unplug it," he said.

"We'd have set it off?" asked Tim.

"Hm." Tabi spoke with puzzlement rather than confidence. "Not one hundred percent sure, but there's some kind of fail-safe in there."

"Can you disarm the device?" asked Gordon.

"Not sure. Anyway, not yet."

The feverish percussion at the keyboard resumed. It continued for minutes. Then fell silent.

353

"Fuck. I can see it all. It's running. Set for seven p.m. – four hours four minutes and counting down. But I've just got kind of read only status, not edit or administrator. I can see the enemy on the battlements, but I can't cross the moat. The drawbridge has been hauled up."

"You can't find a way round it?" asked Helen.

"That's what I've been trying to do. You can open up the laptop, by the way. There's no electronic tripwire on opening it and there are no motion or pressure sensors. But just make sure you don't unplug it."

Helen gingerly opened the computer. The only instantly intelligible segment of the screen was a panel framing a three part clock showing Local Time: 14.57.10, Target Time: 19.00.00 and, beneath these two, Countdown, which – as the seconds spooled away alarmingly – now displayed 04.02.35. The largest part of the screen was taken up with a complex circuit diagram, some parts of which blinked or barrelled as though a process was in motion. Finally, in the bottom right hand corner of the screen, a panel showed a scrolling stream of code.

"That's me bottom right," said Tabi. "Clock obviously ... and then the device. I have a horrible suspicion the drawbridge hasn't simply been pulled up – it's been burnt. I think this is a no-going-back countdown."

"So we need to get this off the island," said Helen.

"Four hours should at least give you a sufficient amount of time, shouldn't it?" asked Gordon.

"I'm not sure about the helicopter, but the police vehicles should be with you very shortly if they've found the route," added Margaret.

"Sounds like we just have to be patient for a short while till the police get here," said Helen. "We might as well sign off on this phone and then call you back in a minute when the police arrive. Shah, we'll leave you running on the other phone in case you can find a way round the defences."

"I'll keep trying. Just don't do any unplugging."

Helen and Tim went round to the back of the hut on the forest side where it was shady and a little cooler. They sat on the ground and leant back against the stone wall of the hut. Helen produced a plastic bottle of mineral water from her bag, took a few draughts and offered the bottle to Tim. He gladly accepted. They were both parched, though had barely recognised their thirst so intensely had they been concentrating on the task at hand. Tim noticed a renewed trickle of blood on Helen's thigh. Helen removed the old dressing, cleaned the wound and, with Tim's help, replaced the dressing and bandage.

They sat in silence. At first, it was the safe removal of the nuclear weapon which occupied their thoughts, but in both cases other thoughts inveigled their way in. In fact, in both cases it was a similar train of thought which preoccupied them. The circumstances of the past week – was it only a week! – had brought an intimacy which neither of them would have expected before the unfolding of recent events. They had been colleagues in arms, but slightly prickly colleagues and in their private lives virtual strangers, for so many years, yet now seemed suddenly to have fallen into a companionship which was more than common cause.

A roar from the slope shocked Tim and Helen from their reverie – it was not the mountain awakening, but the clattering tumult of diesel engines. They scrambled to their feet and rounded the side of the hut.

ONE HUNDRED AND TWO

Two police Land Rovers came thundering and juddering across the rough pasture. They ground to a halt in front of the hut and several police officers leapt out. In the lead was an officer in his mid-forties who wore a uniform with creases of such paper-cut sharpness that it might have been donned only seconds before straight from the press. His hair was similarly barbered to the millimetre. The officer was as darkly handsome as a screen idol and, despite the formality of his appearance and the seniority marked by the crown and crossed swords on his epaulettes, had a boyish eager-to-please air which shone through the current seriousness of his expression. He snapped into a salute of geometric precision. Shambling behind him came his apparent deputy, several centimetres shorter, of agricultural mien and rather of the Tim Lemon school of dress and coiffure. Seeing his senior officer snap to attention, this second officer belatedly improvised a salute.

"Madam, sir," said the senior officer, "General de Brigada Juan Hernández at your service. All the facilities of the island are at your immediate disposal."

Helen and Tim came forwards to introduce themselves and warmly shook hands with the two officers. Tim noticed that standing rather sheepishly to the rear of the other policemen was the young officer with the artfully raked back mop of black hair who had provided so little help in the early hours of the morning. Brigadier Hernández had clearly been briefed en route and quickly took stock of the situation. He noted the countdown – now at three hours and thirty-seven minutes.

"The helicopter is unfortunately delayed, but ..." – he indicated the Land Rovers – "... we will have you at the airport in less than forty-five minutes."

Tim turned to Helen. "Now let's get that frigate onto bloody Draper."

While Helen made a call to update London, Hernández ordered his men to back one of the Land Rovers up to the hut.

356

"We mustn't unplug the computer," warned Helen, interrupting her phone call, as two of the policemen carefully lifted the metal cylinder.

With the utmost care, Tim disconnected the satellite phone and the solar charger from the laptop and then picked up the computer. He kept close beside the two officers as they took shuffling steps to the backed-up Land Rover. Another officer brought the metal trestle and set it ready in the back of the vehicle. The discarded tea chest was taken to the second Land Rover to be retained as evidence of the chain of delivery from Andropov's yacht to Draper's. The two policemen carefully set the cylinder back on its trestle while Tim simultaneously leant into the back of the Land Rover to place the laptop beside the nuclear device. As Tim reached forwards, the computer lead snagged on a torch bracket on the inside of the vehicle. Tim – and Helen, who was standing beside him – saw the moment in slow motion and froze. The USB plug popped out of the socket in the nose of the cylinder. The two policemen nursing the device stared wide-eyed. No one spoke for two or three seconds.

Hernández came forwards. "What happened?"

Helen nodded towards the unplugged cable.

"But we are still okay?" asked Hernández.

Helen gave a grimace of uncertainty. She gently prised open the laptop. The screen had also frozen – countdown included. She spoke into her phone.

"Shah, we've accidentally disconnected the laptop from the bomb."

"No prizes for guessing who that was," said Tim self-deprecatingly through gritted teeth behind Helen.

"As you can tell," resumed Helen, "it hasn't gone off – and in fact the countdown seems to have stopped. Was it as simple as that after all?"

"That doesn't sound right," said Tabi. "I mean, thank God it hasn't detonated … but, no, something will have happened. Plug me back in again. And plug the laptop back into the bomb."

Helen reconnected the device and the second phone and dialled Tabi back into the laptop. On her handset, she could hear Tabi battering his keyboard.

"Fuck," said Tabi.

At the same moment, the screen sprang back to life. The countdown clock leapt forwards to 00.57.10, 00.57.09, 00.57.08 ...

"By unplugging, you've jumped the clock forwards to just one hour – or now fifty-seven minutes. I guess Suskin wanted to make sure if anyone interfered, he was allowing himself, Draper and the other two as much time as possible to get clear while not allowing anyone else sufficient time to get the device off the island. Shit ..."

"We've got time," said Helen. "The bomb is already in the Land Rover; there's a plane standing by at the airport ..." She looked around at her companions and yelled, "WE'VE GOT FIFTY-SEVEN MINUTES TO GET THIS THING OFF THE ISLAND AND TO A SAFE DISTANCE."

Hernández barked at his men. All piled into the vehicles, which set off at speed bouncing over the tufted pasture. The Land Rovers went scudding down the half mile of dirt track and hit the main road with lights flashing and sirens wailing. The diesel engines gunned to one hundred miles per hour on the straights, tyres smoked as the vehicles braked and skidded around the bends. Within a very few minutes, Tim and Helen saw the beginning of the dirt track up which they had laboured with Alfonso – with barely any detour, Alfonso could have saved them a good ninety minutes! They sped through El Charco, Los Canarios ... Fortunately, there was barely any traffic – the population of these villages still seemed unaware of the unfolding drama and was observing the siesta hour or continuing about its daily business. The occasional motorist trundling along stared in astonishment at the hurtling police convoy – an unprecedented sight on the normally tranquil island. A few miles after Los Canarios, the Land Rovers diverted from the LP1 main road, instead taking a lower coast road which was signposted for the airport. As they roared through the hamlets of Lomo Oscuro, San Simon and Callejones, the airport came increasingly into view. Approaching the perimeter fence, they saw more police vehicles – a car and two motorcycles, all with lights flashing – awaiting their arrival. With the motor bikes in the lead and the additional police car falling in behind, the motorcade raced along the perimeter fence. Security barriers were already thrown open in readiness as they turned into the restricted section of the airport and hurtled out onto the runway. Glancing down, Helen saw that the laptop now showed thirty-one minutes.

A couple of mid-sized passenger jets were parked at their gates at the terminal building. Through the panoramic windows of the terminal building, Helen and Tim could see a dense throng of people apparently in a state of commotion – the outlying villages might still be peaceful, but it seemed the capital of the island had heard the news of the seismic threat and a panic-stricken crowd was now competing for the few places on the two passenger planes which might take them to safety. Meanwhile, a lone Gulfstream G200 executive jet stood some distance apart on the tarmac. Two figures stood in front of the private jet at the foot of the steps descending from the cabin. The police convoy swung round and pulled up in a line parallel with the jet.

As Helen and Tim disembarked from their Land Rover, the captain of the jet and his flight attendant strode to meet them. The uniformed pilot was around fifty years of age. Though a little below average height, he carried himself with military bearing. His grey hair was close cropped and his cheeks glowed pink and smooth as though just shaved and then wrapped in a hot towel. His colleague was a few inches taller than him and in her late twenties. She wore a navy jacket and skirt over a white blouse. Most noticeably, she had a turbulent stack of brown hair. She had a rather stern face and exuded an air of down-to-earth competence.

The pilot extended a hand. "Miss Stride, I presume. And Mr Lemon. Bill Trumper, RAF retired – and this is Cheryl, my flight crew."

They were joined by Brigadier Hernández, who snapped into a salute. His deputy followed behind with what might have been a salute or might just have been a hand raised in greeting.

"Co-pilot's gone AWOL, I'm afraid," continued Trumper, "but in the circumstances I guess we'll just have to ignore the regs and do without. Cheryl, on the other hand, has bravely volunteered to help us see this assignment through."

"Pleased to meet you," said Cheryl, as she offered a firm handshake. She spoke with an estuary twang.

"Nice to meet you too," said Tim, "but, Cheryl, you really don't need to be on the plane. We're far from out of danger and you'll be much safer remaining here on the ground."

The policemen had unloaded the bomb and now set it on its trestle in front of the aircraft.

Cheryl nodded towards the bomb. "Looks to me as though you could do with an extra pair of hands when ditching that and, more to the point, it's not immediately obvious how to operate the cabin door when the plane's in flight."

"If you show us, I'm sure we'll manage," said Helen.

"Concern noted, sentiments appreciated," said Cheryl. "But you'll need my help. Clock ticking. End of. Let's get the little bastard onto the plane."

"I say, Cheryl," said Trumper, "was that a clever little historical allusion?"

Cheryl looked blank.

"Hiroshima was 'Little Boy'," explained Tim.

Cheryl lifted her chin in recognition. "Hotel delivered all your kit, by the way," she said to Helen and Tim. "All safely stowed on board already."

Hernández meanwhile was staring at Cheryl. "Miss Cheryl, you are happy to accompany them? I can assign one of my men."

"Job needs doing by someone familiar with the aircraft," reiterated Cheryl, while declining the offer with a shake of the head.

Brigadier Hernández, with mist in his eyes, stood ramrod straight and flung his arm into a whip-crack salute. "¡Señorita!"

"Am I correct in understanding the clock jumped forwards and we now have less than thirty minutes?" asked Trumper.

"Unfortunately, yes," confirmed Helen.

"Best look sharpish, then."

The policemen loaded the bomb onto the aircraft and disembarked. Hernández stepped forwards again. Helen, Tim, Trumper and Cheryl rushed to shake his hand before he knocked himself out with another salute.

"Good luck," said Hernández, on the verge of tears, "and safe return, when you will be the most honoured guests of the Canary Islands!"

ONE HUNDRED AND THREE

"Buckle up," said Cheryl to Helen and Tim and then disappeared from the passenger cabin to join Trumper in the cockpit.

Trumper had the Gulfstream off the ground in the shortest take-off Helen and Tim had ever experienced. The plane lunged upwards out of the more humid and dense lower atmosphere to hit an initial cruising altitude of just a few thousand feet. La Isla Bonita and, in the distance, the islands of La Gomera and Tenerife receded from view. A helicopter, a distant speck, could be seen traversing the sea passage between Tenerife and La Palma.

Helen and Tim sat opposite each other in tense silence as the jet arrowed towards the open ocean. They barely noticed the deep comfort of the upholstered leather seats and the luxurious trim of the aircraft's fittings – all rather of a piece with Draper's yacht. Instead they were transfixed by the menacing canister, balanced on its trestle and wedged in the aisle, and the laptop, which now showed fifteen minutes remaining. The aircraft started to descend towards the ocean.

As the countdown hit twelve minutes, the aircraft levelled. Cheryl reappeared.

"Captain reckons we're over deep ocean and clear of shipping lanes here and we're nearing the limit of what's safe for us. Let's do it."

"Safe to disconnect the laptop?" asked Tim.

"Shah reckoned the damage was already done the first time," replied Helen.

Tim hesitated, but then pulled the laptop cord from the canister. The counter stopped at 00.11.11. Tim and Helen lifted the cylinder while Cheryl brought the trestle. They carried the bomb and set it on its stand in front of the main door to the aircraft.

"Hold on to something while I open up," said Cheryl.

She punched a sequence of buttons on a control panel, swung a lever on the door and then heaved the door open. Gusts of cold air buffeted into the cabin sending Cheryl's heap of hair into even wilder disarray.

"Ready?" shouted Helen against the noise of the wind.

Tim nodded. They each took a hold of the cylinder.

"One, two, three," called Helen.

They lobbed the bomb through the door and watched for a brief second as it disappeared from sight.

"And good riddance!" yelled Tim. For good measure, he tossed the metal trestle after the bomb.

"Better not celebrate just yet," shouted Cheryl. "Got to make our getaway." She hauled in the door, closed the lever and punched the buttons in reverse sequence. "Right, strap in tight. Captain's going to push the pedal to the floor."

Helen and Tim returned and sat side-by-side as Cheryl disappeared into the cockpit. Within moments of their buckling up, the aircraft lifted its nose to a forty-five degree angle and hit full throttle. Helen, who was in the aisle seat, craned over Tim and the two of them looked out of the porthole at the fast receding whitecaps of the Atlantic. They pulled down the window blinds and settled back in their seats. In the same instant, with heart-stopping suddenness, a huge flash of incandescent green lit a vast expanse of ocean from beneath with searing brightness. Within a fraction of a second, the ocean surface began to boil and then a mighty plume of water and steam spurted skywards. Helen gripped Tim's hand. Instinctively, they pressed themselves into their seats. Abruptly, the aircraft began to shudder, slightly at first, but then more violently; it bucked and began to rattle in terrifying fashion as though it might fly apart; for one blood-chilling second, the jet even seemed to be dragged backwards into the vacuum created by the pressure wave, before it resumed its turbulent course. As the shuddering continued, the aircraft held level, but then the cabin lights went out and ... it seemed the engines had fallen silent. The aircraft appeared to hold an impossible equilibrium, teetering unsupported in the air.

Cheryl appeared at the passenger cabin door. "Captain says we've lost everything – power, hydraulics, electrics. Might regain it on the way down, so hold tight. But if we don't, it's been a privilege." Cheryl vanished back to the cockpit.

Tim slid open the nearest window blind. Helen tightened her grip on Tim's hand and pulled his arm in to hers. The plane seemed to balance for a few more impossible seconds and then toppled from the horizontal. Clutching Tim's arm, Helen pressed the back of his hand to her lips. With an ever increasing whine, the jet began to hurtle towards the ocean. Jackhammer vibrations tore at Tim and Helen's joints and the pressure change pounded their eardrums to bursting point. The plane screamed in its descent. But now there was a sudden choking and sensation of braking and – yes! – the engines had come back to life and the lights flickered back on. Yet the recovery of power merely accelerated the precipitous descent! Through the porthole, the ocean was flashing towards them. The plane began to judder even more violently, but seemed ... surely seemed to be levelling. Still, the ocean rushed at them. Was the nose pulling up fast enough? ... No, they would ditch, in seconds they would ditch ... Spume flecked the porthole, salt waves were upon them ... The jet hurtled over the face of the ocean at the height of wave-tossed spray. After a few moments, the Gulfstream lifted its nose and eased into a leisurely climb. Helen and Tim exhaled – they had held their breath for however many seconds or minutes the descent had taken. Their hearts thundered in their chests. They fell back in their seats, drenched in sweat.

By the time the jet reached cruising altitude, their breathing had returned more or less to normal and their heartbeats had settled to a thump. Helen relaxed her grip on Tim's hand, but still kept hold of him. Cheryl reappeared at the door to the passenger cabin. Her hair was more than ever an unruly haystack, yet she spoke calmly and matter-of-factly, as though this day were not so different from any other.

"Well, job done, I reckon. High fives?"

She presented her palms to Helen and Tim who, though a little taken by surprise, reciprocated the gesture. Cheryl pulled a table out from the bulkhead and secured it in place in front of Helen and Tim.

"Probably three and a half hours or so to London. We've got a great little menu." She pulled a card from a seat pocket. "Champagne, some very nice wines – maybe champagne after all that, don't you think? Some great canapés – foie gras, lobster, caviar and such. That Draper character liked to look after himself."

Tim was staring at Cheryl. He shook his head in wonder. "I'm very impressed."

"It is a good little menu, isn't it?" said Cheryl.

"No, no, not with the menu – with you!"

"Uh?" Cheryl looked genuinely nonplussed.

"I mean, ten minutes ago we were disposing of a nuclear bomb, five minutes ago we were in a death dive … and here you are – business as usual."

"We like to provide a good service," said Cheryl, as though she were still not quite sure what Tim was driving at. She paused. She saw that Helen was still holding Tim's hand. "Or," she said, "I could just leave you two to yourselves, if you prefer."

Helen released Tim's hand and folded her hands in her lap.

"Anyway, I'll give you a minute or two to consider. Just ping me when you've made your choice." Cheryl stepped back out of the cabin.

"Remarkable young lady," observed Tim.

Helen took a deep breath and exhaled over several seconds – as though she were trying to expel a lifetime's burden. She stared straight ahead for a few moments and then turned to Tim.

"I owe you an apology," she said.

Tim looked puzzled. "I hardly think so."

Helen nodded in affirmation of her point, but took a further moment before continuing. She looked Tim directly in the eye. "I apologise profoundly for taking eight years to call you Tim."

Epilogue

LATER

A black cab drew up in Pall Mall. Helen stepped out followed by Tim. Helen was wearing a midnight blue satin sheath dress and Tim a dinner jacket – with a spotless white dress shirt beneath. Helen had bought the shirt for Tim and had suggested that he not put it on until a few minutes before he left his flat on his way to collect her. She had limited expectations that the shirt would get back to the flat in the same condition, but at least Tim would start the evening looking presentable. As Tim paid the cab driver, Helen saw Tabi and Trevor come marching along the pavement, also in dinner jackets.

"Evening, Tabi. Evening, Trevor."

Tabi and Trevor stopped in their tracks and looked at each other.

"I just can't get used to this," said Tabi.

"I think we must be imagining it," said Trevor. "Or maybe we've slipped into some Panglossian altered state where we suffer the delusion that everything is miraculously right with the world."

"I rather put it down to battle trauma on Helen's part," rejoined Tabi, perhaps not altogether frivolously.

The four ascended the steps into Gordon's club. None of them had been here before, so they were mildly surprised when the uniformed elderly retainer in reception seemed to know immediately and without need of explanation who they were and whose guests for the evening. He escorted them through a whisper-quiet reading room – oak panelled, hung with oil portraits and occupied mostly by mouldering and ruddy-faced old gents seemingly misshapen through centuries of inbreeding, buggery, meat and potatoes and alcoholic excess. The bar through which they passed next, on the other hand, though also oak panelled and hung with oil paintings of hunting scenes, had been colonised by a group of braying young thrusters. Passing through a corridor into a deserted anteroom, the elderly servant opened a wood panelled door and ushered the team into a private room. Gordon, Maggie and Luke were already there – the men in dinner jackets and Margaret in an ivory evening dress.

"Welcome, everybody." Gordon advanced, shaking hands and giving Helen a kiss on the cheek.

"Are we all here?" asked Luke, looking expectantly at a waiter standing unobtrusively to one side with champagne bottle and flutes at the ready.

"Two more," said Gordon. "Ah, here they are!"

Bill Trumper made a tiny adjustment to his bowtie and dinner jacket and stood aside at the door to allow Cheryl Burton to enter first. Cheryl wore a sparkling and ruched black mini dress. Her pile of hair was at least partially restrained by a black velvet ribbon. Gordon greeted his remaining guests and then called for attention.

"First things first. I trust everyone was given a clean bill of health this afternoon?"

Helen, Tim, Bill and Cheryl nodded.

"Apparently, radiation gathers in the thyroid," said Helen, "so running a Geiger counter over the thyroid gland gives a fair indication of whether you're likely to have been affected. We all came up clean."

"Excellent. That's the most important thing. Having said which..." Gordon assumed a grave expression. "... one of our number is of course not with us this evening." Gordon turned to Bill and Cheryl. "A young colleague of ours was killed in the line of duty only ten days or so ago." Gordon once more addressed the group as a whole. "There will be a proper memorial service in due course, but before we settle down to enjoy ourselves, I think we should perhaps take a moment to remember Nick. And while we do so, perhaps we should also spare a thought for the poor young woman whose untimely death first put us on Draper's trail. I suggest we observe a minute's silence."

There were murmurs of assent. Heads were bowed and the minute observed in stillness.

"Well," Gordon resumed, at the same time nodding to the waiter to begin filling the champagne glasses, "on this occasion the Mountie didn't quite get all his men, but I think we can congratulate ourselves on having averted what would have been a cataclysm of quite unprecedented proportions. You will all know that messages of thanks have been pouring in from all quarters. The PM and the

368

Spanish ambassador have both said they will join us for a brandy at the end of the evening and you may know that the President has said he would like to host a private dinner in our honour at the American embassy next time he is here. And the Director General, by the way, sends his best wishes for this evening from Washington." Gordon adopted a more sombre tone. "On a more personal note ... Tim and Helen, I've just received a message from Henry and Juliet Trenchard. They ask if they could have a private meeting with you tomorrow. They'd like to thank you for putting the record straight on poor Lucy." Gordon allowed a brief moment's pause as a further mark of respect for the dead young woman's memory. He drew a breath, straightened his back and looked around the assembled gathering. "I know the gongs on these occasions – the knighthood and I hear there's talk of a Presidential Medal of Freedom – I know that these tend to get dished out to those who labour under the burden of high office. But all of us here know who played what part. Tim, you might have given us a scare or two along the way and even now I'm not quite sure how you managed to piece all this together, but it's your remarkable detective work which laid bare the conspiracy. Helen and Tim, you both showed tremendous courage and resourcefulness in your respective ordeals on the boat. Bill and Cheryl, caught up in this by chance and yet stepping up without a second thought and displaying nerves of steel – Bill, you demonstrated extraordinary airmanship in regaining control of the stalled aircraft and, Cheryl, I gather you insisted on staying on the plane even when told you should remain in safety on the island. And on that note, by the way, I have a little announcement to make." Gordon beamed as he looked around the group. "Cheryl, I have your vetting papers on my desk. You'll be pleased to hear we can find nothing to hold against you other than the occasional drink on a Saturday night!"

There were smiles and chuckles from the assembled group.

"If you'd care to come by the office tomorrow, I have a contract of employment for you."

The team applauded and offered their congratulations with handshakes and kisses.

"And ..." Gordon held up a hand. "... let me not forget the rest of you. Every person here played an essential part in unravelling this plot

369

and averting disaster. I owe all of you my personal thanks. Indeed, on this occasion, not only our own nation, but a very long list of other nations as well, owe you all an extraordinary debt of gratitude. Ladies and gentlemen – Tim, careful, there's a champagne glass at your elbow – ladies and gentlemen, team, here's to all of you!"

The toast was drunk. The waiter refilled glasses and then discreetly withdrew from the room.

Bill Trumper spoke. "Gordon, I have of course seen what's been reported in the press, but do we actually know for sure what happened to Draper?"

"No," said Gordon. "As you will have gathered, the frigate and the SBS caught up with the yacht a few miles from Agadir in Morocco, which seemed to be where the boat was heading. The Russians put up a firefight. The younger one was killed. Markov is unlikely to survive his injuries. And Draper … as you've no doubt read, he was found half clothed in the master suite with a bullet in the head. But, in answer to your question, Bill, no, we don't know for sure whether he took his own life or whether the Russians decided he had become a liability. My own instinct would be the latter, but that's just a guess."

"And Andropov?" pressed Bill.

"The Russian government is officially disclaiming all knowledge of the affair; however, according to the financial media, Taiga Oil has already been placed under the control of Yevgeny Berezin and there's talk that Ruza Bank will be subsumed into one of the Russian state banks, while Siberian Minerals Corporation will be taken under the wing of some other avatar of the Russian state prior to auction or re-listing. Meanwhile, both Andropov himself and his *éminence grise* Vasiliev have vanished, but the Russian government seems to be encouraging rather than denying rumours that they're now occupying less than well-appointed accommodation in the depths of the gulag. And MI6 also tells me some black market kingpin who may have supplied the bomb was killed in a major gun battle with Russian special forces at his bolthole in the godforsaken middle of nowhere." Gordon drained his champagne glass and set it down. "Anyway, ladies and gentlemen, *à table*."

Acknowledgements & afterword

Thank you to all my early readers – Tom, Arthur, Sarah, Andy, Joff, Tom, Betsy and Sophia. Your immeasurably helpful comments and suggestions over the course of several drafts have made this a much better novel than it would otherwise have been. Sophia, thank you too for the cover design. Mimi, thank you for the translation into Spanish. Matt, thank you for the smuggling reference (for anyone interested in the subject, I would strongly recommend Matt Tiner's learned treatise *Smuggling in the late eighteenth century. Was it a profitable business in Devon and Cornwall?*). Lars, thank you for the Swedish reference.

I have fictionalised the debate concerning La Palma and Professors Jenkins, Rodriguez and Plomp and Dr Pfeiffer are my inventions; however, the controversy is real. Academics from University College London (but not my Assistant Professor Jenkins) and others, among them an academic at the Swiss Federal Institute of Technology (but not my Dr Pfeiffer), did put forward in a BBC Horizon programme the theory that La Palma is susceptible to collapse in the event of a volcanic eruption and could unleash a mega-tsunami. An opposing camp, including an academic at the Delft University of Technology (but not my Professor Plomp), has argued against this theory. I do not know whether the venerable Complutense University of Madrid has entered the debate – its inclusion here is my invention. The transcript of the BBC programme can be found on www.bbc.co.uk/science/horizon/2000/mega_tsunami.shtml and the opposing case on www.lapalma-tsunami.com. In creating my fictional debate, I have drawn upon these two sources and am indebted to them.